Praise for the Christmas stories of
#1 *New York Times* bestselling author
Linda Lael Miller

"Stuff a copy in the stocking of every romance fan
you know!"
—*USA TODAY* on *A Lawman's Christmas*

"Brimming over with memorable characters both
human and animal, Miller's novel incorporates
the magic of Christmas and the true meaning of
romance."
—*RT Book Reviews* on *A Lawman's Christmas*

"Miller liberally sprinkles Christmas magic
throughout...this quintessentially warm and cozy
slice of small-town life."
—*Publishers Weekly* on *Christmas in Mustang Creek*

"Sweet, homespun, and touched with angelic
Christmas magic, this holiday romance reprises
characters from Miller's popular McKettrick series
and is a perfect stocking stuffer for her fans."
—*Library Journal* on *A McKettrick Christmas*

"Miller delivers a holiday heartwarmer her fans are
sure to adore."
—*Publishers Weekly* on *A Creed Country Christmas*

LINDA LAEL MILLER

A SNOW COUNTRY
Christmas

HQN™

HQN™

ISBN-13: 978-1-335-04115-9

A Snow Country Christmas

Copyright © 2017 by Hometown Girl Makes Good, Inc.

The publisher acknowledges the copyright holder of the individual work as follows:

Glory, Glory
Copyright © 1990 by Linda Lael Miller

Recycling programs for this product may not exist in your area.

www.HQNBooks.com

Printed in U.S.A.

CONTENTS

A SNOW COUNTRY CHRISTMAS

December 23rd

*The young lady sat with her chin on fist, the fire-
light shining off her dark hair. She was reflective but not pensive, content in her solitude on
this cold evening. A log in the old stone fireplace
snapped and crackled and there was the smell of
pine in the air. Her father's old dog lay asleep at
her feet, gently snoring; the sound comforting.
Two days to Christmas and she'd spend it alone
for the first time.*

From the opening paragraph of The Aspen Trail
Matthew Brighton, 1965

CHAPTER ONE

RAINE McCALL FIRST frowned at the screen and then stared at the clock.

Her computer was right. Two in the morning? No way.

Oh, she'd be the first to admit that when she was working she lost track of time, but she was always there to put her daughter on the school bus and make sure Daisy had done her homework and had a healthy breakfast.

She'd always suffered from what she called WSS. Whimsical Sleep Schedule.

Awake at all hours, losing track of time if the muse was in the mood, and she'd been guilty of falling asleep in the chair at her desk. Daisy had told her more than once, with a maturity beyond her years, she thought she worked too hard, but then Raine didn't really think of it as work. Spinning dream images into reality was a unique joy and she felt sorry for every person in the world that had a job they disliked.

She wasn't the only one awake, either. Taking a break, she checked her email and was startled. Mick Branson? *The* Mick Branson had sent her a message? Hotshot Hollywood executive, way too focused, and no sense of humor—though come to think of it, he did smile now and then. He was good-looking, but she couldn't get beyond the sophisticated polish. She was a Wyoming girl through and through and thousand dollar suits weren't her preference. Give her a hat, jeans, and some worn boots.

Of course she'd met the man quite a few times at the ranch because he was the driving force behind the documentaries that Slater Carson, her ex-boyfriend and the father of her child, made, but getting an email from him was a definite first. Sent five minutes ago? She was too intrigued not to open it.

I'm going to be in Mustang Creek for the holidays. Can we have a business meeting? Maybe over dinner?

That *was* interesting, but currently she was up to her ears in deadlines trying to produce artwork for the labels for Mountain Vineyards wines. Her graphic design business had really taken off, and she wasn't sure she could handle another project.

From what she knew of Mick Branson, it wouldn't be a small one, either.

She typed back. When did you have in mind?

Tomorrow night? If you don't already have plans, that is.

On Christmas Eve?

Well, Daisy did usually spend that evening with her father's family and Raine spent it alone with a nice glass of wine and a movie. They always invited her, but she went the next day instead for the big dinner celebration and skipped the night before in favor of solitude. It was never that they made her feel like an outsider; quite the opposite, but Slater needed some time with his daughter to make memories without Raine always in the background. So while she appreciated the invitation, she'd always declined. It had been difficult when Daisy was little to spend such a magical evening away from her, but he was entitled. He was a wonderful father.

She typed: On the 24th of December, I assure you no place is open in Mustang Creek. This isn't California. You'd have to come to my place and I usually just eat a hamburger and drink wine.

He wrote back: That sounds fine. I like burgers and I enjoy wine. Let me bring the beverages. Please excuse me if I'm inviting myself.

She couldn't decide if he had, or if she'd done it. She really did need to get more sleep now and then. She typed: Mountain Vineyards for the wine.

You got it.

Have a safe flight.

Thank you, but I'm already here. See you tomorrow. Don't mention to anyone, especially Slater, that I'm in town please.

Raine sat back and let out a breath. She hadn't ever anticipated spending an evening with someone like Mick Branson, much less Christmas Eve.

Luckily, she thought, she'd thoroughly cleaned the house the day before when she realized that sound she abstractly heard in the background was the vacuum. Daisy was *voluntarily* doing a chore she usually argued over? Raine decided then and there—once she recovered from her shock—that maybe she had been spending too much time in her office. Sure enough, the house needed dusting, the kitchen floor had crumbs on it and the laundry room was in dire need of a workout.

Not that someone like Mr. Hollywood Executive Mick Branson, who probably lived in a mansion in Beverly Hills, would be impressed with her small and eclectic house anyway, no matter how tidy. Wait until he got a look at her Christmas tree. There was no theme to the ornaments; if something caught her eye, she bought and it put it up. There were owls, glittery reindeer, a glass shrimp with wings wearing a boa, all right alongside her grandmother's collection of English traditional antique glass orbs in brilliant colors. Those heirlooms were hung up high thanks to Mr. Bojangles, her enormous Maine coon cat. He was somewhat of a reclusive character, but he became positively playful when the Christmas tree went up. Walking past it usually meant an unexpected guerilla attack on your ankles because he considered it his covert hiding place every December. Therefore the ornaments on the bottom were soft stuffed squirrels and bunnies with a few fake pine cones he could bat around. Add in Daisy's giant dog, Samson, who accidentally knocked an ornament off every time he walked by, and her tree had no hope.

"Definitely not a designer tree, unless a deranged leprechaun arranged it" was how Daisy described it.

Raine loved it.

It was exactly her style. There was nothing wrong with being quirky. She went and switched off the lights and headed off to bed, wondering how she'd gotten roped into this situation.

Hollywood Hotshot Mick Branson eating hamburgers at her house on Christmas Eve?

Slater Carson was going to laugh himself into a fit.

THE PLANE HAD touched down on a snowy runway and Mick had said a small prayer of thanks for an experienced pilot and maybe some luck of the season as the snow continued to pile up. It had been a bumpy ride and he wasn't at all a nervous flyer, but coming over the mountains he'd had a moment or two.

He'd been everywhere. Asia, Africa, South America, Australia, Europe...he lived in Los Angeles, but he liked Wyoming. It felt like being on vacation and he could really, really use a vacation.

It wouldn't be a hardship to see Raine McCall again, either.

The thought surprised him because she was *so* not his type. Frothy skirts, and as far as he could tell she thought makeup was optional, or maybe forgot it altogether, and if she owned a pair of heels he'd be surprised. Her artistic temperament was the antithesis of his rigidly corporate lifestyle, but he somehow found it intriguing. She was naturally beautiful without trying. Maybe that was it. There was no artifice to Raine—what you saw was what you got. Not to mention he had a feeling she could care less how much money he made. Material things, he guessed, to her, were little more than a necessity now and then.

Anyway, he had planned this trip with a dual purpose.

He wanted to surprise Slater, who was not just a colleague but a friend, with the television premier of the documentary of *Wild West... Still Wild*—and he wanted to see Raine. Two separate goals but also intertwined, since Slater and Raine had a past and shared a daughter. Slater was now happily married to someone else, but through a few very casual questions, Mick knew Raine wasn't seeing anyone.

This might get complicated and he hated complications. Business deals were a dance back and forth but he kept his personal life as simple as possible.

Raine was far from simple. Her art was exemplary and over the top, and the vivid mermaid label she'd created for the Carson winery's sparkling wine had resulted in more bottles sold in one day upon release than were sold of all their other wines combined, and they had been doing quite well before. Somehow he doubted Raine even registered the triumph.

But he wasn't interested in her for her talent—well, he was impressed, but that wasn't first and foremost in his mind. Maybe opposites did attract, though if you'd told him that before he'd met her through the Carson family, he'd have laughed it off.

He wasn't laughing now. It wasn't that he didn't have a good reason to be in Wyoming at the moment anyway, but he was essentially there because of a certain woman he couldn't seem to get off his mind.

Grace Carson met him in the dining room of the Bliss River Resort and Spa, her eyes sparkling, and gave him a welcoming hug. Slater really did have good taste in women because his wife was a stunning red-head with a confident air. She also apparently had a good memory, because almost immediately a waiter came over with coffee and a rack of rye toast, which was his favorite.

She joined him, pouring coffee for them both. "Do

you have any idea how hard it is to not tell Slater about Christmas Day?"

"I've actually struggled with it myself, so maybe I do." He admired the view of the snow-capped mountains out the huge windows as he sipped his coffee and thought about all the strings he'd pulled. Considerable was the answer. He looked back at Grace, which was also a pleasure. "The time slot was the hardest part. But everyone is pretty much home, and hopefully by then Christmas dinner will be over and there will be a worldwide desire to watch something other than the old classics."

She added cream to her coffee. "I think it's a brilliant idea. You do realize you just usurped my gift to him, which was a new saddle. He'll probably kiss *you* under the mistletoe instead of me."

Mick chuckled. "I doubt it, but if it happens, let's not catch that on film." Not knowing remote cameras were taking footage, Slater's younger brother Drake had gotten caught in a romantic moment with his now wife, Luce, and was none too happy about it being used in the film, but had grudgingly signed the release.

"Maybe Raine will kiss you instead." Grace took a sip from her silver-rimmed cup, a knowing look in her eyes.

He'd never understood how women had magical powers when it came to sensing a possible romance. Men just blundered on, unaware, and females were like wolves sniffing the air. He was a man who played angles, so he admitted noncommittally, "I can't imagine any man minding that. How is the resort business these days?"

She caught on to that just as easily. "Subject

changed. I can take a hint. It's going well. Ski season is in full swing. We're packed. The spa is booked out two months. The owner is pleased and it keeps me busy and, well, I'm expecting again. Luce is also in baby mode. We're just waiting for the same kind of announcement from Mace and Kelly. Then all the cousins can grow up together."

Mick pictured a bunch of toddlers running wild around the sprawling Carson ranch. To his surprise, the image was immensely appealing. He hadn't had much exposure to babies; his only brother was childless by choice even though he'd been married a long time. He and his wife tended to spend the winter in France or at their house in the Caribbean, and as an investment banker, Ran could work from anywhere, so their attitude reflected their sophisticated lifestyle.

Prior to his business association with Slater, he hadn't thought about it much, but Mick had to acknowledge that his upbringing had left a hole in his life. Warm family gatherings had just never happened. His parents traveled widely when his father was alive and now it was tradition to meet his mother at the country club for Christmas dinner.

Elegant, but not exactly cozy. He'd been to celebrations at the Carson ranch before and they were usually quite the boisterous experience. He said, "Congratulations. Slater is a lucky man all the way around."

"He'll certainly be one tomorrow," Grace replied with a smile. "I haven't said a word to anyone—although Blythe knows, which means Harry knows."

"Raine knows I'm in town." He gave what he hoped was a casual shrug. "We have a business meeting tonight and she said no restaurants would be open, so she invited me over."

Arched brows rose higher. "Did she now? She's breaking her burger and glass of wine tradition?"

"No. I was informed that's the menu."

Grace gave a laugh of real merriment. "Only Raine would serve Mick Branson a burger. I love Raine but she is on the eclectic side. That's why I was surprised the two of you hit it off so well. She's right about Christmas Eve, by the way—we even close the restaurants here at the resort and the spa. Guests can pre-order special bags with gourmet sandwiches and salads that will be delivered via room service, but quite frankly, I just don't believe in making anyone work who would rather be with their family on Christmas. A few staff members would rather work for holiday pay, so the resort is open, but not the dining choices. In town everything is closed."

Vaguely he registered her words about the holiday, but his mind was caught on what she'd said about Raine. *Hit it off?* He chose not to comment. He could negotiate deals involving millions of dollars, but personal discussions were not his strong suit. "Los Angeles is a little different."

"Oh, I bet." Grace was definitely amused. Her phone beeped and she rose. "Excuse me, but that sound means something needs my attention. I'll see you tomorrow."

After she left he finished his toast and coffee, checked his email via his phone, and headed out to his rental car. It was lightly snowing and briskly cold, the car dusted over in white, and he wished he'd thought about bringing some gloves. It wasn't something that occurred to him back in L.A. when he packed for the trip.

The wine shop was on the main street and some-one had done an artistic job of decorating the windows with snowflakes. The bells on the huge wreath on the door jingled as Mick walked in. There were several other customers and he noted Kelly Carson, Slater's sister-in-law, was the one sitting behind the old pol-ished counter. She looked cute wearing an elf hat and a surprised expression.

Good, his lucky day.

Or so he hoped, but it was yet another person to swear to secrecy. Her eyes had widened as she recog-nized him.

There was just no such thing as a secret in Mustang Creek. He'd heard that the last time he'd been in town and really hadn't believed it, but was now starting to feel like living proof.

"Merry Christmas, Mick," Kelly called as he ap-proached.

"Merry Christmas," he said. "Let me make an edu-cated guess and assume you're working because you wouldn't ask any of the employees to so they could be with their families."

She nodded and the fuzzy tassel on her hat bobbed. "You're right. Absolutely. We're only open until noon today anyway, holiday hours… I guess I didn't realize you were in town. No one mentioned it."

"No one knows." Well, not true. Grace, Blythe, Harry and Raine knew, and now Kelly. He smiled wryly. "Let me rephrase. I'd prefer if Slater didn't find out I'm here. It's about both business and friendship, so if you can keep it to yourself until tomorrow, I'd appreciate it."

She sent him a wink. "My lips are sealed."

"I knew I could count on you. Now, tell me, best wine to go with a burger would be…what?"

"I hate to disappoint you, but Bad Billy's won't be open."

The biker bar was legendary for its burgers. "I'm not actually getting my burger from Billy's."

She blinked. "Oh…oh! Raine?"

It was tempting to deny it, but…well, why bother? Clearly her Christmas Eve burgers tradition was well-known. "We have a business meeting tonight. What kind of wine does she usually buy?"

"The Wildfire Merlot." Kelly said it promptly, her expression alight with humor. "She also likes Soaring Eagle Chardonnay. Either one would be fine. At the end of the day, Mace always tells me to drink a wine you like with food you like. Don't worry about the rest of it. He thinks snobbish pairing is overrated."

"People all over California just fainted dead away because you said that."

"People all over California buy our wines," she countered with a mischievous elfin grin that matched her festive hat. "So he seems to know what he's doing."

Tough to argue with that. "I'll take a few bottles of each, plus some for the Christmas gathering tomorrow, including the new sparkling wine. Just give me a case."

CHAPTER TWO

IT WASN'T LIKE she didn't consider what she wore, but on a scale of one to ten she would rate herself maybe a five when it came to how much thought and time she usually put into her attire.

Tonight for some reason, Raine was on the higher end of the scale.

The long red skirt and clingy black blouse looked nice, but were not exactly hamburger-worthy, she decided with a critical eye before she changed into jeans and a teal blue silk sweater. Except it occurred to her that if she dribbled ketchup or spilled even a drop of wine the sweater would be toast and she'd have to toss it—she'd known at the time it was an impractical purchase but had loved it too much not to buy it—so she changed for a third time. Black leggings and a patterned gray sweater dress won the day, comfortable but certainly dressier than she'd usually choose for a night home alone.

Well, she wasn't going to be alone. She even set the table—which would never have happened on her traditional Christmas Eve—with what she called her December plates, white with tiny candy canes on them. Daisy had seen them when they'd been out shopping when she was six years old and begged, so Raine caved and bought them. Every year when the plates came out, it signaled the holiday season for her daughter and the sentimental value was priceless. Even though she'd been a classic example of a starving artist and had been trying to launch her business at the time, she'd also bought a set of silverware whose handles were etched with reindeer and a sleigh.

It was ironic in a good way to think someone as successful as Mick Branson wanted to meet with her on a professional level and would eat off the dishes that she'd bought when she really couldn't afford them. Now she was so busy she doubted she could accept whatever it was he wanted to discuss even if she was interested.

Mr. Bojangles wandered past with a feline yawn, headed for his food bowl, but stopping to be petted. It was like a royal decree when a cat of his size demanded to be scratched behind the ears. Raine stroked his head. "What do you think of the table? Fancy enough for a hotshot executive?"

He yawned again, his gold-green eyes reflecting doubt. She said defensively, "Hey, I paid twenty bucks for those dishes."

His furry face expressed his skepticism that the plates were worth even that. She argued his point. "Daisy loves them."

He didn't disagree, just headed off to the kitchen to chomp loudly out of his bowl. His ample backside was normal for his breed, but his love of food didn't help matters. His vet, Jax Locke, had been diplomatic in suggesting she could maybe curtail the cat treats.

Raine agreed, but Jangles—as she called him face-to-face—was a contender when it came to getting his way. There was not much in the way of compromise on his part.

The snow was beginning to blow a little and she had started a fire in her fireplace with the push of a button. She liked ambiance and watching the flames, but as a single female didn't want to haul in logs, so she'd had a gas insert put in a few years ago. Bypassing Christmas music, she put on some soft classical in the background, and without the World's Largest Puppy—Samson—tearing around, the house felt downright serene. Daisy always took him with her to the ranch and he loved running free with the other dogs. The backyard at Raine's just wasn't as exciting as herding cattle with Drake and the other hands. Maybe when he got a little older Samson would be content to just bask in the sun. As it stood, he wanted to run amok.

Red, the head ranch hand, called the dog a log-legged galoot. That seemed about right.

When Raine saw the arc of headlights in the big front window and glanced at the fairy tale clock on the mantel, Cinderella's glass slipper was pointed right at six sharp. Mick Branson was right on time.

She, on the other hand, was perpetually late to everything. Maybe being awake at two in the morning was the only thing they had in common. She opened the door before he knocked and in return got a capricious swirl of snow blowing into the tiny foyer.

"Thanks," he said as he came in. "The wind is really picking up. A Merry Christmas with all the appropriate special effects." He studied her as he wiped his boots on the mat inside the door. "It's nice to see you again."

"And you as well." She shut the door, peering through the side panel of glass. "It is coming down out there, isn't it? So pretty."

"From safe in here, it's very pretty," he said with

his all too fleeting smile. "The wine is in this bag, and where do you want my coat?"

She recognized the bag because she'd designed the print on it. The M for Mountain Vineyards was flanked by pine trees and a hawk sat on a branch on one side. "I'll take your coat, and the kitchen is through that doorway right there. It's impossible to get lost in this house."

"It's charming." He glanced around as he slipped off his wool coat.

She wasn't used to men who used the word *charming* in regular conversation, but he did have nice wide shoulders, so she'd cut him some slack. Actually, everything about him was attractive: dark hair, striking dark eyes, and what she'd define as an aristocratic face that spoke of a lineage that was Old World, probably Spain or Portugal. She had an admitted fascination for history, so she'd love to know his story. "I'll be right back. There's a corkscrew and glasses on the counter. Go for it."

He took her at her word, she discovered after she'd deposited his coat on the bed in the spare bedroom— one drawback to her quaint little house was no coat closet—and poured them both a glass of wine.

"Merlot," he told her as he set the bottle on the counter. "I took Kelly's advice and bought the wines I like best and didn't try to match hamburgers."

"She's pretty good at that sort of thing." Raine accepted a glass, looking at him as she did. "I've never had a business meeting on Christmas Eve, but you probably have. What's the protocol? I don't have a table in a conference room, but we could sit by the fire."

"I'm not all business, just so you know. Conference tables are overrated, and the fire sounds nice."

"I thought business was why you were here."

"Come on, Raine, I think you know that's not entirely it. I do have something I want to talk to you about, but I just wanted to see you."

Well, at least he was direct. She liked that, even as the admission surprised her. "The fire it is then."

She led the way and he followed, and as luck would have it when they passed the tree, Jangles decided on a drive-by attack to defend his territory. Maybe she should have issued a warning, but she was so used to the giant cat's antics she didn't think of it, and though obviously startled, Mick managed to not spill his wine even with claws in the hem of his no-doubt expensive slacks. She apologized as the cat unhooked and retreated back into his lair. "By the way, meet my cat, Mr. Bojangles. He has a perimeter staked out around the tree and he guards it. Sorry, I should have warned you."

"That's a cat? I would have guessed African lion."

"You should see the dog the Carson family gifted me. Mace made the mistake of suggesting Daisy help him pick out a puppy. She and that dog fell instantly in love. He's hers now. I think one day you'll be able to slap a saddle on that bad boy and ride out on the range. I have a sack of dog food in my pantry so big I need a furniture dolly to carry it in." In an attempt to be a proper hostess, she asked, "Shall we sit down?"

And get the business part done so we can relax a little. It was, after all, Christmas Eve.

MICK WASN'T SURPRISED at all by her house. Raine's taste showed, well…everywhere. It was so different from the elegance of his childhood home, he tried to restrain his smile. No settees, no polished tables, no imported rugs or pricey oil paintings…

There was a poster of wine labels she'd created above the fireplace and the mantel was a hand-hewn log of some kind. A ceramic frog sat on the brick hearth, and there was a rusted antique toy truck on the other side. Her couch was ruby red and suited the dark wood floors, and a coffee table with a distressed finish added an artistic touch. A craftsman glass lamp patterned with butterflies and brilliant flowers adorned a bookshelf. Nothing matched, yet the décor oddly fit together.

He liked it better than his own perfectly decorated house, which he'd hired someone expensive to put together. Raine's house was comfortable and lived-in; his place might look like it was straight out of a magazine, but it was hardly homey.

"This is nice."

"This is probably about a tenth of the space of your house, but thank you," she said drily. "Daisy and I don't need more. She can get that at the ranch. I'm not really into personal possessions, which is a good thing since she acquired that enormous puppy. Along with my favorite pair of shoes, the rug in the kitchen has been a casualty. I happened to like that rug but I had no idea it was a culinary canine delight. He chewed it to pieces when my back was turned for about eight seconds."

He had to laugh as he settled next to her on the couch. "Slater mentioned every time Mace went to acquire a pet, someone else in family became latched on to it and he had to try again."

"It's like visiting a zoo," she agreed, also laughing.

"The moment the infamous Mrs. Arbuckle-Calder became involved, game over. That woman makes an executive decision over whether or not you might need a pet, and if you are deemed pet-worthy, she'll pick one out for you and just show up with it and drop it right inside your door. You don't really get to say yes or no. How do think I ended up with the lion?"

He liked the way she kicked off her black flats and propped her feet on the coffee table, wineglass in hand. A gust of wind hit the rafters, but the fire balanced it nicely. "I wasn't allowed pets growing up. My mother was opposed to the slightest hint of pet hair in her house, plus my parents traveled a lot, so pets were an inconvenience she didn't want to suffer."

Raine furrowed her brow. "No pets?"

"None."

"Daisy would be desolate without her cat and dog."

He'd had some moments of desolation, too, but he'd survived.

"Everyone is different. This is what I wanted to talk to you about. I know someone who produces Pixel motion pictures and I mentioned you were a graphic artist. I showed him your work, and he's interested in talking about it. He's fairly sure Wyoming is the end of the earth, but he's willing to come here to meet with you."

She stared at him. "What?"

Raine had the most beautiful unusual eyes. Not green and not gold, but a starburst mixture of of both colors.

"Pixel. Motion pictures. I—"

"I know what they are," she interrupted, groaning and briefly closing those eyes. "Oh man, I swore I was going tell you *no* to anything…but that changes the game."

"Anything?"

"Stop with the sexual innuendo, I'm processing here. I don't have the time in my day to add another thing, but I can't possibly pass that up. I thought you liked me. How could you dangle this in front of me?" She shook her head in disbelief. "I'm not even that qualified. I took some animation classes in college, but that's it."

He smiled. "My personal feelings about you aside, from what I've been able to see, you're really talented. I'd never have mentioned your name otherwise. But I'm glad I did, because the producer agrees with me. He thinks you could be a valuable addition to the team."

Raine glared at him from those vivid hazel eyes. "You knew this would be a graphic artist's dream. This is a calculated move."

"Of course I did. Never underestimate me." He had known. He understood a lot about being driven. Why else would they be exchanging emails at two in the morning?

"What kind of company are we talking about?"

She wasn't a fool, but he already knew that. "Let's just say you'd recognize the name."

She blew out a breath. "I knew you were trouble. I'm so busy right now as it is—"

"All you have to do is think about it and let me know if you want a face-to-face. I'm investing, so I want it to be topnotch. It's in my financial best interest to help him find the best artist possible." She opened her mouth again, undoubtedly to protest further, and he held up a hand. "That's enough business for one night, especially when it's Christmas Eve. I'm declaring the meeting portion of our evening officially over."

Raine blinked, then raised a brow. "In that case, I think it's time for the dinner portion of our evening. I hope you can stand spicy food." She got to her feet. "Bring the wine, please."

"I thought we were having hamburgers." He followed her toward the kitchen, bottle in hand. "But yes, I do like spicy."

Her kitchen was as interesting as the living room. A row of unmatched antique canisters sat on the polished counter. The appliances were modern but the vintage hutch in the corner held what looked like a beautiful set of old dishes and pink crystal glasses. A mobile made from tarnished silver forks hung over the farmhouse sink—another piece of décor that was quintessentially Raine and suited the room perfectly.

His mother would undoubtedly faint at the sight, but Mick again found himself both charmed and amused.

"Good." Raine moved efficiently between the refrigerator and the counter as she set down a plate and several containers. "Green chili cheeseburgers are my indulgence on Christmas Eve. Questionably traditional, I know, but I love them."

He grinned for what felt like the thousandth time that night. "Are you kidding me?" he said incredulously. "I'm from New Mexico. We didn't move to California until I was fifteen. My aunt and uncle still live in Las Cruces. I have done some self-analyzing to try and figure out if I go to visit them, or just for the food."

She gave him a surprised look that probably mirrored her own. "Are you serious? My cousin lives in Santa Fe. I love it there. She sends me the chilis every late August or early September and I hoard them like a miser."

"The real deal? From Hatch? Don't tease me."

"Oh yeah." Raine nodded, no doubt inwardly laughing at his expression. "I roast them myself and freeze them. I would save Daisy and the pets first in a fire, but I might consider going back in for my chilis."

He'd just gone straight to heaven. "You've just given me quite the Christmas present. If I can help, let me know. Otherwise I'll just stand here and drool."

She pulled out a cutting board from a side cupboard. "Somehow I suspect your culinary skills are limited to making reservations, but if you can slice an onion, you have a job to do."

"That I can do." She was right, he didn't cook often, but then again, he traveled constantly and home-cooked meals were hard to come by when one wasn't often home. Maybe that was part of what he liked about Mustang Creek—every aspect of the community felt welcoming and homey. If you walked into an establishment like Bad Billy's Burger Palace, you'd be greeted by name.

He hadn't even realized until recently that that appealed to him.

Maybe he was just getting a little restless in his life. Something was missing, and he knew he was in Mustang Creek for Christmas for more than just work.

Standing in Raine's kitchen, admiring the shapely curves of her body under that silvery sweater, he wondered again what it was about her that had caught his attention. It had served him well in the business world to play hunches and go with his instincts, and his instincts had started humming the instant he'd first laid eyes on her. Raine wasn't classically beautiful but she was one of those women who, whenever she walked into a room, unconsciously made everyone turn to look. Her vitality was part of the appeal, and since he himself was reserved and self-contained, he'd been fascinated from the start.

"Knife is in the drawer." She looked up and caught him staring. Wiping her hands on a towel, she looked down as a sudden faint hint of color bloomed in her cheeks. "What?"

"You're just so—" he cast about for the word "—alive."

"I hope so, since the alternative is pretty undesirable." The smile she gave him was quizzical this time.

He wasn't about to elaborate. "True enough, Ms. McCall."

"Knife is in the drawer, by the way."

"You mentioned that." He tugged open the drawer she indicated and found the object in question. "On the job."

Mick chopped onions while she dropped the burgers in the grill pan and in less than a minute, his mouth was watering from the tantalizing smell of sizzling meat. Outside, the snow was thickening, draping the trees and the wooden fence out back in a festive wardrobe of white. The whole scene was relaxing in a way he didn't often allow himself, a respite from the world, and the music softly playing in the background didn't hurt one bit.

Fire in the hearth, a concerto in the background, a glass of wine, a home-cooked meal and a beautiful woman...

The perfect way to spend Christmas Eve.

CHAPTER THREE

"THAT WAS A real treat. I felt like I was home again."

For someone who obviously hit the gym, Mick could eat on a par with the Carson brothers, and that was a high bar. As Red, the head hand at the ranch would say, he could really strap on the ole feed bag. Raine was happy she'd decided to make three burgers instead of just two because that third one disappeared quickly. Mick's manners were meticulous, of course, but he had devoured his food with flattering enthusiasm.

"I warn you," she informed him when she got up to clear their plates, "I learned all about how to make dessert from Blythe Carson. Ice cream is going to be all you get."

"That sounds just fine to me."

"Once you taste Bad Billy's Lemon Drop Ice Cream, you'll be hooked for life." She wasn't kidding. "There's a reason I don't dare keep it on hand all the time. That would be a desire to keep my girlish figure."

He gave her a slow once-over as he rose, plate in hand. "There's nothing *I'd* change, trust me. Let me help with the cleanup."

She'd argue, but had a feeling Mick Branson didn't lose verbal battles very often, maybe ever. He was the epitome of cool, calm and collected, with a good dose of masculine confidence thrown in. It was telling that she wasn't sure how to handle his obvious interest, because she'd decided a long time ago to just live her life as she wished and that her untraditional approach was a healthy outlook on life, at least for her. She'd sat down with her daughter and explained that the reason she'd never married Slater was that they were too fundamentally different for it to work out, and Daisy seemed to accept that, perhaps because she saw how much her parents loved her and respected each other.

But no one was more different from her than Mick Branson, so Raine had to question why, when their fingers brushed as she handed him the ice cream scoop so he could do the honors, there was an electric flicker of awareness between them.

He wasn't her type.

She was definitely not his type. She wasn't sure what his type might be, but she imagined a cool, polished blonde who'd feel right at home in pearls and a stylish black dress. Someone who'd fit in at corporate functions and with the Hollywood set.

Mick interrupted her musings as he scooped out the creamy lemon mixture into the two Victorian glasses she'd inherited from her grandmother. "Daisy is a great kid from what I've seen. Spunky and self-confident."

She smiled. "That she is. It's hard to believe she's half-grown already. I don't know where the time goes."

He concentrated on scooping. "Have you ever thought about having more children?"

Raine's expression must have reflected her surprise at the unexpected question. He caught her gaze and for a moment she found herself trapped in those dark eyes. "I just meant you're a wonderful mother, according to Slater. You're young, so it just occurred to me. Plus I talked to Grace this morning and she told me her news, and also about Luce." He looked not exactly embarrassed but maybe off balance. "I didn't mean to get so personal so quickly. I officially recant."

Raine wasn't about to let him off the hook so easily. "I don't mind the question, but turnabout is fair play. So what about you? Kids?" He was, she'd guess, around forty or so. There wasn't a fleck of gray in that carefully tousled dark hair, but Slater had once remarked that he and Mick were about the same age.

"Do I have any kids? No. Do I want them? Maybe."

"I feel like I don't know that much about you. You've done a good job of keeping your private life, well… private."

"Checking up on me?" He didn't seem to mind— quite the opposite. "I keep it that way as much as possible."

"I might have checked a little when you first showed up in Mustang Creek, but Slater likes you, so I trust you. If I didn't, I wouldn't be wasting BB's Lemon Drop on you."

"In that case, I hope to prove worthy of the ice cream. Sounds like a high bar."

At least he had a sense of humor. She was discovering she liked that about him.

There were quite a lot of things she liked about him. Too many.

"It's an honor, trust me. I don't just give it away all the time."

Without a blink, he returned smoothly, "I didn't think you did."

Raine couldn't help but give him *the look*. "I thought I banned the sexual innuendos."

"Hey, you can take that remark any way you wish."

A man like him didn't look boyish often, but his unrepentant expression was pretty close. And those eyes...

"Just for that, I'm going to make you watch my favorite Christmas movie, unless you have other pressing plans."

"I'm all yours." He deftly wielded the ice cream scoop. "In case you're wondering—and I'm going to guess you are—my brother and his wife are in London for the holidays this year, my mother is in New York with friends, and since I have a little surprise for Slater, I decided Mustang Creek might not be a bad place to spend Christmas this year. I'm almost afraid to ask, but what's your favorite Christmas movie? Please tell me there isn't a lot of singing and dancing."

"Relax. There's none. I usually watch *Big Jake*. You know, John Wayne." She took two long-handled spoons from a drawer. "Not only is it a great movie, but it has sentimental value. My father loved it. I remember sitting on the couch watching it with him after my mother went to bed. Unlike you, she liked the movies with the singing and dancing and he needed a good dose of the Old West afterward. I was allowed to stay up as long as I wanted on Christmas Eve. I still do that."

"You are a big girl, so you can do whatever you want."

She was just going to ignore that. He was deliberately provoking her. "I always have done what I want. Make a note of it. Do you want a cup of coffee?"

"That sounds good. It'll keep me awake for the drive back to the resort later."

The reminder that their evening would come to an

end caused an odd sinking in her stomach, one she immediately chided herself for. After all, it wasn't like she planned to invite him to spend the night, no matter how attractive she found him. The softly falling snow outside might be adding to the ambiance of the evening, but her guarded heart was resistant to even the most romantic of trappings.

She believed in love. In loving your child, your family, and of course, she'd thought she was in love with Slater what felt like a million years ago, but that just hadn't worked out.

It would have been easy to accept his proposal once he knew she was pregnant, to settle into a comfortable life as a Carson, but she'd known from the start that neither of their hearts would have been in it. They were friends—she genuinely liked the father of her child and was grateful for the good relationship they shared—but that wasn't the same as love.

For the life of her, she couldn't figure out why it was Mick Branson who apparently inspired more than friendly feelings in her. She couldn't have picked a man more different from her if she'd tried.

Not in a million years was she Hollywood. Not in a million years was he Mustang Creek.

Though when he settled next to her on the roomy couch, ice cream in hand, he seemed comfortable enough despite the designer slacks and tailored shirt. He took a bite and gave her an incredulous look from those oh-so-sexy dark eyes. "You have to be kidding me."

"I told you. Billy is a burly, tattooed culinary angel."

"I might kiss him the next time I see him." Mick dug back in.

"And he might take exception to that." She took a spoonful from her own dish. The ice cream was smooth, creamy yet tart, and everything she remembered. Billy only made it once a year and she always put in an order early. Picking up the remote, she pushed a button to cue up the movie. "Here we go. The Duke."

"Pure Christmas magic in the form of an old western—sounds great to me. But I guess now would be the time to confess I've never actually seen it. Did you say *Big Jake*?"

"What?" She stared. "Never? That's…incomprehensible."

He shrugged. "If you met my family, well, let's just say John Wayne was not on their radar. I'm sure they would enjoy it, don't get me wrong, but they just wouldn't think of it. I believe I was dragged to a Broadway play as a child before I ever watched a cartoon."

That explained quite a lot. "Is that why you do what you do?"

"It might be. Why are you an artist? I doubt I'm going to get a straight-up answer. There probably isn't one."

She had to concede that one, so she changed the subject. "I can't believe you already ate all of that ice cream." He'd inhaled it. "Haven't you heard of an ice cream headache?"

"I've never had one, but for that stuff, I'd take my chances." He got up to go into the kitchen and she heard him rinse the bowl and considerately put it in the dishwasher.

Considerate? Oh no. That was trouble right there.

Mick Branson was larger than life in some ways. So was Slater, so maybe that accounted for the chemistry simmering between her and Mick. She was attracted to charismatic men.

She savored each spoonful as the opening movie scene unfolded, feeling oddly comfortable. Even though he wasn't a stranger, they'd never spent time alone together before this evening, so the ease between them surprised her.

Everything about the way Mick acted said he was interested and she wasn't positive she was ready for someone like him intruding on the life she'd so carefully built for herself and her daughter.

His life was all about reading signals. Meetings, the stock market, international affairs, how the media was cooperating...

Mick was in tune with the business side of his life. The personal side? Not so much.

Raine was clearly a free spirit but there was a wariness about her that was impossible to miss. It wasn't like he didn't understand being cautious; he tended to tread carefully himself, or perhaps he would have had more long-term relationships rather than just a fleeting romantic entanglement here or there.

Her wary aura aside, he wondered if she had any idea how sexy it was to watch her eat ice cream.

He forced his gaze to remain on the screen rather than her lips. There was no way he'd take advantage of softly falling snow and all the rest of the ambiance to get her into bed, though he had a lot of enthusiasm for a night with the lovely Ms. McCall. Maybe more than one night, and that was food for thought right there.

He was afraid this was going somewhere, and Mick wasn't a man who considered himself afraid of all that much.

Luckily, John Wayne saved him along with everyone else on the screen. Well, not quite everyone, and with an analytical eye he admired the director's decisions on how the plot played out. It was his favorite kind of script, showing people as they really were—not all good, not all bad, but a combination of both. Slater tended to roll that way in his documentaries as well, with villains and heroes side by side. His characters weren't fictional, but balanced, and he made riveting dramas set in real places steeped in history.

"Good movie, but there's no love story," Mick pointed out when the credits rolled.

Raine sat easily with one leg folded under her. He'd already concluded she did yoga from the rolled-up mat tucked in the corner, so the agile pose didn't surprise him. What had surprised him more was when her giant cat had wandered out and jumped on the couch with remarkable grace for a creature of his size, then settled down next to her. "Isn't that what appeals to most men? All action and no sappy stuff."

He shook his head, a faint smile on his mouth. "I think you have it backward. Men are more interested in romance than women are."

"Au contraire, Mr. Boardroom." She waved her hand in dismissal. "Men are more interested in sex."

"I sense a debate coming. Who buys flowers and candy and dutifully mows the yard just to please the woman in his life?"

She shot back tartly, "A man who wants to have sex. I appreciate a thoughtful gesture as much as any woman, but let's not get confused about the motivation here."

"You can't put an entire gender in the same bracket,

Ms. Artist. There are a lot of decent guys I know who would never walk into the bedroom of someone who they didn't have romantic feelings for in the first place. Brains and beauty are all well and good, but if a woman isn't also a nice person, no thanks. I can tell you, in the world I live in, there are plenty of women who use sex as leverage, so it could be argued that your assumption works both ways."

Raine stroked the cat's head and Mr. Bojangles gave a rusty purr. "I'm afraid you're right and I was just pulling your chain. People are too complex to reduce to stereotypes. I don't understand a lot of them, but I think I know more good ones than bad ones. It makes me glad Daisy is growing up in Mustang Creek."

"I've looked at some land in this area," he heard himself confessing. "I haven't found the right combination of house and location, but I have done some research."

She stopped petting the cat, her attention arrested. Mr. Bojangles sent him a lethal stare for interference in the petting process, clearly understanding the interruption was his fault. "Really?"

"It's beautiful country," he said noncommittally. "I have a vacation home in Bermuda, but while it's nice to have sun and sea, I get bored after about two days. I'm thinking about leasing it out or selling it, and building one here, or better yet, buying a place with some history behind it. There's more to do in Mustang Creek than lie on a beach with a drink in your hand."

Raine looked thoughtful. "I'm the same way. I've tried it once or twice, but I can't sit and do nothing for very long. I don't find it relaxing because I feel I should be doing *something*."

"We have that in common then."

"Why do I have the feeling that's about the only thing we have in common? Aside from a love of green chilis, of course."

"Not true," he told her, and gestured toward the TV. "We both like the John Wayne movie we just watched. We both like Mountain Winery merlot. We both would kill for Bad Billy's lemon ice cream. Mr. Bojangles clearly loves us both...the list just goes on."

"You were doing pretty good until the Jangles part. He's really picky. I can tell he hasn't made up his mind yet. He doesn't trust men that easily."

They weren't talking just about the cat, and he knew it. "He just needs to get to know me better. Let me prove how trustworthy I am."

"You want to prove yourself to a cat?"

"Well, he's a really big cat. I'm kind of afraid of him."

There was merriment in Raine's eyes. "His girth is part of his charm, or so I tell the vet when he starts on me about Jangles' diet. Luckily, I feed him, so he adores me."

"He has impeccable taste."

"I doubt you're really afraid of him and I suppose he must like you to come out from under the tree and sit this close."

"I respect his opinion, one male to another."

"That's a good way to handle him. Otherwise Jangles might boss you around."

Mick had to raise a brow. "Maybe like his owner."

"Oh, come on, no one owns a pet. Have you really never had one?"

"I always wanted a dog, but it never worked out."

She only believed him—he was sure of it—because of his matter-of-fact tone. He wasn't shallow enough to ever complain about a privileged childhood but his mother hadn't approved of animals in the house, so they didn't have any. End of story. He'd begged for a dog and the answer was no.

"That's too bad. You missed out. But it's not too late to get one now."

"These days it's a timing issue. Once I was out of college, I immediately joined a firm that sent me to Japan for three years. When I came back to California, I started my own company, and trust me, with the hours I kept I didn't have the time for a dog and still don't."

"You need one." Raine said it firmly as if the whole matter was decided. "Buy the land, build your house, and you'll have no shortage of dog-sitters to pitch in if you're out of town. I can be one of them. Daisy would be thrilled, and Samson is used to other dogs from being at the ranch so frequently. When it comes to the land, do you want real Wyoming?"

It was a generous offer about the dog, and an impulsive one, but he already had the impression that despite Raine's wariness around him, she made a habit of following her instincts most of the time—not in an impractical way, but just acting from the heart. "Yes, that's the plan. Real Wyoming. Solitude and a stunning view. A place where I can sit and read, maybe write something that isn't a memo just for a change of pace, and relax on the front porch with a glass of wine or a cold beer and watch the sunset. I'm at a place in my life where I'm starting to realize that being driven has its perks, but working every second of the day isn't necessarily good for you."

"Write something? Like the great American novel?" She was looking at him like he'd sprouted a second head.

"Believe it or not, Ms. Artist, I do have some imagination." He didn't add that he could easily imagine her soft, warm and naked in his arms, but it was getting harder to banish those images from his mind.

"I have no trouble believing that, actually. Excuse me, Jangles, your new friend and I have someplace to go." She gently scooted away from the cat and stood. "I'll get your coat, Mr. Boardroom. Time for a scenic Christmas Eve jaunt."

"Now?" He glanced at the clock, which had wands for hands and glass slippers in varying colors to represent the hours. Which made him think she'd designed it. It looked like, if he could read it correctly, it was nearly eleven o'clock.

"As good a time as any, right? Snow falling, the mountains in the backdrop and winter magic in the air... I want to show you something. No, now I *need* to show you something."

He had absolutely no idea what she was talking about, but was willing to play along. "Okay, I'm game."

"You might be when you see what I'm going to show you. I'll drive."

"Drive? Where—"

"Let's go." She opened a hall closet and took out a coat, then disappeared to return with his, pulling on fluffy white mittens as he did up his buttons. "This is perfect."

Mystified, he said, "I'll take your word for it. Care to give me a hint where we're going?"

"I'm a show-not-tell kind of girl. You'll find out."

Two minutes later they were in the car, driving toward a destination unknown.

THE PLACE LOOKED as she remembered it the day she put it up for sale, but was also lit by the moon now that the snow had subsided to flurries, and she spotted the twinkle of a star or two as the clouds moved overhead in the brisk December wind.

Maybe fate had smiled on her twice this night.

Raine took in the weathered structure before them and tried to stifle a pang over the prospect of it being torn down. She warned herself that a man like Mick Branson probably wouldn't want the dilapidated wreck, and she could hardly blame him for that, but the setting was incredible.

"If you want Wyoming, this is it," she said as she parked the SUV. "There's a small lake behind the house, fed by a spring. It's so crystal clear, fishing should be a crime there because you can drop a hook right in front of a fish. I know it's frozen over right now, but in the warmer weather it's perfect for swimming in. And you have never seen anything so amazing in your life as the view from the back porch when you sit and watch the sun come up."

He was diplomatic, but she expected that. "The cabin looks really old."

"That's the understatement of the century. The house is falling down." She shut off the vehicle. "It was once just one room, but sections were added on here and there over the past century. Keep in mind the location. It isn't a lot of land, just a hundred acres, but you don't want to run cattle, correct? Just have a place to get away. Let me show you the inside."

"One hundred acres in L.A. isn't even a possibility. Neither is me running cattle, since I'd have no idea what to do. I do just need a place to get away... Raine, why do you have a key?"

"You can tear it all down as far as the buildings go, though I wish you wouldn't, but this is really a nice piece of property."

"That doesn't answer my question."

She sighed and turned to face him. "It belonged to my grandfather."

He paused. "Okay."

"And it belonged to his grandfather before him."

His jaw dropped. "You're joking, right?"

She wasn't. "It was built a very long time ago obviously. Don't those old pictures you've seen strike a chord? Slater featured a before and after of this place in his documentary. I have to say, he made his point about continuity across the generations. It hasn't changed."

Snow was still drifting down as she stood there, reminded powerfully of Slater's film. Mick said, "I remember. He didn't tell me this belonged to your family."

Drily, she remarked, "When Slater is in work mode, the rest of the world just goes away. Plus I doubt he thought it'd matter to you one way or another. Wait until you see the inside." She pulled out the flashlight she'd brought, the powerful beam catching the sagging facade. "No electricity. The water is piped in straight from the lake with no filtration system whatsoever, but since my grandfather grew up here, he just drank it anyway and swore it was better than any city water could ever be. I'd skip that top step—it was dicey the last time I was here and I doubt it has improved any."

Mick had a bemused expression on his face. "This has certainly been an interesting first date. Lead on."

She slanted him a sidelong look and hopped up over the tricky step. The entire porch creaked, but it had done so for as long as she could remember. "Date, huh? I thought it was a business meeting."

"I guess now's the time for me to confess that that was a ploy to get you to have dinner with me. My reasons for talking business with you were genuine, but the minute that discussion was over, it became a date." He was tall enough to step smoothly over the dicey step. "See how devious I am? You fell right into my wicked trap."

"Or you fell into mine." She jiggled the key in the ancient lock. There was an art to cajoling it to cooperate. "Have I mentioned this place is haunted?"

"No, but what would Christmas Eve be without a snowy haunted old cabin? If it wasn't, I'd be disappointed." His tone was dry, but he looked intrigued.

She liked his understated sense of humor. To her that was more important than good looks or money. The door finally decided they could come inside and obediently creaked open. "Here's your slice of history."

CHAPTER FOUR

THE INSIDE OF the cabin was like a time capsule.

Mick couldn't believe what he was seeing. Old wooden armchairs around a table made from what looked like an old trough turned upside down, an ancient washtub in the corner, a very old rifle over the hearth of a fireplace he suspected had been the only source of heat for the place. There was even a tin cup sitting on the table like it had been left there by the last occupant.

And everywhere there were books. In homemade shelves against the walls and stacked on the floor. An ancient dry sink was part of the kitchen area, as was a rusted metal work table and several shelves with some significantly old dishes. In the corner, a wooden bucket right next to it was probably the way to wash them.

Raine stood next to him, her mittened hands in her pockets, and said neutrally, "No electricity, no heat, and if you look around for the bathroom, it's out back. My grandfather was a minimalist. He read Walden and never glanced back. Maybe you've heard of him. Matthew Brighton."

Mick about fell over. "The author?" It would certainly account for all the books...but really?

"That's the one."

"*He* was your grandfather?"

"Yes." She'd put on this cute white knit hat before they left the house and it set off her dark hair. Her nose was tinged pink from the cold.

He couldn't believe it. "My father had some of his books. I read them as a kid. That's how I got hooked on Westerns. Are you serious?"

"Would I lie?"

He didn't think she ever would. In his estimation she was probably as honest as it was possible to hope for a person to be.

He found himself grinning. "I loved those books. My favorite was *Paintbrush Pass*."

She smiled. "Mine, too. Do you realize that was set right here?"

"Here…here? Like on this property here?"

"Exactly."

Oh hell, that intrigued him. "I knew Slater's film emphasized the legacy of a famous Western author and it was Brighton. I liked seeing the town through that lens."

Her eyes suddenly glossed over. "This is where my grandfather wrote. He sat right at that desk." She pointed to the corner. "Impressive, right?"

It wasn't, certainly not by modern standards. But it was perfect—an old wagon wheel on a post covered with pieced together lengths of hand-shaved wood no one had ever bothered to finish other than to roughly plane it with a tool that gave it a moderately flat surface. Brighton's typewriter was still there and should probably be in a museum.

"He told me once that was all he'd asked for in his life. Solitude and a place to write suited his needs perfectly. Central air was an option he didn't worry about, he'd just open the windows. He didn't need a dish-washer since he had two perfectly good hands and that old bucket."

Mick walked over and ran his hand reverently over the surface on the typewriter, coating his fingers with dust. "I can't believe this."

Raine still missed her grandfather. He could hear it in her voice. "He was a rather salty old character, but all in all, a happy man."

"I can imagine. You know, thanks to him I wrote a couple of short stories in college that actually got published. My major was business, but my minor was English. I started a novel, but then I got that fairly high-powered job right after graduation." He lifted his shoulder in a negligent shrug, but life was full of what-ifs and he knew that. "Going that direction certainly made more sense at the time."

"This property would be a great place for a house." She looked him in the eye. "I swear you'd get a bar-gain price if you'd just let the cabin stand. There's lots of space to build. I've tried the Bliss County Histori-cal Society, but they think it's too remote to really be a tourist draw, so they can't justify the funding for a decent road and maybe they're right. Not even Mrs. Arbuckle-Calder can whip up some support. I want someone to enjoy the place and not tear down the cabin. If you want a scenic spot, this is it. Just tell me you won't raze the cabin and I'll practically give it away."

So this was why she'd dragged him halfway up a mountain in the middle of a snowy night. He sensed from the way she looked at him that she was somehow confident he was the man who might be worthy enough to take on this legacy that mattered to her.

He had to admit he was flattered—and humbled. It mattered to him, too. He'd devoured Brighton's books, reading a lot of them in one sitting. He couldn't agree more that the place should stay exactly as it was.

"I'm not quite ready to sign on the dotted line, but I'm definitely intrigued. Second date? We can come back and you can show me the property in the daylight." It was difficult not to confess he'd see footage of it tomorrow, but especially now, he wanted her to be as surprised as Slater and the rest of his family when the documentary aired.

"Second date." Her smile was tremulous and he doubted that happened often with her. "I never wanted to sell it in the first place, but taxes are expensive. And though Daisy and I come up here for a picnic now and then, as ridiculous as this sounds, I think the cabin is starting to get depressed about being abandoned. I want someone who appreciates the history and doesn't just see a dilapidated wreck. If you didn't have vision, you and Slater wouldn't get along."

He needed to set the record straight. "If he wasn't a brilliant filmmaker we wouldn't get along on a business level, but he is, and as a person I like him very much. It has nothing to do with me except I help other people believe in what he has in mind."

Her breath was frosty as she blew out a laugh. "He'd so disagree. I believe he calls you 'the driving force.'"

"Maybe I am, of the funding of the production. He's the inspired one. It's collaboration, a sum of the parts."

"Slater Carson doesn't collaborate with just anyone Take my word for it. I've known him for a while." She suddenly put those fluffy mittens on his shoulders and rose up to give him a light kiss that was very nice but not nearly all he wanted. Her lips were warm and smooth. She whispered, "I'm glad you're here. Merry Christmas."

At that moment a breeze brushed by, ruffling a stack of old, yellowed papers still sitting on the cluttered desk. Startled, he looked around, but the door was firmly shut and so were the windows. She said blithely, "I told you it was haunted. I think he likes you. Let's head back."

One of the pages had floated to the floor and she bent to pick it up.

WELL, THERE WAS no question she was an idiot.

A sentimental idiot, but so it went. The minute Raine heard Mick Branson was looking for property in Wyoming, she thought about her family legacy. That he knew her grandfather's name blew her away. That he'd read his books made it even more special.

Fate, plain and simple.

She was a great believer in spiritual signs, no matter if it was labeled *fate* or attributed to some divine power. If Mick bought the property, maybe he *would* leave the cabin standing. She'd resigned herself to saying goodbye to it someday, and Blythe had kindly offered to have the Carson Ranch pay the taxes, but Raine wanted someone to use the land, to enjoy the breathtaking views, to appreciate and find joy in it like her grandfather had his whole life. She'd thought about someday building a house on it, but it would have to be after Daisy was out of school. Their modest little house suited them perfectly for now.

"Two people have looked at the property in the past three years," she told Mick when they were back in the car and bumping along what didn't even resemble a lane. "Both thought it was too remote and the cost of bringing electricity and making a decent road was prohibitive. The road has to be built in order to bring in supplies for building and fuel. I'd put in a generator and call it a day. Internet might be a bit dicey, too."

Mick was hanging on to the strap on the passenger side. "How did your grandfather handle it? I mean, everyone needs groceries."

"He rode a horse into town. He used saddlebags."

"Of course," he murmured. "I just take the freeway or get on a plane. I guess I forget sometimes where I am. So he didn't just write about it, he lived the life."

"There's something to be said for convenience, but on the other hand, the middle of nowhere is pretty peaceful. There are sacrifices involved in both, I suppose."

"It's tough to get what you want without sacrifice," he agreed quietly. "I'm living proof of that. I worked very hard to please my parents when I would have rather have been one of those daring cowboys in your grandfather's novels."

"Those fictitious cowhands would have thought you were the glamorous one. Ranch life is cold, it's lonely, and you definitely don't get any thank-you notes from the cattle. At least in your line of work you get invitations to the Oscars."

Mick had the grace to laugh. "I wouldn't exactly call my life glamorous, but I get what you're saying."

"I never thought I'd say this, but I really see why Slater likes you. You're very real."

"As compared to being fake?"

"As compared to being a snob because you probably own suits that cost more than some of the pickups people drive around here. I'm surprised the cabin didn't collapse when you walked in wearing a cashmere coat and loafers instead of boots."

"There's a part of me that would rather walk around in worn jeans and a flannel shirt. It's all based on what we get used to, and what works for us." He took a deep, appreciative breath as he looked out the window. "Man, it *is* beautiful here. Aspens in snow are about as Christmas as you can get."

She smiled to herself. He'd mentioned the aspens. That was a sign.

It did look like quite the winter wonderland outside, the trees glistening and, now that the weather was clearing, a moon that illuminated the snowcapped mountains. Something slunk by in the shadow of the trees and disappeared before she could get a clean view beside the gleam of feral eyes. *Big wolf or small mountain lion?* Out here, either was a possibility.

Mick noticed it, too. "What was that?"

"Not sure." The increasing wind picked up some snow and flung it at the windshield. "But I'm fairly certain we'd just as soon avoid it on foot if possible."

He muttered, "Me, too. I don't see how the ranchers out here do it. Drake Carson in particular, riding fence lines after dark every single night."

"Not that I've ever known him to use it, but he carries a rifle and rides a really big horse. And I'm sure he doesn't understand how you're able to endure traveling the crowded L.A. freeways on a regular basis and having three-martini lunches in fancy restaurants."

Lightly, Mick said, "I usually keep it to just two martinis, no olive, just a twist of lemon." She caught his grin in the darkness of the car. "Actually, I tend to stick to a glass of sparkling water. I work long hours. A drink at lunch, much less three, is just bad for productivity."

"I might do business with a winery, but I agree."

"You see? We have another mutual philosophy. What time are you headed out to the ranch tomorrow?"

She turned on the county highway and it felt smooth as glass compared to the rutted, overgrown and disused lane that had never been graded in her memory. "About ten or so. We don't open gifts until the morning chores are done and everyone rides back in. Cattle still need to be fed and the horses taken care of, even on Christmas day."

"I was told dinner was at one sharp."

"My advice is don't be late. You've met Harry." The Carson housekeeper, Harriet Armstrong, was a legendary cook, but also an unstoppable force of nature. All three of the Carson sons considered her a second mother. "If you're late, you get to do all the dishes. Take it from someone who has made that unfortunate mistake. I'm habitually running behind, but not if Harry is involved. I toe the line around her."

"Don't worry, I'll be prompt. I'm really looking forward to tomorrow."

She glanced at the time display. "Today, actually. I'd apologize for dragging you out so late, but I happen to know you're also a night owl. I just forget what time it is. A personal flaw."

"You can get a lot done when it's quiet and your phone isn't beeping, and no one is sending emails."

"*You* emailed *me* at two in the morning."

"I didn't expect you'd be awake."

"I certainly didn't expect to get an email from you, either. Slater had some part in that, didn't he? I know you've never asked me for my email address."

"I asked if he thought you'd be interested. He said you were definitely a woman who made her own decisions, but if an animation film fell into your lap, you might jump on the idea."

"I see."

"There's a firm rule in business. It never hurts to make a proposition."

"Just in business?" She raised her brows, knowing it was probably more than a little dangerous to flirt with this man, but somehow unable to stop herself.

"Timing is everything."

At least he was reading the signals with unerring accuracy. She wasn't ready for a holiday romance when he would just get on a plane afterward and head back to California.

He wasn't serious, she told herself; he was just casually interested. She'd run across that before. Careless bachelors that came around, most of them shying away when they discovered she had a daughter, but Mick knew about Daisy already so she wasn't sure exactly what he wanted.

Mustang Creek definitely looked festive, with the streetlights adorned with wreaths and holiday lights strung in the windows of the closed shops. The streets were utterly deserted and no doubt everyone was snug in their beds. Her eclectic tree looked good from the street, she noticed as she pulled into the driveway. At the sound of the car, an indignant furry face appeared in the window, Mr. Bojangles monitoring—as always—her every move.

Had to love that cat. He was spoiled since she worked at home, but they were definite roomies.

"I think someone believes you've been out past your curfew," Mick said with a laugh. "He probably scared Santa Claus half to death while we were gone when Santa tried to put presents under the tree."

"Jangles wouldn't hurt a fly. He just looks fearsome." She'd invite him in, but it really was late, and he still had to drive to the resort.

"I won't argue that point." Mick studied her for a moment, as if reading her mind. "I had a very nice evening. Thanks again for the burgers and ice cream, and for introducing me to *Big Jake*. See you later today."

He walked her to the door and then everything changed. "By the way, nice kiss earlier but I think maybe we could go it one better." His dark eyes really could smolder, and she'd thought that was just a creative myth.

It was irrefutable that his kiss was more memorable than her brief impulsive peck back in the cabin. He was really good at it too, but then again, he was probably good at just about everything.

However, he seemed almost more off balance than she was when he finally let her go. He left without a word, getting swiftly into his rental car and backing out of the driveway, and she was almost amused as she watched him drive off. Raine went inside and sat down on the couch, Jangles immediately snuggling close. She remembered the piece of paper that she'd absently picked up in the cabin, and retrieved it from her pocket, wondering what it would say.

It was the end of a chapter.

The old man tentatively approved of the greenhorn,

though he wasn't sure city folks were quite his type. Maybe he had real promise.

Raine laughed and scratched under the cat's chin. "You see," she whispered, "I knew Grandpa liked him."

CHAPTER FIVE

FOR GIFTS, RYDER had been easy. Mick had once been a teenaged boy, so he had a fair idea of what they liked, but times changed. He'd opted for a gift card to a very popular online store.

Daisy had been more of a challenge.

He really knew nothing about a girl her age, and his childless sister-in-law was no help. In the end, he'd asked his mother's opinion.

"A purse," she announced promptly. "I have plenty of friends with granddaughters, not that I have any yet, so I will ask what brands are popular right now."

He ignored the implied criticism. "I'd appreciate it, but I can't pick out a purse."

"Sure you can. You have wonderful taste."

Well, he *had* asked, he thought as the call ended. The idea was better than nothing, which was all he'd had before. So he'd gone into the closest trendy store and asked the young clerk if she was Daisy's age what she might want. Directly she went to a rack, selected a purse he would never have picked out in a million years, and handed it over. "She'll faint over this," she informed him. "If we hadn't gotten a shipment in today we wouldn't have it on the shelf."

He took her word for it and had it gift-wrapped, along with some nail polish the knowledgeable clerk promised with a dimpled smile was popular with girls Daisy's age. For Blythe, a small Victorian tabletop greenhouse because she was the ultimate gardener, and for Harry, who always had a cup around as far as he could tell, a genuine English antique tea set. Grace and Luce were getting robes his sister-in-law swore by, since she claimed they were just the right weight, yet warm and cozy, and the Carson men were getting handmade leather gloves.

Raine had taken some thought. He wasn't trying to impress her; he was trying to show he was thoughtful enough to understand what she might like. In the end he'd stumbled upon the perfect gift—or he hoped it was, anyway. He'd found an obscure but original print of the infamous Sirens luring sailors to their demise when he was recently in Athens, the color faded because he had no idea how to date it. But the detail was so beautiful he thought she'd love it. He'd had it framed, and after seeing her house, he was sure it would fit right in. He'd liked her imaginative décor.

Packing up the gifts he'd had shipped to the hotel, Mick got in the rental car, checked his phone one last time, and shut it off. It was Christmas Day. London was hours different, his mother was in New York so he'd call her later, and no one else needed to talk to him in Wyoming.

The resort really was quiet, but Mick noticed the bar was full as he walked past, and there were a lot of skis in the lobby propped against the wall and a fire going in the giant stone fireplace. It made him reflect on how the season was celebrated, and if one person wanted to sit by a fire and another wanted to brave the slopes because the powder was perfect, that was the quintessential to-each-his-own. Both of those sounded pretty good to him, depending on the company. The Alps at Christmas that year he was sixteen had been an experience, but he preferred this homey atmosphere hands down.

He was very much looking forward to the company he would be in today.

The Carson ranch looked festive as he pulled up, the veranda of the big house decorated with twinkling lights and a garland, and there were two small trees complete with ornaments on either side of the doors. The row of cars spoke of a gathering in progress.

It was overcast and a few flakes floated down, landing on his shoulders and hair as he walked up the steps. Blythe answered the door, her smile gracious. "Mick, Merry Christmas. It's so good to see you."

"And you. I hope I'm not late."

"The fear-of-Harry factor is a powerful thing." Blythe took his coat. "You come bearing gifts. How nice of you. We were just about to start the gift exchange. Brace yourself for the usual male Carson competition. They are ridiculous. It isn't a monetary thing at all, it's just their nature. They have a built-in need to outdo each other whether it's through throwing a rope on a horse or buying a toy for a child."

"Hopefully I'll be a contender, since I made a few educated guesses." He stepped farther into the foyer. "But I make no promises."

As it turned out, he won the competition.

At least with Daisy. The purse was a leaping-up-and-down hit. She gasped as she opened the package and came over and gave Mick an exuberant hug, clinging to that purse like it was made of pure gold.

He made a mental note to thank his mother later.

Grace poked him in the shoulder with an accusing finger. "How'd you manage to find that? I tried to order one online three months ago. I'm still on a waiting list."

Raine studied him, clearly equal parts intrigued and annoyed. "Four months ago for me. Stop showing off, Branson." She wore dark jeans and a yellow top that brought out the gold in her eyes, and looked delicious against the sweep of her hair at her shoulders.

"I probably shouldn't tell you that all I had to do was walk into a store and there it was." He grinned as he sat back carelessly in his comfortable chair and took a sip of the smooth merlot Blythe had handed him. He had to admit that the spirited gift exchange had been much preferable to the stuffy country club dining room where he usually spent his holiday.

Both women glared at him.

Slater told him flat-out that if he would give up his shopping secrets, they'd be friends for life. "I don't think her first car is going to make her as happy as that purse did."

"I thought we already were friends for life." Mick was going to go back and give the clerk the bonus of her life. The joy of giving was defined by Daisy's excited smile.

Slater acknowledged that with a nod of his head and a chuckle. "At least you beat out my brothers. For that, I'll forgive you. They would create a favorite uncle pendant and ride around an arena brandishing it until next year. Boys are simple. Give them a video game or some sports equipment and you're good to go. If Grace has a girl this time, the games will begin again. If Luce has a girl there might be an amusement park in the front yard with spinning teacups and a roller coaster."

Mick could envision it. "A unique addition to a working ranch. And maybe worth a brand-new documentary on how fatherhood can soften even the toughest cowboy."

"What can I say? We like to please our ladies."

"Having gotten to know your ladies pretty well recently, I can't say I blame you."

Slater caught his eyes drifting to Raine and said neutrally, "My wife didn't tell me until this morning you'd be here, but she was all too delighted to tell me about your Christmas Eve dinner plans. So how'd last night go?"

"Well. I told Raine about the animated film. She seems interested."

Slater rubbed his jaw and laughed. "Not quite what I was asking, but that's good."

"She also showed me her grandfather's cabin. I can't believe she's related to Matthew Brighton. I've been thinking about buying property here, but it was pitch-dark so I couldn't get a feel for the view or anything else. You know the territory. Give me your opinion."

"That's so Raine. She took you there on a snowy Christmas Eve when there isn't even a real road to the place? You two could have easily gotten stuck there."

Mick couldn't help it. "That would have been just fine with me."

"So I gathered," Slater said drily. "As for the property, it's a wonderful piece of land but you can't run cattle there, it needs a road, there's no electricity, and that old cabin is supposed to be haunted now. That's nonsense I usually don't believe in, but I was up there once because Raine asked me to check on it and I'll be damned if I didn't hear someone say in a deep male voice: *Howdy, Slater.* I knew I was alone, so I about jumped out of my skin." He shook his head, chuckling at himself. "On the positive side, that lake is so scenic you could make a fortune just selling postcards and the view of the mountains just can't be beat. You'd wake up to bears and elk wandering past the decaying front porch, but when it comes to peace and quiet, if that's what you're after, you'd have it in spades."

Mick refrained from mentioning the sudden breeze that had swept through the cabin last night. He was also a skeptic but that had been an odd moment. He took a sip of wine and studied his glass thoughtfully. "I don't think I'd mind sitting on a porch with a cup of coffee in the morning and waving hello to a bear. I'd build a house with all the modern amenities, but the cabin would stay."

"That would make Raine really happy, but I think you just did anyway." Slater pointed.

She'd unwrapped the illustration and her rapt attention was emphasized by the reverence with which she ran a finger over the glass, tracing an outline of one of the figures. Raine was sitting cross-legged on the floor by the enormous tree. She looked over at him. "Mick, *where* did you get this?"

"Santorini. I was in Athens on business. I couldn't skip a tour of the island while I was already in Greece."

"It's gorgeous."

He held her gaze for a beat. "Maybe that's why I thought of you."

WELL DONE.

Raine was fairly sure that smooth compliment was overheard by almost everyone in the room. If nothing else, Mick Branson had style down pat.

It was unsettling to be under the Carson microscope at this particular moment. She was grateful for the extended family for both her daughter and herself, but the scrutiny that accompanied it was a bit much. Slater was fine, they'd come to an understanding a long time ago, and she was genuinely happy he was married to Grace. She loved Drake, Mace and their wives as well, but she wished they'd focus on their own gifts right now.

Instead, all eyes were on her and Mick.

She was keenly aware of it, and so was he from his expression.

The framed print he'd given her was simply priceless. No matter what he'd spent—and she didn't want to think about what it had probably cost him—it was the fact that he'd seemed to know exactly what she'd love that moved her the most. She figured she could forgive him the purse triumph. She was touched he'd thought of Daisy at all.

Both gifts were the perfect choice.

The same was true for what he'd selected for Ryder, and everyone else; he'd clearly put some time into it, and no small amount of thought.

No one had ever managed to gain her attention in quite this way. It wasn't his money. She was fine all on her own. For that matter, if money was a draw for her, she'd have married Slater all those years ago when he asked.

Mick had read her grandfather's books. He could

easily name his favorite, and since it was hers, too, well…

A small voice in her head said: *Watch yourself, McCall.*

"And now yours." She took a box from under the tree, wading through the sea of wrapping paper. Drake and Mace were supposed to be keeping up with gathering the discarded colorful paper and putting it into bags as each gift was eagerly unwrapped, but there was quite the crowd, a ridiculous amount of gifts, especially for the kids, and they'd finally looked at each other and declared jointly they'd pick it up afterward.

"Mine?" Mick raised his brows. "You didn't have a lot of shopping time."

"I didn't need it." She perched on the edge of his chair, sharing it with him. She wanted to see his expression when he opened it.

Delilah, Ryder's little long-haired mutt, had taken a shine to Mick and was currently draped over his expensive shoe and his gentle attempts to dislodge her merely made her wag her floppy tail, so he'd evidently resigned himself to her adoration and the amount of hair being deposited on his tailored pants. Samson was having a ball attacking discarded wads of paper, while Drake's two well-behaved German shepherds watched with superior resignation, as if inwardly they were shaking their heads. Blythe's cat was used to the turmoil enough to doze on the top on the couch, having an afternoon siesta.

A man like Mick Branson probably thought he was having Christmas at a zoo. He accepted the box with a look of protest. "You didn't have to—"

"Give? None of us *have* to, we want to. Now open it."

He obligingly tore open the paper and lifted the lid on the box. His expression went from curious to stunned. "You're kidding. An original manuscript? I don't recognize the title."

"It's never been published," she explained as he stared at the manuscript, reverently touching the title page. "Grandpa started it right before he died. *The Aspen Trail* was something he thought about for a long time, one of the books that run circles in your head, he told me once. He still used that old typewriter, so you'll find some penciled-in corrections."

He tore his gaze away from it to look at her. "You can't give me this. It's probably worth a small fortune."

"I just did. But, well, it comes with a catch."

"What?" He was understandably wary.

"Could you maybe finish it?"

"What?"

"Read it. I want to know what happens next."

"I can't possibly—"

"Put that English minor to good use. You said you have imagination. So prove it."

Harry emerged from the kitchen right then and saved Mick by making the grand announcement. "Okay, ladies and gents, it's time."

The males in the room rushed to help her carry in food, which wasn't surprising since they would eat most of it. And it wasn't like Harry just roasted a turkey; she'd made prime rib, Swedish meatballs, ribs, fish…a variety of side dishes in order to please everyone, and Blythe had baked her legendary rolls, so it was quite a varied feast, as Raine had come to expect.

Ask for it, and you got it as a special Harry gift. Dessert was a miracle, too, with everyone's favorites on the table, but then again, with all the leftovers, Harry would get a few days off to balance all the marathon baking and cooking.

Today, she also got another special gift.

When Harry sat down with the inevitable cup of tea, she picked up the envelope that had mysteriously appeared on her placemat during her last trip into the kitchen. "What's this?"

It was almost as much of a pleasure to see her open that envelope as it was to see Daisy sitting with her precious purse at the table, trying to eat one-handed because she didn't want to let go of it.

Harry's eyes widened. "A European River cruise? Airline tickets?"

"For you and your sister." Blythe smiled. "It's from all of us, so don't just thank me. You've always said you wanted to go, so go. I can manage this house alone for a couple of weeks and Raine is going to do lunches for the hands. Everyone is pitching in so you can just relax and enjoy. Take pictures of the castles, please."

"Stephano has volunteered to cook," Grace added, as Harry continued to look stunned. "I'm bringing home dinner from the resort's restaurant every night. You do realize he'll try to outdo you, right?"

"I'm making my famous chili on the weekends," Luce said. "In exchange for river pics. I hope you'll throw in some vineyards snaps for Mace."

Kelly piped up, "Yes, do. I'd like to frame one for the store. By the way, I'm in charge of dessert. If you'd leave out a few recipes I'd appreciate it."

"I will." Harry looked endearingly touched, maybe

even teary-eyed, as she opened the brochure. "My sister is going to love this."

That translated to Harry loving it. Raine suspected Harriet Armstrong could be the most sentimental woman on this earth, but she was too stubborn to admit it.

Seated next to her, Mick whispered, "Is she a wizard or something? How many people does it take to fill her shoes?"

Raine whispered back, "A tyrant wizard. I believe that's her official job description. You've eaten her food, so you know she has magical powers."

He was way too handsome, especially when he smiled. Hearts probably fluttered all over California, and apparently in foreign countries as well, since she assumed business didn't take up all his time there.

But he'd evidently thought of her on his travels.

"I agree."

"Why do you keep checking the clock?" She had to ask because she'd seen him keeping a close eye on it. Not that she was watching him or anything like that… no, not at all.

Right.

Mick just said in a neutral tone, "I have a good reason, and no, I won't explain. Trust me, it will be worth it."

"Promise?"

"Yes, and I always keep my promises. Just wait."

CHAPTER SIX

IF THERE WAS one thing Mick knew, it was that surprises didn't always go according to plan. Still, he was pleased with the way his unfolded.

Dinner was over, the table cleared and the adults sipped wine. Snow had begun to fall again, so the ranch looked like an idyllic cowboy poster.

"Slater!" Ryder rushed in, waving his hands. "Dude, your movie is about to come on."

Mick smiled. It would've been fun to spring the news himself, but the teen's wide-eyed announcement added a nice hint of drama.

Slater, by contrast, was calm when he replied, "Don't call me *dude*, Ryder. I don't play on your basketball team and have the locker next to you. And what film do you mean?"

"*Wild West... Still Wild.* Your documentary. I just saw an ad for it."

Mace perked up. "Really?"

Mick hoped he was pleased. There was a short ad for the winery at the beginning of the film, and also an ad for the resort and spa Grace managed.

"Yeah, du... I mean, Uncle Mace, really."

"But it isn't out for another month."

Mick cleared his throat. The cat was officially out

of the bag. "Actually, it might be premiering in...oh, about twenty-eight minutes."

It wasn't surprising Slater was visibly taken aback. "Mick, that's why you're here?" He turned to his wife, who was beaming smugly. "You knew, didn't you? And you didn't tell me?"

Grace, looking unrepentant, lifted her slim shoulders. "If you think I'd spoil a great surprise, think again. Surprise!"

"Christmas Day?" Slater looked floored, staring at Mick. "How'd you pull that off?"

"I have strings I tighten now and again." Mick wasn't lying about that. Those were some hard-won tug-o-wars.

"It isn't possible. Not for a documentary."

"Tell me that again in twenty-seven minutes."

"I just saw the ad. Like a major commercial!" Ryder was jacked up, his thin face alight. Mick could swear the kid had grown about four inches since his last visit to Bliss County and when he filled out, he was going to be quite the broad-shouldered man. "I was watching football."

So far the films had all made a good profit and that's why Mick could still get investors on board, but that ad had taken a lot of money and some true finesse. Everyone involved had agreed that maybe it was time to notch it up, especially once they'd viewed the film. They'd thought the investment would pay off.

"During a football game on a major network?" Drake wasn't a wine drinker so he lifted his bottle of beer in a salute. "Look at you, Showbiz."

"I think you're the one we'll be looking at," Mick informed him, enjoying the moment. "Remember how the film opens? I think millions are about to get a peek at you kissing your lovely wife."

"Oh, hell," Drake muttered in obvious chagrin. "I'd either forgotten or blocked that out of my mind. Tell me you aren't serious."

Luce laughed. "Relax, you're not being rocketed into instant stardom, honey. In that footage no one can really tell it's us, and besides, they'll all be looking at the wild stallion in the background. I'm sorry, but I think Smoke is the one who will steal the show."

"He's welcome to it," her husband responded darkly.

Maybe it was the Hollywood in him, but Mick had always thought each of the Carson brothers would make a fascinating leading man in his own way. All three were intense, but he'd describe Slater as artistic, Drake as the quiet cowboy, and Mace the wildcard.

What was he?

Focused, maybe. Not artistic, that was for sure. Though he appreciated art in all forms, he couldn't draw so much as a square. "The gloves were just for show, Showbiz," he told Slater. "Your real gift is going to be the next couple of hours. I don't know how you're going to outdo this one, but you should have the opportunity if this doc goes over like I think it will. The backers loved it enough that the commercial was a sell."

"They loved it?"

"Of course. I held a showing. This is business, Carson. Don't look so surprised that they enjoyed it."

Raine was the one who elbowed him. "I'm with Slater. This is like having someone tell you if your child is ugly or pretty, Branson. It's nerve-wracking stuff."

He did get that. He really did, at least on an intellectual level. Defensively, he murmured, "He doesn't make movies just to make them. He wants people to watch them. Slater knows what he's doing."

"Yes, but no," she corrected. "He really does make movies just because he loves them. Having people watch and enjoy them is a bonus. But without someone like you, he could never do it on this scale."

Raine was an intellectual challenge at times. Maybe that was why he liked her so much. No agenda. "What's the point of doing it if no one sees it?"

"Because of the sheer joy of creation. I have artwork I've done I wouldn't sell even if offered a fortune for it."

"A private showing of those pieces would interest me a great deal." He made his tone deliberately suggestive.

Raine looked amused. "Please tell me you're usually more subtle when you flirt, Branson."

"You're harder to flirt with than most women, Ms. McCall."

"I'd like to think I'm not most women."

"You've got that right."

Her beautiful eyes softened. "That's improvement right there. I'm going to help clear the table. I think we all have a movie to watch."

THE FILM WAS BRILLIANT, but Raine had expected that. Though she and Slater hadn't ended up on the same page in life, they certainly connected on different levels, and one of them was their mutual understanding of the emotional significance of vision.

The documentary was a love letter to Mustang Creek, taking viewers on a journey through its rich history. There were pictures of the old hotel that was there before the new resort, and video of a snowboarder in mid-air doing an Olympic-style flip, and then photos of cowboys digging a path for their horses out of the snow. Ranch hands around a table wearing chaps and drinking coffee from tin cups, and the same table a hundred years later, same cups, different men. The main street of Mustang Creek back in the day, and the similarity to the modernized version, including the wine store, before and after. Elk grazing next to cattle, the wild horses at full gallop, fluttering fall leaves and an eagle soaring above, a mountain lion perched above a walking trail…

And her grandfather's cabin, so unchanged from when it was built except for the slow process of aging. She drew in a breath at the picture of him when he was a boy happily playing on the steps, and later a picture she'd provided of an old man sitting on the front porch smoking a pipe—that child grown and weathered by time but still content. In the latter photograph there was a book on a simple table next to him; one of his, of course.

Her mother had taken the picture and Raine wasn't immune to a nostalgic moment. It was telling that even the kids didn't get restless, but watched intently. When it was over, there was a resounding silence.

Then Blythe began to clap, Daisy jumped up to run and kiss her dad, and everyone was talking at once.

The beginning of the film had been fantastic, with an unintentional shot of Drake leaning in to Luce for a passionate kiss, accidentally captured by remote cameras but, fortunately for the couple, entirely in silhouette. Luce had been right—the setting took over.

But the ending was astounding.

The wild horses were being herded off and Slater

had taken gorgeous footage of the warrior stallion stopping to nudge a gangly colt, gently urging the youngster into the herd because he wasn't quite able yet to keep up.

It was so well done, emphasizing the continuing cycle of life.

"Let's hope the ratings reflect the quality of the work." Mick sounded optimistic, his long legs extended, Delilah yet again camped out on his foot.

"They will." Raine was able to say it with utter conviction.

Mick didn't hesitate. "I loved the idea, loved the execution, and Slater's style and his sense of timing are distinctive. I could tune in and know right away who ran the production. That isn't easy to come by."

"He's a bright man," Grace interjected, snuggling into her husband as he grinned and ran a hand over Daisy's hair.

"He has excellent taste," Raine agreed. She glanced at Mick's feet. "And apparently so does a certain small, floppy dog."

"Thanks." Mick eyed his snoozing new best friend, and the sleeping giant at *her* feet. "Raine, you do realize you're going to need a larger yard for that beast."

Samson had come over and collapsed at her feet mid-movie and, even at his young age, he already snored. His head was significantly bigger than her foot. She offered helpfully, "If you decide you want my grandfather's property, I'll throw him in for free. Problem solved. That's one big yard."

Mick chuckled. "Oh yes, I bet your daughter would let that fly. And I might have always wanted a dog,

but I'm not sure about a rambunctious horse in canine form."

"Yeah, I guess I'm stuck with him. But there's one
thing I can give you." She was impulsive and she knew
it. It was exactly how she ordered her world. Follow
the heart. If she had a motto, that was it. Raine took a
breath and blurted out, "What if I just deeded the property to you on the proviso you keep the cabin as it is?
Yours, free and clear."

It wasn't hard to see Mick was flabbergasted. He
looked at her like she was insane. "That is the most ridiculous thing I've ever heard."

She stood her ground. "I don't agree. I think it
makes perfect sense."

"Raine...the property is like what I'm looking for
and I can afford to *buy* it."

"I believe I already told you that I want someone
who appreciates it to have it. If you can afford to buy
it, you can afford the taxes and to put in a decent road.
Fix that top step on the porch, too, will you? Say you'll
keep the cabin. We'll call it even."

It seemed like he was searching for words. "You...
you can't *give* a hundred acres and a historical cabin
away."

The more she thought about it, the better the idea
seemed to be. "You want land in this area, and you'd
have it." She needed to make her position clear so she
chose her next words carefully. "I'm really being selfish. Mick, I don't want to sell it. But I can't justifiably
keep it either and let it fall apart. This seems a lot more
right to me. You'd be doing me a favor. The guilt of
having it on the market has been eating away at me. I
think, given your friendship with Slater, you'd let Daisy

come out there every once in a while to visit the cabin. That's so much better than a stranger buying it and not caring that he was Matthew Brighton, the author, and getting rid of it."

"If you get that animated movie deal I mentioned, *you* could afford all of that."

"That's a big 'if.' And I assume these things take time. I would have given it to the Carson family, but they really don't need more land. For them, it would just be taxes and something else to manage. They would do it, but it would be an imposition on my part."

"You *are* part of the Carson family."

He was right, and he was wrong. "My daughter is. I've been made welcome, no doubt about it, but there's a reason I spend Christmas Eve on my own."

"Not this year."

She held his gaze, remembering that brief kiss that was still a spine-tingling experience, the second one even better. "No. I want you to know I don't share my green chilis with just anyone."

"That was a Christmas gift all its own. If a genie had popped out of a bottle and asked what I wanted for dinner, that selection would have been my choice."

There came that heart-stopping smile again. She pounced on the moment. "So we have a deal then? Take the land, keep the cabin, and I'll make you green chili cheeseburgers every Christmas Eve if you want."

"Okay, we have a standing date."

"Mom, Mom." Daisy rushed in and flopped down on the floor next to Samson, who promptly rolled over to get his belly rubbed. Her blue eyes were alight. "Dad and Uncle Mace are going to take me and Ryder for a midnight ride in the snow tonight. Is that okay? I can just stay over again, unless you mind."

At least they'd spent the day together, and it was Christmas after all. "I don't mind." But Raine had to ask, "Are you going to take your purse on the ride?"

Daisy was appalled. "No. What if snow got on it?"

"Oh no, hadn't thought of that. It would be a tragedy." She bent to kiss her daughter's head. "Go and have fun."

"Thanks, Mom." She jumped up and ran off, and Samson decided maybe something was afoot and followed in a lumbering gait, clumsy but somehow still cute despite his size.

"Don't look smug," Raine informed Mick. "She loved my gift, too."

"I'd love to take credit but I can't." He didn't heed her request but looked smug anyway. "There's a very efficient clerk who understands both retail and young girls and does an excellent job for her company. Daisy should really thank her for the purse. So now you're free for the evening?"

What she said next might be life-changing. Raine thought it over—letting him know she wasn't *always* impulsive. She trusted him absolutely with her grandfather's property. Her heart was a different matter, because it also included her child. So when she spoke, her tone was cautious. "It seems like I am."

"Can we spend it together?"

"Are we talking the entire night?" She looked him squarely in the eyes.

He looked right back. "You just don't pull punches, do you? I'm talking whatever you want."

"I hope you can accept I'm not sure."

"I'm fairly aware there's a guarded side of you. Kind of like a prickly pear cactus."

"Those plants have beautiful flowers, so I'll take that as a compliment." She shot him her sweetest smile.

"I meant it as one," he replied. "I know you have reason to be cautious, and that you're used to being independent."

"I think learning to rely on yourself is a very valuable lesson. I remember as a child once asking my grandfather if he wasn't lonely sometimes, all alone in that old secluded place, and he answered that it never even occurred to him. He was happy with himself for company. I think I took to that mentality."

Mick regarded her intently. "You certainly seem to have done just that."

Maybe it was the season, because she wasn't usually that open with her feelings. "I'm not very conformist. I've met handsome men I would never give a second glance because they just aren't my type. I don't like them shallow, and I don't like arrogance. I'm not into cocktail parties and getting a manicure, but would rather mow my yard or tackle fixing a leaky faucet. That's not very feminine, I guess. If you're looking for someone who will put on a little black dress and stay on your arm at Hollywood parties, you'd better move on."

He just seemed amused. "If you think for a minute I haven't already figured that one out, you underestimate me. I hate to disabuse you of the notion that all I do is rub elbows with the elite, but I like quiet evenings in even more."

"Then how about a fire and a glass of wine?" She really wasn't sure what she was getting into, but it was going past the ankle-deep level and she might be up to mid-calf. "Maybe some philosophical discussion about life, and I'm sure Jangles will want to give his two cents. He might even think about sitting on your lap."

Mick lifted his brows in mock alarm. "I think I've had enough of animals sitting on me for one day." Then he added, "Otherwise, it sounds perfect."

CHAPTER SEVEN

HE COULDN'T VERY well tell the truth, so Mick said neutrally, "It's certainly been an interesting trip so far. How's New York?"

His mother answered, "Busy, brilliant, definitely full of holiday spirit. There's nothing like seeing The Nutcracker at Rockefeller Hall. What was so interesting in the wilds of Wyoming?"

Well, he should have known he wouldn't get off the hook so easily. "A certain woman that, oddly enough, I think you might like."

He was sitting in his car outside Raine's house, gazing at her enchanting but unusually decorated tree through the large front window.

"Why would it be odd if I liked her?"

"She's definitely a small-town girl, an artist, and though I bet she could catch one without any problem, I doubt she owns a set of fish forks to serve the trout. By the way, thanks for the tip on the purse. Her daughter is now my biggest fan."

"She has a daughter?"

"She does."

"So she's divorced."

"Actually, no."

There was a judgmental pause. He expected nothing else. Better to get it out in the open now.

"I see."

"No, you don't. Raine turned down Slater's proposal because she thought in the long term that a marriage between them wouldn't work. They parent together and have remained friends. It seems like a reasonable arrangement and Daisy is a happy, well-adjusted kid."

"Slater…as in Slater Carson?"

"He's Daisy's father, yes."

"That's sounds complicated, Michael. Don't you handle a lot of the backing for his films?"

To his friends he was Mick, but to his mother he would always be Michael. As patiently as possible, he said, "He's happily married, has another child, and in fact, a third on the way. He cares about Raine as the mother of his daughter but he doesn't have an issue with my having feelings for her."

"You sound definite enough," she said, but it was grudgingly. "I'll have to trust your judgment."

Considering he'd been a grown man for over two decades, he could point out that she had no say one way or the other—but then again, he'd always believed that it was a mistake to become involved with someone your family disliked. It added an unwelcome dimension to something that was supposed to enrich your life and make you happy.

It surprised him that the big, sometimes boisterous Carson family was comfortable for him when he'd grown up very differently. It also surprised him that he was so attracted to Raine when she was the antithesis of the women he'd dated before, and it surprised him even more that she seemed to feel the same way about him. He wasn't a free-spirited artist, or a tried-and-true cowboy.

"She's—" he sought the right description "—like a warm breeze on a sunny afternoon."

"Oh no, now you're getting poetic? It must be love. Darling, have a wonderful evening. Now I need a martini. Merry Christmas."

He couldn't help laughing at himself all the way up the snowy sidewalk, but he thought it was a good description and would stand by it. When Raine opened the door at his knock, she gave him a quizzical look. "What's so funny?"

He smiled. "Let's just say I think my mother likes you."

"Um, I'd ask why you were talking about me to your mother, but something tells me I'd rather not know. Come on in. Fire and wine are in place. If I eat again in this lifetime I'll be surprised, but Harry sent cookies and turkey sandwiches. If you get hungry, speak up."

"I will." He was certainly hungry, but he wasn't thinking that much about food and he had a feeling she knew it. He really wasn't like this with women, more pursued than the pursuer most of the time, but there was some serious chemistry going on his part anyway.

He was lucky that the lion didn't have an entire pride waiting for him. Mr. Bojangles barely let him get in the door before he launched a sneak attack, darting out from his super-not-so-secret hiding place and nailing his ankle again. It added comic relief that when the critter went back under the tree, his bushy tail was fully visible, even if his ample body was hidden.

"He must have trained with the special forces. The ambush was perfect, but he may have skipped class on hiding day."

Raine observed wryly, "He's not quite figured out

that his size is a problem. I've thought about getting a bigger tree just to make sure he doesn't get insecure about his ability to be stealthy."

"That would be the compassionate thing to do."

She'd changed into soft, drawstring pajama pants, a flowing top with the same pattern, and slippers with raccoon faces on them. How that could be sexier than a slinky nightgown he wasn't sure, but it worked for him. There was a nice fire, and two glasses of wine on the coffee table.

The mixed signals were driving him crazy. He was invited—or maybe he'd invited himself by suggesting they spend the evening together—and yet she was dressed like she was going to a sorority slumber party. She'd told him flat-out she was unsure how she viewed things between them, but agreed to have him over again anyway.

The agreement was good. The rest of it was up in the air.

"What smells so good in here?"

"That candle from the local store that Grace bought for me. She knows I love vanilla." Raine sat down and visibly relaxed, cradling her wineglass in her slender fingers, propping her feet on the coffee table and wiggling her toes in those ridiculous slippers. "I love Christmas at the ranch, but a little peace and quiet afterward is nice, too. I always manage to forget how exhausting a big crowd can be. I go out to lunch with friends now and then, but mostly I'm by myself all day, at least during the school year." She smiled. "I love my daughter—that goes without saying—but the quiet is nice. Feel free, by the way, to take off those Italian loafers and put your feet up. *Formality* is almost a dirty word in this house."

"My mother would faint if I put my feet on your coffee table, but taking off my shoes sounds great." He slipped them off. "Solitude can be a friend or an enemy, depending on the person. I know far too many people who can't stand to be alone, almost never eat at home, and in general love the bustle of a big city." He relaxed, too, just enjoying the view, and he wasn't looking at the sparkling tree or the fire. "Is this the beginning of our deep philosophical discussion?"

"Or maybe just two people talking. You still worry about what your mother thinks of you?"

"I wouldn't say worry, exactly. But I try to keep on her good side."

"Good for you." Her tone was approving. "I like that."

"Hopefully that isn't the only thing you like about me."

"No." She smiled playfully. "You have great hair."

He shot her a look. "Not quite the compliment I was angling for. I was hoping to hear my intellect amazes you and my charm is unsurpassed in your experience."

"Both those things could be true, but I just can't get past the hair. Do you have a stylist?"

"You think you're so funny, don't you."

She laughed, hiding her mouth behind her hand. "Kind of."

"No, I don't have a stylist. I get it cut and I wash and comb it. Surely there's something else you like."

She pretended to think it over. "Now I suppose I have to mention those gorgeous movie-star eyes and high cheekbones. Nice shoulders, too, unless there's padding in your shirts."

"And here I thought I wasn't in Hollywood...throw me a bone here." He was laughing, too, but also serious.

Her smile faded as she held his gaze. "I trust you are a good man. If I didn't, you wouldn't be sitting here right now."

It was exactly the type of compliment he might have expected from Raine—frank and straightforward—but he was aware that she meant what she said. "And you wouldn't be giving me your grandfather's property. We'll have to talk over that one again later. You really can't do that."

"I talked to Slater. He said it was a sound idea. Drake agreed and Mace was with it, too. One of the reasons I like you so much is that they all trust you. Those are some pigheaded, stubborn men, but they're some of the best judges of character that I know. And lucky for me, they don't even think about your hair."

"But you do?"

"In the context of maybe running my fingers through it, I do."

"Feel free." He certainly meant that. *Time to carefully consider your next words, Branson.* He studied the flames in the fireplace for a moment. "I don't think it's a secret I'd really like to spend the night making wild, passionate love with you, but that's entirely your call."

"Are you wild and passionate, Mr. Boardroom?"

"I was more thinking about *you* being that way. I've thought about it quite a lot. After making a spreadsheet detailing your personality traits and comparing them to mine, I've come to the conclusion that you are in the lead in those departments."

She almost spat out her sip of wine and swiped her mouth with the back of her hand, laughing. "Damn you, Branson, don't do that to me."

"Do what?" He put on his most innocent face, but he was laughing as well.

"We could be the most unlikely couple in the world."

"Maybe," he acknowledged. "But I never did like doing the predictable."

She set aside her wine. "I think your hair might be pretty messy in the morning."

WHAT *WAS* SHE DOING?

It could be foolish, but it didn't seem like that. Maybe she'd regret it in the morning, but Raine really wanted to lie in his arms as the snow fell softly outside.

And tumble head over in heels in love.

Not too much to ask, right?

Maybe it had already happened.

She had to admit that Mick was deliciously male lounging on her couch, and she'd never before been tempted to stray over the line she'd drawn for herself.

Nothing casual.

No males who would love her and leave her. That was for her own well-being.

No long-distance relationships. They didn't work as far as she could tell.

No one who would break her daughter's heart if he decided to decamp. It wasn't like Daisy didn't have a grounded support system, but still she had parents who lived separate lives and introducing Mick into the mixture was a risk. Mick could be all of those things. A love-'em-and-leave-'em sort, a potential scoundrel, as her grandfather would have put it, but maybe something else also…

"Do you have the manuscript I gave you in your car?"

"Of course." He looked like Daisy had when Raine had asked about the infamous purse on the snowy ride. "Why?"

"I need to see it."

"Sure, fine, if you've changed your mind about giving it away—"

"No, I haven't changed my mind. I just need to look at it."

He seemed baffled but obligingly went out in the snow and a minute or two later returned with the box. Flakes of snow glistened on his hair and dusted his shoulders. He set the manuscript on the table. "It's still just coming down lightly and there isn't even a breath of wind but I get the feeling it's going to really snow. I think they'll enjoy their midnight excursion."

Daisy would love it. Her sense of adventure had made her a handful as a young child, but Raine had that same enthusiasm, so she could hardly fault her daughter for her eagerness to experience new things and maybe take a risk now and then. "I would bet on it. She's a pretty happy kid and Slater is a wonderful dad." She gestured to the box on the table. "Pick a page."

"What?"

"Just pick one at random out of the manuscript and hand it to me."

"Raine. Why?"

"Because I asked you to?"

"Fair enough." He shuffled through the manuscript. "Any page?"

"Yes. Just pick one."

He flipped through the manuscript, selected one and shrugged. "Here."

She stepped to him, plucked the page from his fingers and read the first line: *He kept his emotions close, like a beloved jacket, worn and well-used, the one he would wear out into a howling storm. He was not a man easy to read, yet she trusted him.*

So she should.

Raine handed back the page. "That was what I wanted to see."

"A random page?"

"It sure seems that way, doesn't it? Kiss me."

He'd fallen into a dream.

There was Raine, pressed against him, her mouth soft against his, warm arms around his neck and he couldn't be more enthusiastic about the idea. This wasn't like the brief kiss at the cabin either, or the more arousing one as he'd left the night before. It was hot, and he didn't need the encouragement.

At all.

What made her go from wary to passionate he wasn't sure, but he wasn't going to argue, either. She kissed him back with sensual promise and he didn't miss the signal.

He tightened his arm around her waist to bring her body more fully against his so he could feel every curve, every nuance. She did like vanilla. Her hair held a sweet scent of it, and was like fine silk under his fingers.

"Bedroom?" he murmured against her mouth when they both came up for air.

She whispered back, "I think that's the best idea you've had all day."

"You lead the way."

Her choice the whole time. This was what he wanted, hands down, but she needed to be on the same page.

She was. She ran her fingers through his hair. "Um, we do have one problem though. I'm not on birth control. I think I mentioned I'm kind of a hermit most of the time."

He traced the curve of her cheekbone with a finger and figured he might as well confess. "I have condoms. I'm not saying I thought this would be a sure thing, but I was hopeful anyway. Boardroom executives are master planners and always arrogantly anticipate the best outcome possible. I took two flights and endured a four-hour layover just because I was hoping for the kiss of a lifetime. I got it."

Oh, whoa, did I just say that?

"Of a lifetime? No pressure." Her eyes held a knowing look.

He was used to calling the shots, but she was definitely in charge. "Trust me, you didn't disappoint."

"Bedroom is this way."

He followed her. She could have been leading him off a cliff and he probably wouldn't have noticed anything besides the sway of her hips and her fluid stride.

As she walked in front of him, she took off that loose, less-than-sexy pajama top he found so inexplicably arousing, then tossed it down on the hallway floor. The graceful curve of her back almost did him in right then and there.

"Raine." It was said on a groan.

She glanced back. "Don't lag behind."

"Are you kidding? I'm following at warp speed."

Her laughter was warm and infectious, and he couldn't help but think that this was what life should be about. The joy of another person's presence, and definitely the magic of their laugh.

Raine's bedroom was a reflection of her personality, from the colorful artwork on the walls right down to the unusual black bedspread that was patterned with bright red poppies. The headboard looked antique, intricately carved, and he'd examine it later but right now that wasn't his focus at all.

Raine was shimmying out of her drawstring pants. "You seem kinda overdressed to me, Branson."

She was stunning with every stitch on, and naked... he'd dream about that image. Long legs, firm breasts, a taut stomach...heaven.

His hands had forgotten how to follow brain signals. Mick fumbled with the buttons on his shirt and finally got enough undone to be able to strip it off, though he was fairly sure at least one button went rolling. Socks next, then pants, and by this time Raine had pulled back the exotic bedspread and her dark hair was spilled enticingly over the pillow.

He even surprised himself when he said, as he joined her on the bed, "This is what falling in love should be about."

She brushed his hair back. "You didn't just say that."

"I think I just did."

"I'm so not ready for your direct approach."

He nuzzled her throat. "You aren't ready for us, and I'm not either, but I'm ahead of the game as I've been thinking about my options for quite some time. I can pretend you haven't captured my interest like no woman I've ever met, but it doesn't work. The first time I saw you I was sixteen again and my locker was next to the one of the prettiest girl in school."

"Do you say that to all—"

He stopped her with gentle fingers on her lips. "Raine, you have it all wrong. There are really no 'all.' I'm not wired that way. I'm selective. I always have been. Sex should mean something intimate and special between two people. If you think differently then you're not the person I thought you are, and I'm usually a pretty good judge of character."

"You know the right things to say, don't you?"

"I'm just speaking from the heart. Really."

She bit his shoulder lightly. "Then seduce me right now or I'll haul off and slug you. I don't know what I want long-term, but I do want you right this red-hot second, so you'd better make a note of it."

"Slugging is legal in Wyoming?"

"Probably not, but we like to make our own rules out here."

"I believe I just watched a film about the Wild West, so I'm going to take your word for it, ma'am."

"Hold on a second." Her eyes were luminous. "I have something I want to do first."

Her fingers ran through his hair again. How that could push him toward the edge, he wasn't sure, but it certainly did, even though he knew she was just teasing him.

Two could play that game.

He started with her breasts, firm and luscious, her nipples already taut, and when he drew one rigid tip into his mouth she shivered and let out a small moan of pleasure. He explored the valley between them with his tongue, gave due attention to the other nipple, and kissed his way downward.

She liked that too and wasn't shy about expressing it.

He discovered she wasn't really shy about anything and that just tipped fuel right on the fire to create a skylight blast. The dance between them was natural and beautiful; when he moved, Raine did too, and the heat level started to scorch the roof.

Her climax involved a small scream and then it was his turn. He managed to remember the condoms he'd brought so carefully at zero hour, slipped one on, and then there was nothing but pleasure and deep satisfaction as he joined their bodies and sank deep inside her.

Mick had been waiting for her his entire adult life. There was no question. He knew it all the way down to his heart.

CHAPTER EIGHT

SHE WAS IN his arms, he was in her bed. Jangles had decided to join them at some point and was sleeping peacefully in a large furry ball at the foot, taking up a good deal of space. Outside the wind had begun to pick up; she could hear the whisper under the eaves.

Raine was physically content, no doubt about that, but emotionally she wasn't yet she'd made the right decision. Mick had lapsed into a deep sleep, and was breathing peacefully, his tanned chest quite the contrast to the stark-white sheets she preferred.

There was no way she considered her relationship with Slater a mistake because it had given her Daisy, but it had made her cautious about choosing future partners. This man was far more dangerous because he didn't live nearby, and she liked him too much. Maybe gifting the property to him hadn't been an act of altruism but a selfish move to get him to spend time in Wyoming.

This relationship was evolving too quickly for her comfort. Mick Branson was a wild card she hadn't seen in her hand. How to play that hand was the real question. Discard him? No, he didn't deserve that. Up the ante? That was a definite possibility.

He was intimidating in many ways, but she was used to men like that. All the Carson men were confident, forthright and driven, and she was around them often. Mick was more understated, but he got his way just as effectively, even if he used a memo and not a lasso.

There was more than one kind of cowboy in this world.

She looked at Jangles, who sensed her uncertainty and lifted his head. "What am I supposed to do?" she whispered.

He answered with a very obvious reply by lowering his head and closing his eyes: *Just go to sleep.*

Sage advice. She took it by relaxing next to Mick and nestling in closer.

SNOW. OVERNIGHT? NEARLY two feet of it. Mick had obviously rented the wrong type of car. He had to admit he wasn't used to shoveling snow in L.A., so the waist-high drift by his luxury car wasn't a very welcome surprise. He wasn't positive a big truck could handle it, either.

He accepted a cup of coffee—Raine informed him it was something called Snake River Chocolate Peppermint blend, but it tasted just like coffee to him so he was fine with it—and he settled into a chair in her homey kitchen and took a sip. "I could be snowed in for a bit."

"No way." She looked cozy in a long soft pink sweater and worn jeans, her eyes sparkling. "I have backup. I *want* you to see the cabin in the deep snow like this. We aren't staying put because of a little snow."

"A *little* snow?"

"Hey, it happens here now and then."

It definitely qualified as the classic winter wonderland outside. The tree in her backyard was like a giant white sculpture. "You're serious?"

"I am. If it doesn't move you to see the place after a fresh snowfall, you aren't the man I think you are."

"What kind of man do you think I am?"

She put both elbows solidly on the table. "I've already pointed out I trust you. If I didn't, last night wouldn't have happened."

It was easy to say softly, "Then I'm glad you do."

"Me, too."

That was the response he was hoping for, and damn if this Snake River Chocolate stuff wasn't pretty good. He'd woken first and Raine had been half draped across him, deliciously nude and disheveled. The lion had been curled up at the foot of the bed and gave him the old stink-eye, but he interpreted approval there, so there had been a telling sense of contentment. Mick smiled lazily. "So, how do you propose we get out to a place that has no real driveway?"

"I have Alice for a reason."

"Do I even want to know who Alice is?"

"More like a what than a who. My snowmobile. It's very handy around these parts." She daintily sipped her peppermint coffee.

"You named it?" He was amused but not surprised. Raine would do something like that.

"Of course. We'll go look at the property in the daylight and then we can go pick up Daisy."

It wasn't his usual mode of travel but he wasn't without a sense of adventure. "I assume you know how to drive one, since I don't."

"I was practically born on one. I'm a December

baby. My father took my mother to the hospital on a snowmobile. I can drive it in my sleep."

At least he was in good hands. "I bet she enjoyed that."

"I'm sure she enjoyed getting to the hospital, either way."

"There's a valid point."

"How would you know? You're male."

No way was he going to let her get away with that. "I have feelings, too. Male and childbirth translates to helpless in most cases to control the situation. We'd love to fix it, but we can't always, and it makes us crazy."

"You all are crazy anyway, and what would you know about childbirth?"

"I lost a child once." It was the truth, but he kept it as low key as possible. "That was tough. Like you and Slater, apparently we weren't meant to be together forever. She got pregnant then miscarried. Our relationship didn't weather the storm. The child certainly wasn't planned, but I'd gotten used to the idea of fatherhood, gone to a few appointments, even heard the heartbeat. The sense of loss was acute."

Her eyes were full of sympathy and she reached over to touch his hand. "I had no idea. I'm so sorry."

"I don't tell anyone. But you aren't just anyone. I thought maybe you should know."

Raine was predictably direct. "Is that why you asked me if I'd ever considered having more children?"

Was it?

He still wasn't sure why he'd asked that personal question out of the blue. He did what he did best and equivocated. "I asked because you and Daisy seem to have a wonderful relationship. I wouldn't mind a second cup of coffee, but I can get it for myself." He stood, cup in hand. "When's your birthday?"

She clearly knew he was deflecting, but went along with it. "The thirtieth."

He hadn't planned on staying that long, but maybe he should change his mind. "We need to do something special then."

"Like?" Her brows went up.

"Paris? Rome? How about Key West? We could watch the famous sunset over the ocean, and escape the snow. You choose."

No one should look so gorgeous in the morning, bedhead and all.

Mick could be stuck on the cover of a magazine in just his boxers and it would sell a million copies. She'd be the first one in line to buy an issue.

Raine waited until he returned with his coffee before she'd formulated her response. "Those are all nice options, but I can't just pick up and jet off with you, so right here would be better if you have the time."

She was touched.

In the head.

Don't fall in love with this man.

Too late.

"I can make the time." He leaned back and his smile was boyish. "I certainly have it coming to me. And it doesn't hurt being my own boss, I suppose."

"I work harder than most people I know and I'm my own boss, too. I don't think I could make the time."

"Sweetheart, if you don't think I work hard, think again."

It wasn't like she didn't know he did. This was a pointless argument, and probably one she was instigating in order to distract herself from worrying thoughts of love and forever after. She smoothed her fingers across the fringe of the placemat. "I know for a fact you do. What I don't know is what you want from our... er...friendship." She'd searched for a word and settled on that one, though as soon as she said it she was fairly sure a kindergartener would have chosen something more sophisticated.

Apparently he agreed, his mouth curving in amusement. "I think after last night we're a bit more than friends, don't you? I'm not positive what you want either, so we'll have to figure it out together."

He'd done a lot better than she had in the words department.

Jangles strolled into the kitchen and made a familiar sound. It was something between a growl and a screech. Mick looked startled and slightly afraid for his life. "What was that? Is he sick?"

"He wants to be fed. He's very vocal about it and emits that special noise so there's no misunderstanding. If it's any consolation, I wondered the same thing the first time I heard it. I assume, Mr. Boardroom, you can use a can opener? While you do the honors, I'll go get Alice. The food is in the pantry and the opener in that drawer right there." She pointed and got up. "I'd move fast if I were you. He can get cranky if it takes too long. I'm going to go put on my coat. When you're done, put on something warm and meet me out front."

"Cranky?"

"Very."

The smooth, urbane Mick Branson could get out of

a chair and scramble across a room with impressive speed when faced with a large demanding cat. Jangles had his solid behind already on the floor by his bowl and his body language said he meant business. Raine was still laughing when she slipped into her favorite parka and went out back, wading through the snow.

The sleek snowmobile started sweetly. She'd gotten it from a friend of Blythe's whose husband had unexpectedly passed away, and much like her grandfather's property, the woman wasn't going to use it, but didn't want to sell his beloved possession. When Raine mentioned to Blythe that she was thinking of getting a sled—it was what her father had always called his snowmobile—suddenly she had one. The woman refused money for it, so Raine had done a graphic image of the vehicle and framed it as a gift.

She understood entirely not wanting to place monetary value on a possession so near and dear to someone you loved, but giving it to someone who would appreciate it was completely different.

Mick would appreciate the cabin property, especially on a day like this that Mother Nature had handcrafted to show it off. Brilliant blue skies, deep snow, and the mountains looked surreal, like something from a fairy tale. The skiers would be in seventh heaven, that was for sure. This was pure powder, the kind they lived for. Grace would be busy today, with the week between holidays and the resort always jammed full in this sort of weather.

When she pulled around, Mick was already on the sidewalk—probably to escape Jangles—and when she stopped he came down the steps and jumped on behind her. "Why do I think I'm going to need to hang on for dear life?"

"I like speed," she said. "Remember last night?"

He wrapped his arms around her waist and said exactly the right thing. "I'll never forget it. I trust you, so go for it."

She'd said the same thing. Trust was very important to her. Then he swept back her hair and kissed the nape of her neck just as she hit the throttle.

He had good technique and timing, she'd give him that.

Excellent technique, she recalled, thinking again of last night. Her burning cheeks appreciated the cold bite of the air as they took off. They were clearing the streets now, but not with big plows, more ranchers with trucks and blades, and they blew past without effort and were hardly the only ones on a snowmobile. The minute they were out of town she hit the back trail. Of course her phone started to vibrate and she fished it out of her pocket and held it over her shoulder. "Mind answering this?"

Mick objected. "It's your phone."

"I don't have a lot of secrets and it could be my daughter. So please do it with my complete permission."

He did, though she couldn't really hear the conversation too well, but she had the feeling he'd just met her grandmother.

Clara was not a Slater Carson fan, which was much more a reflection of her old-fashioned values than the man himself, and Raine had patiently explained time and again that he'd offered marriage. The opinionated woman didn't like the fact they'd slept together before

Raine had stood in a frothy white dress in front of an altar, wearing a lacy veil and flanked by six bridesmaids as a grave minister made her repeat vows.

The truth was, Raine hadn't ever really coveted that scenario. An image of Mick in a tux flashed into her mind and she quashed it as quickly as it appeared.

"Tell Gran I'll call later," she said over the sound of the engine.

A minute later he handed back the phone. "She said she liked the sound of my voice."

"She *did*?"

"What? I don't have a nice voice? She asked me to tell you Merry Christmas."

This wasn't the moment when she could go into a long convoluted explanation about how her grandmother formed opinions first and asked questions later. Instead she said, "Look at that view."

The soaring vista before them was incomparable, and just one of the many reasons she loved where she lived. The streets of Mustang Creek gave way to a county road as they breezed through, and within fifteen minutes they were gliding along toward her grandfather's property.

Trees; leafless now but he should see them in the spring, summer, and fall. Even now their branches were decorated with white, making them graceful and glistening. The background behind it all was beyond imagination. The Grand Tetons were very grand indeed after a snowfall like last night's.

His arms tightened briefly. "You're beautiful. The mountains look wonderful, too."

Well, he'd survived feeding Jangles and talking to her grandmother—sometimes a lesson in patience—so she'd skip pointing out that that was a tired line. The man was probably just plain frazzled. "Wait until we go around the curve."

They crested the hill where she'd put the lane to the property if it was her decision, even if it was a steep incline and there would be a curve. Although the snowmobile was loud, she had the satisfaction of hearing Mick catch his breath.

So he should. The unobstructed view of mountains, a frozen lake, and the quaint little cabin could have been straight out of one of her grandfather's books. She was fairly sure the chimney needed to be rebuilt and cleared, since birds considered it a wonderful place to nest and over time part of it had toppled over, but it was definitely picturesque.

If Mr. Boardroom had ever wanted to be a cowboy, he could fulfill that dream right here.

"Raine."

"I know, right?"

"You could get a million dollars for this."

"I don't need a million dollars. I need someone who will keep it intact and let my daughter come visit. I need someone who won't develop it, won't tear down the old corral and won't destroy the cabin." She stopped the sled in a flurry of disrupted snow. "Call me crazy, but I think that person could be you."

CHAPTER NINE

THE VIEW FROM the Carson ranch was spectacular.

This view might very well be better, if that was possible.

Mick had to admit he was wowed. Yes, the cabin was beyond quaint with its sagging porch and drooping, snow-laden roof, like a framed picture of a holiday card you might pick up at a boutique and mail to your friends, but the lake and the mountains took his breath away.

Stately firs stood in stands sprinkled with the aspens that had no doubt inspired Matthew Brighton's manuscript, and there was no one around for literally miles.

And miles.

Taking in the spectacular scenery, sensing the peace that came from such solitude, Mick knew Raine was right about this place being perfect for him. He'd been thinking for a long time about a change in venue to Wyoming, and certainly Slater's documentary influenced him, but he'd never quite envisioned anything quite like this. He could build the house of his dreams right here. They got off the snowmobile and stood knee-deep in drifts and he inhaled the quiet.

"Thoughts?" Raine read his expression perfectly. It was there in her eyes.

"I'm afraid that you already know what they are."

"Does it get any better than this?"

"I'm doubting it."

"You accept my terms then?"

He huffed out a breath. "Raine, you essentially have no terms. I'd walk over thin ice to save Daisy with or without the property, and your grandfather is a hero of mine. I'll leave the cabin as it is, of course, if you're serious about this."

"That will be all you need to do then."

"Why is it I think arguing with you is just a lesson in futility, but let me try one more time. This is exactly what I've been thinking about and then some, but let me have an appraiser put a fair price on it and—"

"No." She shook her head vehemently. "It's cathartic, giving it to you. Here, let me show you where I'd put a house."

They waded through the snow for a few hundred yards and then she pointed. "There."

The spot was idyllic to say the least, with a stream that was partially frozen right next to it, groves of trees, and a level area with a view that would support a house the size he was considering. A big one. Wraparound porch, a hot tub in the back, second level deck, and maybe three guest suites. He wanted to invite his family, but also use it for business purposes, and inside he wanted the real deal. Log detail, soaring ceilings, stacked fireplace, ultimate bathrooms...

"I agree it's perfect." He wanted to invite her to live with him and that was telling of itself. But he wasn't necessarily there yet, and his spidey senses said she wasn't either, so he left it alone.

"I assume you won't go modest, so this would be perfect." Raine nodded, her cheeks rosy from the cold.

It would be. "Lots of space…yes."

Only perfect if you choose to share it.

Dangerous thinking for a confirmed bachelor, but the image was still in his mind. "You have artistic vision, so maybe you could help me design the house."

That brought her head around. "I did study architecture in college. Just a few classes though. Are you serious?"

"Unfortunately, make a note. I'm always serious."

That was true. He could kid around, but didn't do it often or spontaneously.

Raine considered him thoughtfully. "If I have artistic vision, you have an artistic soul. Otherwise you wouldn't catch on to what Slater wants to do so easily. I would love to help design your house here. It's a dream come true for me. You'll still need an architect, but we could at least draw up the idea of what you have in mind."

We have in mind.

He wanted nothing more. "Let's do it together. That aside, this is my night. Let me cook for you. I'll have to borrow your kitchen, of course. I asked Harry if Daisy would eat lobster mac and cheese. She seemed to think that would go over very well."

Of course she argued. "Lobster? You can't get lobster in Wyoming in December. Last I checked they don't abound around these parts. The local grocery certainly doesn't have them."

"I haven't been in there but I'll take your word for it. On the other hand, you can get it if you know the right people." He tried to not sound smug and failed.

She pounced on it. "Grace."

"Not Grace so much as her chef."

"Stephano? He's making it… Well then, I'm in."

Such confidence. She was right, of course, Stephano adored Daisy so he'd been right on board when Mick had called. He said with mock indignation, "First you doubt the quality of my voice, and now this. How do you know I can't cook?"

Raine gave him a gamine grin. "I know *he* can. You haven't proven yourself."

Mick just gave it up with a laugh. "I can't cook usually but I spent a week in Maine when I was in college, hiking Acadia National Park. One of the rangers recommended this little restaurant and I had lobster mac there for the first time. The owner gave me the recipe when I ordered a second helping and she learned I lived in this godforsaken place called California. She felt sorry for any young man that didn't live in Maine. The recipe is apparently an old family favorite."

"My daughter loves lobster *and* she loves mac and cheese. Daisy will be thrilled."

"Can we pretend it isn't the only dish I can make?"

"Um, if you think you can fool her, think again, but go ahead and try. She's a smart cookie. That kid figured out the Easter Bunny, Santa Claus and the Tooth Fairy way before any of her friends. I'm proud to say she let them go on believing but she sure was on to me. When asked flat out, I cannot tell a lie."

"Good to know." He said it lightly, but didn't mean it lightly. Honesty was important to him. He kissed her cool cheek. "I mean that."

"I take it we need to stop off at the resort before we pick up Daisy. The road crews will have been out by now."

"We do." He said it with a straight face. "A lobster waits for no one."

Raine burst out laughing and picked up a handful of snow and tossed it at him. "Okay, now you *do* win for the worst line ever."

He reached down and retaliated. "If you want a snowball fight, I'm in."

"In that case, I should probably warn you I'm vicious."

"I have good aim."

Raine pelted him with another snowball. "Good luck, cowboy. I was born in snow country."

He needed luck. She was pretty accurate as well. After the third one caught him right in the chest he surrendered, arms in the air. "Mercy."

Of course she pelted him again.

He tackled her and the resulting kiss made him forget about the cold even though they were both lying in the snow.

"I'm falling in love with you." He definitely hadn't meant to admit that, but it was true and she already knew it.

"If you haven't figured out we have the same problem, then you aren't paying attention." Raine looked reflective lying beneath him. "We're both idiots."

"I don't think I am."

"I don't think I am, either." Her eyes were suddenly shiny. "But I've been wrong before."

"Raine, do you really think Slater was a mistake?"

She sat up and shook snow out of her dark hair. "No, of course not. I wouldn't have Daisy if it wasn't for him, and I'll always care about him. It's just that

I keep hoping to find gold in a muddy river bed, but I haven't had a strike yet."

He probably had snow in his hair as well but didn't care. "You sure about that? I'm going to finish that manuscript, by the way. I don't know if I can do it justice, but maybe *I'll* get a strike."

She kissed him then, snowy mittens on his cheeks but her mouth was warm and giving. "I'm so glad."

"I won't know what I'm doing."

"You'll do great. I feel it."

"I'll trust you to tell me if it's terrible."

"Oh, don't you think you'd be the first to know?" Raine gave him a merry glance before getting to her feet. "I'm not shy with my opinions in case you haven't noticed. I believe *blatantly outspoken* is the Carsons' preferred term for me. I have bad news for you, though. Their head ranch hand, Red, is a die-hard Matthew Brighton fan. It's his opinion you really need to worry about, because he won't pull his punches if you can't tell a snake hole from the Grand Canyon."

"Great. Well, I guess I know who my expert consultant will be if I need help with research." Mick got up also and tried to brush off his jeans. "I'm probably nuts even to try this, but I do like a challenge."

The look she gave him was only half-teasing. "Is that why you fell for me? Because I'm a challenge?"

"Maybe it started that way," he admitted, catching her hand as they made their way back to the snowmobile. "You do keep me on my toes. But if you haven't figured out that I'm crazy about everything that makes you you, then you're the one who's not paying attention."

"Likewise, cowboy." She started the snowmobile

again. "Climb on board. Isn't there a lobster with your name on it?"

CREAM, CHEESE, PASTA, GARLIC…there was no way to go wrong with a meal like that, so Mick was cheating. He did let Raine do the salad and got the bread from the restaurant, but otherwise he prepared everything himself. And if the purse he'd given Daisy had won her over, the dinner he served them made her his devoted fan for life.

That was so important to her, Raine thought as she watched her daughter interact so naturally with Mick. Daisy's face was animated as she described the midnight ride in the snow, and she'd definitely cleaned her plate so his dinner choice had been about as popular as Harry's cooking, which was saying something.

Clever man.

"Remind me to kiss Stephano next time I see him," Raine declared during a lull in the excited conversation. "That lobster was the perfect touch."

"How about you kiss the actual cook, not just the ingredient-supplier?" Mick gave her a look of mock reproof. "Besides, I'm way better looking than he is."

"Maybe a tinge." Raine gave him a dreamy smile. "But he has that Latin air, you know?"

DAISY JOINED HER mother in giggling at the expression on Mick's face. Raine knew she was taking it all in— their unexpected guest, the overt affection between them. What Raine wanted her daughter to walk away with from tonight was a sense that love was supposed to be fun. It wasn't supposed to be easy all of the time, but fun was very important.

MICK THREW UP his hands. "In that case, how's an or
dinary guy supposed to compete?"

She shouldn't say it so softly, but she did anyway.
"Oh you aren't ordinary by any means."

"No?"

"No."

Enough said. Daisy was clearly paying attention to
the nuances of the conversation, listening avidly. The
good news was that purse aside, she seemed to really
like Mick. That hadn't been the case last time she'd in-
troduced her daughter to a man she'd briefly been dating, a doctor from a nearby town. Daisy had instantly
pronounced him boring and that put an end to that. She
might not have known him long enough to give him
a fair shot, but Raine trusted her daughter's instincts.
Besides that, any man who was a part of her life would
be part of her daughter's as well. Her opinion counted.

Daisy jumped up. "Who wants ice cream? I'll get
it." She began to eagerly stack the plates. They had an
agreement. Raine cooked and cleaned up the kitchen,
but Daisy cleared the table.

"Her grandmother is Blythe Carson," Raine confided. "According to Blythe, ice cream is an essential
food group all by itself. Beware."

Mick lifted a brow. "Beware? I love ice cream."

"Good. Get ready to prove it."

He ended up with brownie fudge with cherries and
marshmallow topping in a massive bowl, not to mention various kinds of sprinkles in rainbow colors. Before he dug in he muttered, "Beware. Now I get it. I'll
have to go to the gym fifteen times to work this off."

"I'll go with you." Her bowl was half the size.

"You can go with me anywhere."

There was that smooth Hollywood charm again. She scooped up marshmallow and cherry on her spoon. "You see, our problem is I'm *not* going anywhere. I can't. That's why I want to contact my Realtor's office the minute it's open, yank the cabin property off the market, and tell them to set up a closing."

"Cabin? You mean Grandpa's house?" Daisy had seemed to be focused on her own heaping spoonful, but Raine knew she was listening to their every word.

"That's right. I'm giving it to Mick."

"That's a pretty good idea."

Raine smiled. "Mick is a writer. He'll love it there."

That was a full-out dare. Daisy actually stopped eating ice cream, and that was something. Her eyes were wide. "You are? Like him?"

He blinked. "No." Then relented. "Well, I'm afraid I'm nowhere near as talented as your great-grandfather, but I've tried a time or two."

"He's been published in literary magazines." Raine couldn't resist imparting that information and ignored the quelling look from the man across the table. "And he's read the Matthew Brighton books."

"Have you really?" Daisy grinned, obviously delighted. "My favorite is *Mountain Sunrise*."

"I liked that one, too." Mick acted nonchalant, but Raine sensed his passion for finishing the manuscript. No matter how it turned out, she was glad to have played a small role in encouraging him to explore the creative side he didn't often get to give free rein to.

Raine got up. "I'm going to go clean the kitchen. I truly can't eat another bite. I might need to go for a walk but someone should probably carry me."

Daisy pointed out, "Then it wouldn't be a walk."

"I'll help you clean up since I made the mess, and then I'll take you on that walk." Mick rose as well. "Beautiful moon out there."

Raine probably should have predicted the total chaos that ensued when Mick took a step toward the kitchen.

Jangles did a daring guerilla move and went for his ankles, but now Samson was back in residence and wanted part of the action. Raine was almost swept off her feet—not in the romantic sense—as a giant puppy chased a giant cat and both of them nearly took her out, the cat dodging right in front of her and the dog accidentally slamming into the backs of her legs. Mick managed to keep his balance during the mayhem and caught her shoulders, steadying her at the last second as the animals dashed past.

"Such a peaceful household," she said darkly. "Bunch of wild critters that don't realize if they break your leg you can't get to the grocery store to buy them more food."

They went by again at full speed, careening into walls and not caring, playing a classic game of circling the house. It was endearingly funny, but she made sure her computer wasn't plugged in when they really got going because Samson could easily catch that cord. One day he might not be so clumsy, but for now she was taking precautions.

"I like it," Mick said and kissed her swiftly out of Daisy's sightline. "Full of life. I'm starting to think my house in California is entirely too quiet."

"Then move here. I promise no peace and quiet at all."

She was really losing it if she'd just said that. So she

just blundered on. "You can't live in the cabin while the house is being built."

"Sure I could. I've also read Walden."

"You wear Italian shoes."

"So? Stop harping on my shoes and focus on the man." He caught her playfully around the waist. "But invitation accepted. Where would I sleep? With you?"

"I'm thinking that might be the case." She went serious because she might as well make her position clear. "But only on the nights when Daisy is at the ranch. I'm not so naive as to think she hasn't cottoned on to the fact that there's something going between us, but I also know Slater and Grace kept their feelings for each other off her radar until they understood where they were headed, and I appreciated that. Daisy likes you, and so do I—"

"Glad to hear it." He was busy nuzzling her neck. "I can always stay at the cabin."

"Don't you have business on the West Coast?"

"That's the beauty of modern technology. I can work from anywhere, to a certain extent." He kissed her again.

"No plumbing." She whispered it against his mouth, not quite sure why she was trying to warn him off when she so badly wanted him to stay.

"Versus no you? That's hardly a contest."

"I have to think of my daughter."

"I will always think of her, too, I promise. And then there's the other females in our lives to think of. We'll have to handle my mother and your grandmother, Blythe, Harry, and the rest of the bunch."

"The interferers. Grace, Luce and Kelly will be just as bad."

"Exactly."

She couldn't help but laugh at his grim expression. "They'll be fine. They interfere, but mean well."

"Women just don't operate like men."

"Do you think?"

His grin was instant. "Think? Your presence seems to impair the process. No offense intended."

"None taken." She disengaged from his embrace. "If you can rinse dishes and hand them to me while I load the dishwasher, I'll be yours for life."

"Hey, I thought I was the one that made the deals. Don't try and show me up." He picked up a plate and flipped the lever on the faucet. "Obviously I accept your terms. We can negotiate the details."

CHAPTER TEN

THE SKIERS WERE out in full force and Mick sat in a comfortable chair and watched out the window of his room as they careened down the slopes while he sipped a cup of coffee. It was clear and brilliant outside and he was in a reflective mood, watching the sunlight bounce off the sparkling snow.

I'll be yours for life.

Now that was a thought.

She'd probably meant it in a different way than he took it, joking, not serious at all, but it had certainly struck a nerve.

He sat there and seriously considered marriage for the first time in his life.

That word had always scared him. It wasn't the permanence of it, since half the people he knew were divorced—it was the emotional investment. Yet the true problem was that he was convinced it scared Raine even more. She'd opted out once already. Slater was a great guy but she'd given him a firm no when he proposed, and changing her mind was going to take more than the two of them enjoying a night in bed together.

So he really considered it over a second cup of coffee, and then called his brother. Ran answered pretty swiftly but he lived by his phone, even at this time of the year. Mick said, "Hi. How's London?"

"Covered in white. Snowed last night. How's Wyoming?"

"Ditto."

"An ocean away and the same story. It must be Christmas. So what's up?"

"I think I need a ring and Ingrid is no slouch in that department. Could you ask her to pick one out? I'll write you a check when you're back in the States, or I can send you the money now. We can get it sized here."

His brother's wife had been a jewelry store buyer before the two of them got married and remained a consummate gem shopper. They kept her jewelry in a safe.

"What kind of ring?"

"Engagement."

"Are you joking around?" Ran sounded stunned. "*You're* proposing to someone?"

"I'm going to give it a try. And if she says yes, moving to Wyoming full-time. I do half my business by phone or email, not to mention I have to fly from Los Angeles all the time anyway for meetings. I can do that from here."

"You'd *live* in Wyoming?"

He chuckled at his brother's horrified tone. "I realize Mustang Creek doesn't have a ballet company or symphony orchestra, but the scenery alone makes up for that, and yes, I'd live here because she's here and isn't going anywhere and I wouldn't ask it of her. I like it here anyway, you know that."

"I know you keep going back and now I finally understand why."

He thought about Bad Billy's Burger Palace and Harry's cooking, not to mention the resort. "Lots of good food choices, great schools, all the peace and quiet a man could want, and I doubt the sunsets could be beat by any place on earth. No shortage of beautiful women, either." Grace, Luce, and Kelly certainly qualified, as did the wives of Slater's friends he'd met. Not that he had eyes for anyone but Raine. "And I'm talking the type that don't need a salon and expensive make-up artist to make it happen."

His brother wasn't without a sense of humor. "I might just visit then, to check out the scenery."

"You'll be welcome anytime. Tell Ingrid that Raine would probably like something different for the ring. She's an artist. I don't think she'd go for a two-carat marquis. She might turn me down on that one. Something really eclectic would work. Tell Ingrid I implicitly trust her and Raine has hazel eyes and dark hair."

Randal Branson had never been all that imaginative. "The color of her hair and eyes matters...why?"

"I have no idea, but I figure it doesn't hurt to arm Ingrid with enough information to find the perfect ring. Tell her to make it unusual, one of a kind even. Just like Raine."

"I thought the romantic ideal was the man should pick out the ring."

He wasn't easily fooled. "Who picked out Ingrid's? I've seen it. It's tasteful, so don't try to claim it was you."

"Okay, you got me. She chose it herself and I was happy to let her."

"I rest my case," Mick said. "You'll bring the ring back from London?"

"Ingrid has a lot of associates here. I think she'll enjoy shopping for it and be really picky about the stone and setting. I've seen her in action. We fly back tomorrow and she wants to do some last-minute shopping so we were going out anyway. We're invited to the Austins' famous annual New Year's party."

Mick had been, too, but he was spending the holiday right where he was. Those glitzy affairs had lost their gloss even before he'd become so involved with Raine.

"I was thinking New Year's Eve is the perfect night to propose."

"Not waiting around."

"I thought you'd just intimated I'd waited around too much in my life already."

"I'm just happy for you." Ran sounded sincere. "Ingrid will find you the perfect ring and I'll have it insured and overnighted."

"That's all I could ask for. Tell Ingrid thanks in advance from me."

They ended the call and he settled back, amazingly content with his decision. He was used to such a fast-paced life he found he liked just sitting there and watching the ski runs. It was interesting to take time to contemplate the life-changing curve in the road of his future.

He'd have an instant daughter if Raine said yes. Maybe more children; a subject they would need to discuss later.

If she said yes.

It would certainly affect the plans for the house he was going to build.

If she said yes.

It was going to completely change his life.

If she said yes.

Not a given.

Suddenly restless, he got up to pace the length of

the room. He'd always considered himself more a man of controlled contemplation than action, but right now he needed to walk off this unexpected insecurity. It was probably a good sign it meant so much to him, but he wasn't enjoying the myriad emotions. He was nervous, a concept that was foreign to him. Usually, when awaiting the outcome of a deal he'd negotiated, he was confident and straightforward, and if it fell through—which happened now and then for various reasons—so it went.

He couldn't shrug this off if Raine decided he wasn't the one.

The break-up after the miscarriage had been painful, but they would probably have only stayed together for the baby, so that was something else he and Raine had in common. Like Slater, he would have offered marriage, but if his ex-girlfriend had said yes, he wasn't sure at all it would have lasted. The experience did teach him something about himself and that was that he was much more traditional than he thought, but it also made him realize he valued relationships in a long-term way.

Double-whammy right there.

He wanted a wife, family, and roots.

Speaking of roots…if he was going to make good on his promise, he might as well get started on reading *The Aspen Trail*. What better way to spend a snowy morning, especially since he knew Raine was working, though she'd agreed to lunch. She'd already had plans to meet with friends for dinner. They sponsored a college scholarship at the local high school and between them formed a committee each year to review the applications and select a recipient. The Carson Ranch

matched their contributions and people from all over
the state applied for it, and Raine had said with a definite tinge of emotion in her voice that it was wonderful to support higher education. He agreed. Already
it had occurred to him to maybe set up a college fund
for Daisy in her grandfather's name to offset the property gift.

So he sat back down, told himself to forget everything else for the moment, and he started to read.

Chapter One

The haze of the sun hit the leaves in a slanted
light and cast shadows on the ground. The cowboy nudged his horse forward with his heel, the silent communication as natural as words between
them. They understood each other without effort.

The cowboy wished it was half that easy with
women.

His sweetheart was an independent sort with
a mind of her own, and had little use for him unless she was so inclined.

He needed to win the lady but wasn't sure how
to go about it.

Mick laughed quietly and sat back, his feet propped
up. That seemed all too appropriate to his current situation. He'd won his way into Raine's bed, but he wasn't
sure about her heart.

That dark-haired beauty didn't want his help,
hadn't asked for it, and was as dangerous as a
loaded pistol ready to go off. Part of him admired

her feisty spirit, but a bigger part wished she'd agree to lean on him just a little more. Maybe his days as a drifter were coming to an end, because he wasn't going anywhere. This valley felt like home and whether she admitted it or not, she needed someone like him around.

There was a reason for the price on his head in Arkansas. He was damned handy with a gun. A man needed to be able to defend himself, and others if it came right down to it. Maybe someday he'd even tell her that story. But now there was trouble coming. He could smell it in the air and hear it in the whisper of the aspen leaves.

Could he write in a voice like Brighton's, one that was all the more powerful for its simplicity? Mick wasn't sure, but he *was* sure he was interested to find out what trouble was coming and how it worked out with the dark-haired beauty and the cowboy. What was the danger?

He was taking mental notes.

So he read on.

"We need more details."

Hadleigh Galloway, Melody Hogan and Bex Calder all stared her down. They'd known each other since childhood, and the tight-knit threesome were the first people Raine had thought of when she'd come up with the idea of the scholarship. All successful businesswomen and mothers, they'd done what she hoped and, despite their busy schedules, embraced the idea. Bex's wealthy in-laws had handed over a large sum of money as well.

It was no longer just one scholarship, they'd decided over appetizers and then an array of salads varying from shrimp to garlic chicken. They could now safely give out five from the current endowment. They had their usual table at Bad Billy's and the place was hopping due to the influx of skiers. The old jukebox was getting a definite workout, with an emphasis on Patsy Cline and Willie Nelson.

"Details?" Raine tried to look like she didn't understand the demand. "Of what?"

"Nice try," Hadleigh said after a sip of iced tea. "Let's talk you and Mick Branson. Don't ask how we know, because of course we do."

Drake was probably to blame, since he played poker with Tripp Galloway and Spence Hogan once a week, and he regularly bought horses from Tate Calder, so all their husbands were probably a font of information.

"I'm not sure what you want to know. He's…nice." Raine took another shrimp and popped it in her mouth to avoid the conversation. Billy's poppyseed dressing was so good it should probably be illegal.

Melody wasn't letting her off the hook. "In the looks department, I agree. Better than nice. Let's upgrade it to deliciously handsome. And there's no doubt he's successful. He seems to be spending a lot of time here in Bliss County all of a sudden. He spent Christmas Eve at your house and I'm guessing there was mistletoe involved. What's up?"

"He just came so he could see Slater's movie with the family as a surprise Christmas gift."

"I watched it, of course. It was fabulous. But nope." Bex shook her head. "A phone call at the right moment could have done the trick. Speculation has it he came here to see *you*. I have it on good authority."

"Whose?"

"Blythe's, via my mother-in-law. The networking around here is incredible."

Lettie Arbuckle-Calder *was* connected. "Like I don't know that," Raine muttered.

"I'd say he's not your type, but maybe I'm wrong." Melody, a jewelry artist, spoke thoughtfully. "I've met him and he has a soulful aura."

Hadleigh snorted. "You should have been a hippie, you know that? A soulful aura?"

Melody wasn't one to take anything from Hadleigh without arguing, even if they were fast friends. "Hippie, huh? Let's talk about someone who makes quilts for a living. There's hippie for you. I think you're the only person I know with an incense burner."

"That's an air freshener."

Bex said mildly to Raine under her breath, "I'll put a stop to this. Been doing it for years now. Otherwise it could go on for an hour." Loudly, she interrupted, "I think we were talking about Mick Branson, right? Tell us about him."

Too bad putting a stop to the bickering meant shining the spotlight back on Raine. "He's creative and imaginative, once you see beneath that corporate businessman image. Yes, he raises money for Slater's films, but that's because he sees the vision."

"Or the money." That was Bex, so practical.

"Nope. To see his face when the documentary came on at prime time on a day that isn't easy to secure was priceless. Mick did it for all of us. I'd say he moved heaven and earth to make it happen."

"You're in love with him." Hadleigh looked delighted. "I can see it."

"You can't see love," Raine argued, sidestepping an actual answer. She'd only just begun to admit her feelings to herself and to Mick. She wasn't quite ready to share them with others yet, not even friends.

"Yes, she can," Melody disagreed, jumping right into Hadleigh camp. "She has a special magic."

"She can. She's a wizard." Bex pointed a finger at her friend. "She's got a potion or something she takes."

"I do not," Hadleigh protested despite her grin. "There's no simmering pot, no incantations."

"Wizard." They said it accusingly in unison.

"I'm empathic and gifted with insight," she corrected loftily, then turned to Raine. "Do we have wedding plans yet?"

"No!"

"We will soon," the wizard decreed. "The resort will be perfect as a venue. Elegant enough for out-of-town guests, but convenient for everyone else. Blythe wouldn't dream of anyone else doing the bridal shower but her."

"He hasn't asked me." Raine had to point it out.

"What would you say?" That was Bex.

"It doesn't matter, he won't ask. If he wanted to get married, he would have by now."

The three of them looked at each other, and then burst out laughing. Melody was the one who said, "Honey, take it from three married women, it doesn't work that way. They only cave when they find the right woman."

"And once they do, they're pretty wonderful," Hadleigh informed her in a theatrical whisper. "Don't tell Tripp I said that because I'll deny it. Those cocky pilot types are full enough of themselves already."

"I agree." Bex's husband had also been a pilot before he decided to become a horse breeder. "And they're wonderful, only if given some instruction," she explained with a cheeky smile. "They need guidance."

Raine needed to rein in all this speculation. "Mick's well beyond the time in his life when he's going to ask without careful consideration, and he certainly would not ask *me*. I come with a daughter, a giant cat and a big blundering dog. Most of the time I live in faded jeans that are genuinely faded from being washed like a million times, and a handful of T-shirts. I decided when I was about twenty that high heels were overrated and haven't looked back. Besides, I live here and he lives somewhere very different. I will never be glamourous and I don't apologize for it, but he could get glamourous if he wanted it."

"Do you think that's the type of woman he wants?" Hadleigh considered her carefully. "It doesn't seem to me it is. He could have had that at any time. He's dated actresses, debutantes, and if I remember correctly, a very famous professional female athlete."

Raine weighed her words. "He's fallen in love with Wyoming."

"Or you."

Bex added, "Or both."

She wasn't convinced yet, despite his earlier declaration. "Maybe. I could be a passing fad, like when we were in high school and decided blue mascara was the way to go. That didn't last too long."

He'd said it though. *I'm falling in love with you.*

Her artistic bent seemed to fascinate him, and his

desire to write did the same for her. Mick Branson had layers, and she needed that. He wasn't just Mr. Boardroom, he was also polite and thoughtful. That he'd wanted to make dinner for both her and Daisy was a winning strategy, that was for sure. He'd earned some definite points there.

She added, "He did fix me dinner."

All three of her companions glanced at each other and said in unison, "We know."

Of course they did.

Melody commented, "He's a goner. Ask the wizard."

"Goner," Hadleigh confirmed sagely, and Raine smiled, shook her head and gave up.

CHAPTER ELEVEN

MICK READ THE entire manuscript in one day. Other than an extremely quick lunch with Raine that had ended with a brief and unsatisfying goodbye peck on the cheek because she was in a hurry and they were in a public place, he'd spent the rest of the time reading in his room. Dinner was room service, eaten almost absently as he read.

It was an indulgence for him and the unfinished work was fantastic.

No pressure.

It brought him back to his childhood when he'd read those first Matthew Brighton books. Being reminded of his father was welcome when he was now committed to changing his life.

Loyalty. Fidelity. Integrity.

He'd absorbed those lessons without need of a lecture. He'd bet most people thought his parents were frivolous due to their wealth, but they absolutely were not. His father had been demonstratively diligent as a family man, and as a businessman. Both he and Ran had learned a lot from him. Their father wasn't successful because it came naturally, it was because he worked at it, and his example had stuck.

Don't ever screw someone over and think that's okay.

They didn't.

When it goes south, regroup and think about how to fix it. It might seem like the end of the world, but it isn't.

Deal with hard guidelines but make them fair. No one loses that way.

Take time every single day to make sure you appreciate what you have. Ambition is fine, but avarice is not.

Raine was 100 percent on that one. It was clear she liked her life. Mick liked his, too, but recognized that the missing elements had nothing to do with money and everything to do with taking more time to simply enjoy himself. He didn't like busy airports and congested freeways yet had to put up with both on an almost daily basis and both of his houses were nice by any standard and luxurious by most, but a waste since he didn't use even half the space.

It was time to just sell them and move on. He realized now he'd been thinking about it for some time, even before his keen interest in this part of Wyoming had arisen. Maybe ever since he'd picked up his first Matthew Brighton novel and sat down to read.

His father would no doubt approve.

The last paragraph of the manuscript was: *He was a man of action and it wasn't in his nature to sit idly by and just let things happen. They happened on his terms and that was that.*

Mick dealt with talented people on a constant basis. That was his job, to win sponsors, to create backing for plays and films like the ones Slater did so well, to decide what was innovative and new, and what wasn't going to go over with a large viewing audience.

Now the tables had turned and he was the one sitting there on the creative edge...

Tentatively he opened a document on his computer and began to type. He was daunted, yes, but it was out of the question to not at least give it a try. Two hours later he had some words down and wasn't displeased with the result—not that he was impressed with himself, but it had come far easier than he imagined.

He sent Raine an email. Mission Aspen Trail conclusion has begun.

It was now after midnight, and of course she typed right back immediately. You've been busy.

How was the meeting?

It was good. We're all pleased with the number of applicants. The scholarship is evolving into more than we imagined. There are a lot of good students out there who deserve the chance to make their dreams come true.

A very Raine sort of sentiment. The woman who preferred to give away an expensive piece of property.

Good cause, he typed back. I'll help, of course. You should get my mother involved.

Had he really just said that, in writing, no less?

Instantly he recanted. He loved his mother but she had a tendency to take charge and definite ideas on how things should be done. *Or maybe not. She might take over.*

We were talking about how we need someone to maybe run a foundation. Do you think she would?

Oh, I think you'd maybe raise a monster from the depths, but if you want meticulous management, she's your woman. That was honest.

Monster or not, she could be just what we need.

I can obviously get you in touch with her. Can we have dinner tomorrow?

We can but I have something else in mind. Call me in the morning.

Like?

Just call. And sweet dreams.

She didn't write anything further.

If he knew Raine she'd gone right back to work. He did the same, not returning to the manuscript but instead answering emails and checking his messages since he'd basically taken the day off. No news, no stock market updates, none of his usual routine, just moonlight on the snow and a sense of personal well-being.

He had no illusions that this was all going to be simple. Making a major change never was an easy process, but if he trusted his instincts at all, he had to accept that it was time.

OCCASIONALLY SHE GOT some pretty harebrained ideas.

Raine had to admit this could be one of them. She strapped the toboggan to the top of her SUV and Daisy clapped, her eyes shining. She was going to be taller than her mother, Raine had already figured out, taking more after Slater in that regard, and had that coltish lack of grace that would change as she matured. In any case, she was young enough to still think sledding was big fun, and maybe Raine was too, since she agreed. Samson seemed just as excited, romping through the snow.

Some kids never grew up.

Some grown-ups—namely her—just wanted to see Mick Branson rocket down a wicked hill on a toboggan. She could probably sell pictures of that. She knew the steep hill, and since she doubted he had a proper coat for this experience, had asked Slater if she could borrow one. They were very close to the same build. Of course the answer had been an amused yes once she explained why she was asking. He even said he'd love to film it, but his crew was all off on Christmas break.

"That's what my phone is for," she'd assured him. She could catch a short video of the urbane Mr. Branson careening down the slope if he had the fortitude to accept the challenge.

She somehow thought he would. So far he'd proven to be unshakable, even in the face of the entire Carson family, Jangles and his sneak attacks, talking to her grandmother, whipping up a dinner extraordinaire...

She'd see if those nerves of steel held up.

Red called it Dead Man's Hill and it was certainly a wild ride. He was the first person to point her in that direction with the admonishment it was not for the faint of heart. He was right. But the snow was perfect and it wouldn't be winter if she didn't at least go down that hill once a week, and Daisy loved it. Mick could decline if he wanted, but she had a feeling he would be game.

Raine doubted anything tripped him up, but she had to admit she was eager to see the look on his face when he first saw that slope. If a person didn't have a moment of doubt, then they just weren't sensible. What they decided after they stared down that 45 degree angle and thought it was maybe a bad decision but looked like it might be really fun, well, that was up to them.

Red had wisely counseled that if you didn't panic like a sheep that had eaten loco weed then you would be fine. Raine was uncertain how a sheep that had ingested that plant did act, but it sounded like solid advice to just enjoy the experience.

Mick pulled up, right on time as usual, and got out of his fancy rental, eyeing the contraptions strapped to the top of her car. "You've been out sledding?"

"No. Not yet."

"I'm beginning to see the light. This is why you told me to wear jeans."

"Yep," she responded cheerfully. "Hop in. I have the right kind of coat for you and Mace offered up a spare pair of snow boots since some hiking is involved. The good news for you is you get to carry the big toboggan. Don't worry, I have a thermos of hot cocoa."

"It had better have some whiskey in it," he said darkly, but gamely climbed in the passenger side on the car.

She jumped in and started the vehicle. "Has Mr. Boardroom ever been sledding?"

"Maybe when I was about thirty years younger. Are you sure my feeble body can take this?" He buckled his seat belt.

She eyed his muscular frame and broad shoulders with true appreciation. "I think you'll survive."

"I guess I have no choice but to find out. I'm being...what's the expression out here in the wilds? Railroaded?"

"That's the one." She pulled out onto the street, which was clearing nicely after being plowed. The abundant sunshine helped, too, even though the temps were still below freezing.

Samson woofed from his spot next to Daisy in the back seat. "We're bringing the *dog*?"

"He loves it. I think he can ride down the slopes with you. At the bottom you get a special bonus since he always licks your face in exuberant gratitude."

"That takes dogsledding to an interesting level." He looked resigned. "This just gets better all the time. I was thinking a fire and maybe a glass of wine."

"We'll get to that. I'm making homemade pizza, by the way."

"That sounds fabulous." Mick scooted his seat back a few inches, careful not to jar Samson, who was curled up on the seat behind him. "Let me guess—smoked salmon and caviar on crème fraîche."

"This isn't Beverly Hills, hotshot. How about sausage, pepperoni, onion and green pepper."

"Or sardines, Gouda and watermelon." His tone was so serious she heard Daisy draw in a disbelieving breath from the back seat. "It's my favorite."

"Be careful," she said as she turned onto main street. "Or I'll get Stephano to fix that just for you."

"You guys are joking, right?" Daisy asked suspiciously from behind them. "Sardines are fish. That doesn't go with watermelon. And I've never had watermelon on pizza. It sounds gross."

"We're definitely joking." Mick gave a mock shudder. "I tried sardines once in college. I still have night-mares about it. Cans of sardines are following me around on tiptoe, begging me to give them a second chance."

"You're funny," Daisy informed him with the giggle Raine never got enough of hearing.

He did have a good sense of humor once a person caught on to the droll delivery. Raine was happy about that. Raine was...*happy*, she realized. Before he'd come breezing back into town she'd been very content. After all, she had a wonderful daughter, friends, a satisfying career...but this was different. She had to tamp down the hope that maybe Hadleigh the Wizard was right, and try to stay practical.

Even with the property and cabin he wouldn't be around much because he was a busy man. For that matter, she was pretty busy, too. So did their lives collide in the right way?

They might.

Let's see how he handles Dead Man's Hill.

"We're getting close." She headed for the road opposite the ski slopes. "You might want to try on the boots."

He toed off the loafers and picked up the boots she'd left on the floor on the passenger side. "I take it this will be an Olympic event of some kind. Call it a hunch."

"Depends on the snow. There's fast snow and slow snow."

"You'll have to teach me the difference."

"One will cause a sardine-like experience and the other is just fun."

"More nightmares?"

"Only if it's the fast snow."

He sent her a keen glare. "You're deliberately trying to scare me, aren't you?"

"Shoot, you found me out. Let's see if you're up for it."

The drive was scenic by any standards, and right there it was an especially high bar. The curvy road wound up toward the mountains and was crowded by trees, and for most people that alone was harrowing. Luckily she'd driven it enough times to know just when to slow down and take it easy. Some kindly good-old boy had plowed one lane with the blade on his truck and she hoped they wouldn't meet a car coming the other direction, but otherwise the climb was breathtaking. They parked at a scenic outlook the state had put there years ago, and turned to Mick. "Here's the hard part. It's easy to walk to the hill, but we have to hike back up towing the toboggans."

"It seems to me you've done this before, so we can certainly handle it together. I don't really see a hill though."

She sent him a mischievous grin. "You will."

CHAPTER TWELVE

THE WOMAN WAS trying to kill him.

That wasn't a hill. That was a champion alpine slope. Mick pointed at the bottom. "There's a stream down there."

Raine was blasé about that observation, looking absurdly attractive in earmuffs and a scarf. "You're going so fast and with the angle you sail over it, that's part of the fun."

"Uh, I think I weigh a little more than you do."

"No problem. I've seen Drake, Slater and Mace float right over it. Just brace yourself."

"Is this some kind of Grand Teton test?" He hefted the biggest toboggan off the roof.

She flashed a mischievous grin. "Trial by fire."

"I'm going to trust you."

"I think we've already trusted each other quite a bit."

She certainly had a point there. They had. She'd slept in his arms and he wanted a repeat performance in the worst way.

Daisy had bounced out of the car and was impatiently waiting. Samson seemed equally trusting this wasn't a suicide mission and was gamboling in the snow, so Mick had no choice but to take it on faith as well.

That was one hell of a steep mini-mountain. It

looked neck-break worthy. "People have survived this?" he asked dubiously.

"You're looking at some of them right here."

"How many dead bodies buried at the bottom of Dead Man's Hill?"

"Hard to say. Headstones are covered with snow. You gonna chicken out?"

"Never." He wasn't about to give up that kind of dare. "Promise me a night together if we both survive?"

"Deal." Her hazel eyes held a teasing light.

"I'll risk anything for that."

"Then hop on for the ride of your life."

"I thought we were just negotiating for that to come later."

She gave him the look he probably deserved for that comment. Daisy had already gotten on the smaller sled with the ease of someone who had definitely done it before. Samson had climbed on behind her and was furiously wagging his tail, a canine grin on his face, and she gave a whoop and pushed off.

"She's going to lord it over us if they win. Hurry."

Raine sat her very shapely behind down on the bigger toboggan and waved him on. Mick had to admit that despite having scuba dived off the Great Coral Reef and canoed on the Amazon, this had to be up in the top ten of adventurous things he'd done in his lifetime. He gamely got on behind her, wrapped his arms around her slim waist and said a small prayer she knew what she was doing.

The snow was deep enough they had a smooth trip, but they picked up speed at a blood-racing rate and he was pretty sure he didn't need the parka she'd provided because he broke out in a sweat. Their sled was heavier with two adults so they caught up with Daisy and passed her, Raine giving her daughter a cheery wave, and when the slope flattened out, they finally came to a halt in a swoosh of snow and triumph.

Daisy arrived about two seconds later, spinning around in a circle as she too came to a halt, breathless but laughing. "Hey, that's not fair. You had ballast."

Mick wasn't sure if he was more surprised she knew the word and could use it, or if he was insulted. "Big word for a small fry. And you had a little ballast yourself."

His mistake was to point at the dog. Samson took it as an invitation to come leap all over him, his enormous snowy paws dancing with such enthusiasm Mick actually staggered backwards.

Raine didn't quite succeed in hiding her merriment with her mitten clamped over her mouth.

Daisy was as saucy as her mother. "I may be a small fry, but at least I know how to handle a big dog."

He burst out laughing, trying unsuccessfully to fend off the dog's burst of affection. "You have a point there. Too bad he didn't help you win the sledding race."

"We'll see what happens next. Have fun carrying that big toboggan up that hill, Mr. Branson. Come on, Samson."

It *was* imposingly steep. "We have to walk up that? Maybe I should have ridden up on Samson."

"Great cardio workout," Raine replied without apology, handing him the rope to the toboggan. "Think about your heart."

"I have been lately." He gave her a meaningful look.

"Don't do that." Her gaze softened. "I'm already afraid I'm in too deep."

"Why be afraid?" It was hard to believe he was standing knee-deep in snow having this conversation.

"You don't even live close."

"I'm considering selling both my houses and moving here. I have a cabin apparently. I'm going to build a house. Remember, you're going to help me design it. I'll even buy myself a parka. Talk about *in deep*."

"A parka? That *is* deep."

"Almost like a promise ring with weatherproof lining."

"Those are the best kind. That way you don't get cold fingers."

"I thought it was cold feet."

"What are we discussing?"

"You tell me."

"Branson," she said, starting to trudge up the hill— and it took some trudging; he definitely had his work cut out for him carting up that sled, "your love of talking in circles has to go. I'm sure that works well in Hollywood, but in these parts we prefer a more direct approach."

"You want direct? I'll give you direct. We might be too old for promise rings, but not for a more committed relationship. I'd like you to start thinking it over."

He wasn't quite what Red would call a straight-shooter. The kind of man who slapped down his glass on the counter and asked for more red-eye, straight up.

He was tailored slacks, a linen shirt and a persuasive voice.

Well, he had on jeans at the moment, but he looked great in them. His dark hair was every which way, thanks to Samson, and he hauled up the toboggan without missing a breath, so he clearly had more facets to him than just boardroom suaveness. If she had to label his style, she'd call it tousled elegance.

He was also the creative, sensitive man who would finish an old Western novel.

Trouble on the horizon.

She thought maybe he'd just proposed. Or suggested it anyway.

The wizard was perhaps spot-on.

Raine pointed out softly, "We've slept together once."

"It was more than just sex, at least to me."

She was instantly out of breath and it had nothing to do with the steep slope of the hill. "To me as well, but—"

"I'm bringing to the table that I have some social and historical connection to this area. I like your daughter, I even like your beastly dog and that lion of a cat."

"This isn't a business meeting," she said, laughing. "Mick, we're walking up a nearly perpendicular hill in knee-deep snow. You really don't have to sell yourself at this moment."

"Hey, I'll have you know just coming down Mount Everest was a demonstration of my affection for your comely person."

"Comely?" Her brows shot up.

"I've reading some old-fashioned Westerns lately. They use *comely*. That's a word that needs to be brought back. I'm just the man to do it. Consider yourself comely, ma'am."

"You might want to work on your Western drawl, cowboy."

"I can't fire a six-shooter, either. Never touched a cow in my life, and oddly enough I don't have the desire to herd one anywhere. I think you'd better go back to Mr. Boardroom."

It was quite the hill to climb, so her laugh was just an expulsion of frosty breath. "Please tell me you can ride a horse."

"That I've done. In several countries, including Argentina. And in Patagonia those vaqueros are a critical bunch."

"Where haven't you traveled?" she asked curiously as they soldiered up the incline. "Somehow I think that's a shorter list than the opposite question."

Blithely, he said, "I've skipped Siberia and Antarctica. Too cold, though Mustang Creek in winter might just give them a run for their money." He sent her a wink. "I'm joking, but in reality, my parents dragged me all around the world. As I got older, I had to travel for business, so I ended up pretty much everywhere at one time or the other."

That was so different from Raine's conservative upbringing of childhood church camp and the occasional spring break vacation when she was in college. He came from money and she certainly didn't. Her parents were just hardworking middle-class people who weighed their finances based on what they could afford and what they couldn't, were practical and dependable and always there for her. What more could she ask for?

"We really couldn't be more different."

"So?"

"Would it work with you here?"

"My business schedule? Not all the time."

At least he told the truth. "I can't ask you to make that commitment."

"I think I'm asking *you*." He plowed through a deep

pile of snow. "I've never asked anyone before, so maybe I mean it."

"Maybe?"

"That was ill-phrased. I meant, you should consider maybe I really mean it."

"Do I seem hesitant?"

"Do I?" He tugged the sled over a big rock. "Glad we didn't slam into that on our way down."

"I knew it was there." Raine only wished she could avoid emotional pitfalls so easily. "No, you don't seem hesitant. That might scare me the most."

"On the same page then?"

"We could be."

She felt her heart warm despite the fact that there was snow in her boots and her toes were cold. Was it possible she'd just gotten engaged?

No.

Well, maybe. After all, the man *had* slid down Dead Man's Hill because he trusted her. He was going to *move* to Wyoming.

"Oh, I say 'maybe' and get in trouble, but you can say 'could'?"

This wasn't best time for verbal sparring because she was getting out of breath. Deep snow was great for sledding, but it was hell on wheels trying to walk through, especially up an incline like this one. Five seconds to get down and twenty minutes to climb back up. "We'll debate that over the glass of wine by the fire, okay?"

"I think we just came to an agreement on something."

"Can we agree on resting at the top of the hill for at least a few minutes before we attempt to become professional daredevils again? I felt like I was fleeing the bad guys in an action movie."

"Would we have escaped?"

"Oh, definitely. No one would be stupid enough to follow us down this hill, not even bad guys. At least we didn't crash into any of the headstones."

"Like the rock, I know where those are, too, but I admit with ballast it is a little harder to steer."

He laughed and hauled the toboggan the last length of the climb. "Maybe I should sit this next trip out then."

"Not on your life, Mr. Boardroom."

CHAPTER THIRTEEN

WARM, COMFORTABLE AND there was no harrowing hill right in front of him. True, a very large and still-wet dog sat at his feet, not to mention the giant cat beneath the tree, but he'd started the fire while Raine made her pizza dough, and he had a glass of merlot in his hand.

When he'd gotten back to the resort, he'd even managed to write a few pages, including the ending paragraph to a chapter: *Her adventurous spirit never failed to captivate him, and the fascination didn't end there. She was comely, but he'd met other beautiful women. She was intrepid.*

If going down that slope at warp speed wasn't intrepid, he didn't know what was. He felt somewhat intrepid himself, so Raine definitely qualified.

He was starting to wonder if Matthew Brighton hadn't modeled this last novel's heroine after his lovely granddaughter.

It sure seemed like it.

Was Mick the hero?

A tall, dark-haired greenhorn was the main male character. He was starting to wonder. He didn't really believe in premonitions but he was changing his mind. These days, he couldn't help but feel that something was going on and he might be a part of it.

And he got to write his own ending.

Raine came in from the kitchen. "I didn't have watermelon. Or Gouda or sardines. I'm afraid you're stuck with my original recipe."

"I suppose I can live without sardines just this once."

"Harry makes the pizza sauce from scratch. Just wait. She could bottle it and retire. We all just hope she never will."

He couldn't see the always-bustling Harry ever content with retirement. "Was she ever married?"

Raine settled in next to him on the couch. "Harry? I think so. She's like Red. You can't ask too much. I skirt around those subjects like they're a rattlesnake ready to strike."

"Interesting analogy. Maybe you should be the one writing the rest of this book."

"I'll stick to graphic design, thanks. But my philosophy has always been that if something is private and a person doesn't want to talk about it, then they shouldn't have to. Life's too short. Don't stir the pot if there's no need." She planted her bare feet on the coffee table and wiggled her toes. She'd changed into plaid pajama pants and a faded shirt with a picture of Goofy on the front. "The fire is nice."

"After practically flinging myself off a cliff three times, I agree. I felt like I was competing in the luge at the Olympic Games."

Raine elbowed him. "Admit it, you had fun."

He slipped his arm around her shoulders. "As long as Samson enjoyed himself, that's what matters most."

"He did. Jangles is jealous. Look at him, all out of sorts."

"No offense, but he always looks all out of sorts." A pair of unwinking amber eyes was watching them stealthily through the branches of the Christmas tree. "I think he's spying on us."

"Probably wondering if we're going to make out on the couch, just like a suspicious father. That isn't a bad idea by the way. Daisy's not going to venture out from her room until her movie is done playing."

He'd never heard a better idea in his life. "I don't know if I have the strength after walking up that hill three times, but I'm willing to give it a try."

Raine's mouth curved. "I somehow think you'll manage."

He wanted one hell of a lot more than a kiss—or two—but would take what he could get. A beautiful woman in his arms and a crackling fire was his true idea of holiday cheer, and Raine kissed him back with her usual audacity, her fingers trailing along the back of his neck with tantalizing slowness.

If Daisy hadn't been in residence, and Jangles watching their every move, he might have at least tried to slip off her shirt and caress what he knew to be very lovely breasts, but he settled for just pulling her closer so he could feel them against his chest.

Naturally Samson decided to join them then, bounding onto the couch with great enthusiasm, not exactly adding to the romance of the moment, and both he and Raine were the recipients of kisses of the doggic variety.

So much for the romantic mood.

"It's a zoo here." She laughingly pushed Samson away to prevent another attack of affection. "I warned you."

"There are worse things than to be loved." He picked up the dog—no small feat—and set him on the floor.

That animal weighed about a ton and it wasn't done growing. Samson was a fitting name.

"I couldn't agree more." Neither could Samson, who decided to join them again. Mick gently but firmly set him back on the ground, avoiding another slobbering sign that the puppy stood behind him one hundred percent. "Don't get too flattered," Raine warned him wryly. "He loves everyone. Now if Drake's dogs love you, you're part of a special club."

"I want to be a part of a different club entirely," he told her quietly. "The 'If Raine Loves You' club."

She met his gaze squarely. "Aside from Daisy, I'm starting to think you could be the founding member."

"What about Slater?"

She considered the glass in her hand. "I'll always care about him. But we were more in lust than in love. When he offered to marry me it was just because he's a good old-fashioned nice guy. We'd already mutually gone our separate ways when I discovered I was pregnant. Luckily for both of us, I'm not an old-fashioned girl. You've seen how happy he is with Grace."

He had, and he wouldn't mind that for himself at all. He thought about Grace and Luce and the serene glow that currently seemed to surround them both. He'd always thought that was a myth, but had changed his mind. Their happiness came through loud and clear.

"I want children." Those were his cards, right on the table. A straight flush, no request for more of the deck. He was afraid to be so blunt, but she deserved to know it. Besides, she had encouraged him to be more direct out on the hill.

Raine didn't bat an eye. "Slater and I...we were really young when I had Daisy. I've been thinking about it more closely now than I did then. I'm past thirty. I might not *get* pregnant. Can you live with that?"

"Of course." He squeezed her hand. "Life is a gamble. But one thing that's certain is how I feel about you. I risked Dead Man's Hill just to gain your admiration. I bought a purse to win over your daughter. When a grown man is willing to buy a cute purse, you know he's serious."

With a straight face, she agreed. "We'll put the purse in as exhibit A."

"Exhibit B might be making out on a couch like a teenager. That isn't boardroom behavior. You might be a bad influence."

Raine's eyes sparkled. "Just wait. Now, tell me about the book. Gramps was working on it when he passed away, so I haven't been able to bring myself to read it. I'm not going to ask if it's good, because I know it must be. What's the storyline?"

She was admittedly curious.

Mick sounded very neutral. "A Tenderfoot imagines he's a cowboy and falls in love with a dark-haired independent woman and is determined to win her heart. There's some conflict with a neighboring rancher who wants her land. Sound familiar?"

How was it she'd imagined something exactly like that? Tears stung her eyes. "I miss him. It would have been so nice if you could have met him."

"No one could agree more."

"He would have thought you were a fine man."

"I hope he would have been right."

She smiled through her tears. "I know he would."

"That might be the best compliment I've ever gotten." He lifted her hand and kissed it. "I might comment that you now smell vaguely of giant puppy, but I think I might too, so I'll let it go just this once."

Raine was conciliatory. "You might want to get used to that. I don't think Samson will improve as he gets older. Plus your dog will be added to the mix. What were you thinking about? Giant dog, or a small one? Medium breed? What's our plan?"

"I can't ask you—"

"You didn't. I offered." She raised a hand. "So what was that boyhood dream?"

"Collie."

"Done." He seemed like a collie sort of man. It fit. "Long hair, just my luck. I'll tell Blythe, who will tell Mrs. Lettie Arbuckle-Calder and you'll have a collie rescue pup in no time. That woman will scour the state for one. She's a wonder. And don't tell me how you can afford to buy one, because rescue it is."

Mildly, he said, "You can be on the bossy side at times. Just an observation."

He was right. "I'm really used to running my life all on my own, and also making most of the decisions concerning my daughter. If it's anything big, of course I ask Slater, but we don't have a custody agreement because we've never needed one. Ultimately it falls to me to make the day-to-day choices. I warn you, like your heroine, I'm used to being independent."

"If you weren't, I doubt I'd be so interested. Not only do I have my hands full running a company and my own life, no matter how *comely* she might be, I don't want someone who just wants me to take care of her."

Raine practically spit out her sip of wine laughing but managed to swallow in the nick of time. "*Comely*, again. You and that word."

He shrugged. "A man on a mission, I tell you. Soon teenagers will be using it, nudging each other in the football stands on Friday nights. *Dude, look at that comely girl over there. Check her out.*"

"If anyone can do it, I think you can."

"Thanks for the vote of confidence." He was looking gorgeous, and cowboy-like in his denim shirt and jeans. Except for the hair. He needed a hat to really mess it up, and a set of boots and a horse. She'd get Tate Calder to help her with that last one.

Wedding present?

What else to give the man who probably had everything? She couldn't top that beach house in Bermuda.

An old six-shooter?

She did know Bad Billy had a friend who dealt in antique guns. Maybe she'd see what he could negotiate for her. Billy knew everyone.

If Mick finished this book, he certainly deserved something like that…unique and special. Very Old West. Something to hang on the wall of his new house.

She thought he'd love it. Hat and boots aside, he'd really go for the six-shooter. Raine got up. "Let me check on my pizza dough."

"It will have risen about two millimeters, Raine." He captured her waist and pulled her back. "Stay here with me."

She traced the line of his nose with her fingertip. "You are entirely too dangerous."

"I'm entirely yours if you want me."

"Mick." Her voice was hushed.

"I'm right here."

"I know. Your hands are doing interesting things."

"Nice?"

"Too nice. Jangles is still watching us."

"I'm going to have to get used to him giving me the stink-eye, right?"

"You are taking some risks. I wish I could invite you to stay the night, but like I said, I can't. Daisy is certainly old enough to understand why you would. I need to talk to her before anything like that happens."

It was almost disappointing that he immediately let her go and settled back into a more relaxed pose with a sigh. "My intellect is telling me I agree one hundred percent, but another part of me has a different take on the situation. Maybe you shouldn't dress so provocatively."

"These pajama pants and the T-shirt really are a little over the top. I'll try to tone it down."

"See that you do if you want me to behave. Maybe you could shave your head or get a giant tattoo of an elf on your forehead. I'm not positive even that would turn me off, but it would be a good start."

Raine laughed. "You've got the holiday spirit, I see. The elf might look strange in July, so I think I'll skip that one, and I happen to like my hair right where it is."

"There lies the crux of the problem, so do I."

At that moment Jangles prowled stealthily out from beneath the tree—which really meant he lumbered out, because he definitely could not pull off a quiet approach—and launched himself onto the couch between them, but couldn't quite fit. Mick reached for his wine-glass and scooted away enough to give the cat room to settle down. "I think he's decided to help us out with the self-control issue."

"He's a very wise feline." He was. He definitely

liked Mick. She did, too. "So what's Slater's next project? I haven't asked him yet."

"Becoming a father for the third time comes first, I think, but I've heard some musings about the Snake River. After this last film, he'll be able to choose just about anything, I'd guess. Backers will be lining up."

"I like the idea." Raine was sincere. "It's beautiful country there. He'll absolutely remind people we moved west gradually."

"And the setting will win the day."

"I think so. His films work that way."

"He does have an eye for beautiful things. I'm looking at one of them right now." He held her gaze.

It was a nicely done compliment. "Thank you, but I'm hardly beautiful."

"Maybe not in a traditional blonde bombshell sense, but you're striking, and your eyes are unforgettable. I know I couldn't stop thinking about you. Slater is a smart man, so I was surprised he ever gave you up, but I didn't really know the whole story."

"I'm glad I got to share it with you." She hadn't been able to get him out of her mind, either. "Now, if you can chop some onions and green peppers, we'll really be on the same page. Follow me."

He could and he did, and she liked the sight of him in her kitchen, the Hollywood executive with a knife in his hand, frowning over the cutting board in concentration.

It might be a different kind of board than he was used to, but she was starting to think he'd adjust to the change.

CHAPTER FOURTEEN

She bent over to dip water out of the river, her hair in a makeshift knot that had come half-loose, her skirt hiked up over a pair of the prettiest ankles he'd ever seen as she waded in.

He'd die for her.

It was a possibility. There was a small local war going on as the ranchers squabbled over their land and she was vulnerable, a woman alone with a child, a lovely widow doing her best to hold on to what she'd fought to build. He wasn't about to let her lose it all.

Maybe he wasn't a fast draw yet, even though he'd been practicing, but he was a fair rifle shot, he'd discovered, and he could put food on the table. She'd made venison stew the night before that was so tender it melted in his mouth, and despite her guarded stance, he could tell she was starting to trust him. He now had his bedroll on that old front porch.

He felt like he'd gained something special right there.

The war wasn't over, but a skirmish had been won.

MICK EYED HIS computer screen thoughtfully, read it

over again, and decided it fit the voice well enough, but wondered if it was too sentimental.

Maybe not. Men were every bit as sensitive as women were, they just didn't express it in the same way. His father had refused to get rid of the old rocker in the corner of the living room because his grandmother had given it to him, despite his mother's objections to the impact on her otherwise perfectly furnished space. It did stick out like a sore thumb, but he'd stood firm.

Though she came off as highbrow most of the time, Mick had certainly noted his mother had left it there even after her husband had died. That antique rocker stayed put. Maybe she was more sentimental than he thought.

So maybe he'd leave the writing as it was for now. He liked it. If a man would sleep on a woman's front porch, he was really into her, and willing to protect her. Hopefully Matthew Brighton would agree.

Especially on a day like today. The wind had picked up, he could hear it whistling by the windows, and even the ski slopes were empty. It was getting later, or maybe just felt like it because the skies were so gray.

He was trying not to crowd Raine too much, but he slipped out his phone and thought about it and then touched the screen. She answered almost at once. "Hi. What do you need? I'm swamped."

He grinned at her tone. Even clearly distracted, she was appealing. "This might sound crazy, but what if I asked Stephano to make a few sandwiches and throw in whatever other genius side dishes he has and we took dinner to the cabin? Daisy could come, too, of course, but I need... I don't know, a sense of place. You said the woodstove still worked, right?"

"There's probably a zillion nests in the chimney, even though I had it cleaned, so the whole place could go up in a plume of smoke, but as far as I know, yes. Slater just picked Daisy up so she can't come along, but I'm up for it. I need a break. Tell Stephano I'd love some of that garlic artichoke dip he's so famous for. I'll come get you. What time?"

He glanced at his phone. "Is two hours too soon?"

"No, perfect."

"Great. I'll call when I'm on my way."

He then phoned down to the room service number and asked for Stephano himself if possible. Probably thanks to his association with the Carson family, it was. "Can you make me whatever you think is your best sandwich, the artichoke dip Raine apparently loves, and anything else you'd add to an alfresco dinner for two in an old cabin? I'm putting myself in your hands."

"You have chosen wisely." Stephano sounded delighted as he announced, "I will wipe your socks off."

Mick almost mentioned that "knock your socks off" might be the more appropriate description, but he refrained. Stephano's English was sometimes as creative as his cooking. "I look forward to the meal."

"You should."

He hung up with an inward shake of the head and a grin. There was nothing wrong with self-confidence. Mick normally had a decent dose of it himself, but lately he couldn't count on it.

It didn't help that the front desk called and said a special delivery had arrived for him via special courier, and as he went down and signed the confirmation of delivery he knew that his life had just changed forever. Raine had turned down Slater flat. At the moment Mick was decently hopeful that that wouldn't happen to him. Although she'd pointed out how different they were, an observation he didn't disagree with, they'd then discussed marriage, even children and some future plans, so he took that as an encouraging sign. But he hadn't actually *asked* yet.

He'd implicitly trusted Ingrid to choose a stunning ring and he wasn't disappointed. Nestled in the satin lining inside the small box was a chocolate diamond exquisitely cut and anchored on a platinum band. The name of the jeweler making him lift his brows. The assumption she'd spent quite a chunk of his change on it was a given, but he planned on only doing this once in his life.

He felt Raine would love it. He sent off a quick text to his brother. Tell Ingrid I'm smiling. Thanks.

Ran texted right back. Good luck, loverboy.

He went back to his room, wondered what a man wore to propose at a haunted cabin at night, and finally decided maybe he should go shopping at some point because the best he could do was dark, tailored slacks and a white shirt along with his infamous loafers. Definitely vintage Mr. Boardroom, but then again, he was living out of a suitcase at the moment. He hadn't known exactly what to expect from this visit to Mustang Creek.

More writing was out of the question. Instead he paced, tried to watch the news and turned it off since it was the wrong night to hear about what was awry in the world, and instead turned on a classical music station and checked his email. Not much going on during a holiday week and he was enjoying the respite from his normally hectic schedule, so that was just fine with him.

It was ridiculous, but he was nervous. Like he was seventeen and about to pick up his first prom date.

But he was far from seventeen, he reminded himself as he clicked off the computer screen. And he needed to get a grip. He took a calming breath, deep and slow.

He could handle this. Ask the question, hopefully get the right response, and if she chose to be as pigheaded as a feisty mule—a description he'd undoubtedly picked up from Red somewhere along the line—he'd reconsider his tactics.

The elegant bag with Stephano's latest masterpieces was delivered right on time and he was more than ready to make the call. "I'll be there in a few minutes with the requested dip in tow."

"I'll be ready."

I'll have the ring and the question.

He didn't say it, but he certainly thought it as he left the resort and got in his car. He did make one stop in town before he drove to her house, and when he pulled up the light was a warm, welcoming glow in her window.

He knocked and walked in when he heard her call out a welcome. Jangles of course went in for the kill, but by now Mick was ready for it and dodged away. Raine was smiling. "Nice move for a city boy. But he's going to mope. Give him a couple of treats to make him feel better while I grab my keys."

Of course, the cat understood every word. He followed Mick into the kitchen and stared unwaveringly at the correct jar on the counter.

Message received.

He got out a handful of treats and put them in the bowl. Jangles devoured them in about two seconds. Mick had an impulse to deal out more, but Raine came in then and said, "No, that's enough, he's playing you. He does that. Let's go."

She jiggled the keys.

He wasn't positive he was composed enough for this evening, but he decided to take his cues from Jangles, who had collapsed into a relaxed sprawl on the floor, his eyes half closing. His pose screamed: *stop worrying.*

Mick escorted Raine out the door. "Let's go while the food is still at least semi-hot. It smells like heaven."

"What is it?"

"No idea."

"You ordered it, right?"

He held her elbow as they made their way down the snowy sidewalk. "I gave Stephano carte blanche, though I did specifically request the dip you wanted. He promised I would be impressed—at least I think that's what he was saying."

"He does have a way with words, doesn't he?" She pushed a button to unlock the vehicle. "One of the many things I love about him."

He set the bag in the back and got in. "You don't mind driving in this weather?"

"No." She didn't, he could tell. "Wow, it does smell amazing in here."

"That man loves you right back. Whatever is in there is because I mentioned your name. I can take zero credit."

She backed up the car and they tackled the street.

"I'm already starving. The cabin, huh? I appreciate your enthusiasm but you should be forewarned this could be an interesting journey. The snow has somewhat melted off, but it's blowing around more than a little. Luckily this little buggy can handle just about anything." She patted the steering wheel. "I've been there a thousand times. I think I could find it blindfolded."

MAYBE SHE'D BEEN OPTIMISTIC.

It wasn't whiteout conditions, but it was very near, and in broad daylight it was a challenge without a road of any kind, so in the dark it was close to impossible.

Mick seemed pretty determined that the cabin be their destination though, and she sensed it had something to do with the manuscript. She was pretty good at reading people and more in tune with him than most—and Mr. Cool, Calm and Collected was wound up about something. There was tension in his shoulders and a set to his jaw that said something was certainly on his mind.

Maybe it was just that he was making some big decisions, but she didn't think so. Mick Branson did that every single day and didn't even blink about it. He made up his mind and sailed on that ship full-steam ahead.

"There's a big drift by the porch," she noted out loud. "We'll be walking the last bit. Luckily there's still firewood piled inside. I brought a lighter for the lantern in case all the matches are damp and you should put on those boots Mace gave you."

"I bought some for myself, and a sleeping bag, some candles, and a fire log to get things going for our impromptu camping trip."

No wonder he'd loaded several bags besides the food into the back of her car. She'd wondered if they were going off to safari in deepest Africa.

Snow swirled around them in ghostly forms, circling the windows, brushing the hood, occasionally obscuring the entire structure. Raine put up her hood. "I'll go unlock that reluctant door if you'll bring the stuff in. I've got the food, so don't take too long, or it will all be gone. Just a friendly warning."

"Consider me warned. Stephano would never forgive me if I moved too slowly to sample his latest creations."

"The artichoke dip alone will make you weep with joy."

"I'm going to take your word for it, and get inside as soon as possible."

The first blast of wind hit her square in the face. She'd watched the forecast and knew it was supposed to calm down, but it about knocked her over. She scrambled for the doorway, almost forgot the bad top step, and then struggled with the key.

The door opened like magic and she practically fell inside, first because she'd braced for its usual resistance and was caught off guard by its easy surrender, then because another gust propelled her from behind.

By some miracle Raine managed to keep her balance as she stumbled in, and despite the dark, she avoided the old couch that undoubtedly had mice in it and made it to the table. The lantern helped as soon she managed to get it lit, and just then Mick came through the door like a pack mule, loaded down with everything a man could carry and maybe more.

He panted, "I thought the wind was going to die down. I think it's getting worse."

She watched him dump the bags on the floor. "It is supposed to calm by dawn. I think we're spending the night right here."

"Well then, let's get the fire started."

Her grandfather never would have dreamed of using anything as modern as a fire log to light that old wood-stove, but then again, it was remarkably handy. Mick knelt there, dusted in snow, and the log caught with one touch of a match. She was happy to see it seemed to be venting properly because the room didn't instantly fill with smoke.

"I brought a tablecloth from home. For all I know there's a bear hibernating in the single closet where things like that are kept, and I'm not going to look. Clean utensils and paper plates as well, since every-thing gets so dusty when it isn't used."

Mick agreed. "Let's not go bear hunting."

He was a typical man and had brought candles, but nothing to put them on, so she dug out a couple of old plates, and set the table and it was…well, nice. Table-cloth, candlelight and an undeniably attractive man. What more could a girl want?

Food, for one, and maybe some heat. Fortunately, the stove was starting to take care of the temperature, and the howl of the wind outside did add to the cozy ambience.

She was even able to take off her coat as they sat down to discover what wonders Stephano had prepared for them. One sandwich consisted of watercress and smoked salmon with aioli on French bread, the other one roast beef layered with what had to be artisan cheese and served in some sort of homemade rye that had flecks of fennel, too. There was also a pasta salad with tiny shrimp and Kalamata olives, not to mention Raine's prized artichoke dip, and to top it all off, a key lime cheesecake.

It looked delicious.

Quite the alfresco picnic. It was hardly a wild guess that food like this had never been eaten in the cabin before. "I suspect my grandfather subsisted on pemmican or something similar," she told Mick jokingly. "He did like good whiskey and believe it or not, applesauce. There are several groves of apple trees on the property. I remember the smell of applesauce simmering on the stove from my childhood."

"That stove has to be from the Civil War era. I've never seen anything like it."

"It isn't new, that I can promise you. But it works just fine."

"I can tell, since it is warming up in here."

The candlelight played nicely off the masculine lines of his face. If she hadn't seen him interact with Daisy and Ryder, holding babies, laughing with Blythe and Harry, and joking with the Carson brothers, she might worry more that she was influenced by his good looks. Being her, she blurted out what she was thinking. "Don't get all full of yourself, but you're as handsome as this dip is delicious."

Amusement lit his eyes. "Now there's a rare compliment. Because you made a really good call on the dip."

"I always make good calls." She shamelessly took another helping. "But lucky for you, there's plenty. Even I can't eat all of this. Stephano must like you."

"I'm starting to believe that. Just try the pasta salad. I want that at our wedding."

She was still mid-bite when he slid a small box

across the tiny table. His smile was wry. "I would be on bended knee, but have a feeling that part isn't as important to you as the question itself. I would love it if you would agree to marry me, Raine. You'd have the last vote on the pasta salad being served at the reception, of course. The dip is a given."

"Yes." She didn't even hesitate, which spoke volumes to her.

And to him, which was reflected in his expression. "You're sure."

"I didn't sound sure just now? What about you?"

"Absolutely. Now that's settled, maybe you'd like to open that." He nodded toward the box.

She complied and took in a deep breath. The ring was both gorgeous and unusual, and in the candlelight the gem in the exquisite setting winked with tones of brown and bronze. It was Mick Branson–style over the top, and she had no idea what to say.

"Mick."

He reached over. "I take it you like it. I think I'm supposed to put it on your finger, but I've never done this before. If I mess it up, let me know."

He definitely didn't mess it up.

He must have slid the ring on the right finger and said the right words because he was engaged.

Officially.

"Wedding date…when do you have in mind? Just wondering since I'm one hundred percent certain my mother will ask that question."

For the first time since he'd proposed, Raine looked uncertain. "I haven't even met her."

"Oh, she'll consider that an unimportant detail. She'll be so thrilled I'm finally getting married that she'll get immediately involved. I, for one, would like something very understated. But it's your day. I'll just be tagging along."

"Not so. You've promised to bring the dip. You'll be the star. As for the date, I'd like mid-May. It's so gorgeous here at that time of year."

"Done. Stephano can cater. Perfect. That's settled."

"I loved Bex Calder's wedding dress. I might count it as my borrowed item, if she doesn't mind. We're about the same size."

"Food, dress, ring, date. Our work is done. As for my wardrobe, I'll wear pants, I promise. No one will be looking at me anyway, not with you in the room. My brother as best man, Slater, and Ryder as groomsmen and I think we have a wedding all planned. Let's keep it simple."

"You do remember you're Mick Branson, right?" She laughed and shook her head. "I somehow think it won't be simple. I believe celebrities will be invited and Ryder would be the most nervous groomsman on the face of the planet, and Drake would bring his dogs. My bridesmaids would all be pregnant—"

"So how about we set the date for sooner, with just me and you instead? I'm good with that." He was more than good with it. He'd marry her standing in a muddy field in a rainstorm. "Apply for a marriage license at the Bliss County courthouse and have it over and done?"

It was what he wanted. Simple. The fanfare held no appeal. If she wanted the big event—then of course, yes, every bride was entitled to that—but if he was given a choice…

He'd keep it low-key.

Raine put the last scoop of dip on his plate. "How

offended would your family be? No movie stars, no corporate executives except you, not even them."

That he could assuage her on. "You do realize that being Mick Branson really isn't my agenda."

"You know, I do. I *love* that about you."

"There will be a party." He confessed that tidbit almost reluctantly. "My mother will want to throw a reception at some point, but quite frankly, everyone in my family travels so much that getting them all together at the same time probably means planning the wedding out a year or so, and I don't want to do that. I have zero desire to wait."

"If you think Blythe and Harry won't throw a shindig, you're dreaming, cowboy. So we're looking at two parties, and I doubt they'll be quite the same. I'll have to buy heels for one, and will be able to wear my favorite pair of comfortable old flats to the other. They could do that in May instead."

"We could just not tell anyone and let them believe we're living in sin."

"If you think Daisy wouldn't spill the beans, then think again, and I would tell her the truth." She took a bite of her sandwich and after she swallowed, said, "Oh my gosh, Stephano must *really* like you. We might have to set the cheesecake out on the front porch to save it for breakfast."

Raine would do that. She'd eat key lime cheesecake for breakfast without a thought.

She'd accepted his proposal in a run-down cabin in Wyoming during what he expected was now a whiteout snowstorm. The entire structure shook with the next gust of wind.

But unlike in the book he was writing, Mick mused with a private grin, he was not going to have his bedroll on the front porch this particular night.

CHAPTER FIFTEEN

HE WANTED TO marry her.

She wasn't every man's ideal of a perfect bride. She had a child, a past, and her unconventional approach to life was hardly traditional.

But he had no doubt he loved her and that was all that mattered.

She'd said yes.

He didn't ask her the traditional way but while they were eating dinner. He didn't mean to quite blurt it out like that, but his emotions got the best of him.

It was every girl's dream.

A beautiful ring, a romantic proposal and killer artichoke dip.

Not to mention a wind velocity that measured off the charts. It was amazing that she couldn't envision a more perfect evening. If the roof stayed on she'd be amazed at the workmanship of those long-ago craftsmen that nailed it on.

While there was the probability of a rodent drive-by, and Raine wasn't unaware of it because they'd heard rustling all evening, the room was nice and toasty, and when Mick rolled out the sleeping bag and started to undress her, she was willing.

Extremely willing.

He shucked off his clothes just as quickly, joined her

under the warm folds of the sleeping bag and kissed her softly. Not passionately, but with a gentleness that melted her heart. He said, "I've waited for you. I don't think I knew what I was waiting for. Now I understand."

She'd waited for him, too. "Right there with you. A man with good hair in a haunted cabin is a rare find. You're so warm. Hold me closer and protect me from the possible rodent population."

"I'm your knight on a white steed. No mouse will bother you on my watch."

He was a very aroused knight. She wasn't at all averse to that, either. "I'm petrified, but with you to save me from fearsome rodents…say no more."

"No problem there. And warm? I'm alone with you, so call it what it is. I'm on fire. Can we stop talking and do something else entirely? I want to make love to you and I suspect your car will be blown away at any minute and the cabin will fall down around us and I won't care."

No condom. She didn't ask for one and he didn't use one. They'd had that conversation. He was…perfect. Insistently passionate but not less than thoughtful and understood her every response to each touch and whisper, and afterward the wind keening outside was almost as sexy as the way her leg sprawled over his thigh when it was said and done.

Raine rested her head on his damp chest. "I do love you."

"I hope so, since we're engaged."

"That part doesn't matter to me as much as that I *love* you. I can't believe it."

"Can't believe it? I'm trying to decide if I should be insulted or not. You sound uncertain."

"About my feelings, not about you." She gave him a playful slap on the shoulder. "Give me some latitude. This hasn't happened to me before."

"Never found the right man? I, for one, am pretty glad of it. You waited for me." His fingers sifted through her hair. "I'm going to christen you my best Christmas gift ever."

"I intend to be."

"Good, because you succeeded."

"How are you going to finish the book? The last I read, our hero was sleeping on the front porch in a raging snowstorm."

"I think he moves inside. She would never leave him out there in the cold."

"Of course not. I bet he likes it better inside."

"They hook up."

"I think you need to put it more eloquently than that." She nestled closer, knowing he would take her words for the teasing they were. Mick would never be crude.

"Easier said than done, especially for a rugged, solitary cowboy like him. He likes the fact that he found her—he likes it a lot. He just isn't too good at saying it."

"She needs him to say it."

She heard him take in a breath. "I'm guessing you're talking about us. I honestly think the moment I met you I knew I was falling pretty hard."

"I was talking about the book, Mick. I would never play you like that. You made a distinct impression as well, I might add. As far as I can tell, everyone in the entire Carson camp immediately cottoned on to how we were feeling. I don't think we should play poker with them until we work on our technique. Now, back to the book. How does it end?"

"I'm not going to tell you, because I don't really know yet. You'll have to read it yourself when it's finally done. I don't know if my writing is on a par with your grandfather's, but I'm really enjoying it. It's coming more naturally than I might have guessed, probably because I've read pretty much all his books. He's so descriptive. Maybe that's why I have such a connection with this part of the country. I'd been here in my imagination often enough before my first visit."

"Well, this cabin certainly qualifies as the real deal. I'm surprised there isn't a musket mounted on the wall somewhere. On a night like tonight I'm surprised there *are* still walls."

It was wicked out there. She was warm and cozy enough in the afterglow, but the weather wasn't very friendly. Raine was glad Daisy was safe and sound at the ranch. If she had to call it, she suspected they might be stranded for longer than anticipated—the drift by the front door wasn't getting any smaller. "We could have a hard time leaving in the morning."

"Fine. I'd stay like this forever."

That was as good as *I love you*.

"This is a nice sleeping bag."

He chuckled. "I forgot pillows. I didn't think of it. I don't camp too often."

"I'll use you as my pillow. You're actually quite comfortable."

"That type of high praise is likely to win my heart."

"I had that in the bag already, right?"

"I thought that went without saying."

Raine rolled on top of him, which was very easy to do since they were sharing a single sleeping bag. She said simply, "I'm happy."

"That's what we're supposed to do for each other."

"I hope I'm holding up my end of the bargain."

"You have no idea."

She touched his lower lip, their mouths just inches apart. "Oh, I think I have some idea. Otherwise I'm guessing you wouldn't be quite so enthusiastic about one small sleeping bag with two bodies and no pillows."

"I thought I was your pillow." He held her closely, lightly stroking her back, those long fingers taking some definite liberties.

"And you're a good one. If you could market you, the stores would sell out. Women would flock in."

"Unfortunately, I think I'm taken, correct?"

"You got that right, mister."

HANDS DOWN, IT was the most erotic night of his life.

In bed—well, technically in a sleeping bag—with a very sexy woman, and she'd fallen asleep all draped across him, not that she had much choice because there was nowhere else to go. It gave him some time to reflect on his recent life decisions.

If he sold both his other houses he could build her the house of any woman's dreams, but he didn't think she'd go for it. Raine would probably prefer something modest, but a dream artist's studio was a definite must. Maybe after Daisy graduated high school Raine would be willing to move to the cabin property full-time.

His wife. He was starting to get a real charge out of the notion.

Water, electricity, internet, a decent road… He could arrange all of that.

He had an idea forming in his head about the floor plan. As long as Raine basically agreed with it, he was in a very good place. She was focused on details and he was focused on what would work. A one-time-only construction project was his goal and he thought it was hers, too.

He liked pairing the right backer with the right film, and the right artist with the right project, because he could spot solid worth. He'd probably shot himself in the foot by even proposing that Raine consider doing the pixel film. She would be busier than ever, but *he* was ready to slow down and take a look around. His frenetic working pace couldn't go on forever, he'd always known that. If he cut back, he could be there a lot more of the time for Raine and Daisy—and any kids he and Raine might have together.

It seemed to him they'd started working on that tonight.

Those select casual relationships he'd had in the past amounted to nothing and he knew why now. He'd known something was missing, but just not how to define it.

Raine had settled all that.

And now he knew how the book ended.

"I did something wrong." He knew he had. She was quiet, and maybe not distant, but certainly distracted.

"No," she told him in a resigned voice, "you did something too right, I'm afraid."

How was that possible? he argued in his mind,

but the spitfire was good at calling his hand. "The land dispute is settled. That varmit won't ever threaten you or this place again. What now?"

She put her hands on her hips, but at least now there was laughter in her eyes. "*Varmit?* Eastern boy, you need to learn a great deal about how to say a word like that. You can't pull off cowboy just yet, but you're pretty good, I'll grant, at solving a real problem without just taking out a gun."

"A man can use his brain now and then instead of force. I still don't understand why you're mad at me."

"I'm not mad, just pretty sure I'm going to have a baby."

He'd known it was possible, but he was still stunned. "What?"

"That isn't necessarily all your fault, I was there too, but in case you haven't noticed, we aren't married."

He recovered after a moment. And he could solve that problem, too. "There's a preacher in Mustang Creek. Let me hitch up the horses. We can pay him a quiet visit and take care of that right away."

She was going to be stubborn to the last minute, but was so beautiful every time he looked at her she took his breath away. "The last time you did that it didn't work out so well. I seem to remember sitting in the buckboard and watching you jump out to chase the loose horses down."

"Sweetheart, I remember. Thanks for reminding me you were laughing so hard I thought you might fall off the seat."

"I'm not sure I should marry a greenhorn."

He went over and kissed her. "I'm positive you should."

Her smile was predictably saucy. "I think I will. I'll hitch up the horses."

EPILOGUE

December 24th, one year later

Was this a mistake?

Maybe it was—it was going to be hard to tell until it all settled out, but still Raine had fingers and toes crossed.

It was official, she was nuts for even thinking of this, but then again, Stephano and Harry had done most of the work. In a rare truce, they'd coordinated the menu and though they hadn't necessarily cooperated with each other, they'd grudgingly come to an agreement on what to serve.

The new house was complete, if not quite ready for guests since she'd been more than a little busy, but Hadleigh, Melody and Bex had put up decorations and Grace, Luce and Kelly were on kid patrol.

Mick had mentioned he was looking forward to green chili cheeseburgers and an old Western movie.

Not this year. His entire family had agreed to come.

Was she nervous? Oh yes. Not because she was worried the party wouldn't go smoothly, but because she wasn't sure how her surprise was going to be received. Mick seemed to accept just fine that his family didn't spend Christmas together, but she wanted to give him this special gift.

A really wonderful gift hopefully, with a small bonus.

She'd talked it over with Blythe and gotten full Carson approval on the idea. So he had no idea his family was coming, and everyone was forbidden to tell him.

The new house did look wonderful with all the decorations. The tree was from the north end of the property and at least twelve feet high, but a ladder and three Carson men squabbling over who was ascending it took care of the top part and Daisy and Ryder had fun decorating the rest. Ryder was getting to the age where that sort of thing was no longer his idea of fun… He'd rather be taking cute girls to the movies, and—she wasn't a fool—maybe thinking about stealing a beer or two here or there by his age, but he obligingly hung up a snowman on a branch that Daisy wasn't tall enough to reach, asking if it was where she wanted it. She imperiously made him move it over three inches.

He really was the nicest kid and humored Daisy without protest.

The Bransons were the first to arrive. Raine had met them on a swift trip to California that combined personal affairs with business, since she also met with the director of the pixel movie. Mick's mother was cool and poised, but still warmer than expected. Not haughty, just assessing. His brother was very businesslike but equally likeable, and his sister-in-law was unexpectedly a kindred spirit with her keen eye for art. They'd met for dinner at some trendy restaurant so conversation hadn't been very personal, but Raine had started exchanging emails with Mick's mother, which he found quite amusing. She'd sent pictures of the house construction, of the sun rising over the mountains, of Mustang Creek's fall festival, of Mick and Daisy absorbed in a game of chess, all designed to give her mother-in-law a glimpse into their lives.

To her surprise, it worked. She got back not just replies, but photos of vineyards, theater signs, and even a Halloween photo of Mick's mother dressed up as Scarlet from *Gone with the Wind* for a fancy party. They might be many miles apart but they were finding a way to get to know each other.

Raine was convinced that while Mick shrugged it off as if his family never spending Christmas together since his father died didn't bother him, it did. She was hardly a psychologist, but she had to wonder if it didn't bother all of them and scattering to different locations was a way to avoid the emotional impact.

Time to start better memories, or so she hoped.

When Mick walked in the door, looking wiped out after a trip to Germany that took three days longer than planned, he was greeted by the sight of a houseful of people having cocktails and nibbling on artichoke dip. He stood for a minute in the doorway before he said calmly, "I saw the cars, so I guess I'm not surprised at the crowd. Raine, I talked to you last night. You failed to mention we were having a party."

She kissed him. "Surprise! It was really your mother's idea. Welcome home."

He kissed her back, taking his time about it. "My mother wanted me to have a party? Now I have two women conspiring against me—three, if we include Daisy. I feel outnumbered."

"Well, maybe we'll have a boy to help tilt the odds. I'm due in July."

"What?" He looked like he might fall over. "Can you repeat that? We're having a baby?"

"It seems like we are. We've been trying, remember? Don't look quite so incredulous."

"*I* certainly have been doing my best." He scanned the room and froze. "Is that my *brother* pouring himself a drink? He's here? On Christmas Eve? In Wyoming?"

"Don't look now, but your mother is right there in the corner, talking to Blythe and Ingrid. I have no idea what they're saying but I'm going to bet you're the main topic of conversation."

"That's a bet I'd be crazy to take. And nice job trying to change the subject. Raine, really? We're pregnant?"

"I'm pregnant and you're the father, so the answer to that is yes."

"I'm… I don't even know what to say. Why didn't you tell me?"

"It seemed like the perfect present to surprise you with. Last year you got a haunted cabin. How is a girl going to top that one? It was a high bar."

"I think you just cleared it." He reached for her again, but laughing, she pushed him away.

"Tonight you can tell your family face-to-face. Let's go celebrate. Mace made a non-alcoholic wine drink just for me, called Bran-Son. Drake has a new foal about to drop he's going to call Brandy. You know those two. The race is on, boy or girl."

"My family isn't up for this crowd. Or for Mustang Creek. This isn't Paris or Rome."

"No." Raine hooked her arm through his, her eyes shining. "It sure isn't. But I think they'll find they prefer it here."

He certainly did.

* * * * *

From #1 New York Times *bestselling author*
Linda Lael Miller and MIRA Books
comes a sweeping new saga set against the backdrop
of the Civil War.

Read on for an exclusive sneak preview of
The Blue and the Gray...

PART ONE

"…entreat me not to leave thee, or to return from following after thee: for whither thou goest, I will go…"

Ruth 1:16

ONE

Jacob
Chancellorsville, Virginia
May 3, 1863

The first mini-ball ripped into Corporal Jacob Hammond's left hand, the second, his right knee, each strike leaving a ragged gash in its wake; another slashed through his right thigh an instant later, and then he lost count.

A coppery crimson mist rained down upon Jacob as he bent double, then plunged, with a strange, protracted grace, toward the broken ground. On the way down, he noted the bent and broken grass, shimmering with fresh blood, the deep gouges left by boot heels and the lunging hooves of panicked horses.

A peculiar clarity overtook Jacob in those moments between life as he'd always known it and another way of being, already inevitable. The common boundaries of his mind seemed to expand beyond skull and skin, rushing outward at a dizzying speed, flying in all directions, rising past the treetops, past the sky, past the far borders of the cosmos itself.

For an instant, he understood everything, every mystery, every false thing, every truth.

He felt no emotion, no joy or sorrow.

He simply *knew*.

Then, so suddenly that it sickened his very soul, he was back inside himself, a prisoner surrounded by fractured bars of bone. The flash of extraordinary knowledge was gone, a fact that saddened Jacob more deeply than the likelihood of death, but some small portion of the experience remained, an ability to think without obstruction, to see his past as vividly as his present, to envision all that was around him, as if from a great height.

Blessedly, there was no pain, though he knew that would surely come, provided he remained alive long enough to receive it.

Something resembling bitter amusement overtook Jacob then; he realized that, unaccountably, he hadn't expected to be struck down on this savage battlefield or any other. Never mind the unspeakable carnage he'd witnessed since his enlistment in Mr. Lincoln's grand army; with the hubris of youth, he had believed himself invincible.

He had, in fact, assumed that angels fought alongside the men in blue, on the side of righteousness, committed to the task of mending a sundered nation, restoring it to its former whole. For all its faults, the United States of America was the most promising nation ever to arise from the old order of kings and despots; even now, Jacob was convinced that, whatever the cost, it must not be allowed to fail.

He had been willing to pay that price, was willing still.

Why then was he shocked, nay *affronted*, to find that the bill had come due, in full, and his own blood and breath, his very substance, were the currency required?

Because, he thought, shame washing over him, he had been willing to die only in *theory*. Out of vanity or ignorance or pure naivety, or some combination of the three, he had somehow, without being aware of it, declared himself exempt.

Well, there it was. Jacob Hammond, husband of Caroline, father of Rachel, son and grandson and great-grandson of decent men and women, present owner of a modest but fertile farm outside the pleasant but otherwise unremarkable township of Gettysburg, Pennsylvania, was no more vital to the operation of the universe than any other man.

Inwardly, Jacob sighed, for it was some comfort, however fleeting, to know that his mistake was, at least, not original.

Was the cause he was about to die for worthwhile?

Reluctant as he was to make the sacrifice, to leave Caroline and Rachel and the farm behind, Jacob still believed wholeheartedly that it was.

Surely, the hand of God Almighty Himself had guided those bold visionaries of 1776, and led the common people to an impossible victory against the greatest army on the face of the earth. In nearly a century of independence, there had never been a time without peril or strife, for the British had returned in 1812 and, once again, the nation had barely prevailed.

How, then, could he, dying or not, withdraw his faith, his last minuscule contribution, from so noble an endeavor?

So much hung in the balance, so very much; not only the hope and valor of those who had gone before, but the freedom, perhaps the very existence, of those yet to be born.

In solidarity, the United States could be a force for good in a hungry, desperate world. Torn asunder, it would be ineffectual, two bickering factions, bound to divide into still smaller and weaker fragments over time, too busy posturing and rattling sabers to meet the demands of a fragile future, to take a stand against the inevitable rise of new tyrannies.

No, Jacob decided, still clearheaded and detached from his damaged body, this war, with all its undeniable evils, had been fated from the day the first slaves had set foot upon American soil.

We hold these truths to be self-evident, that all men are created equal...

That one phrase had chafed the consciences of thinking people since it flowed from the nib of Thomas Jefferson's pen, as well it should have. Willing or unwilling, the entire nation had been living a lie.

It was time to right that particular wrong, Jacob thought, once and for all.

And if by chance there *were* warrior angels, he prayed they would not abandon the cause of liberty, but fight on until every man, woman and child on the North American continent was truly free.

With that petition made, Jacob raised another, more selfish one. *Watch over my beloved wife, our little daughter, and Enoch, our trusted friend. Keep them safe and well.*

The request was simple, one of millions like it, no doubt, rising to the ears of the Creator on wings of desperation and sorrow, and there was no Road-to-Damascus moment for Jacob, just the ground-shaking roar of battle all around. But even in the midst of thundering cannon, the sharp reports of carbines and the fiery blast of muskets, the clanking of swords and the shrill shrieks of men and horses, he found a certain consolation.

Perhaps, he had been heard.

He began to drift then, back and forth between darkness and light, fear and oblivion. When he surfaced, the pain was waiting, like a specter hovering over him, ready to descend, settle upon him, crush him beneath its weight.

Consequently, Jacob took refuge in the depths of his being, where it could not yet reach.

Hours passed, perhaps days; he had no way of knowing.

Eventually, because life is persistent even in the face of hopelessness and unrelenting agony, the hiding place within became less assessable. During those intervals, pain played with him, like a cat with a mouse. Smoke burned his eyes, which he could not close, climbed, stinging, into his nostrils, chafed his throat raw. He was thirsty, so thirsty; he felt as dry as last year's corn husks, imagining his life's blood seeping, however slowly, into the ravaged earth.

In order to bear his suffering, Jacob thought about home, conjured vivid images of Caroline, quietly pretty, more prone to laughter than to tears, courageous as any man he'd ever known. She loved him, he knew that, and his heart rested safely with her. She had always accepted his attentions in the marriage bed with good-humored acquiescence, though not with a passion equal to his own, and while he told himself this was feminine modesty, not disinterest, he sometimes suspected otherwise.

Caroline shouldered the chores of a farmwife without complaint, washing and ironing, cooking and sewing, tending the vegetable garden behind the kitchen-house and picking apples and pears, apricots and peaches in the orchards when the fruit ripened. She preserved whatever produce they did not sell in town, along with milk and eggs and butter, attended church services without fail, though she had once confided to Jacob that she feared God was profoundly deaf. Caroline was an active member of the local Ladies Aid Society, a group devoted to making quilts and blankets for soldiers and gathering donations of various foodstuffs, including such perishables as cakes and bread, all to be crated and shipped to battlefronts and hospitals all over the North. She did all this, and probably much more, while mothering little Rachel with intelligence and devotion, neither too permissive nor too stern.

In addition, Caroline endured every hardship—crops destroyed by rain or hail, the death of her beloved grandfather and several close friends, the two miscarriages she'd suffered—with her chin up and her shoulders back.

Of course she'd wept, especially for the lost babies, but she'd done so in solitude, probably hoping to spare Jacob the added sorrow of seeing her despair. Now, with death so close it seemed palpable, he wished she hadn't tried to hide her grief, wished he'd sought her out and taken her into his arms and held her fast, weeping with her.

Alas, there was no going back, and regret would only sap what little strength that remained to him.

Besides, remembrance was sweet sanctuary from the gathering storm of pain. In his mind's eye, he saw little Rachel running to meet him when he came in from the fields at the end of the day, filthy and sweat-soaked and exhausted himself, while his daughter was as fresh as the wildflowers flourishing alongside the creek in summer. Clad in one of her tiny calico dresses, face and hands scrubbed, she raced toward him, laughing, her arms open wide, her fair pigtails flying, her bright blue eyes shining with delighted welcome.

Dear God, what he wouldn't give to be back there, sweeping that precious child up into his arms, setting her on his shoulder or swinging her around and around until they were both dizzy. Caroline usually fussed over such antics—she'd just gotten Rachel clean again, she'd fret, and here that little scamp was, dirty as a street urchin—or she'd protest against "all this rough-housing," declaring that someone was bound to get hurt, or any one of a dozen other undesirable possibilities—but she never quite managed to maintain her dour demeanor. Invariably, Caroline smiled, shaking her head and wondering aloud what in the world she was going to do with the two of them, scoundrels that they were.

It was then that the longing for his wife and daughter grew too great, and Jacob turned his memory to sunsplashed fields, flourishing and green, to sparkling streams thick with fish. In his imagination, he stood beside Enoch once more, both of them gratified by the sight of a heavy crop, by the knowledge that, this year anyway, their hard work would bring a reward.

"God has blessed our efforts," Jacob would say, quietly and with awe, for he had believed the world to be an essentially good place then. War and all its brutalities merely tales told in books, or passed down the generations by old men.

In his mind's eye, he could see the hired man's broad black face, shining with sweat, his white teeth flashing as he grinned and replied, "Well, I don't see as how the Good Lord ought to get *all* the credit. He might send the sunshine and the rain, but far as I can reckon, He ain't much for plowin', nor for hoein', neither."

Jacob invariably laughed, no matter how threadbare the joke, would have laughed now, too, if he'd had the strength.

He barely noticed, as he lost consciousness for what he believed to be the final time, that the terrible din of battle had faded to the feeble moans and low cries of other men, fallen and left behind in the acrid urgency of combat.

He dreamed—or at least, he *thought* he was dreaming—of the Heaven he'd heard about all his life, for he came from a long line of church-going folk. He saw the towering gates, studded with pearls and precious gems, standing open before him.

He caught a glimpse of the fabled streets of gold, too, and though he saw no angels and no long-departed loved ones waiting to welcome him into whatever celestial realm they now occupied, he heard music, almost too beautiful to be endured. He looked up, saw a dazzling sky, not merely blue, but somehow *woven*, a shimmering tapestry of innumerable colors, each one brilliant, some familiar and some beyond his powers of description.

He hesitated, not from fear, for surely there could be no danger here, but because he knew that once he passed through this particular gateway, there would be no turning back.

Perhaps it was blasphemy, but Jacob's heart swelled with a poignant longing for a lesser heaven, another, humbler paradise, where the gates and fences were made of hand-hewn wood or plain stones gathered in fields, and the roads were winding trails of dust and dirt, rutted by wagon wheels, deep, glittering snows and heavy rain.

Had it been in his power, and he knew it wasn't, he would have traded eternity in this place of ineffable peace and beauty for a single, blessedly ordinary day at home, waking up beside Caroline in their feather bed, teasing her until she blushed, or to watch, stricken by the love of her, as she made breakfast in the kitchenhouse on an ordinary morning.

Suddenly, the sweet visions were gone.

Jacob heard sounds, muffled but distinct. Men, horses, a few wagons.

Then nothing.

Perhaps he was imagining things. Suffering hallucinations.

He waited, listening, his eyes unblinking, dry and rigid in their sockets, stinging with sweat and grit and congealed blood.

Fear burned in his veins as those first minutes after he was wounded came back. He recalled the shock of his flesh tearing with visceral intensity, as though it were happening all over again, a waking nightmare of friend and foe alike streaming past, shouting, shooting, bleeding, stepping over him and upon him. He recalled the hooves of horses, churning up patches of the ground within inches of where he lay.

Jacob forced himself to concentrate. Although he couldn't see the sky, he knew by the light that the day was waning.

Was he alone?

The noises came again, but they were more distant now. Perhaps the party of men and horses had passed him by.

The prospect was a bleak one, filling Jacob with quiet despair. Even a band of rebs would have been preferable to lying helplessly in his own gore, wondering when the rats and crows would come to feast upon him.

An enemy bullet or the swift mercy of a bayonet would be infinitely better.

Hope stirred briefly when a Federal soldier appeared in his line of vision, as though emerging from a void. At first, Jacob wasn't sure the other man was real.

He tried to speak, or make the slightest move, thus

indicating that he was alive and in need of help, but he could do neither.

The soldier approached, crouched beside him, and one glimpse of his filthy, beard-stubbled face, hard with cruelty, put an end to Jacob's illusions. The man rolled him roughly onto his back, with no effort to search for a pulse or any other sign of life. Instead, he began rifling through Jacob's pockets, muttering under his breath, helping himself to his watch and what little money he carried, since most of his pay went to Caroline.

Jacob felt outrage, but he was still helpless. All he could do was watch as the other man reached hurriedly for his rucksack, fumbled to lift the canvas flap and reach inside.

Finally, the bummer, as thieves and stragglers and deserters were called, gave in to frustration and dumped Jacob's belongings onto the ground, pawing through them.

Look at me, Jacob thought. *I am alive. I wear the same uniform as you do.*

The scavenger did not respond, of course. Did not allow his gaze to rest upon Jacob's face, where he might have seen awareness.

The voices, the trampling hooves, the springless wagons drew closer.

The man cursed, frantic now. He found Jacob's battered Bible and flung it aside, in disgusted haste, its thin pages fluttering as it fell, like a bird with a broken wing. The standard-issue tin cup, plate and utensils soon followed, but the thieving bastard stilled when he found the packet of letters, all from Caroline. Perhaps believing he might find something of value in one or more of them, he shoved them into his own rucksack.

Jacob grieved for those letters, but there was nothing he could do.

Except listen.

Yes, he decided. Someone was coming, a small company of riders.

The thief grew more agitated, looked back over one shoulder, and then turned back to his plundering, feverish now, but too greedy to flee.

At last, he settled upon the one object Jacob cherished as much as Caroline's letters, a small leather case with a tarnished brass hinges and a delicate clasp.

Wicked interest flashed in the man's eyes, as he fumbled open the case and saw the tin-types inside, one of Caroline and Jacob, taken on their wedding day, looking traditionally somber in their finest garb, the other of Caroline, with an infant Rachel in her arms, the child resplendent in a tiny, lace-trimmed christening gown and matching bonnet.

Caroline had sewed every stitch of the impossibly small dress and beribboned bonnet, made them sturdy, so they could be worn by all the children to follow.

No, Jacob cried inwardly, hating his helplessness.

"Well, now," the man murmured. "Ain't this a pretty little family? Maybe I'll just look them up sometime, offer my condolences."

Had he been able, Jacob would have killed the bummer in that moment, throttled the life out of him with his bare hands, and never regretted the act. Although he struggled with all his might, trying to gather the last shreds of his strength, the effort proved useless.

It was the worst kind of agony, imagining this man reading the letters, noting the return address on each and every envelope, seeking Caroline and Rachel out, offering a pretense of sympathy.

Taking advantage.

And Jacob could do nothing to stop him, nothing to protect his wife and daughter from this monster or others like him, the renegades, the enemies of decency and innocence in all their forms.

With the smile of a demon, the bummer snapped the case closed and reached for his rucksack, ready, at last, to flee.

It was then that a figure loomed behind him, a gray shadow of a man, planted the sole of one boot squarely in the center of the thief's back, and sent him sprawling across Jacob's inert frame.

The pain was instant, throbbing in every bone and muscle of Jacob's body.

"Stealing from a dead man," the shadow said, standing tall, his buttery-smooth drawl laced with contempt. "That's low, even for a Yank."

The bummer scrambled to his feet, groped for something, probably his rifle, and paled when he came up empty. Most likely, he'd dropped the weapon in his eagerness to rob one of his own men.

"I ought to run you through with this fine steel sword of mine, Billy," the other man mused idly. He must have ridden ahead of his detachment, dismounted nearby, and moved silently through the scattered bodies. "After all, this is a *war*, now, isn't it? And you are my foe, as surely as I am yours."

Jacob's vision, unclear to begin with, blurred fur-

ther, and there was a pounding in his ears, but he could
make out the contours of the two men, now standing
on either side of him, and he caught the faint murmur
of their words, a mere wisp of sound.

"You don't want to kill me, Johnny," the thief reasoned, with a note of anxious congeniality in his voice,
raising both palms as if in surrender. "It wouldn't be
honorable, with us Union boys at a plain disadvan-
tage." He drew in a strange, swift whistle of a breath.
"Anyhow, I wasn't hurtin' nobody. Just makin' good
use of things this poor fella has no need of, bein' dead
and all."

By now, Jacob was aware of men and horses all
around, though there was no cannon fire, no shouting,
no sharp report of rifles.

"You want these men to see you murder an unarmed
man?" wheedled the man addressed as Billy. "Where I
come from, you'd be hanged for that. It's a war crime,
ain't it?"

"We're not 'where you come from,'" answered
Johnny coolly. The bayonet affixed to the barrel of
his carbine glinted in the lingering smoke and the dust
raised by the horses. "This is Virginia," he went on,
with a note of fierce reverence. "And you are an intruder here, sir."

Billy—the universal name for all Union soldiers, as
Johnny was for their Confederate counterparts—spat,
foolhardy in his fear. "I reckon the rules are about the
same, though, whether North or South," he ventured.
Even Jacob, from his faulty vantage point, saw the terror behind all that bluster. "Fancy man like you—an
officer, at that—must know how it is. Even if you don't

hang for killin' with no cause, you'll be court-martialed for sure, once your superiors catch wind of what you done. And that's bound to leave a stain on your high-and-mighty reputation as a Southern gentleman, ain't it? Just you think, *sir*, of the shame all those well-mannered folks back home on the old plantation will have to contend with, all on your account."

A slow, untroubled grin took shape on the Confederate captain's soot-smudged face. His gray uniform was torn and soiled, the brass of his buttons and insignia dull, and his boots were scuffed, but even Jacob, nearly blind, could see that his dignity was inborn, as much a part of him as the color of his eyes.

"It might be worth hanging," he replied, almost cordially, like a man debating some minor point of military ethics at an elegant dinner party far removed from the sound and fury of war, "the pleasure of killing a latrine rat such as yourself, that is. As for these men, most of whom are under my command, as it happens, well, they've seen their friends and cousins and brothers skewered by Yankee bayonets and blown to fragments by their canon. Just today, in fact, they saw General Jackson relieved of an arm." At this, the captain paused, swallowed once. "Most likely, they'd raise a cheer as you fell."

Dimly, Jacob saw Billy Yank's Adam's apple bob along the length of his neck. Under any other circumstances, he might have been amused by the fellow's nervous bravado, but he could feel himself retreating further and further into the darkness of approaching death, and there was no room in him for frivolous emotions.

"Now, that just ain't Christian," protested Billy, conveniently overlooking his own moral lapse.

The captain gave a raspy laugh, painful to hear, and shook his head. "A fine sentiment, coming from the likes of you." In the next moment, his face hardened, aristocratic even beneath its layers of dried sweat and dirt. He turned slightly, keeping one eye on his prisoner, and shouted a summons into the rapidly narrowing nothingness surrounding the three of them.

Several men hurried over, though they were invisible to Jacob, and the sounds they made were faint.

"Get this piece of dog dung out of my sight before I pierce his worthless flesh with my sword for the pure pleasure of watching him bleed," the officer ordered. "He is a disgrace, even to *that* uniform."

There were words of reply, though Jacob could not make them out, and Jacob sensed a scuffle as the thief resisted capture, a modern-day Judas, bleating a traitor's promises, willing to betray men who'd fought alongside him, confided their hopes and fears to him around campfires or on the march.

Jacob waited, expecting the gentleman soldier to follow his men, go on about his business of overseeing the capture of wounded blue-coats, the recovery of his own troops, alive and dead.

Instead, the man crouched, as the thief had done earlier. He took up the rucksack Billy had been forced to leave behind, rummaged within it, produced the packet of letters and the leather case containing the likenesses of Jacob's beloved wife and daughter. He opened the latter, examined the images inside, smiled sadly.

Then he tucked the items inside Jacob's bloody coat,

paused as though startled, and looked directly into his motionless eyes.

"My God," he said, under his breath. "You're alive."

Jacob could not acknowledge the remark verbally, but he felt a tear trickle over his left temple, into his hair, and that, apparently, was confirmation enough for the Confederate captain.

Now, Jacob thought, he would be shot, put out of his misery like an injured horse. And he would welcome the release.

Instead, very quietly, the captain said. "Hold on. You'll be found soon." He paused, frowning. "And if you happen to encounter a Union quartermaster by the name of Rogan McBride, somewhere along the way, I would be obliged if you'd tell him Bridger Winslow sends his best regards."

Jacob doubted he'd get the chance to do as Winslow asked, but he marked the names carefully in his mind, just the same.

Another voice spoke then. "This somebody you know, Captain?" a man asked, with concern and a measure of sympathy. It wasn't uncommon on either side, after all, to find a friend or a relative among enemy casualties, for the battle-lines often cut across towns, churches, and supper tables.

"No," the captain replied gruffly. "Just another dead Federal." A pause. "Get on with your business, Simms. We might have the blue-coats under our heel for the moment, but you can be sure they'll be back to bury what remains they can't gather up and haul away. Better if we don't risk a skirmish after a day of hard fighting."

"Yes, sir," Simms replied sadly. "The men are low

in spirit, now that General Jackson has been struck down."

"Yes," the captain answered. Angry sorrow flashed in his eyes. "By his own troops," he added bitterly, speaking so quietly that Jacob wondered if Simms had heard them at all.

Jacob sensed the other man's departure.

The captain lingered, taking his canteen from his belt, loosening the cap a little with a deft motion of one hand, leaving the container within Jacob's reach. The gesture was most likely a futile one, since Jacob could not use his hands, but it was an act of kindness, all the same. An affirmation of the possibility, however remote, that Jacob might somehow survive.

Winslow rose to his full height, regarded Jacob solemnly, and walked away.

Jacob soon lost consciousness again, waking briefly now and then, surprised to find himself not only still among the living, but unmolested by vermin. When alert, he lay looking up the night sky, steeped in the profound silence of the dead, one more body among dozens, if not hundreds, scattered across the blood-soaked grass.

Just so many pawns in some Olympian chess match, he reflected, discarded in the heat of conflict and then forgotten.

Sometime the next morning, or perhaps the morning after that, wagons came again, and grim-faced Union soldiers stacked the bodies like cordwood, one on top of another. They were fretful, these battle-weary men, anxious to complete their dismal mission and get back behind the Union lines, where there was at least a semblance of safety.

Jacob, mute and motionless, was among the last to be taken up, grasped roughly by two men in dusty blue coats.

The pain was so sudden, so excruciating that finally, *finally*, he managed a low, guttural cry.

The soldier supporting his legs, little more than a boy, with blemished skin and not even the prospect of a beard, gasped. "This fella's still with us," he said, and he looked so startled, so horrified, and so pale that Jacob feared he would swoon, letting his burden drop.

"Well," said the other man, gruffly cheerful, "Johnny left a few breathin' this time around."

The boy recovered enough to turn his head and spit, and to Jacob's relief, he remained upright, his grasp firm. "A few," he agreed grudgingly. "And every one of them better off dead."

The darkness returned then, enfolding Jacob like the embrace of a sea siren, pulling him under.

TWO

Caroline
Washington City,
June 15, 1863

Nothing Caroline Hammond had heard or read about
the nation's capital could have prepared her for the reality of the place, the soot and smoke, the jostling crowds
of soldiers and civilians, the clatter of wagon wheels,
the neighing of horses and the braying of mules, the
rough merriment streaming through the open doorways
of plentiful saloons and pleasure houses.

She kept her gaze firmly averted as she passed one
after another of these establishments, appalled by the
seediness of it all, by the crude shouts, the jangle of
badly tuned pianos and rollicking songs sung lustily
and off-key, and, here and there, fisticuffs accompanied by the breaking of glass and even a few gunshots.

More than once, Caroline was forced to cross the
road, a gauntlet of ox carts and ambulance wagons
and mounted men who took no evident notice of hap-
less pedestrians.

A farm wife, Caroline was not a person of delicate

constitution. She had dispatched, cleaned and plucked many a chicken for Sunday supper, helped her husband Jacob and Enoch Flynn, the hired man, butcher hogs come autumn, and worked ankle-deep in barn muck on a daily basis.

Here, in this city of poor manners, ceaseless din and sickening stenches, the effects were, of course, magnified, surrounding her on every side, pummeling her senses without mercy.

Runnels of foaming animal urine flowed among the broken cobblestones, and dung steamed in piles, adding to the cloying miasma. On the far edge of her vision, she saw a soldier vomit copiously into a gutter and felt her own gorge rise, scalding, to the back of her throat. The man's companions seemed amused by the spectacle, slapping their retching friend on the back and chiding him with loud, jocular admonitions of an unsavory nature.

Seeing the disreputable state of these men's uniforms, intended as symbols of a proud and noble cause, thoroughly besmirched not only by all manner of filth, but by the indecent comportment of the men who wore them, sent furious color surging into her cheeks. Only her native prudence and the urgency of her mission— locating her wounded husband, lying near death in one of Washington City's numerous makeshift hospitals, or, if she had arrived too late, in a pine box—kept her from striding right up to the scoundrels and taking them sternly to task for bringing such shame upon their more honorable fellows.

How dare they behave like reprobates, safe in the shadow of Mr. Lincoln's White House, while their great-hearted comrades fought bravely on blood-drenched battlefields all over the land?

She was mortified, as well as grieved, but anger sustained her. Kept her moving toward the rows of hospital tents just visible in the distance.

Toward Jacob.

She thought of the long-delayed telegram, tucked away in her reticule. She'd read it over and over again from the day it had been placed in her hands, read it during the long train ride from Gettysburg, the small, quiet town in the green Pennsylvania countryside she had lived in, or near, all her life.

By now, the missive was tattered and creased, an evil talisman, despised and yet somehow necessary, the only link she had to her husband.

The information it contained was maddeningly scant, indicating only that Corporal Jacob Hammond had fallen in battle on May 3, at Chancellorsville, Virginia, and had since been transported to the capitol, where he would receive the best medical attention available.

As the granddaughter of a country doctor and sometimes undertaker, Caroline knew only too well what Jacob and others like him had yet to endure: crowding, filth, poor food and tainted water, too few trained surgeons and attendants, shortages of even the most basic supplies, such as clean bandages, laudanum and ether. Sanitation, the most effective enemy of sepsis, according to her late grandfather, was virtually nonexistent.

The stench of open latrines, private and public privies and towering heaps of manure standing on empty lots finally forced Caroline to set down her carpetbag long enough to pull her best Sunday handkerchief from the pocket of her cloak and press the soft cloth to her nose and mouth. The scent of rosewater, generously applied before she left home, had faded with time and distance, and thus provided little relief, but it was better than nothing.

Caroline picked up her carpetbag and walked purposely onward, not because she knew where she would find her husband, but because she didn't dare stand still too long, lest her knees give way beneath her.

Thus propelled by false resolution and a rising sense of desperation, she hurried on, through the mayhem of a wartime city under constant threat of siege, doing her best to convey a confidence she did not feel. Beneath the stalwart countenance, fear gnawed at her empty, roiling stomach, throbbed in her head, sought and found the secret regions of her heart, where the bruises were, to do its worst.

She had no choice but to carry on, no matter what might be required of her, and she did not attempt to ignore the relentless dread. That would be impossible.

Instead, she walked, weaving her way through the crowds on the sidewalks, crossing to the opposite side of the street in a mostly useless effort to avoid staggering drunkards and street brawls and men who watched her too boldly. Having long since learned the futility of burying her fears, she made up her mind to face them instead, with calm fortitude—as well as she could, anyway.

As she'd often heard her grandfather remark, turning a blind eye to a problem or a troublesome situation served only to make matters worse in the long run. "Face things head-on, Caroline," the old man had lectured. "Stand up to whatever comes your way and, if you are in the right, Providence will come to your aid."

Lately, she had not seen a great deal of evidence to support the latter part of that statement, but, then again, Providence was under no discernible obligation to explain itself or its ways to questioning mortals, particularly in light of the stupidity, greed and cruelty so far displayed by the human race.

One by one, Caroline confronted the haunting possibilities, the pictures standing vivid in her thoughts, nearly tangible. In the most immediate scenario, she could not find Jacob, even after the most arduous search imaginable. There had been a mistake, and he had been taken to some other place entirely, or died in transit, and been buried in an anonymous grave, one she would never be able to locate.

In the next, she *did* find her husband, but she had not arrived quickly enough to hold his hand, stroke his forehead, bid him a tender farewell. He had already succumbed, and all that was left of him was a gray, waxen corpse lying in a ramshackle coffin. When she touched him, in this vision, his flesh was so cold that it left her fingertips numb and burning, as if frostbitten.

But there was one more tableau to face and in many ways, it was the most terrible of all. Here, Jacob was alive, horribly maimed, helpless, forced to bear the unbearable until death delivered him from his sufferings in days, weeks, months—or years.

The thought tormented Caroline.

If only she knew what to expect, she might be able to prepare somehow.

But then, how *could* one prepare for the shock of seeing a beloved husband, broken and torn? Suppose

Jacob was so disfigured that she did not recognize him or, worse yet, allowed shock or dismay to show in her face, her manner, her bearing?

She swayed, not daring to draw the deep breath her body craved, lest the dreadful smells of disease and suffering and death finally overwhelm her, render her useless to Jacob just when he needed her most.

And that would not do.

GLORY, GLORY

CHAPTER ONE

GLORY PARSONS'S GLOVED hands tightened on the steering wheel when the familiar green-and-white sign came into view. *Pearl River, Oregon. Population: 6710.*

All it would take was one U-turn, and she could be headed back toward Portland. She'd find another job, and she still had her apartment. Maybe she and Alan could work things out....

She swallowed hard. She would be in Pearl River three weeks at the outside, then she could join her friend Sally in San Francisco, get a new job and start her life all over again. As for Alan, she hoped his teeth would fall out.

The feed store was festooned in lights and sparkling green garlands for Christmas, like the five-and-dime and the bookstore and the newspaper office. The street was thick with muddy slush, but fat puffs of new snow were falling.

Glory passed the diner and smiled to see the cheap plastic Santa and reindeer perched on the tar-paper roof. She touched her horn once, in a preliminary greeting to her mother, and drove on.

The cemetery was on the other side of town, overlooking the river. Glory parked outside the gates, behind a green police car, and made her way up the curving driveway. She left her purse in the car, carrying a bouquet of holly she'd picked along the roadside earlier in the day.

A crisp breeze riffled the drifting snowflakes and Glory's chin-length silver-gold hair. She pulled up the collar of her long woolen coat, royal blue to match her eyes, and made her way carefully along a slippery walk.

Dylan's grave lay beneath a white blanket of snow, and Glory's throat thickened when she came to stand beside it. "Hi, handsome," she said hoarsely, stooping to put the holly into the metal vase at the base of his headstone. Her eyes filled with tears, and she wedged both hands deep into her coat pockets and sniffled. "You had your nerve, dying at twenty-two. Don't you know a girl needs her big brother?"

She dusted snow from the face of the stone, uncovering Dylan's name and the dates of his birth and death. He'd perished in an explosion soon after joining the air force, and Glory didn't want anyone to forget he'd lived, even for the space of an afternoon snowfall.

She drew a deep breath and dried her eyes with the back of one hand. "I swore I'd never come back here," she went on miserably, "even to see you. But Mama's getting married, so I had to come to her wedding." She took a tissue from her pocket and dabbed at her nose. "I got myself hooked up with a real jerk back in Portland, Dylan. If you'd been around, you probably would have punched him in the mouth. He pretended to love me, and then he stole my promotion right out from under me."

She paused to look up at the cloudy sky. The bare limbs of maple and elm trees seemed to splinter it.

"I quit my job and had my furniture put in storage,"

Glory confided to her brother, gazing at the marble headstone again. "And after Christmas and Mama's wedding, I'm going to San Francisco to make a life for myself. I don't know when I'll be back to see you again."

A swishing sound in the slush alerted Glory to someone's approach. She looked up, and her blue eyes went wide.

"Jesse."

He was standing on the other side of Dylan's grave, dressed in the standard green-and-brown uniform of the sheriff's department. He wore no hat, and his badge, pinned to his jacket, gleamed in the thin winter light. Like Glory, he was twenty-eight years old.

His caramel eyes moved over her frame then swept back to her face. "What are you doing here?" he asked, as though he'd caught her in a bank vault after-hours.

Glory had known she couldn't come back to Pearl River without encountering Jesse—she just hadn't expected it to happen this soon. Her temper flared, along with an old ache in a corner of her heart she'd long since closed off, and she gestured toward Dylan's headstone. "What do you think I'm doing here?" she retorted. "I came to see my brother."

Jesse hooked his thumbs through the loops on his trousers, and his brazen brown eyes narrowed slightly. "It's been eight years since the funeral. You were really anxious to get back."

Eight years since the funeral, eight years since Glory had laid eyes on Jesse Bainbridge.

Pride forced Glory to retaliate. She took in his uniform and then said, "I see you've been promoted to sheriff. Did your grandfather buy the election?"

His jawline tightened for a moment, but then he grinned in that wicked way that had broken so many hearts in high school. "Why not? He bought you, didn't he?" Like everyone else in Pearl River, Jesse probably believed old Seth Bainbridge had paid her to leave town; Glory was fairly certain he'd never learned about the baby.

Without waiting for a reply, Jesse settled his hat on his head and walked away.

Glory barely resisted the urge to scoop up a handful of snow and hurl it at his back. Only the awareness of where she was kept her from doing just that.

When Jesse was out of earshot, Glory put her hands on her hips and told Dylan, "He really burns me up. I don't know why you liked him so much."

You liked him, too, she heard Dylan's voice say, way down deep in her heart. *You had his baby, Glory.*

"Don't remind me!" Glory snapped, folding her arms. "I was barely eighteen, and my hormones were out of control!"

She thought she heard Dylan's laughter in the chilly winter breeze, and in spite of the unpleasant encounter with Jesse Bainbridge a few minutes before, she smiled.

"I love you, Dylan," she said, touching the headstone again. Then, with her hands in her pockets, she turned and made her way down the walk to the driveway and the towering wrought-iron gates.

It was time to face Pearl River, something she hadn't done since Dylan's funeral, and she was reluctant for more than one reason.

Glory's sports car, the one great extravagance in her life, started with a comforting roar, and she drove slowly back into town, telling herself to take things one moment at a time. Before she knew it, Christmas and the New Year's wedding would be over, and she could get on with her life.

She parked in front of Delphine's Diner just before an orange snowplow came past, flinging a picturesque fan of slush at the sidewalk. Glancing up at the life-size plastic Santa and reindeer, Glory remembered Dylan sliding around on the roof to put them in place for Christmases past, deliberately clowning because he knew his mother and sister were afraid he'd fall.

The little bell over the door jingled when Glory went inside. Her mother, as slender and active as ever, lit up brighter than the Santa over their heads when she saw her daughter.

"Glory," she whispered with a choked sob of pleasure. And then she was hurrying across the brown-and-white linoleum floor, with its swirls of fresh wax, to embrace her.

The hug brought a lump to Glory's throat and quick tears to her eyes. "Hello, Mama."

"It's about time you got here," boomed a male voice from one of the stools at the counter. Harold Seemer, the good-natured plumbing contractor who had finally persuaded Delphine to marry him after a five-year courtship, beamed at his future stepdaughter. "We were about to send the sheriff's patrol out after you."

Glory tried not to react visibly to the indirect mention of Jesse. She didn't want thoughts of him interfering with her visit. "Hi, Harold," she said, giving the well-fed balding man a hug. He and Delphine had visited her in Portland on several occasions, and she'd become very fond of him.

"You look skinny," Delphine commented, narrow-

ing her green eyes as Glory took off her coat and hung
it on one of the chrome hooks beside the door.

Glory laughed. "Thanks, Mama. I've been dieting
for two months to make up for all the food you're going
to force me to eat."

Harold finished his coffee and replaced the beige
china cup in its saucer, with a clink. "Well, I've got
to get back to work. I'll leave you two to catch up on
everything."

When he was gone, Glory took a stool at the counter,
sighed, and pushed back her hair. "No customers," she
commented, looking around at the six Formica-topped
tables. The chrome legs of the chairs glistened, and so
did the red vinyl seats.

Delphine shrugged and, stepping behind the counter,
poured a cup of coffee to set in front of her daughter.
"The lunch crowd's been and gone. Things'll be quiet
until dinnertime."

Glory reached for her cup and saucer and pulled
them toward her, feeling the steam caress her face and
taking comfort in the familiar aroma, but she didn't
drink. "I saw Jesse," she said, and her voice was shaky.

"Did you, now?" Delphine's voice was light as the
feathery snow falling past the window with its neon
"We Serve Pepsi-Cola" sign. "How did that happen?"

"I stopped by the cemetery to leave some holly
for Dylan, and he was there." Glory raised her eyes,
watched her mother's face pale slightly at the mention
of her lost son. But Delphine recovered her composure
rapidly, like always. She was nothing if not a survivor.

"Jesse's brother, Gresham, is buried there, along
with his sister-in-law, Sandy, and his folks. Must be
some special day to him, or something."

Glory recalled the plane crash that had taken the lives of Gresham Bainbridge, promising young state senator, and his pretty wife, Sandy. The tragedy had been big news in Oregon. "They left a child behind, didn't they?" Glory asked, because thinking about the Bainbridges' misfortune was better than remembering her own and Delphine's.

Delphine busied herself rinsing out a glass pot and starting a new batch of decaffeinated coffee brewing. "A little girl," she said quietly. After a few more moments, she turned to face her daughter, leaning against the spotless counter, her shrewd eyes inviting—even demanding—confidences. "Tell me about this Alan man. What did he do that made you uproot yourself like that?"

Glory ran her tongue over her lips and fiddled with a paper napkin. She still hadn't touched her coffee. "He was a rat, Mama," she answered after a long time. "He cozied up to all my clients while I was away taking a training course in Chicago, and when I came home, the board had given him the promotion they promised me."

"So you just threw your resignation in their faces, cleared out your desk and left?" Delphine put the question in a nonchallenging way, but it still made Glory's cheeks flame.

And she definitely felt defensive. "What should I have done, Mama? Stayed and brought Alan pencils and files in my teeth? I worked night and day for *four years* to earn that job!"

Delphine shrugged, leaning on the counter again. "I think maybe you just wanted out of the relationship and that was the best excuse that occurred to you. In fact, I wouldn't be surprised to learn that you've never gotten over Jesse Bainbridge."

Glory's hands shook as she picked up the coffee and took an angry gulp. It burned her tongue and the roof of her mouth. "Well, I have!" she sputtered moments later. It still hurt that Jesse hadn't come for her at the unwed-mothers' home in Portland and brought her home to have their baby, even though she knew the scenario was woven of pure fantasy. Jesse couldn't have come for her because he hadn't known she was pregnant. "It was nothing but a childish high-school infatuation in the first place."

Delphine's eyes took on a sad look. "It was more than that," she insisted softly, resting one well-manicured hand on Glory's arm.

Glory pulled away, went to the jukebox and busied herself studying the titles of the songs imprisoned inside. They were all old tunes she couldn't bear to hear when her feelings were so raw.

She turned to the window instead.

Mr. Kribner came out of the drugstore across the street and hung an evergreen wreath on his front door.

"Merry Christmas," Glory muttered, wishing she'd never left Portland. She could have made some excuse for the holidays, then dashed into town for the wedding and out again after the reception.

Her mother's hands gripped her elbows firmly. "You're tired, sweetheart, and I'll bet you didn't have any lunch. Let me fix you something, and then you can go upstairs and rest a while."

Glory nodded, even though she had no appetite and hadn't really rested for days. She didn't want Delphine to worry about her, especially during this happy time, with the wedding and the holidays coming up.

"Harvey Baker was just in the other day," Delphine called sunnily from the kitchen, as Glory stood hugging herself and watching the snow swirl lazily past the diner windows. When it got dark, the Pepsi sign would make a pink glow on the white ground. "He's looking for an assistant over at the bank, you know. Allie Cordman left to take a job in Seattle."

"Smart girl," Glory murmured. Pearl River was a nowhere town, with nothing to offer. Anybody who deliberately made his home here ought to have his head examined.

Delphine hummed in the kitchen, happy with her world, and for one difficult moment Glory envied her profoundly. She wondered what it was like to be in love with a man she could trust and depend on, and to be loved by him in return.

Presently, Glory's favorite lunch—a clubhouse sandwich with potato salad—appeared on the counter, along with a tall diet cola with extra ice.

Glory would have sworn she wasn't hungry, but her stomach grumbled as she got back onto the stool and pulled a fresh napkin from the holder. "Thanks, Mama," she said.

Delphine was busy wiping the already immaculate counter. "There's an old-movie festival at the Rialto tonight," she told Glory cheerfully. "Jimmy Stewart in *It's a Wonderful Life* and Cary Grant in *The Bishop's Wife*."

A poignant sensation of nostalgia came over Glory. "Jimmy Stewart and Cary Grant," she sighed. "They don't make men like that anymore."

Delphine's green eyes twinkled, and she flashed her diamond engagement ring. "Don't be too sure," she said coyly, and Glory laughed.

"Mama, you're hopeless!" But she couldn't help thinking, as she ate her sandwich and tangy potato salad, that it would be nice to have a handsome angel turn up in her life, the way Cary Grant had appeared in Loretta Young's.

Two teenage boys came in, raising a great ruckus lest they go unnoticed, and plunked quarters into the jukebox. A lively old Christmas rock tune filled the diner, and they piled into chairs at one of the tables.

Suddenly wanting to relive her after-school waitress days in that very diner, Glory abandoned her sandwich and reached for a pencil and an order pad.

"What'll it be, guys?" she asked.

The young men ran appreciative eyes over her trim blue jeans and gray cashmere sweater.

"Will you marry me?" asked the one with braces.

Glory laughed. "Sure. Just bring a note from your mother."

The other boy hooted at that, and the first one blushed. The name on the sleeve of his letter-man's jacket was Tony.

"I want a cheeseburger, a vanilla shake and an order of curly fries," he said, but the look in his eyes told Glory he had bigger things in mind than food.

Glory was writing the order down when the bell over the door jingled. She looked up to see Jesse dusting snow off his shoulders onto Delphine's clean floor.

His gaze skirting Glory as though she'd suddenly turned invisible, he greeted the boys by name and took a place at the counter. "Hi, Delphine," he said, as the woman poured his coffee. "How's my best girl?"

Glory concentrated fiercely on the second boy's order, and when she'd gotten it, she marched into the kitchen and started cooking. She had to keep herself busy—and distracted—until Jesse finished his coffee and left the diner.

"What's he doing here?" she whispered to her mother, when Delphine joined her to lift the basket out of the deep fryer and shake the golden fries free of grease.

Delphine smiled. "He's drinking coffee."

Glory glowered at her. "I'm going upstairs!" she hissed.

"That'll fix him," Delphine said.

In a huff, Glory took the cheeseburgers off the grill and the shakes off the milk-shake machine. She made two trips to the boys' table and set everything down with a distinctive *clunk*. All the while, she studiously ignored Jesse Bainbridge.

He'd just come in to harass her, she was sure of that. He probably bullied everybody in Pearl River, just like his grandfather always had.

The jukebox took a break, then launched into a plaintive love song. Glory's face was hot as she went back to the kitchen, hoping Jesse didn't remember how that tune had been playing on the radio the first time they'd made love, up at the lake.

She couldn't help glancing back over one shoulder to see his face, and she instantly regretted the indulgence. Jesse's bold brown eyes glowed with the memory, and his lips quirked as he struggled to hold back a smile.

Glory flushed to recall how she'd carried on that

long-ago night, the pleasure catching her by surprise and sending her spiraling out of her small world.

"That does it," she muttered. And she stormed out to her car, collected her suitcase and overnighter, and marched up the outside stairs to her mother's apartment.

The moment she stepped through the door, Glory was awash in memories.

The living room was small and plain, the furniture cheap, the floor covered in black-and-beige linoleum tiles. A portable TV with foil hooked to the antenna sat on top of the old-fashioned console stereo.

Glory put down her luggage, hearing the echoes of that day long, long before, when Delphine had taken a job managing the diner downstairs. Dylan had been fourteen then, Glory twelve, and they'd all been jubilant at the idea of a home of their own. They'd lived out of Delphine's old rattletrap of a car all summer, over at the state park next to the river, but the fall days were getting crisp and the nights were downright cold.

Besides, Delphine's money had long since run out, and they'd been eating all their meals in the church basement, with the old people and the families thrown out of work because of layoffs at the sawmill.

Dylan and Glory had slept in bunk beds provided by the Salvation Army, while Delphine had made her bed on the couch.

Pushing the door shut behind her, Glory wrenched herself back to the present. It was still too painful to think about Dylan twice in one day, even after all the time that had passed.

Glory put her baggage in the tiny bedroom that was Delphine's now, thinking that she really should have rented a motel room. When she'd suggested it on the telephone, though, her mother had been adamant: Glory would stay at the apartment, and it would be like old times.

She paced, too restless to unpack or take a nap, but too tired to do anything really demanding. After peeking out the front window, past the dime-store wreath with the plastic candle in it, to make sure Jesse's car was gone, she went back downstairs for her coat.

The cook who took Delphine's place at two-thirty had arrived, along with a teenage waitress and a crowd of noisy kids from the high school.

Delphine handed Glory her coat, then shrugged into her own. "Come on," she said, pushing her feet into transparent plastic boots. "I'll show you the house Harold and I are going to live in."

The snow fell faster as the two women walked along the familiar sidewalk. Now and then, Delphine paused to wave at a store clerk or a passing motorist.

They rounded a corner and entered an attractive development. The houses had turrets and gable windows, though they were modern, and the yards were nicely landscaped.

Glory remembered playing in this part of town as a child. There had been no development then, just cracked sidewalks that meandered off into the deep grass. The place had fascinated her, and she'd imagined ghost houses lining the walks, until Dylan had spoiled everything by telling her there had been Quonset huts there during World War II to accommodate workers at the town smelter.

Delphine stopped to gaze fondly at a charming little mock colonial with a snow-dusted rhododendron bush growing in the yard. The house itself was white, the shutters dark blue. There were flower boxes under all the windows.

Glory's eyes widened with pleasure. This was the kind of house her mother had always dreamed of having. "This is it?" she asked, quite unnecessarily.

Proudly Delphine nodded. "Harold and I signed the papers on Friday. It's all ours."

Impulsively, Glory hugged her mother. "You've come a long way, baby!" she said, her eyes brimming with happy tears.

Both of them stood still in the falling snow, remembering other days, when even in their wildest dreams neither of them would have dared to fantasize about owning a house such as this one.

"Are you going to keep the diner?" Glory asked, linking her arm with Delphine's as they walked back toward the center of town.

Delphine's answer came as no surprise. After all, she'd worked and scrimped and sacrificed to buy the place from her former employers. "Of course I am. I wouldn't know what to do if I couldn't go down there and make coffee for my customers."

With a chuckle, Glory wrapped her arm around her mother's straight little shoulders. "I imagine they'd all gather in your kitchen at home, they're so used to telling you their troubles over a steaming cup."

Back at the apartment, Delphine immediately excused herself, saying she had to "gussy up" for the Stewart-Grant festival at the Rialto.

"Sure you don't want to come along?" she queried, peering around the bathroom door, her red hair falling around her face in curls. "Harold and I would be glad to have you."

Glory shook her head, pausing in her unpacking. "I feel as though parts of me have been scattered in every direction, Mama. I need time to gather myself back together. I'll get something light for supper, then read or watch TV."

Delphine raised titian eyebrows. "You're getting boring in your old age, kid," she said. "Just see that you don't eat over at Maggie's. Last week one of the telephone linemen told me he got a piece of cream pie there that had dust on top of it."

"I wouldn't think of patronizing your archrival, Mama," Glory replied, grinning. "Even though I do think serving pie with dust on it requires a certain admirable panache."

Delphine dismissed her daughter with a wave and disappeared behind the bathroom door.

As it happened, Glory bought spaghetti salad in the deli at the supermarket and ate it while watching the evening news on the little TV with the foil antenna. Downstairs in the diner, the dinner hour was in full swing, and the floor vibrated with the blare of the juke-box.

Glory smiled and settled back on the couch that would be her bed for the next several weeks, content.

She was home.

After the news was over, however, the reruns of defunct sitcoms started. Glory flipped off the TV and got out her mother's photo albums. As always, they were tucked carefully away in the record compartment of the console stereo, along with recordings by Roy Orbison, Buddy Holly, Ricky Nelson and Elvis Presley.

Delphine probably hadn't looked at the family pictures in years, but Glory loved to pore over them.

Still, she had to brace herself to open the first album—she was sitting cross-legged on the couch, the huge, cheaply bound book in her lap—because she knew there would be pictures of Dylan.

He smiled back at her from beside a tall man wearing a slouch hat. Glory knew the man's name had been Tom, and that he'd been mean when he drank. He'd also been her father, but she didn't remember him.

The little boy leaning against his leg, with tousled brown hair and gaps in his grin, was another matter. Gently, with just the tip of one finger, Glory touched her brother's young face.

"When am I going to get over missing you, Bozo?" she asked, in a choked voice, using the nickname that had never failed to bug him.

Glory stared at Dylan for a few more moments, then turned the page. There she made her first photographic appearance—she was two months old, being bathed in a roasting pan on a cheap tabletop, and her grin was downright drunken.

She smiled and sighed. "The body of a future cheerleader. Remarkable."

Her journey through the past continued until she'd viewed all the Christmases and Halloweens, all the birthdays and first days of school. In a way, it eased the Dylan-shaped ache in her heart.

When she came to the prom pictures of herself and Jesse, taken in this very living room with Delphine's Kodak Instamatic, she smiled again.

Jesse was handsome in his well-fitting suit, while she stood proudly beside him in the froth of pink chiffon Delphine had sewn for her. The dress had a white sash, and she could still feel the gossamer touch of it against her body. Perched prominently above her right breast was Jesse's corsage, an orchid in the palest rose.

She touched the flat, trim stomach of the beaming blond girl in the picture. Inside, although Glory hadn't known it yet, Jesse's baby was already growing.

Glory closed the album gently and set it aside before she could start wondering who had adopted that beautiful little baby girl, and whether or not she was happy.

The next collection of pictures was older. It showed Delphine growing up in Albuquerque, New Mexico, and there were photographs of a collage of aunts, uncles and cousins, too.

Glory reflected as she turned the pages that it must have been hard for Delphine after she left another abusive husband. Her family had understood the first time, but they couldn't forgive a second mistake. And after Delphine fled to Oregon with her two children, she was virtually disowned.

Saddened, Glory turned a page. The proud, aristocratic young face of her Irish great-grandmother gazed out of the portrait, chin at an obstinate angle. Of all the photographs Delphine had kept, this image of Bridget McVerdy was her favorite.

In 1892, or thereabouts, Bridget had come to America to look for work and a husband. She'd been employed as a lowly housemaid, but she'd had enough pride in her identity to pose for this picture and pay for it out of nominal wages, and eventually she'd married and had children.

The adversities Bridget overcame over the years were legion, but Delphine was fond of saying that her grandmother hadn't stopped living until the day she died, unlike a lot of people.

Glory gazed at the hair, which was probably red, and the eyes, rumored to be green, and the proud way Bridget McVerdy, immigrant housemaid, held her head. And it was as though their two souls reached across the years to touch.

Glory felt stronger in that moment, and her problems weren't so insurmountable. For the first time in weeks, giving up didn't seem to be the only choice she had.

CHAPTER TWO

THE NEXT MORNING, after a breakfast of grapefruit, toast and coffee, Glory drove along the snow-packed streets of Pearl River, remembering. She went to the old covered bridge, which looked as though it might tumble into the river at any moment, and found the place where Jesse had carved their initials in the weathered wood.

A wistful smile curved Glory's lips as she used one finger to trace the outline of the heart Jesse had shaped around the letters. Underneath, he'd added the word, *Forever.*

"Forever's a long time, Jesse," she said out loud, her breath making a white plume in the frosty air. The sun was shining brightly that day, though the temperature wasn't high enough to melt the snow and ice, and the weatherman was predicting that another storm would hit before midnight.

A sheriff's-department patrol car pulled up just as Glory was about to slip behind the wheel of her own vehicle and go back to town. She was relieved to see that the driver wasn't Jesse.

The deputy bent over to roll down the window on the passenger side, and Glory thought she remembered him as one of the boys who used to orchestrate food fights in the cafeteria at Pearl River High. "Glory?" His pleasant if distinctly ordinary face beamed. "I heard you were back in town. That's great about your mom getting married and everything."

Glory nodded. She couldn't quite make out the letters on his identification pin. She rubbed her mittened hands together and stomped her feet against the biting cold. "Thanks."

"You weren't planning to drive across the bridge or anything, were you?" the deputy asked. "It's been condemned for a long time. Somebody keeps taking down the sign."

"I just came to look," Glory answered, hoping he wouldn't put two and two together. This had always been the place where young lovers etched their initials for posterity, and she and Jesse had been quite an item back in high school.

The lawman climbed out of his car and began searching around in the deep snow for the "condemned" sign. Glory got into her sports car, started the engine, tooted the horn in a companionable farewell, and drove away.

She stopped in at the library after that, and then the five-and-dime, where she and Dylan used to buy Christmas and birthday presents for Delphine. She smiled to recall how graciously their mother had accepted bottles of cheap cologne and gauzy handkerchiefs with stylized *D*'s embroidered on them.

At lunch time, she returned to the apartment, where she ate a simple green salad and half a tuna sandwich. The phone rang while she was watching a game show.

Eager to talk to anyone besides Alan or Jesse, Glory snatched up the receiver. "Hello?"

The answering voice, much to her relief, was female. "Glory? Hi, it's Jill Wilson—your former confidante and cheerleading buddy."

Jill hadn't actually been Glory's best friend—that place had belonged to Jesse—but the two had been close in school, and Glory was delighted at the prospect of a reunion. "Jill! It's wonderful to hear your voice. How are you?"

In the years since Dylan's funeral, Glory and Jill had exchanged Christmas cards and occasional phone calls, and once they'd gotten together in Portland for lunch. Time and distance seemed to drop away as they talked. "I'm fine—still teaching at Pearl River Elementary. Listen, is there any chance we could get together at my place for dinner tonight? I've got a rehearsal at the church at six, and I was hoping you could meet me there afterward. Say seven?"

"Sounds great," Glory agreed, looking forward to the evening. "What shall I bring?"

"Just yourself," Jill answered promptly. "I'll see you at First Lutheran tonight, then?"

"Definitely," Glory promised.

She took a nap that afternoon, since she and Jill would probably be up late talking, then indulged in a long, leisurely bubble bath. She was wearing tailored wool slacks in winter white, along with a matching sweater, when Delphine looked her up and down from the bedroom doorway and whistled in exclamation.

"So Jesse finally broke down and asked for a date, huh?"

Glory, who had been putting the finishing touches on her makeup in front of the mirror over Delphine's dresser, grimaced. "No. And even if he did, I'd refuse."

Delphine, clad in jeans and a flannel shirt for a visit to a Christmas-tree farm with Harold, folded her arms and assembled her features into an indulgent expres-

sion. "Save it," she said. "When Jesse came into the
diner yesterday, there was so much electricity I thought
the wiring was going to short out."

Glory fiddled with a gold earring and frowned. "Really? I didn't notice," she said, but she was hearing that
song playing on the jukebox, and remembering the
way her skin had heated as she relived every touch of
Jesse's hands and lips.

"Of course you didn't," agreed Delphine, sounding
sly. She'd raised one eyebrow now.

"Mother," Glory sighed, "I know you've been watching Christmas movies from the forties and you're in
the mood for a good, old-fashioned miracle, but it isn't
going to happen with Jesse and me. The most we can
hope for, from him, is that he won't have me arrested
on some trumped-up charge and run out of town."

Delphine shook her head. "Pitiful," she said.

Glory grinned at her. "This from the woman who
kept a man dangling for five years before she agreed
to a wedding."

Delphine sighed and studied her flawlessly man-
icured fingernails. "With my romantic history," she
said, "I can't be too careful."

The two women exchanged a brief hug. "You've
found the right guy this time, Mama," Glory said softly.
"It's your turn to be happy."

"When does *your* turn come, honey?" Delphine
asked, her brow puckered with a frown. "How long
is it going to be before I look into your eyes and see
something besides grief for your brother and that baby
you had to give up?"

Glory's throat felt tight, and she turned her head.
"I don't know, Mama," she answered, thinking of the

word Jesse had carved in the wall of the covered bridge. *Forever.* "I just don't know."

Five minutes later, Glory left the apartment, her hands stuffed into the pockets of her long cloth coat. Since the First Lutheran Church was only four blocks away, she decided to walk the distance.

Even taking the long way, through the park, and lingering a while next to the big gazebo where the firemen's band gave concerts on summer nights, Glory was early. She stood on the sidewalk outside the church as a light snow began to waft toward earth, the sound of children's voices greeting her as warmly as the golden light in the windows.

Silent night, holy night
All is calm, all is bright...

Glory drew a breath cold enough to make her lungs ache and climbed the church steps. Inside, the music was louder, sweeter.

Holy Infant, so tender and mild...

Without taking off her coat, Glory slipped into the sanctuary and settled into a rear pew. On the stage, Mary and Joseph knelt, incognito in their twentieth-century clothes, surrounded by undercover shepherds, wise men and angels.

Jill, wearing a pretty plaid skirt in blues and grays, along with a blouse and sweater in complimentary shades, stood in front of the cast, her long brown hair wound into a single, glistening braid.

"That was fabulous!" she exclaimed, clapping her

hands together. "But let's try it once more. Angels, you need to sing a little louder this time."

Glory smiled, brushing snow off her coat as Jill hurried to the piano and struck up an encore of "Silent Night."

The children, ranging in age from five or so to around twelve, fascinated Glory. Sometimes she regretted studying finance instead of education; as a teacher, she might have been able to make up, at least in a small way, for one of the two major losses in her life—she would have gotten to spend time around little ones. As it was, she didn't even *know* any kids—they just didn't apply for fixed-rate mortgages or car loans.

Joseph and Mary looked enough alike to be brother and sister, with their copper-bright hair and enormous brown eyes. Two of the wise men were sporting braces, and the third had a cast on his right arm.

Glory was trying to decide who was an angel and who was a shepherd when her gaze came to rest on a particular little girl. Suddenly she scooted forward in her seat and gripped the back of the next pew in both hands.

Looking back at her from beneath flyaway auburn bangs was the pretty, pragmatic face of Bridget McVerdy, Glory's great-grandmother.

For a moment the pews seemed to undulate wildly, like images in a fun-house mirror, and Glory rested her forehead against her hands. Almost a minute passed before she could be certain she wasn't going to faint.

"Glory?" A hand came to rest with gentle firmness on her shoulder. "Glory, are you all right?"

She looked up and saw Jill standing over her, green eyes filled with concern. Her gaze darted back to the child, and the interior of the church started to sway again. Unless Dylan had fathered a baby without ever knowing, or telling his mother and sister...

"Glory," Jill repeated, sounding really worried now.

"I—I'm fine," Glory stammered. She tried to smile, but her face trembled with the effort. "I just need some water—"

"You sit right there," Jill said in a tone of authority. "I'll get you a drink."

By the time she returned with a paper cup filled with cold water, Glory had managed to get back in sync with the earth's orbit, and the feeling of queasy shock in her stomach had subsided.

Talk about your forties movies and Christmas miracles, she thought, her eyes following the child that had to be her own.

Jill excused herself and looked at her watch as she walked up the aisle. Parents were starting to arrive, peering through the sanctuary doors and congregating in the back pews.

"All right, showstoppers," Jill said, "it's a wrap, for tonight, at least. Angels, practice your songs. You were a little rusty on 'It came upon a Midnight Clear.'"

Glory wondered if she'd be able to stand without her knees buckling. She fumbled through her purse for aspirin and took two tablets with what remained of her water.

Just then, the little girl on the stage broke away from the other angels and shepherds and came running down the aisle, grinning.

Glory's eyes widened as her daughter drew nearer and nearer, turned slightly in her seat to see her fling her arms around a man clad in blue jeans, boots and a sheepskin coat.

Jesse.

"Hi'ya, Munchkin," he said, bending to kiss the child where her rich, red-brown hair was parted.

Glory's mouth dropped open. He knew, she thought frantically. Then she shook her head.

He *couldn't* know; fate couldn't be that cruel. His grandfather wouldn't have told him, Dylan hadn't known the truth, though he might have guessed, and Delphine had been sworn to secrecy.

At that moment Jesse's maple-colored eyes found Glory's face. They immediately narrowed.

Glory felt no more welcome in the First Lutheran Church than she had in the cemetery the day before. She sat up a little straighter, despite the fact that she was in a state of shock, and maintained her dignity. Jesse might be sheriff, but that didn't give him the right to intimidate people.

He opened his mouth, then closed it again. After raising the collar of his macho coat, he turned his attention back to the child, ignoring Glory completely.

"Come on, Liza," he said, his voice sounding husky and faraway to Glory even though she could have reached out and touched the both of them. "Let's go."

Liza. Glory savored the name. Unable to speak, she watched Jesse and the child go out with the others. When she turned around again, Jill was kneeling backward in the pew in front of Glory's, looking down into her face.

"Feeling better?"

Glory nodded. Now that the initial shock had passed, a sort of euphoria had overtaken her. "I'll be fine."

Jill stood, shrugged into her plaid coat and reached for her purse. "Jesse's looking good, isn't he?"

"I didn't notice," Glory replied as the two women made their way out of the church. Jill turned out the lights and locked the front doors.

Her expression was wry when she looked into Glory's eyes again. "You were always a lousy liar, my friend. Some things never change."

Glory started to protest, then stopped herself. "Okay," she conceded, spreading her hands wide, as Jill led the way to a later-model compact car parked at the curb. She was too shaken to offer an argument, friendly or otherwise. "He looks terrific."

"They say he's never gotten over you."

Glory got into the car and snapped her seat belt in place. Strange, she'd spent the past eight years thinking about Jesse, but now a gangly child with auburn hair and green eyes was upstaging him in her mind. "The little girl—Liza. Where did she come from?"

Jill started the engine and smiled sadly before pulling out into traffic. "You remember Jesse's big brother, Gresham, don't you? He married Sandy Piper, from down at Fawn Creek. They couldn't have children, I guess, so they adopted Liza."

Glory let her head fall back against the headrest, feeling dizzy again. The car and Jill and even the snowy night all fell away like pages torn from a book, and suddenly Glory was eighteen years old again, standing in Judge Seth Bainbridge's imposing study....

She was pregnant, and she was scared sick.

The judge didn't invite her to take a chair. He didn't even look at her. He sat at his desk and cleaned out his pipe with a scraping motion of his penknife, speaking thoughtfully. "I guess you thought you and your mama and that brother of yours could live pretty high on the hog if you could just trap Jesse, didn't you?"

Glory clenched her fists at her sides. She hadn't even told Jesse about the baby yet, and she figured the judge only knew because he and Dr. Cupples were poker buddies. "I love Jesse," she said.

"So does every other girl between here and Mexico." At last, Jesse's grandfather raised sharp, sky-blue eyes to her face. "Jesse's eighteen years old. His whole life is ahead of him, and I won't see him saddled to some social-climbing little chippie with a bastard growing in her belly. Is that clear?"

The words burned Glory, distorted her soul like some intangible acid. She retreated a step, stunned by the pain. She couldn't speak, because her throat wouldn't open.

The judge sighed and began filling his pipe with fresh tobacco. The fire danced on the hearth, its blaze reflected in the supple leather of the furniture. "I believe I asked you if I'd made myself clear, young lady."

Glory swallowed hard. "Clear enough," she got out.

The defiance he'd heard in her tone brought the judge's gaze slicing to Glory's face again. He and Jesse had a tempestuous relationship, but he obviously regarded himself as his grandson's protector. "You'll go away to Portland and have that baby," he said. He waved one hand. "For all I know, it could belong to any man in the county, but I'm taking you at your word that Jesse's the father. I'll meet all your expenses, of course, but you've got to do something in return for that. You've got to swear you'll never come back here to Pearl River and bother my grandson again."

She was trembling from head to foot, though the room was suffocatingly warm. "When I tell Jesse about the baby," she dared to say, "he'll want our child. And he'll want me, too."

Judge Bainbridge sighed with all the pathos of Job. "He's young and foolish, so you're probably right," the bitter old man concluded. He shook his head mournfully. "You leave me no choice but to drive a hard bargain, Missy. A very hard bargain, indeed."

Glory felt afraid, and she wished she hadn't been scared to tell Dylan about her pregnancy. He would have gotten mad all right, but then he'd probably have come with her to answer Judge Bainbridge's imperious summons. "What are you talking about?"

The most powerful man in all of Pearl River County smiled up at Glory from his soft leather chair. "Your brother—Dylan, isn't it? He's had a couple of minor scrapes with the law in recent months."

Glory's heart pounded to a stop, then banged into motion again. "It wasn't anything serious," she said, wetting her lips with a nervous tongue. "Just speeding. And he did tip over that outhouse on Halloween night, but there were others…"

Since Jesse had been one of those others, she left the sentence unfinished.

The judge lit his pipe and drew on the rich, aromatic smoke. He looked like the devil sitting there, presiding over hell, with the fire outlining his harsh features. "Dylan's about to go off to the air force and make something of himself," he reflected, as though speaking to himself. "But I guess they wouldn't want him if he were to be caught trying to break into a store or a house."

Glory felt the color drain from her face. Everybody knew Judge Bainbridge owned the sheriff and the mayor and the whole town council. If he wanted to, he could frame Dylan for anything short of murder and make it stick. "You wouldn't—Judge Bainbridge, sir, my brother doesn't have anything to do with—"

He chuckled and clamped down on the pipe stem with sharks' teeth. "So now I'm 'sir,' am I? That's interesting."

Glory closed her eyes and counted methodically, not trusting herself to speak. She was afraid she'd either become hysterical or drop to her knees and beg Jesse's grandfather not to ruin Dylan's chance to be somebody.

"You will leave town tomorrow morning on the ten o'clock bus," the judge went on, taking his wallet from the inside pocket of his coat and removing two twenty-dollar bills. "If you stay, or tell Jesse about this baby, your brother will be in jail, charged with a felony, before the week is out."

Glory could only shake her head.

Seth Bainbridge took up a pen, fumbled through a small metal file box for a card, and copied words and numbers onto the back of an envelope. "When you arrive in Portland, I want you to take a taxi to this address. My attorneys will take care of everything from there."

She was going to have to leave Jesse with no explanation, and the knowledge beat through the universe like a giant heartbeat. Just that day, out by the lake, they'd talked about getting married in late summer. They'd made plans to get a little apartment in Portland in the fall and start college together. Jesse had said his grandfather wouldn't like the idea, but he expected the old man to come around eventually.

All that had been before Glory's appointment with Dr. Cupples and the summons to Judge Bainbridge's study in the fancy house on Bayberry Road.

"I won't get rid of my baby," she said, lifting her chin. Tears were burning behind her eyes, but she would have died before shedding them while this monster of a man could see her.

Bainbridge's gaze ran over her once, from the top of her head to the toes of her sandals. "My lawyers will see that he or she is adopted by suitable people," he said. And with that he dismissed her.

"Glory?"

She was jerked back to the here and now as the car came to a lurching stop in Jill's slippery driveway. She peered through the windshield at a row of Georgian condominiums she'd seen that morning, while driving around and reacquainting herself with the town. There had been lots of changes in Pearl River over the last eight years; the sawmill was going at full tilt and the place was prosperous.

Jill strained to get her briefcase from the back seat and then opened the car door to climb out. "I know what you're thinking," she said. "You're wondering how I could afford a condo on a teacher's salary, aren't you?"

Actually Glory hadn't been wondering anything of the sort, but before she could say so, Jill went rushing on.

"Carl and I bought the place when we were married," she said, slamming her door as Glory got out to follow her inside. "When we got divorced, I kept the condo in lieu of alimony."

The evergreen wreath on Jill's front door jiggled as she turned the key in the lock and pushed.

"I guess that's fair—" Glory ventured uncertainly.

"Fair!" Jill hooted, slamming the door and kicking off her snow boots in the foyer. "I should hope so. After all, Carl makes five times as much money as I do."

Glory laughed and raised her hands in surrender. "I'm on your side, Jill. Remember?"

Jill smiled sheepishly, and after hanging up her coat and Glory's, led the way through the darkened living room and dining room to the kitchen. "I thought I'd make chicken stir-fry," she said, washing her hands at the sink.

"Sounds good," Glory replied. "Anything I can do to help?" She felt like a mannequin with a voice box inside. She said whatever was proper whenever a comment was called for. But her mind was on Liza, the little girl she'd been forced to surrender to a pack of expensive lawyers nine years before.

Jill shook her head and gestured toward the breakfast bar. "Have a seat on one of those stools and relax. I'll put water in the microwave for tea—or would you rather have wine?"

"Wine," Glory said, too quickly.

Although she didn't make a comment, Jill had definitely noticed Glory's strange behavior.

Nevertheless the two women enjoyed a light, interesting dinner. After a couple of hours of reminiscing, Glory asked Jill to take her back to the diner.

Glory didn't even pretend an interest in going upstairs to her mother's apartment. She plundered her purse for her keys and went from Jill's car straight to her own.

The sports car wasn't used to sitting outside on snowy nights, instead of in the warm garage underneath Glory's apartment complex, but it started after a few grinding coughs. Glory smiled and waved at Jill before pulling onto the highway and heading straight for the sheriff's office.

The same deputy Glory had encountered earlier that day—she saw now that his name tag said Paul Johnson—was on duty at the desk when she hurried in out of the cold.

It took all her moxy to make herself say, "I'd like to see Sheriff Bainbridge, please."

Deputy Johnson smiled, though not in an obnoxious way, and glanced at the clock. "He's gone home now, Glory."

Of course. Glory remembered that Jesse had been dressed in ordinary clothes when he'd come to the church to pick up Liza, instead of his uniform. "He still lives out on Bayberry Road, with his grandfather?" she asked, hoping she didn't sound like a crazy woman with some kind of fatal attraction.

The deputy plucked a tissue from a box on the corner of the desk and polished his badge with it. "The judge has been in a nursing home for five years now. His mind's all right, but he's had a couple of strokes, and he can't get around very well on his own."

Glory skimmed over that information. She couldn't think about Seth Bainbridge now, and she didn't want to take too close a look at her feelings about his situation. "But Jesse lives in the Bainbridge house?"

Officer Johnson nodded. "Yep." He braced his

chubby hands on the edge of the desk, leaned forward, and said confidentially, "Adara Simms will be living out there with him soon enough, unless the missus and I miss our guess. Jesse's been dating her since she moved to town last year. 'Bout time they tied the knot."

Glory did her best to ignore the unaccountable pain this announcement caused her. She nodded and smiled and hurried back out to the parking lot.

The snow was coming down harder than before, and the wind blew it at a slant. The cold stung Glory's face and went right through her coat and mittens to wrap itself around her bones.

The downstairs windows of the big colonial house that had been in the Bainbridge family ever since Jesse's great-great-grandfather had founded the town of Pearl River glowed in the storm. Glory parked her car beside Jesse's late-model pickup truck and ran for the front porch.

She pounded the brass knocker against its base, then leaned on the doorbell for good measure.

"What the—" Jesse demanded, pulling a flannel shirt on over his bare chest even as he wrenched open the door. He was already wearing jeans and boots. "Glory," he breathed.

She resisted the temptation to peer around his shoulder, trying to see if the woman Deputy Johnson expected him to marry was around. "Is Liza here?" she asked evenly.

Grimacing against the icy wind, Jesse clasped Glory by one arm and wrenched her inside the house. "No," he said, on a long breath, after pushing the door closed. "I have legal custody of Liza, but she spends most of the time in town, with my cousin Ilene. I'm always getting called out in the middle of the night, and I don't want to leave her alone." He buttoned his shirt and shoved one hand self-consciously through his hair.

Jesse Bainbridge looked for all the world like a guilty husband caught in the wrong place at the wrong time.

Glory didn't care if she'd interrupted something. "Did you know?" she demanded, taking off her coat.

"Did I know what?" Jesse frowned, looking agitated again.

It was possible, of course, that he really hadn't learned who Liza was, or even that Glory had borne him a child, at all; but it seemed unlikely now. She wouldn't have been surprised to learn that Jesse and his grandfather had been in this together from the beginning.

"I guess the joke was on me, wasn't it, Jesse?" she said. Glory was amazed by her calm manner; inside, she was a raging tigress, ready to claw the man to quivering shreds.

He stood so close that she could feel the heat of his body. "Damn it, Glory, what the hell are you talking about?"

It was then that her control snapped, when she thought of all the Christmases and birthdays she'd missed, all the important occasions, like the appearance of the first tooth and the first faltering step. "God in heaven, Jesse," she spat, all pain and fury, "I hate you for keeping her from me like that!"

His hands came to rest on her shoulders, and their weight and strength had a steadying effect. So did the look of honest confusion in his dark eyes. "I get the feeling you're talking about Liza," he said evenly. "What I *don't* get is why she's any of your concern."

Glory's tears brimmed and shimmered along her lashes, blurring Jesse's features. "Liza's my daughter, damn you," she sobbed. "Mine and yours! I had her nine years ago in Portland, and your grandfather made me give her up!"

Jesse let her go and turned away, and she couldn't see into his eyes or read the expression on his face. "That's a lie," he said, his tone so low she could barely hear him.

CHAPTER THREE

JESSE WALKED INTO the mansion's massive living room, moving like a man lost in a fog, and sank into a leather chair. Glory followed, though he hadn't invited her, and took a seat on the bench in front of the grand piano, her arms folded.

She reminded herself that Jesse was a good actor. He'd been actively involved in the drama club in high school and probably college, too. Surely police work required an ability to disguise his emotions.

It would be no trick at all for him to pretend Liza's identity came as a surprise to him.

"Why didn't you tell me?" he asked, and his voice sounded hollow, raw.

Glory felt as though she'd been wound into a tight little coil. One slip, one wrong word, and she'd come undone in a spinning spiral. "Spare me the theatrics, Jesse," she said, wrapping her arms around her middle to hold herself in. "I know your grandfather let you in on his little secret a long time ago."

Jesse pushed aside a tray on the coffee table containing the remains of a solitary frozen dinner, and swung his feet up onto the gleaming wood. He closed his eyes and rested his head against the back of the couch. "This is crazy. Liza was Gresh and Sandy's child—they adopted her through some agency in California."

Glory stood, shaking her head in angry wonder. "You're incredible," she breathed, bolting from the piano bench and storming back out into the entry hall. Her coat had fallen off the brass tree, and she retrieved it from the floor.

She had one arm in the sleeve when Jesse gripped her by the shoulders and whirled her around.

"Just a minute, Glory," he told her, his brown eyes hot with golden sparks. "You're not going to walk in here and announce that you had my baby and then waltz right out again. Furthermore, you'd better face the fact that Liza isn't that child."

In that moment, Glory made up her mind to stay in Pearl River, even if she had to support herself by working at the diner, and become a part of Liza's life. She'd been forced to give her daughter up once, but she was a big girl now, and it was time she stopped letting people push her around.

Including Jesse.

"You can't get rid of me so easily this time, Jesse. I want to get to know Liza."

A myriad of emotions flickered in Jesse's eyes before he spoke again. "I didn't 'get rid' of you before," he said, his voice husky. "You left me, remember? Without even taking the trouble to say goodbye. My God, Glory, I looked *everywhere* for you. I begged your mother to tell me where you were, and Dylan and I got into three or four fights about it."

Glory didn't try to defend herself. She didn't have the strength. "Dylan couldn't have told you, Jesse, because he didn't know." She paused and sighed. "I guess you and I just didn't have whatever it takes."

She would have turned and walked out of the house

then, but without an instant's warning, Jesse dragged her close and brought his mouth down on hers in a crushing kiss.

At first Glory was outraged, but as Jesse held her in place, his hands cupping her face, all the tumblers inside her fell into place and her heart swung open like the door of a safe. The old feelings rushed in like a tidal wave, washing away all the careful forgetting she'd done over the biggest part of a decade.

"Didn't we?" he countered harshly, when he finally let her go.

Glory was devastated to realize that Jesse still wielded the same treacherous power over her he had when they were younger. She'd been so certain that things had changed, that she was stronger and wiser now, but he had just proven that at least part of her independence was pure sham.

For all of it, she was still Jesse's girl.

She said a stiff goodbye and opened the door.

The snowstorm was raging and the wind caught Glory by surprise, pushing her back against the hard wall of Jesse's chest. She launched herself toward her car, and Jesse was right behind her.

"That glorified roller skate isn't going to get you back to town in this weather!" he bellowed. "Get into the truck!"

Glory considered ignoring his command until she got a glimpse of his face. The look in his eyes, coupled with the rising ferocity of the storm, effectively quashed her plans for a dramatic exit.

She let Jesse hoist her into his pickup truck and sat there shivering and hating herself while he ran back into the house for keys and a coat.

"Don't get the idea that this thing is settled," she warned, when he was behind the wheel, starting the engine and flipping switches to make the heater come on. The motor roared reassuringly, and Glory had to raise her voice. "Liza is my daughter, and I'm not going to turn my back on her a second time."

Jesse shifted the truck into reverse and clamped his teeth together for a moment before answering, "I think it would be better if we talked about this tomorrow, when we're both feeling a little more rational."

Glory folded her hands in her lap. She was overwrought, on the verge of screaming and crying. She desperately needed a night of sound sleep and some time to think. "You're right," she said, hating to admit it.

"Well, glory be," Jesse marveled in a furious undertone, jamming the gearshift from first to second, and Glory ached inside. Once, he'd used that phrase in a very different way.

She bit down hard on her lower lip to keep from shouting at him for stealing all those minutes, hours, weeks and months when she could have been with Liza. And she wept as she thought of the things she'd missed.

When they finally reached the diner, Jesse got out of the truck and came around to help Glory down from the high running board. She pushed his hand aside, and suddenly she couldn't contain her anger any longer.

She stood staring up at him, her hands knotted in the pockets of her coat. "You cheated me out of so many things," she said coldly. "First-grade pictures, Jesse. Dentist appointments and Halloween costumes and bedtime stories. You had no right!"

His hand crushed the lapels of her coat together, his

strength raised her onto her tiptoes. "I loved you," he seethed. "I would have done anything for you, including break my back at the sawmill for the rest of my life to support you and our baby. I've been cheated out of a few things, too, Glory. I figure we're even."

With that, he released her and climbed back into the truck.

Glory grimaced as he sped away from the curb, his tires flinging slush in every direction and then screeching loudly on a patch of bare pavement.

Delphine was waiting up when Glory let herself into the apartment. A symmetrical five-foot Christmas tree stood in a corner of the living room, fragrant and undecorated.

"Was that Jesse?" Delphine asked without preamble.

Glory sighed. "Yes," she answered despondently, peeling off her gloves and coat and putting them away in a tiny closet.

"He sure had his shorts in a wad about something," Delphine commented, obviously fishing for more information.

"Sit down, Mama," Glory said wearily.

Delphine was sipping herb tea from a pretty china cup as she settled herself at one end of the sofa. "If you're going to tell me that Jesse was the father of your baby, Glory, save it. It's no flash."

Glory had a pounding headache, and she sat opposite her mother in a cheap vinyl chair, resting her elbows on her knees and rubbing both temples with her fingertips. "There's a lot more to it than that," she said wearily, wondering how to start. "Mama, you've lived here in Pearl River all this time. You must know about the child Jesse's brother and his wife adopted."

The teacup rattled against its saucer as Delphine set it on the coffee table. It was plain that she was making some calculations. "Yes," she said in an uncertain tone. "It was tragic when they died. Everybody said that plane crash brought on the judge's first stroke."

Glory nodded glumly. "Mama, the baby they adopted was mine." The tears she had been battling all evening welled up and trickled down her cheeks. "Jesse knew—that's the worst part. He sided with his grandfather."

"Are you sure about that?" Delphine frowned thoughtfully. "I'd have thought it would be more Jesse's style to hunt you down in Portland and confront you with the facts. He was shattered when you left, Glory—it was all I could do to keep myself from giving him the address of that home for unwed mothers you were staying in. He definitely wasn't buying my standard story that you were back East, living with my sister and attending a private school, but I think everybody else did."

Sniffling, Glory thrust herself out of her chair and went into the kitchenette for a paper towel. Her reflection showed in the window over the sink, and she could see that her mascara was smeared all over her face and her hair looked as if she'd just stuck one hand into a toaster.

She mopped her cheeks with the towel, not caring what she looked like, and went back to the living room. Seated in her chair again, she blew her nose vengefully. "You had a lot on your mind that summer, with me pregnant right out of high school and Dylan going off to the air force."

Delphine leaned forward slightly, her voice gentle.

"Why didn't you want Dylan to know about the baby, Glory? We were a family—we shared everything."

Glory sighed. There was no point in keeping the secret any longer; Dylan couldn't be hurt by anything Judge Bainbridge or anyone else might do. "Because Jesse's grandfather said he'd have Dylan arrested for something serious, so the air force wouldn't take him. I was left with only one choice."

The color drained from Delphine's cheeks. "My God. Glory, why didn't you tell me all this *then*?"

"Because you would have told Dylan, and he'd have done something really stupid and gotten himself into even worse trouble."

Delphine reached across to clasp Glory's hand. "All of this is in the past," she said with a sigh and a resigned shrug. "What will you do now?"

Glory took a deep breath before answering, "I'm going to stay right here in Pearl River, so I can be near Liza."

"That might not be wise, dear," Delphine pointed out gently. "Liza's life will be turned upside down. She'll be terribly confused."

Shoving a hand through her rumpled hair, Glory sighed again. "I'm not going to tell her who I am, Mama," she said sadly. "I just want to be her friend."

Delphine rose off the old-fashioned couch and folded it down flat. "It's late, sweetheart," she said, disappearing into her bedroom for a few moments and returning with blankets, sheets and a pillow. "And you don't have to make any decisions tonight. Why don't you get some sleep?"

Together the two made up the bed, and Glory went into the bathroom to change into her nightgown, wash away her makeup, and brush her teeth. When she returned, Delphine was waiting, perched on the arm of a chair.

"Glory, I know you've had a shock," she said quietly, "and I understand that your mind is in an uproar. But please don't forget how hard you worked to put yourself through school and build a fine career. Pearl River isn't going to be able to offer you what a big city could."

There was nothing Glory wanted more than to be close to her child. She would have lived in a metropolis or a remote Alaskan fishing village and given up any job. She kissed her mother's cheek without speaking, and Delphine went off to her room.

Glory got out the photo album and flipped to the page where Bridget McVerdy's picture was displayed. Sitting cross-legged in the middle of her couch bed, she touched the eternally youthful face and marveled. If she hadn't been one to pore over old family portraits, she'd never have suspected the truth about Gresham and Sandy Bainbridge's adopted daughter, even though it all seemed so obvious now.

After a long time, Glory set the album back in its place in the cabinet of her mother's old-fashioned stereo, switched out the lamp and crawled into bed.

Beyond the living-room windows, in the glow of the street lamps, transparent, silvery snow edged in gold drifted and swirled hypnotically.

Glory settled deeper into her pillow and yawned. Tomorrow she would pay a visit to Ilene Bainbridge, who ran a bookstore at the other end of Main Street. Glory had never met Ilene before, since, according to Delphine, the woman hadn't come to Pearl River to live until after the judge's first stroke.

Her mind drifted from the future to the past, back and back, to the night Liza was probably conceived. She and Jesse had gone to the lake for a moonlight picnic after the spring dance, and spread a blanket under a shimmering cottonwood tree....

The leaves above them caught the light of the moon and quivered like thousands of coins, and Jesse's dark eyes burned as he watched Glory take sparkling water, delicate sandwiches and fruit from the picnic basket. The surface of the lake was dappled with starlight, and soft music flowed from the radio of Jesse's flashy convertible.

He caught her wrist in one hand and pulled her to her feet to stand facing him on the blanket. "Dance with me," he said.

She'd already kicked off her high-heeled shoes. Laughing, Glory cuddled close to Jesse and raised her head for his kiss. He took her into his arms at the same time he was lowering his mouth to hers.

As always, Jesse's kiss electrified Glory. She didn't protest when he smoothed her white eyelet dress off her shoulders, his hands lightly stroking her skin as he bared it. She and Jesse meant to get married.

Glory's naked breasts glowed like the finest white opal when he uncovered them. The nipples hardened and reached for him, because they knew the pleasure Jesse could give.

"Glory be," he whispered in a strangled voice. "You're so beautiful it hurts to look at you."

She reached up with both hands to unpin her hair, and while her arms were raised, Jesse leaned forward and caught a coral-colored morsel between his lips.

Glory moaned and tried to lower her arms, but Jesse

wouldn't let her. He closed one hand over both her wrists and held them firmly in place, and he gave as much pleasure as he took.

In the next few minutes, their clothes seemed to dissolve. Jesse lowered Glory gently to the blanket and stretched out beside her. While they kissed, his hand moved restlessly over her breasts and her taut stomach.

"Forever," he said breathlessly, his lips moving against the flesh of her neck. "I'll love you forever."

Jesse had long since taught Glory to desire him— their first encounter had taken place on that very spot just a few months before, and she didn't want to talk, not even about forever. Her young body was hungry, and she couldn't think beyond the moment.

"Make love to me, Jesse," she whispered, teasing him by nibbling at his lower lip, and he poised himself above her with a moan. She tasted his earlobe and kissed his neck, and when he entered her with a sudden, desperate thrust, she received him eagerly.

"Tell me you love me," he pleaded raggedly. His back was moist under Glory's hands, and she could see a fine sheen of perspiration glistening on his forehead and along his upper lip.

Her own body was catching fire, and she was moving faster and faster to meet his thrusts and increase the friction. "Jesse—you know—I do—"

"Say it!"

"I love you," she gasped as her body arched suddenly, like a bowstring drawn taut, and pleasure splintered through her. "Oh, God, Jesse, *I love you*!"

Now, lying on a made-down couch in her mother's living room a full decade later, Glory wept. Those two trusting, innocent children were gone for all eternity, replaced by angry and embittered adults who could barely exchange a civil word.

IN THE MORNING, just as she'd expected, Glory looked terrible. Her eyes were puffy and red-rimmed, and there were shadows underneath them, purple as bruises. She showered, put on jeans and a navy blue turtleneck sweater, and pulled her hair back into a French braid. Knowing there would be no hiding the ravages of the night before, she wore very little makeup—just some blusher and lip gloss.

Delphine presented her with a steaming cup of coffee and a bowl of hot oatmeal when she arrived in the bustling diner. The short-order cook was busy in the kitchen, frying up traditional breakfasts for a hungry crowd.

Glory tried to fade into the wall at the end of the counter, but there was no such luck. People knew she was back in town, and they were anxious to talk with her.

No sooner had the telephone lineman gotten off his stool to go out and battle the weather than someone else replaced him. By the time she'd finished her breakfast, Glory had explained to three people that she'd be staying on in Pearl River for a while and agreed just as often that, yes, it was about time her mother finally remarried.

She was just about to make an escape when the little bells over the diner's door jingled and a stream of cold air swept into the warm, brightly lit interior.

"Good heavens, Jesse," Delphine fussed as she set four breakfast specials down in front of as many customers, "shut the door. The furnace in this place burns five-dollar bills!"

Glory felt her throat go tight, as she watched Jesse push the door closed and grin at Delphine. It seemed to Glory that everyone in the place was either looking at him or at her.

"Sorry," he said, taking off his snow-dusted hat with an exaggerated politeness.

At the same time he was zeroing in on the empty stool next to Glory. Reaching it, he turned and looked at her with eyes as cold as the slush outside in the gutter and said, "I brought your car to town."

She would have stood, but he reached out and caught hold of her forearm, effectively pressing her back down.

"Thank you, Jesse," he coached, and though he sounded as though he was teasing, his dark eyes snapped.

"Go to hell," Glory replied in a normal tone. She wasn't about to forget what this man had stolen from her.

Delphine had always said Jesse's grin ought to be registered as a lethal weapon, and he obviously had no compunctions about using it. He smiled at Glory and, for just a moment, she was a teenager again, willing to share her body and soul with this man.

"There's something on the seat of your car that you might be interested in," he said. Then he pushed away from the counter and strolled toward the door, stopping to joke with some of his constituents as he went.

Glory waited until he'd driven away with the waiting Deputy Johnson before hurrying out to her car. She found a plastic bag lying on the seat, filled with snapshots and school photos of Liza. Glory held the package close to her heart as she sped up the outside stairs to the privacy of Delphine's apartment.

While this unexpected gift might have surprised other people, Glory knew it was typical of Jesse. Even when he was angry with someone, he was still more inclined toward kindness than anything else.

She poured coffee in the tiny kitchenette and sat down at her mother's table to go over the pictures, one by one, noting even the smallest changes as Liza progressed from a plump infant to a shy fourth-grader.

"Don't worry, kid," Glory whispered, smiling through her tears. "You'll get past this gangly stage, I promise. And you'll be the prettiest girl in Pearl River."

After putting the pictures carefully back into their plastic bag, she grabbed her purse and coat and went downstairs once more. The breakfast rush was slowing down, but Delphine and her helper were still pretty busy.

"I'm driving back to Portland today, after I stop by Ilene Bainbridge's bookstore," Glory told her mother.

Delphine looked as though she'd drop the tray of dirty dishes she'd gathered up. "What?"

"I just want to pick up a few things I left in storage, Mama. My resumé, some job-hunting clothes. I'll be back tonight."

"Those roads are icy," Delphine warned. "You be careful, and call when you arrive."

Glory kissed her mother's cheek. "I will. See you."

Five minutes later, Glory's car nosed to a stop in the hard, dry snow in front of Ilene's Book Store. Parallel parking had never caught on in Pearl River; people still left their cars at right angles to the sidewalk, the way they'd left horses and wagons years before.

There were Christmas lights in the window of the bookstore, along with a display of crystals catching the cold winter light.

Glory pushed open the door and walked in.

The place had a friendly ambience; there was a rocking chair, complete with a gray tabby cat curled up on the cushion, and a cheerful fire burned in a small Franklin stove. The selection of books, Glory saw at a glance, was eclectic.

"Hello?" Glory called, when no one appeared to wait on her.

A plump woman dressed in a caftan of gold-and-mauve paisley came out of a back room, smiling. Her brown hair was braided and wound into a coronet at her nape, with a bright yellow feather for accent.

"Jesse's friend, Glory," she said with a smile.

Given the new-age flavor of the place, Glory wondered for a moment if the woman was psychic. "Just Glory," she corrected quietly.

"Ilene Bainbridge," the bookshop owner said, extending a bejeweled hand. "I've been hearing about you for years, and just lately the news has gotten even more interesting. It's good to finally make your acquaintance." She shooed away the tabby cat and gestured for Glory to sit down in the rocking chair. "Would you like a cup of licorice tea?"

Before Glory could respond, Ilene disappeared again. Her voice came clearly from the back room.

"Shall I add sugar?"

Glory was looking out the window, watching as fat snowflakes began tumbling from the sky. "Just a teaspoon, please."

Ilene returned with two steaming cups. Handing

one to Glory, she pulled up a plain folding chair and
sat down. Her kind eyes were eager and warm. "It's
nice to sit by a fire on a day like this," she commented.

Sipping her tea, Glory nodded. "Jesse tells me that
Liza spends most of her time here with you."

Since Ilene didn't look at all surprised at the sudden shift in conversation, Glory assumed Jesse had
told her about their relationship and her claim that Liza
was her child. The other woman, who was probably in
her late thirties, smiled. "Liza and I have a little apartment upstairs."

Glory sensed that Ilene was a gentle, even-tempered
woman. She was probably very good to Liza. "I take it
she's had a difficult life so far," she said, feeling guilty.
In those moments, Glory sorely regretted not standing
up to Judge Bainbridge and going straight to Jesse with
the news of her pregnancy. In trying to protect Dylan,
she had caused her daughter a lot of pain and upheaval.

Ilene's smile was gentle. "It's been eventful, that's
for certain. But we love Liza, Jesse and I, and she
knows it. That goes a long way toward making a child
feel secure. Lately, though, she has developed a tendency to speculate almost incessantly about her birth
parents."

Glory thought of the house her mother and Harold had bought, and suddenly she wanted with all her
heart to live in a place like that with Liza and Jesse.
Of course she knew it was impossible—just a Christmas fantasy. She would never trust Jesse again, and
he'd never trust her.

"I want Liza to be happy," Glory said, near tears
herself.

Ilene reached out and patted her hand. "Jesse told me

you were planning to stick around, and I think that's a good idea. You never know what might happen."

Glory set her teacup aside and smiled at the tabby cat, who was curled up a few feet away on the hooked rug in front of the stove, waiting for the human intruder to get out of the rocking chair. "Thank you," she said to Ilene, standing.

The other woman rose and took Glory's teacup. "You'd be welcome to stop by any time," she said. "Even if you weren't shopping for books."

Glory got the message. When she wanted to see Liza, she would be a welcome guest at the bookstore. That was certainly more than she could say for any reception she might get at Jesse's place. "I'll remember," she replied.

She left the store and got back into her car, cranking up the heat and turning on the tape deck. It was a three-hour drive to Portland, and if she wanted to be back before nightfall, she would have to hurry.

Accordingly, five minutes later, Glory was speeding down the open road. The highway had been sanded, and although there were lots of cars in the ditch from the night before, driving conditions were good. The snow had stopped and patches of blue sky were visible in the distance, along with clouds that looked like well-used cotton balls.

She drove straight through, except for a brief stop at the drive-in window of a fast-food restaurant for lunch, and when she reached the storage place, it took a long time to locate the particular boxes she wanted. She found an expensive gold bracelet Alan had given her in the pocket of a tweed blazer.

On impulse she drove to his apartment building,

meaning to leave the piece with one of his neighbors, but his car was parked in the lot, so she knocked on the door. Something inside made her want Alan to know she was all right; that she had hopes and plans, that he hadn't destroyed her.

"Come in, it's open!" he called out, and when Glory stepped inside, she saw that he was packing up his books.

Glory felt only a slight ache in her heart at the sight of him. He was a good-looking man, with his dark hair and blue eyes, but she knew she didn't love him. Maybe she never had.

"Hi," she said, closing the door. "I thought you'd be working." She held up the bracelet. "I just wanted to leave this."

Alan nodded, a sad grin lifting one corner of his mouth. "The bank is sending me to work in one of its outlying branches. You can probably appreciate the irony of that."

Glory was taken aback. If what Alan said was true, she could probably return to her old job right there in Portland. She'd been decisive when she gave notice, but not rude.

Just a few days ago, that position had meant everything to her, but now she could hardly wait to be in Pearl River again. "I'm moving back to my hometown," she said. It seemed strange that she'd once thought she loved this man desperately. Now he seemed insipid, even a little on the wimpy side.

Alan paused in the packing of books to rest his hands on his hips. "Ah, yes—Pearl River. The heartbeat of the American financial community."

Glory ignored his sarcasm, drew a deep breath,

and took a step backward, reaching for the door knob. "Well, Alan—goodbye, and good luck in your new job."

He stretched out a hand toward her. "Glory, stay. At least have dinner with me—we can part friends."

"We can never be friends," Glory responded, and then she opened the door and went out. The moist, chilly wind felt good on her face.

Alan followed her all the way to her car. "I suppose you arrived in the old hometown and found out none of the local women had managed to sink their claws into Jesse Bainbridge," he said, his arms folded across his chest.

She swallowed. "This has nothing to do with Jesse," she said. It wasn't the complete truth, but none of this was any of Alan's business, anyway. "Besides, I think I'm a small-town girl. The cutthroat ways of big-city banking are not for me."

Alan jammed the fingers of one hand through his hair. "Damn it, Glory, I only wanted that promotion so you and I could finally get married and start a family. I knew that wouldn't happen if you were up to your eyeballs in loan applications and appraisals—"

"You *knew*," Glory corrected, "that I'd studied and slaved for that job for years. And when my back was turned, you elbowed your way in."

"Glory, I'm sorry," he said.

She opened the car door. "Gee," she replied cuttingly, batting her eyelashes at him. "You're *sorry*. Well, why didn't you say so before, Alan? That just changes everything."

With that, she got behind the wheel and slammed the door.

Alan slammed his hands down on the hood of her car in pure frustration, and although Glory had never known him to be violent before, she was angered and frightened by the action. She shoved the engine into reverse and sped away.

Reaching the edge of the city, she stopped at a busy restaurant for a cup of coffee and a sandwich. While she was waiting for her order, she borrowed the phone and dialed Delphine's number at the diner.

"Hello, Mama," she said, when her mother answered. "I arrived safely, and now I'm ready to leave again. I'll see you in a few hours."

Delphine's quicksilver sense of humor came through just at the moment when Glory needed it most. "Who is this?" she asked.

CHAPTER FOUR

GLORY ARRIVED BACK in Pearl River, as promised, before nightfall. She and Delphine and Harold had dinner out in nearby Fawn Creek and went Christmas shopping at the mall, another new addition since Glory had first left home.

The next morning she put on a suede suit in a pale shade of rose, accented with a cream-colored silk blouse and gold jewelry, and went down the street to the bank to pay a call on Harvey Baker. Glory hadn't forgotten her mother's remarking, that first day, that Mr. Baker needed an assistant, since the old one had taken a job in Seattle.

Mr. Baker was a substantial man with a full head of white hair and exceptional manners. And he'd already heard that Glory was looking for a job. He took her into his modest office, looked over the resumé she presented, and hired her on the spot.

Glory left the bank feeling almost euphoric. Now all she needed was a place of her own, so she could get out of her mother's way. She called the town's only motel, but it was full. Then she telephoned the real-estate agency and learned there was a one-bedroom place available in an old Victorian house down by the river.

By the time she went into the diner for a very late lunch, Glory not only had a job but a place to live. She would make arrangements for her furniture and personal belongings to be moved as soon as possible.

"Don't you think you're being a little hasty, here?" Delphine asked, when they were alone in the diner after the lunch rush. The fry cook was outside in the alley, arguing with the man who delivered fresh produce. "Glory, maybe it would be better if you just went on with your life and tried to forget about Liza."

"Forget her?" Glory's spoon rattled in her coffee cup as she stirred unnecessarily. The two women were sitting at a table close to the counter. "Mama, could you have ever forgotten Dylan and me?"

"Of course not, but it wasn't the same. I didn't just give birth to you, I raised you." For a moment she averted her eyes, displaying great interest in the rusted metal thermometer affixed to the outside window casing. The snow was coating it, hiding its imperfections. Finally Delphine looked back at her daughter again. "Glory, Jesse's involved with somebody. Her name's Adara Simms and she owns the beauty shop."

Although she wouldn't have shown it, the reminder made Glory feel as though she'd just been slammed in the stomach with a board. She *had* been fostering a fantasy that included Jesse and Liza, whether she wanted to or not, neatly ignoring Adara's existence, and she realized now what dangerous emotional ground she'd been on. "Why didn't you tell me this the other night," she asked moderately, "when you were so sure I had a date with Jesse?"

Delphine sighed. "That was before Mavis Springbeiger came in and told me Jesse planned to give Adara an engagement ring for Christmas."

Glory closed her eyes tightly for a moment. Lord,

but it hurt, the idea of Jesse slipping a ring onto someone else's finger. She didn't dare imagine the wedding itself. "I see," she said woodenly.

Her mother reached out and closed her hand over Glory's fingers, to still their trembling with a squeeze. "Honey, you're young, you're beautiful—you're smart and educated. You don't need Jesse, or even Liza, to make your life complete. There are other men to love you, and you can still have all the babies you want. *Please*, don't limit yourself by staying here and living for the occasional glimpse of your daughter!"

Glory understood what her mother was saying, and it all made sense to her intellect. But her heart, never very amenable to logic, was balking. She sniffled. "If I didn't know better, Mama, I'd swear you were trying to get rid of me."

There were tears in Delphine's eyes, even though she was smiling. "Heaven help me, Glory Parsons, if my conscience would allow it I'd beg you to stay. But I love you very much, and I want you to have the best possible life."

The bell tinkled over the door, and long habit made Delphine stand up and smooth her crisp apron. When she saw that the visitor was Jesse, however, she didn't offer any of her standard greetings. She tossed her daughter a meaningful look and disappeared into the kitchen.

Without being invited, Jesse dragged back Delphine's chair and sat. The expression in his caramel eyes was guarded, and there was a stubborn set to his jaw. Glory sensed that he was full of questions, that beneath his calm exterior was an urge to grab her and shake her until she told him everything about her past.

"You sure know how to clear a room," Glory said, because somebody had to say something and it was clear Jesse wasn't going to extend the courtesy first.

He managed a rigid smile, and Glory noticed that there were snowflakes melting in his glossy brown hair. Jesse had never liked hats. "Ilene told me you visited her yesterday."

Glory drew a deep breath and let it out slowly. "Guilty," she confessed, raising one hand as if to give an oath.

He sat back in his chair for a long moment, regarding Glory as though he expected her to do or say something outlandish. Then he muttered, "I'm prepared to concede that Liza is our child."

"That's big of you," Glory replied smoothly, getting up from her chair and going behind the counter for a cup and a pot of coffee. She poured a cupful for Jesse, refilled her own, and returned the pot to its place before going on. "I assumed you'd come to terms with the idea, when you gave me those pictures of Liza. Thank you for that, by the way."

Now Jesse leaned forward, ignoring the steaming coffee before him. "What I'm *not* willing to concede," he went on, as though she hadn't spoken, "is that you have any right to interfere with Liza's life now. She's been through enough, as it is. I don't want her upset."

Glory's hands trembled as she lifted her cup to her mouth and took a sip. Delphine's coffee was legendary, since she added a secret ingredient before brewing it, but the stuff passed over Glory's tongue untasted. "I've never said I would tell Liza who I am," she said evenly, once she'd swallowed. "I just want to spend time with her. And I will, Jesse, whether you like it or not."

Again, Jesse's jawline tightened. He took a packet of sugar from the container and turned it end over end on the tabletop. "You gave her up," he said. "You handed her over to the authorities and walked away. As far as I'm concerned you made your decision then, and you can't go back on it now."

Glory's instincts warned her to drop the subject for the moment. Jesse wasn't feeling real receptive just then, and pushing would only make him more stubborn. "I hear you're getting married." She said the words as cheerfully as she could.

He averted his wonderful brown eyes, gazing out at the drifting snow, and for a moment he looked so desolate that Glory wanted to put her arms around him and offer him whatever comfort she could. "You hear a lot of things in small towns," he murmured. Then he pushed back his chair and stood. "You're not going to give ground on this, are you? You're going to insist on hanging around."

Glory felt color pool in her cheeks, and she knew her eyes were shooting blue sparks. She'd tried to be civil, but Jesse evidently wasn't going to allow that. "Yes, Jesse," she said quietly. "I'll be staying in Pearl River. I have a job and an apartment."

"Great," he rasped, shoving a hand through his snow-dampened hair.

"There's an old adage, Jesse, about accepting the things you can't change. This is one of those things."

He bit out a curse word. "I suppose you're planning to drag some big-city lawyer into this."

Glory straightened her shoulders. She was glad she was still wearing her suede suit, because it gave her an added air of dignity. "If necessary, I will. But it doesn't have to be that way."

Jesse turned and walked away without another word. The little bell over the door jangled angrily as he wrenched open the door and left.

Delphine came out of the kitchen. "I have to hand it to you, Glory—you were diplomatic."

"I tried," Glory answered. She wanted to go upstairs, throw herself down on the sofa and sob, but she couldn't face the emotional hangover that would come afterward. She glanced at the clock on the wall behind the counter and sighed. "Do you need any help?"

"Roxy will be coming in at the regular time," Delphine replied sympathetically. "You've had a big day. Why don't you get some lunch and then go upstairs and take a nice nap?"

Glory chuckled, but there wasn't even a hint of humor in the sound. "Mama, it's only eleven-thirty in the morning. Do I look like such a wreck that I should be in bed convalescing?"

"Yes," Delphine retorted. But she was smiling.

"Well, I'm not going to lie around with a rose in my teeth," her daughter said firmly. "I have things to do. The first of which is to call the moving company and ask them to bring my furniture. Then I'd better do a little emergency shopping. I'm going to need some stuff to tide me over, in the meantime."

Delphine's expressive eyes went wide. "Nonsense. You can just stay with me until your things arrive. I don't want you camping out in some apartment, sleeping on the floor and eating your meals out of aluminum trays."

Glory took her coat from a hook by the door and put

it on. Slinging her purse strap over her shoulder, she smiled and replied, "Mama, I called the Stay Awhile Motel, but there's no room at the inn. You're madly in love and about to be married. What you don't need right now is a woebegone daughter sleeping on your sofa."

With that, Glory went out into the biting wind again and up the stairs to her mother's apartment. After making the necessary arrangements for her belongings to be brought to Pearl River, she came back downstairs and climbed behind the wheel of her car. Praying her snow tires were as good as the people in the TV commercials maintained, she set out for the mall in the next town.

There, she bought a sleeping bag and an air mattress, a card table and two cheap folding chairs, towels and other necessary household items. Then she returned to Pearl River, driving cautiously in the ever-wilder flurries of snow to the supermarket at the north end of town.

She couldn't help noticing that people were pointing to her and whispering. Glory was sure none of them knew about the baby she'd borne nine years before, but there was no question that the inevitable small-town speculation was going on. The general population was obviously wondering why she'd left town so suddenly all those years before, deserting "poor Jesse Bainbridge" without so much as a fare-thee-well, and whether or not she'd prove to be a problem where his new relationship was concerned.

After she'd taken everything to her empty, chilly apartment and put it away, Glory went on impulse to Ilene's bookstore. Heaven knew, the woman was nothing if not unconventional, but there was a quiet warmth about her that drew the troubled spirit. Glory had no doubt that the local bookseller was a trusted confidante to many people.

Ilene was busy with a customer when Glory entered, but she still greeted her with a wide and welcoming smile and a "come-in" gesture of one beringed hand.

Glory went to the shelves and busied herself selecting mystery novels. She had a passion for the books, especially if they boasted some unusual element, such as a vampire or a werewolf.

"I take it you've talked to Jesse recently," Ilene said softly, startling her newest customer. Glory hadn't heard her approach.

"You must be psychic," Glory replied with a sigh.

Ilene smiled and glanced at the books in Glory's hands. "You don't have to buy things for an excuse to talk to me," she said. "I consider you a friend, and you're welcome here any time."

Glory felt quick, illogical tears burn behind her eyes, but she managed to hold them back. She held the books a little tighter. "I read a lot," she said in a small voice.

Ilene took her arm and gently ushered her toward the rocker and the warm stove. She shooed away the tabby cat and bid her guest to sit down. "What did Jesse say to you?" she asked, taking the other chair.

After a pause, Glory replied with a despondent shrug, and said, "He thinks I ought to leave town." Although neither woman had ever mentioned the fact, Glory knew Ilene was aware Glory had borne Jesse's child, and that the child was Liza.

Ilene sat forward in her chair, her hands calmly folded. "Will you?"

Glory shook her head, arranging and rearranging the paperback books on her lap. "No. I must admit my mother suggested the same thing—that I just go on with my life somewhere else—but I can't. Something inside insists on staying right here where I can be close to my child."

"Then that's probably what you should do," Ilene commented. "Do you plan to tell Liza who you are?"

"No," Glory replied quickly. "That would only confuse her. I just want to be her friend, and I don't know why Jesse can't understand that."

Ilene smiled. "He's not trying, at least not at the moment. But I'm sure this has all been a terrific shock to him. After all, it isn't every day a man finds out that his niece is really his daughter. Jesse must feel as though he's wandered onto the set of a soap opera."

"I know," Glory agreed with a nod. "Believe me, I didn't expect to come home for Christmas and my mother's wedding and find out that the baby I'd given away was right here in Pearl River, being raised as a part of the Bainbridge family."

With a chuckle and a responding nod, Ilene got up to brew tea. She returned minutes later with two steaming cups.

"This time it's chamomile," she said. "That's really soothing, you know."

Glory was all for anything that would calm her jangling nerves.

"I'll talk to Jesse myself," Ilene said decisively, while her guest sipped herbal tea. "Perhaps I can get him to see reason."

"I'd be very grateful," Glory said. "I don't really want to approach Liza until Jesse gives me some kind of go-ahead, but I can't wait forever."

"Of course you can't," Ilene agreed as an older man bustled eagerly in from the cold.

Glory recognized him as Mr. Pellis, the principal at Pearl River High back when she and Jesse were in school.

"Got any more of that tea, Ilene?" he demanded jovially, in that booming voice that had called a halt to so many food fights and hallway spit-wad barrages. "This weather is enough to chill a man to the marrow!"

Ilene bustled back to brew another cupful, and Mr. Pellis turned his kindly gaze to Glory.

"Aren't you the Parsons girl?" he asked. "The one who took up two pages in your class's senior yearbook?"

Glory smiled, nodded, and started to stand, but Mr. Pellis gestured for her to remain seated. He took off his hat, revealing a perfectly bald head, and then his scarf and overcoat, and hung all the items up.

"I'm retired now," Mr. Pellis went on, taking Ilene's chair. He tapped his temple with one finger. "But I remember things. You dated the Bainbridge boy, didn't you?"

Glory swallowed and nodded again. She supposed she shouldn't be surprised that Jesse found his way into virtually every conversation. After all, this was Pearl River, his hometown, and he was sheriff.

Mr. Pellis chuckled and slapped his thighs with both hands. "Always thought you'd end up in the movies or something, you were so pretty. What do you do for a living?"

"I'm a loan officer," Glory replied, rising from her chair. It was getting late, and Delphine would be watching for her. "As of Monday morning, I'll be working right down the street at the First National."

Mr. Pellis beamed as though she'd just been elected president and he was personally responsible. "Well, good," he said. "I'll stop by and say hello when I drop off my pension check."

Glory's smile was warm. "I'll be expecting you," she said. Then she paid Ilene for her books and went back to the diner.

She was curled up on the couch, dressed in jeans, sneakers and a red turtleneck sweater, reading one of the mysteries she'd bought, when the telephone jangled.

Startled, Glory jumped before reaching out to snatch up the receiver. "Hello?" she said a little uncharitably.

"Hello," responded a voice she immediately recognized. "This is Jesse." He sounded weary and more than a little annoyed, and Glory guessed without being told that Ilene had talked with him. She held her breath, waiting for him to go on.

After a long, electric silence, he did.

"They still have that community Christmas Party every year, with the sleigh riding and everything," he announced, each word dragged out of him by an invisible mule team. "It's tomorrow night, and I was wondering if you'd like to go. I mean, it won't be a date or anything, because Adara will be along, but you've been wanting to spend time with Liza…."

Glory was well aware that, as a beggar, she couldn't be a chooser. "Thanks," she said softly. Sincerely. "I appreciate it."

"I don't want you telling her anything."

Who, Glory wanted to ask, *Liza or Adara?* But she controlled herself because she was in no position to be making smart remarks. "I've already told you, Jesse—I won't say anything to Liza that would upset her. You can trust me."

"I thought I could, once," he responded in a distracted voice, and Glory closed her eyes against the pain of the jibe. "Listen, just meet us at the hill tomorrow night when the sun goes down. We'll be somewhere around the bonfire."

Glory was nodding, and it was a moment before she realized Jesse couldn't see her and said quickly, "I'll be there. Thanks, Jesse."

"Right," he answered in the clipped tone she'd come to expect from him. And then he hung up.

Glory bounded off the couch, upsetting her book and the crocheted afghan she'd spread over herself earlier. "Yippee!" she yelled.

The cry brought Delphine out of the bedroom, where she'd been dressing for a bowling date with Harold. "You won the lottery?" she inquired with a wry grin.

"Better," Glory crowed. "Jesse's going to let me see Liza."

Although Delphine shook her head, her eyes revealed a mother's happiness in her daughter's joy. She came and took both Glory's hands in hers. "Promise me you'll be careful, baby," she whispered. "This situation has a very high heartache potential—especially for you."

Glory was deflated for a moment, but she immediately perked up. "Jesse did make a point of telling me he was bringing Adara, but I'm not going to let that ruin things. He can marry King Kong, for all I care, just as long as I get to see Liza."

Delphine patted her daughter's cheeks. "Like I said,

be careful. Here be dragons, fair maiden. Big ones, with fire in their noses."

Glory chuckled and kissed Delphine's forehead. "I'll get through this without so much as a singed eyelash," she promised.

But Delphine didn't look convinced.

GLORY SPENT THE night at her new apartment, staying up late to finish the first of the mystery novels she'd bought because she was too excited to sleep. The place was freezing cold when she awakened, and she shivered while trying to crank on the ancient steam radiators that stood under each window.

Outside, the world was a wonderland of white velvet strewn with tiny diamonds. Snow mounded on top of the row of mailboxes across the street and the cars parked on the road.

After taking a shower and dressing warmly, with long underwear under her jeans and flannel shirt and two pairs of socks inside her hiking boots, Glory donned a jacket and walked to the diner. Her breath made white plumes in the air, and the cold turned her cheeks and nose red.

By the time she reached her destination, she figured she probably looked a lot like Rudolph.

Delphine greeted her as though she'd spent the night in an igloo in the Arctic, shuffling her to a table, pouring coffee for her, insisting that she have a hot breakfast.

"You're not used to this, after Portland's milder climate," Delphine fretted.

Glory just smiled. She'd been on her own a long time, and Alan had never been much for making a fuss. It was sort of nice to have somebody taking care of her, at least for a few minutes.

After breakfast, Glory insisted on staying to help with dishes and then the noon rush. She was living for that evening when she would see Liza, and if she didn't keep busy in the meantime she'd go absolutely crazy.

Once the lunch clientele had eaten and gone, however, things slowed down considerably. Glory called Jill, and the two of them went to a matinee at the Rialto.

"I've always said Ted Danson was wasted as a bartender," Jill commented as she and Glory left the theater about two hours later.

Glory chuckled. "Are you going to the snow party tonight?" she asked.

Jill shook her head. "Normally I would. But I've got a hot date with a guy over in Fawn Creek. Wish me luck." They crossed the street to where Jill's car was parked—behind a four-foot pile of snow. "The mad plower has struck again."

A teenage boy came out of the hardware store wearing a heavy coat and blushing, either from the cold or from the presence of two women, to shovel a path for Jill. Soon Glory's friend was driving away, tooting her horn and waving.

Glory looked at her watch and groaned. It was still hours until time for the community party.

Finally, however, the time came. She rode to McCalley's Hill, which overlooked the town, with Harold and Delphine, who were bundled up and equipped with hot cocoa in a big thermos bottle. An enormous bonfire was blazing in the big clearing at the bottom of the slope, and already kids and adults alike were racing down the long incline on their sleds.

When Glory spotted Jesse standing with Liza and a slender woman dressed in a pink quilted ski outfit, she was struck by a sudden attack of shyness. Now that the moment she'd been looking forward to for twenty-four hours had finally come, she wasn't sure how to approach the trio, and she had no idea what to say.

Delphine solved the problem by gripping Glory by one arm and fairly propelling her into the cozy little circle. "Hello, Jesse," Glory's mother said with a bright smile. "Liza, Adara, I'd like you to meet my daughter, Glory."

Adara had dark hair and beautiful brown eyes, Glory noticed, but her attention immediately shifted to Liza.

The child looked up at her with an unhesitating, friendly smile. "Hi," she said. "I've seen you in Uncle Jesse's yearbook. It says, 'Glory, Glory, Hallelujah' over your picture."

Adara's gaze came quickly to Glory's face, and there was something sad in it.

"It's just a play on my name," Glory told Liza. "Listen, I'm new in town..." She carefully avoided Jesse's gaze, though she could feel it burning against her face, just like the bonfire. "Well, okay, I'm not new, but I've been away for a long time, and I could use a friend to go sledding with."

Liza, who was apparently a naturally gregarious child, looked delighted and pointed to her nifty Red Flier. "I'll share with you. Come on!"

Glory was intent on following Liza up the hill, when Jesse reached out and took a tight hold on her arm.

"Remember," he said cryptically.

Glory understood him all too well. "Your orders are burned into my gray cells, Sheriff Bainbridge," she replied with a cocky grin and a salute, and then she hurried after the eager little girl pulling a sled behind her.

She and Liza raced down the hill on the sled among a horde of other sledders, and then, laughing, ran up again. They repeated the process until their cheeks, feet and mittened hands were numb.

"I think we'd better stand by the fire for a while and have something warm to drink, don't you?" Glory suggested breathlessly to the sturdy child standing beside her, surveying the hillside with an attitude of conquest.

Liza sighed, her green eyes rising to Glory's face. She smiled, and her freckles showed like specks of gold in the firelight. "Okay," she said. Her gaze was full of generous curiosity. "You said you were new in town. Where do you live? Do you have a job?"

Glory explained about her new position at the bank and her apartment in the blue-and-gray Victorian house near the bend in the river.

Liza was familiar with both places.

Adara was standing next to the fire, sipping cider, when Glory and Liza approached with cups of their own. There was no sign of Jesse, and his girlfriend looked politely uncomfortable.

While Liza was occupied talking to a friend a few feet away, Adara smiled shakily and asked, "Will you be staying in Pearl River long?"

Glory sensed the woman's fears and felt a strange need to reassure her. "Yes, as a matter of fact, I plan to settle here. I'll be working at the bank."

Adara seemed composed, although her hand trembled a little, causing some of her cider to spill over into the snow. "Isn't that nice," she said, and though she didn't speak unkindly, there was no conviction in the words.

Before Glory could reply, Adara spotted some people she knew, trilled out a hello, and hurried off toward them.

Glory was relieved. Adara was probably a relatively new arrival in Pearl River, but she had to know that Jesse and Glory had been high-school sweethearts. Like every small town, this little burg had its busybody contingent.

"Ready to go again?" Liza asked eagerly, just as Glory was finishing her cider.

"Sure!" Glory responded. She was exhausted and cold, but she would have sledded forever if it meant she could be close to her daughter. She would be grateful until the day she died for the child's ready acceptance.

Each of them took hold of the rope and pulled the Flier up the hill, careful to stay out of the way of the sleds zooming down from the top. Once they reached the summit, however, Jesse appeared out of nowhere.

The look he gave Glory was one of annoyance, as though he'd been dragged to the crest of that hill, kicking and screaming. "Once for old time's sake?" he asked, and the words were, of course, unwillingly spoken.

Glory remembered the winters she and Jesse had sledded down this very slope together, and her heart rate quickened by a beat or two. She looked at Liza and tried to speak in a normal tone of voice. "Would that be okay with you?"

Liza looked pleased, and the pom-pom on the top of her blue stocking cap bobbed as she nodded her head.

Glory settled on the front of the sled, instead of the

back as she would have with Liza, and shivered a little
when she felt the warmth of Jesse's breath against her
nape. He wrapped his legs around her and hooked his
heels into the front of the sled, then his arms embraced
her, his hands gripping the rope.

They went careening down the hillside, the wind
rushing in their faces, cold enough to sting. At the bottom the sled suddenly overturned and sent them both
tumbling over the snow.

When they finally came to a stop, Jesse was lying
on top of Glory. He swore and rolled away, but not before she felt the hard evidence of his desire pressing
against her thigh.

CHAPTER FIVE

JESSE DROPPED LIZA off at Ilene's first, then drove to Adara's condo overlooking the river.

She stood waiting for his kiss there on her doorstep, and for the life of him Jesse couldn't give it.

"You might as well tell me about Glory," she said quietly, holding her chin at a proud angle. "I run a beauty shop, remember, and by Monday afternoon I'll know every sordid detail."

He jammed splayed fingers through his hair and swallowed a curse. "We went together in high school, all right?" he finally bit out a few seconds later.

Adara pretended to recoil slightly. "Aren't we defensive?" she inquired sweetly. "I'm not a fool, Jesse. I've already guessed that you loved her."

Loved her? He'd been so crazy about Glory that he couldn't put one sensible thought in front of another. And after she'd left without one damn word of explanation, he'd honestly thought he was going to die of the pain. He'd hounded her family and friends for weeks, trying to find out where she'd gone.

"What do kids that age know about love?" he countered irritably.

"Sometimes a lot," Adara replied.

"I don't want to talk about it."

"That's obvious, Jesse. But I can't let things go at

that. I won't stumble along, thinking you and I have a future together, only to find out that you're still hung up on your high-school sweetheart."

Jesse thought of the diamond engagement ring he'd bought. Until just a few days ago, he'd been sure he'd finally reached the point where he could put Glory out of his mind, get married and start the family he wanted more than anything else. Now he felt as though he'd just collided with a linebacker at a dead run; not only did he hurt everywhere, he no longer knew down from up, or in from out.

"Jesse?" Adara prompted.

He hated himself for the heartache he saw in her eyes. She was a nice person, and she didn't deserve to be hurt. "Maybe we'd better cool it for a little while," he said with extreme effort. "Just until the holidays are over and I can think things through."

Adara kissed his cheek, and her hand shook as she turned the key in the lock. So did her voice. "Call me when you've worked it out," she said. And then she opened the door and went inside.

Jesse stifled a roar of outraged frustration and flung himself down the sidewalk toward his truck, which was parked at the curb and still running.

He guessed that said a lot, right there. He hadn't even bothered to shut the engine off, when even a few days before, he would have stayed until just before the sun came up.

Reaching the truck, Jesse jerked off his gloves and flung them into the cab, one after the other, not giving a damn where they landed. Then he got behind the wheel and sped away.

At home, he brought the truck to a lurching stop in the driveway and stormed toward the front door.

Not only had he wounded Adara, he'd stirred up a whole lot of old sensations he didn't want to deal with. Ever since he and Glory had gone flying off that sled—hell, ever since he'd gotten *on* the damn thing with her—he'd ached in every muscle between his eyebrows and his shins.

He opened the door, went inside and slammed it again. Instead of hanging up his bulky coat, he hurled it in the general direction of the coat tree. Then he marched into the living room, to the liquor cabinet, and poured himself a double shot of brandy.

A few sips settled him down a little, and he ventured into his grandfather's study and squinted at the shelves until he found the Pearl River yearbook from when he and Glory were seniors.

After tossing back a little more brandy, he carried the annual to the heavy rolltop desk, with all its cubbyholes and drawers, and sat down in the swivel chair. His fingers flipped the pages unerringly to the layout honoring Glory.

She'd been homecoming queen that year, and head cheerleader, and there were shots of her wearing a sun top and cutoff jeans at the senior picnic, making a speech on graduation day, sitting on Santa's lap at the Christmas dance.

Jesse couldn't help smiling at the banner headline spread across the top of the adjoining pages. *Glory, Glory, Hallelujah.*

"Amen," Jesse said aloud, his gaze going back to the snapshot of Glory at the class picnic. He'd taken her to his room that sultry afternoon and made slow, hot love to her, and she'd responded without holding anything back.

Just the memory made him harden painfully. He slammed the yearbook closed and tossed it onto the desk.

Whatever he did, he had to remember that Glory was Glory. She'd proven beyond a doubt that she cared only about her own interests and she'd betray people who trusted her, to attain her objectives. As delectable as she looked, all grown-up, it was unlikely that she'd changed in any fundamental way.

She wanted Liza, and that meant he had to be on his guard. Despite Glory's protests that she wasn't going to upset the child, Jesse had no illusions about her conscience.

She probably didn't have one.

Still he needed to see her, talk to her, hold her. He phoned the office to let them know he'd be on the road, put his coat back on, and went out to his truck again.

He knew Glory had taken an apartment, he even knew where it was. But some instinct took him by the diner instead, and he saw her through the snow-trimmed window, sitting there all alone, her head bent over a book or something.

Almost as furious with himself as he was with Glory, he parked the truck and strode over to the door.

The "closed" sign was in place and the door was locked, but Glory came and admitted him right away. Her blue eyes were wide and wary, and standing there, Jesse forgot everything he'd meant to say.

"WHAT HAVE I done now?" Glory asked with a sad smile as she relocked the door and went back to the table where she'd been sitting, going over Delphine's quarterly taxes. Earlier, it had seemed like a good, practical way to pass what remained of the evening, as well as an excuse to get out of her lonely apartment.

Jesse helped himself to coffee behind the counter, then crossed the room to join her. After taking off his jacket and hanging it over the back of his chair, he sat down. "I just wanted to tell you that Liza had a really good time with you tonight."

Glory could tell he hadn't meant to say that, and the bewildered expression in his eyes made her feel strangely jubilant. "She's a wonderful, outgoing child," she replied. "You and Ilene must be doing a very good job with her."

He relaxed at that, and took a sip of his coffee. "Ilene strikes most people as a little weird, at first, but she'd walk through fire for Liza, and the kid knows it. That makes for a lot of security."

It was so nice to be talking civilly with Jesse for once that Glory felt her throat tighten. "We had that, Dylan and I, whatever else we were lacking. We both knew Mama was committed to us with her whole heart."

Jesse shifted in his chair, looking slightly uncomfortable again. "I don't remember my parents very well. Gresh was a lot older than I was, of course, and Gramps had his own fish to fry. As you know, he and I never got along very well."

Glory found it impossible to picture that vicious old man in such a homey context as "Gramps." "I've heard your grandfather suffered a couple of strokes and had to be confined to a nursing home. I'm sorry." And she was, though she felt no remorse for hating Seth Bainbridge for so long, just a certain weariness.

"They take good care of him at the convalescent center," Jesse said. He was avoiding her eyes.

Glory glanced down at her mother's receipts and tax forms, at a temporary loss for something to say, and Jesse's chair legs scraped against the linoleum floor as he stood.

The idea of his leaving alarmed Glory, and she was further upset to find herself wanting him to stay.

But he only went to the jukebox and leaned against it, studying the selections. Delphine believed in moldy oldies, as she called them, and many of the songs dated from the fifties and sixties. The latest offerings were from the early seventies.

After a few moments Glory heard a coin drop into the slot, and she braced herself. Sure enough, Jesse chose the ballad that had been playing on the radio when they'd made love for the first time up at the lake.

She squeezed her eyes shut as an avalanche of emotional pain cascaded down on her.

Then Jesse took her hand, pulled her to her feet and into his arms and they danced. Glory was overwhelmed not only by memories but by the presence and the substance and the scent of Jesse. She wanted to melt against him, become a part of him.

He held her close, and the contact was so excruciatingly sweet that it brought tears to Glory's eyes.

"Don't do this," she pleaded in a bare whisper, certain that he understood his power over her and meant to use it. "Please."

He curved a finger under her chin and lifted. The words he said then were the first gentle ones he'd spared her since her return to Pearl River. "All I want is to hold you, Glory."

It wasn't all he wanted, and Glory knew it. She'd felt his need earlier, when they'd fallen off the sled, and she could feel it now. She fought to reason with him, and with herself. "This isn't right. You're engaged."

He maneuvered them over to the switch beside the door and turned off the lights, so that nothing illuminated the diner except for the multicolored glow of the jukebox. Their song finished and started again, and Jesse bent his head to nuzzle at Glory's neck.

"I'm not engaged," he finally countered, his voice a sleepy rumble, his breath making Glory's flesh tingle under its warmth. "I haven't asked Adara to marry me, and I told her tonight that I needed some time."

Glory swallowed and wondered if he felt the tremor of elation that went through her at this announcement. She was quick to remind herself, however, that it didn't really mean anything. For all that he was holding her so tenderly now, a part of Jesse hated her and he wouldn't hesitate to wreak any kind of vengeance he could manage.

"Jesse, go home," she said thickly. "You shouldn't be here."

He spread his hands over her trim bottom and pressed her close against him and, God help her, she couldn't even take a step back in the interest of self-preservation. Her nipples were throbbing beneath her flannel shirt and winter underwear, and there was a soft, expansive ache where Jesse would enter her.

He found her lips with his own and kissed her treacherously, encircling her mouth with the tip of his tongue and then invading her with it. Instead of fighting, she bid him welcome with her own, sliding her arms up his chest and plunging her fingers into his hair.

The kiss ended, but Jesse didn't withdraw. He bit Glory's lower lip lightly and lifted one of his hands to her breast, cupping it in his fingers, teasing the nipple with his thumb.

"Come home with me," he pleaded in a ragged whisper, "or God help me, I'm going to take you right here."

The words brought Glory abruptly to her senses, and she pushed back out of his arms, gasping for breath as though she'd just surfaced after long minutes underwater. "Damn you, Jesse," she sputtered, "we're not eighteen anymore. And you're not going to get back at me for my supposed wrongs by dragging me off to your bed!"

He hooked his fingers in the waistband of her jeans and hauled her forward, so that she collided with his thighs and the hard heat of his shaft. "Remember how it felt when I was lying on top of you in the snow tonight?" he breathed, and Glory was awash in yearning. "I'm surprised we didn't turn the whole hill to slush."

Jesse was right; there was something hot burning between them, even after all that time and heartbreak. He could take her there in the dark diner if he chose to, and she despised him for that power.

"Get out," she ordered with the very last of her strength.

Miraculously he retreated a step, allowing her to put things somewhat back into perspective again. "I want to take you to dinner Monday night," he said. "We need to talk."

Glory still couldn't manage to speak normally. "J-just about Liza," she stammered. "N-no more dancing."

He reached out and touched the tip of her nose in a gesture that was achingly familiar. "No promises," he said hoarsely. And then he opened the door and went out, just as their song began to play for the third time on the jukebox.

GLORY SPENT SUNDAY working at the diner and then helping Delphine and Harold put away early wedding presents and various personal belongings in their brand new house. The next day she started her job at the bank.

She had a small office and plenty of people wanted to borrow money, since Pearl River seemed to be in some kind of development boom, so the morning went by rapidly. She had lunch in the coffee room with some of the tellers and secretaries, then returned to the pile of work left behind by Mr. Baker's previous assistant.

It was a surprise when, at quarter after three, Glory's office door squeaked open and Liza's bright green eyes peered at her around the edge.

"Am I bothering you?"

Glory couldn't think of anyone she'd rather have seen, though her mind *had* been straying to Jesse with disturbing frequency. Thanks to him, she'd been in misery most of the weekend.

"Of course you're not bothering me," she said quickly. "Come in."

Liza took in the office in a series of thorough glances. "Nice place," she said.

Glory gestured toward a chair. "Sit down, if you'd like."

The child wriggled into the seat facing Glory's desk, unbuttoning her coat at the same time. Although she was the spitting image of Glory's great-grandmother, there were things about Liza that reminded her of Jesse, too, and of herself.

The steady gaze was Jesse's, the tremulous voice her own.

"I'm adopted," Liza announced without preamble.

Glory was grateful for the chair that supported her, because she knew her legs wouldn't have managed it at the moment. "I see," she finally replied after a long time. She remembered then that Ilene had told her Liza thought a lot about her birth parents.

"Susie Harbrecker says my mom and dad didn't want me, so they gave me away."

A momentary desire to find Susie Harbrecker and shake her until her teeth rattled possessed Glory, then she regained her equilibrium. "I'm sure that isn't true," she said as evenly as she could. "There are lots and lots of good reasons why people put babies up for adoption, Liza. Sometimes they're too poor to care for them properly, and sometimes they're too young and immature." *And scared*, Glory added in her mind.

Liza gave a philosophical sigh, apparently willing to accept Glory's words at face value. She seemed naturally drawn to Glory, just as Glory was to her. "I'm going to be in the Christmas program at church."

Glory smiled, relaxing a bit. "I know. I watched you practice one night."

That seemed to please Liza, but then she frowned. "Of course, I'll probably have trouble coming up with an angel costume. Aunt Ilene sewed in one of her past lives, but she doesn't know how anymore."

Before Glory could comment on that startling statement, there was a brisk rap at the door and then Jesse came in. His expression was stormy, as though he'd just caught Glory plotting the downfall of the free-enterprise system.

If Liza picked up any of the difficult undercurrents in the room, she gave no sign of it. "Hi, Uncle Jesse," she chirped, jumping up and throwing her arms around him.

He gave her an easy hug, but his dark eyes were fixed on Glory, and they were full of wariness and suspicion. "Why don't you wait outside in the car?" he asked politely, his hand resting on Liza's shoulder. "I want to talk with Ms. Parsons for a moment."

Somewhat reluctantly, Liza said goodbye to Glory and left.

"That was some pretty fancy detective work," Glory said, when they were alone. "How did you know she was here?"

He braced his hands against the edge of her desk and leaned forward, glowering ominously into her face. "I know everything that goes on in this town, so don't try to pull anything."

Glory snapped the pencil she was holding into two pieces, though her manner was otherwise pleasant. Or at least courteous. "Why are you acting like I was about to kidnap her and head for South America? We were only talking."

"You have a nasty habit of skipping out at the most inopportune moments," Jesse said. "I wouldn't put anything past you."

"Then there would seem to be no point in our going out to dinner tonight and talking this thing over like adults. You've already drawn the battle lines."

Jesse sighed raggedly and turned away to stand at the office's one window. Once again, snow was coming down. "Maybe I did overreact," he conceded in a barely audible voice. He looked back at her over one sturdy shoulder. "I don't know if I can talk this out with you, Glory, when I haven't even managed to work it through for myself yet."

"Have you told Liza that you're her father?"

He rested his back against the sill and folded his arms. "No," he replied. "She's a sharp kid. If I told her, it wouldn't be long before she guessed who her mother is."

"What would be so terrible about that?"

Jesse thrust himself away from the window, crossed the small room, and opened the door. "It would give you a kind of power I don't want you to have," he answered flatly. "I'll pick you up at six and we'll have dinner in Fawn Creek, if that's all right with you. They've got a pretty classy Mexican place."

Glory couldn't imagine why she wasn't refusing to go out with him, why she wasn't telling Jesse Bainbridge what to do with his Mexican dinner. "Okay," she said. "You know where I live?"

He raised one eyebrow. "I know where you live," he responded. And then, to Glory's enormous relief, he was gone.

At five she left the office, bundled up in her coat, laughing and talking with the other employees who were on their way out, too. In just a few minutes she arrived at her apartment.

There, Glory stripped off the blue-and-gray striped suit she'd worn to work that morning, took a shower, blew her hair dry, and put on a black crepe pleated skirt that reached to mid-calf and a long sweater of the same color, threaded through with silver. She had just finished applying her makeup when the doorbell rang.

Glory crossed her empty living room and opened the door to admit Jesse, who looked handsome in charcoal slacks and a cream colored fisherman's sweater. He wore a tweed overcoat, too, and his brash brown eyes moved over Glory's figure with undisguised appreciation.

She longed for an excuse to touch him, but there was none. "You look very nice," she said.

There was something wry about his grin. "So do you," he answered.

At first, it was like old times. Jesse helped Glory into her coat and held her elbow protectively as he escorted her to the classic old luxury car parked outside.

"No truck?" Glory teased, as she sank into the cushiony leather seat.

Jesse shut the car door and came around to get behind the wheel before answering. "Nothing but the best for you," he said, and each word was stretched taut, like a violin string.

Heat flowed out of the vehicle's heater, ruffling Glory's thin skirt, and soft music streamed from its impressive stereo system. "Your grandfather's car," she reflected, just to break the silence. "We went to the prom in this car, didn't we?"

She regretted the question instantly.

Jesse's eyes smoldered as he looked at her for a long moment before nodding and pulling away from the curb. They'd made love that night after the dance, and they'd been so excited that they hadn't even taken off all their clothes. Jesse had set Glory astraddle his lap and, gripping her hips, lowered her onto his shaft...

She was desperate, so she tried again. Reaching out to switch off the heat, she asked, "Do you think it's going to keep snowing like this?"

Jesse was no help, at all. "Until February or March, probably. I guess you're not used to it anymore, since you've been living in the western part of the state."

Glory gave a strangled cry of frustration. "Jesse, don't just leave me dangling. I need some assistance here."

He gave her a teasing glance that did as much to ignite her senses as her memories had. His eyes said assistance wasn't what she needed, though his lips moved only to curve into a half grin.

"So, did you win the election by a wide margin, or what?" she threw out, in another wild attempt at normal conversation.

"Were you in love with that guy you left behind in Portland?" he countered out of the blue.

Glory was instantly defensive, and she was grateful for it. "How did you know about Alan?"

"I asked you if you loved him."

"No—yes—I don't know!" How could she say, straight out, that she'd never loved another man besides Jesse himself? "Damn it, this isn't fair. You said we were going to talk about Liza!"

Jesse was shaking his head, and though his tone was polite, his words were downright inflammatory. "At least I know I'm not the only guy you ever ran out on. How many others were there?"

Glory wanted to slug him, but the roads were slick and she couldn't be sure he wouldn't lose control of the car, so she knotted her fists in her lap and savored the fantasy. "Take me home."

"I'll be glad to—at the end of the evening, when we've settled something. Anything."

They were leaving the city limits and climbing along the well-plowed tree-lined highway that led to Fawn Creek. Glory was startled when Jesse pulled the car off the road into a secluded rest area that was familiar for all the wrong reasons.

He shut off the engine and the lights and, after Glory's eyes adjusted, she could see him fairly clearly in the muted glow from the dashboard. "You're driving me crazy," he said, as though that explained everything.

"Start this car this instant," Glory sputtered, on the verge of panic. She was a strong woman, certainly not promiscuous, but Jesse Bainbridge had always been her downfall. "I want to go home."

"I know damn well what you want, and so do you. And maybe we're not going to get anywhere with the rest of our lives until we've taken care of it."

Glory grabbed ineptly at the door handle, but she never made contact. "Jesse, if you force me—"

"I won't have to force you," he pointed out, his fingers resting lightly on the back of her neck. "And we both know it."

He pushed a button somewhere, and the seat back eased slowly downward until she was lying prone. Before she could cope with that development, Jesse was kissing her, and one of his strong hands was resting on her thigh.

He snapped open her seat belt and laid it aside, then went right on kissing her, while his hand moved her skirt slowly upward.

She managed to free her mouth from his, though

it didn't like its liberty and wanted to surrender. "Jesse—"

Jesse eased her long, glistening sweater up and over her head, and deftly unfastened the front catch on her bra. He was watching, waiting, when her plump breasts spilled out, their tips already seeking him.

With a husky chuckle, he took one nipple into his mouth, and the sensation made Glory moan aloud and stretch out on the seat in involuntary abandon. His hand found the top of her panty hose and began rolling them slowly and surely downward.

Everything was happening as fast as a sleigh ride down McCalley's Hill, but Glory couldn't put on the brakes. She'd been without Jesse's touch for too long, craved it too desperately.

He found the aching center of her femininity and delved under its mat of silk to the quavering nubbin beneath. Glory groaned again as he rolled her between his fingers.

"Oh, Jesse—" she pleaded.

He bent until his head was lying in her lap, and then his lips and tongue replaced his fingers, and Glory gave a lusty shout and thrust her hips high.

Jesse chuckled against her, but he showed no mercy of any kind. His hands clasped her bottom, and he held her to his tender vengeance, taking everything she had to give. He laid her back on the seat, only to ignite the blazes all over again by sucking at her breasts and stroking them.

When she was twisting beneath his hands and mouth, feverish for the union she knew she should deny herself, he shifted her, so that he was lying on the seat and she was kneeling over him. He opened his slacks and lowered Glory onto him.

Her body surged into reflexive action, but Jesse gripped her hips and measured the pace, whispering ragged, senseless words as he sheathed and unsheathed himself in her.

"Jesse—*Jesse*—" She sought his mouth with hers, and he gave her a brief, fiery kiss. But he was caught up in a tender agony of his own, and he finally thrust his head back and uttered an exclamation.

In the next moment, their bodies made a pact independent of their minds, fusing together in a hot, searing thrust. Glory cried out and arched her back when Jesse intensified every sensation by pulling her forward and catching one of her nipples in his mouth.

When she collapsed against him, she was crying. "Damn you, Jesse," she sobbed brokenly. "Are you satisfied now?"

His chuckle was more tender than amused. "A strangely appropriate question," he gasped. And then he wrapped his arms around Glory and he held her for a long time, until they'd both recovered a little.

Only then did Glory realize that Jesse had shed not only his overcoat but his sweater, too. And her coat was jumbled into a corner with them. It scared her that she didn't remember the process of that.

"Oh, God," she sniffled, as Jesse dislodged himself to pull on his sweater and raise the seat back.

"Glory, it's all right," he rasped, as she dried her eyes with some tissue from the glove compartment and did her best to straighten her clothes.

Glory slammed the glove compartment and snapped her seat belt back into place. "Well, now you've proved it," she said, in a furious, singsong voice riddled with tears. "For a good time, a guy just has to call Glory Parsons!"

He silenced her by taking her chin in his hand. His grasp was hard but not painful. "Don't ever say that again," he bit out. "I made love to you because I wanted to, not because I was trying to make a point!" He paused to drag in a deep, ragged breath. "Now, maybe we can concentrate long enough to figure out what the hell we're going to do about our daughter."

CHAPTER SIX

BECAUSE JESSE INSISTED, they went on to the restaurant in Fawn Creek, and Glory headed straight for the women's room to make repairs on her hair and makeup. When she came out, Jesse was waiting for her, and his brash brown eyes smiled even though his lips were still.

"Don't worry," he whispered a few moments later, as they followed a waitress to their table. "Nobody would ever guess that half an hour ago you were having your way with me."

Glory's cheeks burned and she glared up at Jesse, her lips drawn tight across her teeth, as he pulled back her chair for her.

"You did all the seducing," she pointed out, once they were alone with their menus and a flickering candle.

Jesse leaned forward in his chair. "Maybe so." He grinned. "But when you got warmed up, you were plenty willing to play the game."

"We came here," Glory reminded him stiffly, snapping her menu open, "to discuss Liza."

"By the way," Jesse began, drawing his eyebrows together briefly in a frown. "Are you doing anything for birth control, or did we just make the same mistake twice?"

Glory gave a hissing sigh and slapped her menu

down on the table. "It's so typical of you to ask after the fact. Yes, I've got an IUD. And furthermore, I don't consider Liza a mistake."

"I can see we're going to get a lot settled tonight," Jesse replied through his teeth.

The waitress returned, and they both ordered chicken enchiladas with beans and rice. Glory wondered why they couldn't agree on anything besides food and sex.

Neither of them spoke again until their dinner salads had been delivered.

"I guess things must have been pretty serious between you and that Alan character, if you have an IUD," Jesse commented.

Glory took aim and fired back. "I guess things must be pretty serious between you and Adara, too, since everybody in town knows you bought her an engagement ring for Christmas."

"Adara and I are finished," he said, stabbing at his salad with his fork.

Glory smiled acidly. "What a coincidence. So are Alan and I. So why would we want to talk about them?"

Jesse shrugged and tried to look nonchalant, but Glory wasn't fooled. It troubled his male ego to know she'd had a long-term relationship with another man; Jesse had always been a very proprietary animal.

"I think you should tell Liza you're her father," Glory ventured to say, long minutes later, when their dinners had arrived. "I mean, it must have been hard on her, losing Gresham and Sandy."

Jesse sighed, and the look in his eyes was, for a moment, grievously sad. "It was," he said gravely. "I don't mind admitting I had some trouble with it myself. Gresh was busy with politics, even when I was a kid, but he always had time for me."

A knot formed in Glory's throat. She knew how close a person could be to his brother, and how much it hurt to lose him. A part of her was still standing beside Dylan's grave, watching in numb disbelief as they lowered his coffin into the ground, aching because a stupid mistake on another airman's part had robbed him of his life. She nodded, because that was all she could manage.

Accurately reading the expression on her face, Jesse reached out and closed his hand over hers. "If Gresh and Dylan were here," he said quietly, "they'd tell us to stop worrying over the dead and think about the living."

Glory nodded again. "I know."

Over coffee, Jesse was the one to bring up the subject of their daughter. "Why is it so important to you that I tell Liza I'm her father?"

It was a question Glory had thoroughly examined in her own mind. "Kids tend to find out things like that. And when they do, they're devastated because nobody told them the truth."

He arched one eyebrow. "No ulterior motives? Like wanting her to put two and two together and decide that if I'm her father, you must be her mother?"

Glory met his gaze steadily. "I'd love for Liza to know who I am, under the right circumstances. But I care more about her happiness and welfare."

At that, Jesse looked skeptical, and their brief, tenuous truce was over. "Either that, or you have a rich relative somewhere, and the only way you can inherit is by proving you've produced offspring."

Even though his expression had forewarned her, Jesse's words still came as a slap in the face. "Did I hurt you that much?" she asked, when she'd gotten her breath back.

"Yes," he answered coldly. "I was eighteen, Glory, and gullible as hell. You'd told me with words and with your body that you loved me. When you ran off without telling me why it was over, the pain was so bad that I couldn't stand still. When I tried, it consumed me like fire.

"I did everything I knew to find you, but nobody wanted to help me, including Dylan and your mother." He paused, and his eyes, averted from Glory's face, were haunted. "I'll never forget the day I finally had to give up. Gresh had taken me fishing, trying to snap me out of it. He said if I didn't tell somebody about my feelings, they'd never go away, they'd just get worse. I threw my fishing pole down and yelled, it hurt so much. When Gresh put his arms around me, I cried like a two-year-old."

Glory had seen the images vividly in her mind as Jesse was talking, and she ached. Driven to distraction by her own pain, she'd inflicted agony on a person she loved with her whole heart. "I don't suppose it would help to say that I'm sorry, that I was hurting, too?"

Jesse threw two bills down onto the table to cover the cost of their meal and shoved back his chair. His eyes were hot with remembered frustration, as Glory stood with him. "Maybe someday it will," he responded in a low voice. "Right now, I feel like it all happened last Tuesday."

At the coatrack beside the restaurant's front door, he settled Glory's coat on her shoulders, then shrugged into his own. Although he was unfailingly polite, linking her arm with his so she wouldn't fall in the icy parking lot, opening the car door for her, something in his manner chilled Glory through and through.

Shame all but crushed her as she realized that, whatever he'd said to the contrary, Jesse had made love to her that night to avenge himself. He didn't care for her, and probably hadn't even especially wanted her. God knew, Jesse could have had just about any single woman in Pearl River County for the asking.

"We should have left well enough alone, Jesse, and stayed away from each other," she said miserably, when he brought the elegant old car to a stop in front of her building.

He was staring straight over the wheel instead of looking at her, and his profile was rigid. "I tried to tell you that," he answered gruffly after a long, difficult interval. His brown eyes were full of accusations when he turned to her. "For your own sake, Glory, and for Liza's and mine, please let this thing alone. Go back to Portland and your boyfriend and forget we made a baby ten years ago."

Glory's eyes filled with tears. In a way, she thought Jesse was right, she should go, but she knew even then that she wouldn't be able to make herself do it. The knowledge of Liza's existence would haunt her for the rest of her life.

"If you and I never exchange another civil word," she said, unfastening her seat belt and pushing open the car door, "it'll be all right. But I can't leave my daughter. I won't."

She was halfway up the walk when Jesse caught up with her and forcefully took her arm. The irony of it would have made her laugh out loud, if she hadn't been in so much emotional pain. The sheriff of Pearl River County didn't mind ripping out her heart and stomping on it, but he'd be damned if he'd let a lady walk to her door unescorted!

She shoved the key into the lock and would have gone inside without another word, if Jesse hadn't grasped her shoulders and forced her to face him.

"Damn it, Glory," he breathed, his jaw set so tightly it was a wonder he could speak at all, "leave Liza alone! I don't want her in pieces, when you decide you're bored with Pearl River and need to move on!"

Glory longed to slap him, but her fury was too great. It practically paralyzed her. "Sorry, Sheriff," she told him, "but I'm going to be a part of the landscape around here, and you'd damn well better get used to it!" With that, she shoved open the door.

Jesse yelled a swear word, heedless of the neighbors, shoved his hands into the pockets of his expensive overcoat and stalked back to his car.

ALL NIGHT LONG, Jesse tossed and turned, alternately burning to feel Glory beneath him, receiving him, and wanting to strangle her. She was like a fever beginning in his brain and spreading into his body, destroying his reason, changing him from a man of the nineties to a cave dweller.

After a shower and a haphazard shave, Jesse put on his uniform and called the office to let them know where to find him. And then he got into his truck, backed it out of the driveway, and practically floorboarded the gas pedal.

The vehicle fishtailed on the blindingly white packed snow as he drove toward the main road.

A left turn would have taken him into Pearl River, but Jesse turned right. He stopped once to use the winch on his truck to pull a young couple's car out of the ditch.

No one was hurt, but they had a baby with them, and the weather was colder than a witch's nipple. Jesse made sure the old heap they were driving would run before going on.

In a way, he envied those two kids their youth and innocence, as well as the unique young life they'd created together. He hoped they knew they were rich, even if they couldn't afford a decent rig, and that they would fight to hold on to what they had when they hit the inevitable white water.

He set his teeth. At that age, he would have fought any force in the universe to keep Glory and their child at his side—if he'd been given the option.

He was grateful when Twin Poplars Convalescent Home loomed up in the distance; he'd spent the night thinking about Glory, and he needed a distraction.

Vicky Walters, a nurse Jesse had dated briefly before he and Adara had started seeing each other, greeted him with a smile. Only then did it strike him that she bore a faint resemblance, with her blond hair and blue eyes, to Glory.

"Hi, Jesse. Nasty morning out, isn't it?"

He grinned and shivered in reply. "Speaking of nasty, is my grandfather up?"

Vicky laughed. "He's already had his breakfast, and he happens to be in a pretty good mood. He was in his room last time I saw him."

Jesse's grin faded as soon as he got past Vicky. Even on his best days, Seth Bainbridge wasn't an easy man to deal with. And this sure as hell wasn't going to be one of his best days.

Seth sat at the window, slumped in his wheelchair, dressed in his robe and slippers and gazing out from beneath bushy eyebrows at the dazzlingly white world. He still had his hair, though it was mostly gray now, and his eyes were as sharp as ever, like his mind. But the rest of his body had betrayed him by turning feeble.

"Gramps?" Jesse paused in the doorway, his hands braced on either side of the jamb.

The old man wheeled around and scowled at him. "Hello, Jesse."

"Can I come in, or do I have to get a warrant?" Jesse asked, trying to smile. It was tough to keep up a front sometimes, because the old cuss could be so hard and cold. And this was one of his *good* days.

"Come in," the judge grumbled, waving one hand in a desultory gesture. "Come in."

Even after he'd crossed the threshold, Jesse couldn't make himself sit. "How have you been feeling?"

"Like hell," the old man answered gruffly.

Jesse drew in a deep breath, let it out slowly. He had to go carefully here; he didn't want to cause the judge to have another stroke. And yet there were things he needed to know. "Glory Parsons is back in town." He said the words with the same caution he would have used to make sure the ice over Culley's Creek was thick enough to hold his weight.

He'd expected a reaction, and he got one. Seth's gaze snapped to his face and narrowed there, and his gnarled hands clenched on the arms of his chair. "That cheap, lying, little—"

Jesse had a lot of unresolved issues where Glory was concerned himself, but he wasn't about to let the judge insult her. "Hold it," he said firmly, raising both hands, palms out. "I don't want a dose of your venom, Gramps, and I swear to God I'll walk out of here and never come back if you don't watch your mouth."

Seth had few enough visitors, Jesse suspected, because when it came right down to it, he didn't have any friends, at all, except for old Doc Cupples. As for family, Gresham and Sandy were dead, of course, and he'd long since alienated Ilene with his black moods. She refused to subject Liza to the old man's unpredictable temperament, and Jesse backed her up on the decision.

Which left himself and the aging doctor as the only people who ever paid a call of any kind.

"All right," Seth muttered. He was silent for a long time, then he went on. "She shouldn't have come back. She promised she wouldn't."

Jesse's fist knotted; he wanted to slam it down on the dresser top, hard enough to make lamps and ashtrays jump, but he restrained himself. "So you did send her away," he ground out.

"Sit down," fussed the old man. "It hurts my neck to look up at you like that."

Jesse dragged a chair over and sank into it. "All right, you old reprobate, start talking."

"She would have ruined your life," his grandfather insisted. And had Seth been able to close his hands into fists, Jesse figured he would have. As it was, agitation was clearly written in every line of his body. "You wouldn't have gone to college. By God, you wouldn't be sheriff today, with every prospect of entering the state legislature in a few years!"

Jesse rubbed his eyes with a thumb and forefinger and sighed. "Glory was pregnant with my baby, wasn't she? And you ran her off because of your damn family pride."

"The baby was yours," Seth agreed bitterly. "I knew that the moment I saw Liza. But she *could* have belonged to anybody in the county!"

"Watch it," Jesse warned, his voice as rough as two rusty nails being rubbed together. In that moment, Jesse realized that he'd suspected Glory's pregnancy all along; he'd just never been able to get anybody to confirm it.

Seth trembled with frustration and rage and the relative inability to express those emotions. "Glory Parsons wasn't like Gresham's Sandy—she didn't come from a good family. That brother of hers was practically a criminal, and as for her mother—"

"Glory was as good as anybody, Gramps," Jesse interrupted in an angry undertone, "and *better* than you and I put together. Dylan was no worse than any of the rest of us, and let's not mince words here—you didn't like Delphine because you wanted to sleep with her and she told you to go to hell."

For a long time, Seth just sat there, gripping the arms of his chair and swallowing repeatedly. Finally he ground out, "I did the right thing, Jesse. Gresham and Sandy wanted a baby, and I made sure they got one. And I saved you from the mistake of a lifetime, you ungrateful young whelp!"

Jesse rose from the chair, went into the bathroom,

and drew a glass of cold water for his grandfather. Seth was still red in the face when he got back. "Take it easy," Jesse said, holding out the glass.

Seth obviously would have liked to knock the cup out of Jesse's hand, but he didn't because he needed the water to steady himself. He drank it down thirstily. "I paid her to leave," he muttered, and the words were ugly to Jesse, even though he'd long since guessed that Glory had sold him out for money.

Hearing the words from his grandfather lifted them out of the realm of theory and planted them squarely in reality. And they were wounding. He averted his eyes to a naked tree beyond the window, but the old man was ruthless. He knew he'd cornered his prey, and he couldn't resist closing in for the kill.

"She could have come to you, Jesse, and told you about the baby. You would have married her. But we both know why she didn't, don't we? Because I told her I'd cut you off without a nickel the day you put a ring on her finger, and she didn't want you *or* the baby if she couldn't have the Bainbridge money, too."

Jesse thrust himself out of the chair and turned his back. He felt broken inside, just the way he had that long-ago summer day when Dylan had told him Glory had gone away and wasn't ever coming back. Only now he didn't have Gresh to help him get his balance back. He didn't have anybody.

"You ought to be thanking me on your knees!" the old man went on, tearing at Jesse's spirit like a frenzied shark. "*I saved you* from that calculating little tease!"

Not trusting himself to speak, Jesse strode out of the room, his grandfather's bitter words ringing in his ears.

ON HER LUNCH HOUR, Glory left the bank and drove cautiously along the icy roads until she reached the Pearl River cemetery. Then, parking her car outside the gates, she made her way on foot to Dylan's grave.

The headstone was mounded with snow, but the letters of his name were clearly visible. Glory sniffled and shoved her hands into the pockets of her coat. Then, after looking around to make sure she was alone, she started talking.

"Last night Jesse and I went out to dinner," she said, pulling one mittened hand out to wipe her eyes. "We took that fancy old car that belongs to his grandfather and—well—we ended up making love on the seat like a couple of teenagers." Glory paused to sniffle again. "Actually, it wouldn't classify as lovemaking, given the fact that Jesse was just trying to get back at me for hurting him. The Anglo-Saxon term would fit better, but you know me—I can't say that because I think it's so ugly."

An icy breeze swept in among the naked trees, ruffling Glory's hair and stinging her ears. She tried to imagine what Dylan would say if he were there, and it wasn't difficult. He'd have vowed to find Jesse Bainbridge and loosen a few of his teeth.

"Violence won't solve anything, Dylan," she said firmly.

She guessed that then he would have put an arm around her shoulders and told her not to be so hard on herself, that everybody makes mistakes.

"Thanks," she snuffled. Then she took one of the small candy canes the bank was giving away from her purse, stuck it like a little flag in the snow on top of Dylan's headstone, and carefully returned to her car.

She got back to the bank just in time for a staff meeting, and the rest of the afternoon was so busy that quitting time came long before she expected it.

Not wanting to go home to her apartment and sit in a folding chair, staring at a blank wall, Glory went to the diner instead. Delphine was off-duty, and her daughter found her upstairs, curled up on the couch with a romance novel.

"Hi," Glory said brightly. And then she promptly burst into tears.

"I'd ask what's bothering you," Delphine said with gentle wryness, patting her daughter on the back, "but I already know it's Jesse. Sit down, and I'll get you a nice hot cup of tea to settle your nerves."

Glory collapsed into a chair without even bothering to take off her coat, and let her purse tumble to the floor. "He hates me," she said, resting one elbow on the arm of the chair and propping her forehead in her palm.

"Nonsense," replied Delphine from the kitchenette. "He just wants your body, and it's making him crazy."

Glory let out a despairing wail. "He's already had my body!" she sobbed.

Diplomatically, Delphine waited a few beats before responding to that. "I take it we're not talking about ten years ago, when you were young, foolish and hormonal."

"We're talking about *last night*!" Glory ranted.

"Good grief," Delphine muttered, materializing at her side with a glass of water and two aspirin tablets. "Get a grip before you give yourself a headache."

Glory swallowed the aspirin and felt a little better just for having been fussed over. "This would all be so much easier if it weren't for Jesse."

"None of this would have *happened* if it weren't for Jesse." She patted Glory's shoulder distractedly. "Honey, please don't tell me you've come up with some crazy plan to replace Liza by getting pregnant with Jesse's baby all over again."

"Of course I haven't!" Glory cried, getting awkwardly out of her coat and leaving it all bunched up in the chair behind her.

Delphine returned to the stove as the tea kettle began to whistle. "Well, then, how did it happen?"

"I've never been like this with any other man," she marveled furiously. "But for some reason all Jesse has to do is kiss me and I go absolutely wild."

The older woman arched one auburn eyebrow as she handed Glory her cup of tea and then sat down to face her. "You know," she said, her eyes twinkling with mischief as she tapped the cover of her romance novel, "Storm Ravenbrook is having the same problem with her man, if it's any comfort to you."

"It isn't," Glory assured her huffily.

Delphine sighed. "Sweetheart, I warned you about staying here in Pearl River. To quote those old western movies on TV, this town just ain't big enough for the two of you. And since Jesse owns a mansion, the sawmill, and half the real estate in the county, he isn't very likely to move on. That means—"

"I know, I know," Glory interrupted wearily, taking a somewhat unladylike sip of her tea. "I've either got to leave or learn to deal with our illustrious sheriff."

"That's about the size of it," Delphine agreed. Having listened to people's problems at the diner for so long, she'd probably heard more sad stories than the average psycho-therapist. Her basic philosophy was that ninety-seven percent of life was just a matter of showing up, and the other three consisted of rolling with the punches.

"Thanks, Mama," Glory said.

"What for?"

"For not judging me. Until they start a group called Jesse Anonymous, I'm afraid I'm going to have to play this thing by ear."

Delphine laughed. "In your case, I think the affliction may be incurable. Has it ever occurred to you, my darling daughter, that you might still be in love with the man?"

Glory's eyes went wide with alarm at the suggestion. As much as she thought about Jesse, as wantonly as she'd behaved in his arms the night before, the possibility had never crossed her mind.

"No," she said. *"No!"*

Delphine just shrugged and asked Glory if she wanted to stay for dinner. Harold, who was working on a plumbing job in Fawn Creek, was going to stop off on the way home and pick up a big pepperoni pizza.

Glory shook her head and gathered her crumpled coat around her. "I'd just be a drag," she said. Then she stood, bending to kiss Delphine's forehead. "Thanks for everything, Mama. I love you."

Delphine squeezed her hand. "If you decide you want to talk some more or just hang around, I'll be right here until about eight o'clock. Then Harold and I are going over to the new house to put shelf paper in the cupboards."

Glory promised to seek her mother out if she hit another crisis, and left. She was walking back to the bank parking lot, where her car was waiting, when Ilene came out of the bookstore and waved.

"You look half frozen," the woman called. "Come on over, and Liza and I will thaw you out."

After the last twenty-four hours, the offer of time with Liza was irresistible. Glory looked both ways and then hurried across the icy street and into the bookstore.

A lush-looking artificial tree had been set up in one corner of the shop, which was now closed for the day. Lights were strung among the branches, and Liza was decorating the boughs with old-fashioned glass ornaments.

"Hi, Glory," she chimed with a smile that pulled at Glory's insides and almost brought tears to her eyes.

Glory hid her reaction by taking off her coat and hanging it up. "Hi, there," she finally answered, when she was a little more composed. "That's a pretty tree."

"Thank you," Liza replied. "Aunt Ilene says cutting down a live one is senseless slaughter. Uncle Jesse always gets a big spruce for the big house, though."

Amusement at Liza's vernacular saved Glory from flinching, at least inwardly, at the mention of Jesse. The twinkling colored lights on the tree cheered her a little, and she carefully picked up an ornament and handed it to the child.

Liza hung the piece from a branch and looked up at Glory with Christmas reflected on her earnest little face. "Will you stay for supper, Glory? Aunt Ilene said it was all right to invite you, and we're having Chinese."

Glory glanced at Ilene, who smiled and nodded. "I'd like that very much," she said softly, reaching out one hand to touch her child and then drawing it back at the last moment. Embarrassed, she turned to Ilene again. "Is there anything I can do to help?"

Ilene's expression was one of tender understanding. "Just keep this young lady company," she said, gesturing toward Liza, "while I deep-fry the wontons." With that, she turned and left the shop for the apartment upstairs.

"Aunt Ilene's a good cook," Liza confided. "She thinks trying foods from other countries will promote peace, so we eat lots of strange stuff."

Glory smiled and began decorating the top portion of the tree, where Liza couldn't reach. The activity was so ordinary—parents and children did this everywhere, every year—but to Glory it was precious. "What are you asking Santa for?" she inquired casually, not sure whether her daughter believed or not.

"Santa's really Uncle Jesse," Liza confided, leaning close to whisper the words gently, lest they come as a terrible shock. "And I already got what I want."

"What was that?" Glory asked, her voice hoarse because of the lump in her throat.

"For Uncle Jesse not to get married to Adara."

"Don't you like her?"

"I like her all right. I just don't think she's Uncle Jesse's type."

Glory smiled. "I see."

"I want somebody who'll bring cookies to school and come in my room and hug me if I have a bad dream—like Mommy used to do."

Glory's heart twisted, and before she thought, she leaned down and kissed Liza on the crown of her head, just where her bright-penny hair was parted. When she straightened, she saw Jesse standing on the other side of the store's front window, glaring at her.

CHAPTER SEVEN

THE BELL OVER the bookshop door didn't jingle merrily as Jesse came in; it jangled in warning.

"Uncle Jesse!" Liza whooped, flinging herself at the man, apparently never noticing his taciturn expression.

Looking on in silence, Glory envied Jesse the child's wild affection.

"Hi, Button," Jesse answered distractedly, hugging the nine-year-old and then giving one of her braids a little tug. His eyes never left Glory's face the whole time, and their expression wasn't friendly.

She was saved from having to speak to him, at least temporarily, when Ilene appeared, pushing up the sleeves of her bright purple sweater and smiling.

"Hello, Jesse. Want to join us for supper? We're having Chinese."

He rubbed his chin, which was showing a stubble of beard, and at last he turned from Glory. He smiled at his cousin. "No thanks," he answered. "I'm still on duty." He looked down at Liza's face then, and now it was as though Glory were invisible to him. "I'm going out looking for a Christmas tree this Saturday, and I'd like you to come along if you want to."

"*Yes!*" Liza cried, and her eagerness made Glory's heart constrict. "I want to! Could Glory come with us, please? And Aunt Ilene?"

"Saturday's my busiest day, what with Christmas coming on," Ilene interceded with a gentle shake of her head.

Glory stood awkwardly by, embarrassed, not knowing what to say. It was obvious Jesse hadn't intended to include her in the invitation, and she could have gotten off the hook by saying she had to do her holiday shopping that day. But the painful truth was that she wanted, just once, to go on a Christmas-tree-hunting expedition with her daughter and the man who had fathered her.

Jesse narrowed his eyes at Glory, as though he suspected her of making Liza ask to bring her along by ventriloquism, but then he said grudgingly, "I guess it would be all right."

Liza cheered and hugged Jesse again, then scrambled upstairs to get something she wanted to show him. Diplomatically, Ilene went along.

"What are you doing here?" Jesse immediately demanded, placing his hands on his hips.

Glory stepped away from the artificial Christmas tree, realizing only then that she'd unconsciously been trying to hide among its branches. She sighed. "What does it look like I'm doing here, Jesse? I'm spending time with Liza."

He lifted one finger and shook it at her, starting to speak, but Liza reappeared before he got a word out.

"Here it is, Uncle Jesse," she burst out, waving a sheet of paper. "It's my math assignment. I got an *A*."

Jesse grinned. "That's great," he said, taking the child's eager offering. "Can I keep it? I'd like to pin it up on the bulletin board at my office, so all the deputies will know what a smart kid I've—you are."

Liza was beaming. "Okay," she said. And then she

turned her bright green eyes to Glory. "Supper's ready. Aunt Ilene said to lock the door after Uncle Jesse and come up."

With a chuckle, Jesse bent to kiss Liza's forehead. "See you tomorrow, kid," he said. After that, he exchanged a brief look with Glory, silently warning her not to overstep her bounds.

She responded with a grudging nod, and he went out.

That night when dinner was over Glory helped Liza with the dishes and her homework, then read her a chapter of *Little House in the Big Woods* before tucking her into bed. When she'd kissed the child good-night and closed the door of her small room, she sought out Ilene, who was at the kitchen table, tallying the day's receipts for the bookshop.

"Thank you," Glory said.

Ilene gestured toward the colorful teapot in the center of the table with a smile. "Help yourself," she said. "It's herbal, so it won't keep you awake."

Since Ilene had also set out a cup, Glory poured some tea and took a sip. "Why are you so kind to me?" she asked, in a voice carefully modulated not to carry as far as Liza's room. "I mean, I'm a stranger as far as you're concerned."

"I have good instincts about people," Ilene said. "Besides, I believe in families."

Glory swallowed. She simply wasn't up to the topic of families, not after an evening of emotional ups and downs that had left her slightly disoriented and tired to the center of her heart.

Ilene patted her hand. "You've got good instincts, too, Glory," she said softly. "And you loved Jesse once.

If you'll just give him time, he'll come to terms with all of this and start behaving like a human being again."

That brought a wan smile from Glory. "I hope you're right," she sighed, "because it will be very hard to have a relationship with Liza, if Jesse and I can't get along."

After that, the two women drank tea and talked about other Christmases, in other places. Glory was tired and pleasantly relaxed when she left to fetch her car from the bank's parking lot and drive the rest of the way home.

"I GUESS YOU'VE done all the thinking you need to do," Adara said, accurately guessing the reason for Jesse's unscheduled visit. He wanted to leave it at that, to get back into his patrol car and drive away, but his sense of honor wouldn't permit such an easy out.

He entered Adara's apartment when she stepped back to admit him. "I'm sorry," he said, standing there in the middle of her living room, shoving his hands into the pockets of his jacket.

The tears shimmering in her eyes filled him with guilt, because he knew she would have done anything to hold them back.

"It's Glory?" she asked with a despairing lilt in her voice.

Jesse raised his shoulders in a shrug. "I'm not sure. The situation is pretty complicated."

Adara nodded. "I imagine so. Five people must have come into the shop today just to tell me that you took her to dinner last night."

"I'm sorry," Jesse said again. The reminder of the night before, when he and Glory had made love, would be sweet torment for some time to come. He supposed he deserved it.

He went to the door, and Adara followed, speaking quickly. "If you're not happy with her—"

Jesse touched her lips with the tips of his fingers. "Don't say it," he replied quietly. And then he left Adara's apartment for the last time.

ON WEDNESDAY, THE movers stopped at the bank to inform Glory that her furniture and other belongings had arrived, and Mr. Baker gave her the rest of the day off to get things squared away. The moment the movers were gone, she unearthed her espresso maker and brewed herself a *latte*.

She was sipping the mixture of espresso and steamed milk and trying to decide which carton to unpack first, when her doorbell chimed. Expecting Delphine, or perhaps Jill, Glory was surprised to find Liza standing in the hallway, looking slightly ill-at-ease.

Glory never laid eyes on the child without a painful tug at her heart, but she was ready with a smile. "Hi," she said warmly, stepping back so that Liza could come in.

"Hi," Liza answered, stepping over the threshold and then just standing there in her little coat and boots, shifting back and forth from one foot to the other.

"Does your Aunt Ilene know where you are?" Glory asked, reaching out gently to unbutton Liza's coat.

Liza nodded. "I told her. She has a migraine headache and had to go upstairs and lie down."

Glory was concerned. "Is there anything I can do for her?"

Liza shook her head and tugged off her mittens and

stocking cap, all of which Glory laid aside with the coat. "Nothing works but peace and quiet. I'm supposed to wait at the sheriff's office and have supper with Uncle Jesse tonight."

"Did you call him from school?" Glory inquired, wending her way through the stacks of boxes to the kitchen, where she planned to make hot cocoa for Liza.

"No," Liza replied nervously. "He's probably out chasing criminals, anyway. I'll go straight to the office after I leave here."

"I think we'd better call him," Glory said.

Liza stopped her by grasping her hand. "First I have to ask you something."

A chill went through Glory, followed by a wild hope that this bright, perceptive child had already figured out the secret she and Jesse were keeping from her. "Yes?"

"Do you sew in this lifetime?"

Glory chuckled, at once relieved and disappointed. "Yes, a little. Why?"

"Because I'm going to be the only angel in the pageant without a costume if I don't get somebody to help me," Liza blurted out. "Uncle Jesse's got something on his mind—he doesn't even hear half the questions I ask him—and Aunt Ilene used to be a seamstress in France, during a war. It was an unhappy life, and she swears she'll never pick up another needle and thread—"

Glory resisted an impulse to hug the child and laughed softly. "Sure I'll help you. Do you have the directions?"

Liza nodded and threw her arms around Glory. "Oh, thank you!" she cried. While Glory was recovering from that, the little girl hurried to her coat and extracted a folded, much-worried-over piece of paper containing basic instructions and a list of materials for an angel costume.

"The first thing we have to do," Glory reflected, reading over the paper, "is call your Uncle Jesse and let him know exactly where you are. Then we'll drive to Fawn Creek and get the materials we need."

Liza's green eyes were alight at the prospect. "The mall will be all decorated for Christmas!"

Glory nodded, smiling, and went to the telephone affixed to her kitchen wall. After asking Liza for the number, she called the sheriff's department, identified herself and politely asked for Jesse.

Another voice came on the line. "Glory? This is Deputy Johnson. Jesse's out on a call right now. Can I help you?"

Twisting the cord around her finger, Glory frowned. She would have preferred to relay the message directly to Jesse, so there could be no mistake, but she couldn't wait. She'd gotten Liza all excited about the project. "Just tell him, please, that Liza is with me. We'll be out of town for a while, picking up some things in Fawn Creek."

"I'll make sure he knows," Deputy Johnson promised earnestly.

Glory thanked him and hung up. In the process of preparing Liza and then herself for the cold, she forgot Jesse even existed. She couldn't remember the last time she'd looked forward to anything as much as she did those few stolen hours with her child.

The two of them had just passed the city limits in Glory's sports car, happily singing Christmas carols, when a siren sounded behind them and blue-and-red lights flashed ominously in the rearview mirror.

Knowing she hadn't been speeding, Glory frowned as she pulled over to the side of the road.

It shouldn't have surprised her, she guessed, that the officer who strode up beside her car was Jesse.

She rolled down her window and opened her mouth, but he didn't give her a chance to speak.

"Get out of the car," he ordered in an undertone that, for all its even meter, was girded in steel.

Glory glanced at Liza and smiled to reassure the child, who looked surprised and worried. "It's okay, honey," she said. "Your Uncle Jesse obviously didn't get the message that we left, so he and I have to talk."

Liza looked relieved. "Hi, Uncle Jesse," she sang out, wiggling her fingers.

He managed a semblance of a smile, and even though his eyes were hidden behind mirrored sunglasses, Glory knew they were snapping with controlled fury. "Hi," he replied.

Glory opened the door and stepped out onto the snowy roadside, and Jesse immediately gripped her by the elbow and hustled her around to the back of the car.

"Where the hell were you taking her?" he demanded in a hiss, as Glory wrenched free of his grasp.

Outraged, Glory folded her arms and rolled her eyes. "To China, Jesse," she answered. "We were making a break for it!" She flung her hands out at her sides and then slapped them against her thighs. "Too bad you had to catch us."

"Do you know how scared I was, when I couldn't find her?" Jesse rasped.

Glory found it only too easy to put herself into Jes-

se's shoes, and she relented a little. "I'm sorry," she said
grudgingly. "Liza came by my apartment and asked
me if I'd help with her angel costume. I called your
office—I swear it—and left a message with Deputy
Johnson that Liza and I were going to the mall in Fawn
Creek to buy materials."

He turned away for a moment, his hands resting on
his hips, seemingly taking a great interest in the snow-
draped pine trees along the road. Glory knew he was
composing himself.

Finally he looked at her again. "I thought you were
leaving town on the spur of the moment, like before,"
he confessed. "And taking Liza with you."

It was a marvel that she'd been so angry with Jesse
only a moment ago, when now all she wanted to do was
comfort him. She wedged her hands into the pockets of
her black corduroy pants so she wouldn't lay them on
his broad shoulders. "Jesse, I'm not a scared eighteen-
year-old girl, anymore. I'm not going to vanish, and I'd
never, *never* put you or anyone else through the kind
of anguish stealing a child would cause."

He faced her with a heavy sigh and shoved one hand
through his hair. "Have her back in time for supper,"
he said. "And be careful. The roads are slick."

Glory smiled. Ilene had expressed the hope that
Jesse would turn back into a human being, and it did
seem that he was making noticeable progress toward
that end. "You'd better go and tell Liza it's all right,"
she said, gesturing toward the passenger side of the car,
"or she'll worry the whole time we're gone. Pleasing
you is important to her, Jesse."

He gave her a look that might have contained a modicum of amused chagrin, shoved his hands into his jacket pockets, and proceeded to Liza's window.

"Have a good time, kid," Glory heard him say, as she rounded the car to get behind the wheel again. The lights on top of Jesse's patrol car were still splashing patches of blue and red over the snow.

"Were we going too fast?" Liza asked, with innocent concern, as she and Glory pulled back onto the highway. In the rearview mirror, Glory could see Jesse standing there at the side of the road, watching them go from behind those damnable sunglasses of his.

Glory shook her head. "He didn't get the message we left for him, so he was worried. Sometimes when parents—*people*—are scared, they act the same way they would if they were angry."

Liza nodded thoughtfully. "Then Gramps must be scared all the time," she reflected. "He's always mad."

"Gramps?" Glory asked, before it came to her that Liza was talking about old Seth Bainbridge, Jesse's grandfather. The hatred she'd always felt for the man seemed to ebb away, leaving sadness and pity in its wake.

"His son was Daddy and Uncle Jesse's father," Liza explained in that amusingly adult manner she sometimes assumed.

The reference to Jesse's brother as "Daddy," indirect as it was, reminded Glory that her gain was Gresham and Sandy's loss, and she wished there was a way to promise them that she'd keep their memories alive in Liza's mind if she could. After all, for six of the little girl's nine years, they'd loved and taken care of her.

"I miss my mommy and daddy a lot at this time of the year," Liza said with a little sigh.

Glory's eyes burned, and she reached out to touch Liza's knee briefly. "I knew your daddy, though not very well." She thought of how Gresham had comforted Jesse after Seth had driven her out of town all those years before. "He was a nice man. Strong, with a ready smile."

Liza giggled. "He used to chase me around the house trying to tickle me," she said.

From then until they reached the mall at Fawn Creek, Glory kept the conversation turning around Gresham and Sandy, and talking about them seemed to be a great relief to Liza. The words and memories, mostly happy, bubbled out of her.

At the mall, Glory bought cups of cocoa for them both, and they sat at a table on the concourse, planning their strategy.

The stores were decorated, and Christmas music was being piped in over a sound system. Although she'd been something of a Scrooge for the past few years, embittered by her breakup with Jesse, the loss of her child and Dylan's subsequent death, Glory found herself getting into the spirit as she and Liza went from shop to shop.

Mindful of Jesse's edict that she have Liza back in Pearl River in time for supper, Glory didn't linger as long as she would have liked. Snowflakes were falling like big feathers shaken from a goose-down pillow, when the two shoppers left the mall with the makings of an angel costume.

It wasn't hard to find Jesse when they got back to town; his patrol car was parked in front of Delphine's diner, and he was standing at the jukebox when Glory and Liza came in.

"I'm going to be the best angel there ever was!" Liza crowed, hurrying to his side and waving the bag-ful of supplies.

Glory lingered just inside the doorway, very much aware of being outside the circle again. "If Liza could stop by tomorrow sometime, after I get home from work, I'll be able to get started on the costume."

Jesse was holding Liza close against his side, as though he feared to let go, and he didn't look at Glory. "You'll have to talk with Ilene about that," he answered.

After coming close enough to reclaim the shopping bag, Glory turned on one heel, her vision blurred, and hurried out of the diner into the cold and snowy night.

"How come you don't like Glory?" Liza asked, an hour later, when she and Jesse were seated at the table in the mansion's immense dining room, eating her favorite meal of chicken from a bucket.

It occurred to Jesse to hedge, of course, but then he had a strange feeling, as though Gresh were stand-ing in the room with them, urging him to say the right things. He rubbed the back of his neck with one hand. "It isn't that I don't like her, Button."

"You used to be her boyfriend," Liza announced, reaching for a drumstick. "I've seen pictures in your yearbook, and you and Glory were *kissing*."

Jesse chuckled, though he felt sad to the very core of his being. "Yeah. We used to *kiss*," he retorted good-naturedly. "So what?"

"Did you love her?"

He tried hard, but he found that he couldn't lie. "Yes, Captain Quiz, I loved her. Is there anything else you'd like to know?"

Liza caught him off guard by nodding and saying seriously, "Yes. I'd like to know who had me before I got adopted by Mommy and Daddy."

Jesse looked away. So, she was back on that again. He'd hoped the phase was over. "Does it matter? Your mom and dad loved you a whole lot, and they did all the important stuff."

Liza's tone was solemn. "It matters. Someday, I'm going to find my real mom."

"Sandy Bainbridge was your real mom," Jesse said, and though he didn't mean for it to be, his tone was on the sharp side.

His daughter's large green eyes were filled with lingering grief. Maybe it was worse for her at Christmas, knowing Gresh and Sandy were gone forever, like it was for him.

"I just want to ask my mom why she gave me up," she said with gentle defiance, and her lower lip quivered.

Jesse sighed and shoved his paper plate away, then braced his folded arms against the edge of the table. "She was a kid, Liza. She gave you up because she didn't know how to take care of you."

"Gramps told me once that she was eighteen," Liza argued. "Women get married and have babies at that age all the time."

Tonight, of all nights, she had to go into her forty-year-old-midget-posing-as-a-kid routine. "Trust me." Jesse sighed, before slurping up a drink of soda through his straw. "Your mom wasn't mature enough to take care of a baby."

"Did she have a husband?"

"No. I mean, probably not."

Liza narrowed her eyes. "You know what I think, Uncle Jesse? I think you know who my mom is."

How the hell was he supposed to look the kid in the face and deny that? He stood and started gathering up the debris of their dinner, carefully avoiding Liza's gaze. "How would I know that?" he snapped, turning and striding off into the kitchen.

He could feel Liza's suspicious stare following him.

Jesse didn't come back until he'd stood gripping the edge of a counter for nearly five minutes, trying to compose himself. The fact that none of this would be happening if Glory had just stayed in Portland where she belonged did nothing to improve his mood.

When he returned to the dining room, Liza had her school books and a bunch of papers spread out on the table. Jesse was infinitely grateful that the topic of parenthood had been set aside, at least for the moment.

The telephone rang just as they were working the last fraction problem, and Jesse went to the sideboard for the extension. "Bainbridge," he answered, expecting the caller to be someone at the office.

"Jesse, it's Ilene," his cousin said. "The headache isn't improving. Could you please keep Liza tonight?"

Despite his discomfort over the secret he was keeping from Liza, he liked the idea of their being like a real family, at least for one night. "Sure. But maybe I should call Doc Cupples and send him over to have a look at you."

"That old quack?" Ilene retorted. "I wouldn't let him clip my toenails. Besides, I know I'll be better by morning."

"Call if you need anything," Jesse instructed. Then he said goodbye to his cousin and hung up. "Ilene wants you to sleep here tonight," he told Liza. "She's still not feeling well."

Liza relaxed visibly, and Jesse realized she'd been expecting bad news. It broke his heart that the kid was only nine years old and already trained in the adult art of bracing herself against tragedy. "Maybe she needs to go to the hospital."

Jesse kissed the top of his daughter's head. "She'll be fine, Spud," he promised. "Did you work out that last problem?"

The child nodded, closing her books and putting her papers in a neat stack. It was a trait she'd probably gotten from Glory, Jesse reflected, since he tended to leave things scattered about.

"So what do you want to do?"

Liza's face brightened. "Let's get the Christmas stuff down from the attic. That way, we'll be all ready to decorate when we get the tree."

Jesse sighed dramatically, but he liked the idea as well as Liza did. He was looking forward to Christmas this year, though he'd spent the last ten dreading it. "Okay," he said, shaking his finger. "But it's a school night and you're not staying up till all hours."

She grinned. "Don't worry, Uncle Jesse. I'll mind real good."

They brought the nativity scene down first; it had been one of Jesse's mother's most valued possessions, and he carried it carefully. The porcelain figures had been handcrafted in Italy before he was born, but he and Gresham had built the stable out in the carriage house one year, as a surprise.

After the crèche had been set in its place of honor, on the raised hearth of the living-room fireplace, the figures arranged just so, Jesse and Liza went back to the attic for the boxes and boxes of delicate ornaments and lights that always graced the tree.

Jesse was actually humming a Christmas carol as he sat in the middle of the living-room floor, a fire blazing on the hearth, untangling strings of lights. Liza had hooked them all together and plugged them in, and he suddenly found himself surrounded by bright knobs of color.

He laughed. "You're no help, at all."

Liza came and sat beside him, amid the twinkling tangle, and laid her head against his shoulder. Her statement caught him unaware, even though he should have been on the alert after that conversation they'd had earlier. "I think my real dad and mom might live around here."

We got trouble, Jesse thought, *right here in Pearl River. And it starts with a capital G.* "Why do you say that?" he asked, still working with the twisted strings of rubber-coated wire.

"It's just a feeling," Liza answered. But then she pinioned him with those eyes of hers and asked him straight out, "Do you know who my dad is, Uncle Jesse?"

He answered hoarsely, without knowing why he did it. He was sure of only one thing: that lying to this kid was impossible. "Yes, Button. I know."

"Who is he?"

Jesse drew a deep breath, exhaled, and set the lights aside to draw Liza gently onto his lap. She gazed into his face with total trust.

"He's me," he said raggedly, holding her tighter.

She didn't seem shocked. In fact, she didn't even

seem surprised. "How come you gave me to Daddy and Mommy?"

"I didn't, exactly." Jesse tucked her head under his chin. "But it worked out okay, didn't it? I mean, your daddy and mommy really loved you, and they took good care of you."

Liza twisted in his lap, so she could look him directly in the eye again. "But they're gone," she reasoned. "If you're my dad, you know who my mother is. Tell me, Uncle Jesse—please."

Jesse shook his head. He'd had all the emotional strain he could handle for right then, and besides, he needed time to think before he gave Glory a permanent place in Liza's life. She swore she'd changed, but Glory had a habit of disappearing just when somebody started loving her with everything they had. "I can't do that, sweetheart. At least not tonight. For right now, I'm going to ask you to trust me and to believe that I'll tell you when the time is right."

She reached up to kiss his cheek, then settled her head under his chin again. "I love you, Jesse," she said, and for a moment the scattered tree lights blended before Jesse's eyes, making a collage of Christmas colors.

"I love you, too, kid," he answered gruffly.

CHAPTER EIGHT

LIZA ARRIVED AT the bank about five minutes before closing time and waited quietly in one of the chairs in Glory's office. The child seemed distracted, and Glory was troubled by that.

"Is something wrong?" she asked, as she put on her coat and reached for her purse.

Liza's small shoulders moved in a shrug. "Sometimes I wish I could be Nancy Drew and go around solving mysteries."

Glory put a hand on Liza's back and ushered her through the office door. "What mysteries would you solve?"

The little girl looked up with an expression of despairing resignation. "I'd find out who my real mom is, and ask her why she didn't want me."

A painful lump formed in Glory's throat, but she made herself smile in spite of it. "I'll bet she wanted you very, very much," she said.

Liza shrugged again, and the two of them hurried out to Glory's car. Glory turned on the engine and shivered as she waited for the heater to kick in.

At home, Glory made cocoa for Liza and a *latte* for herself. The apartment was warm; evidently the temperamental radiators were having a good day. Since

Glory had spent the evening before putting things away, the place looked relatively tidy.

"You should put your Christmas tree right here," Liza announced, standing by the bay windows that overlooked the street. She turned in a circle, with her arms stretched wide, as though clearing a space in the cosmos.

"I thought I would," Glory agreed, setting the cocoa and *latte* down on the coffee table in front of her pale rose couch.

"When are you doing to put it up?" Liza inquired.

"This weekend, I hope. I'll probably get one while we're out tree hunting on Saturday."

Liza's smile was a little forlorn as she came to sit in Glory's mauve wing chair and reached for her cocoa. It was plain she was trying to work up her courage to say something, and when she did, the words practically stopped Glory's heart. "If a person loses one daddy, and then they get another one, can the second one die, too?"

She set her *latte* on the coffee table so it wouldn't spill over onto the rug. Obviously, Jesse had told Liza who he was, but what had he said about her biological mother? Damn it, he might have warned her! She drew a deep breath and forcibly controlled herself! "Honey, anybody can die, and most of the time we don't know when it's going to happen." She paused, praying silently for the right words. "The thing is, you can't plan your life to avoid pain. You can't say, 'I'm not going to love this person, because if I do, I might get hurt somewhere down the road.'"

Unexpectedly, Liza began to cry. She put her cocoa

down, crossed the distance between their chairs and scrambled into Glory's lap, sobbing.

Glory held her child, her own eyes blurred with tears. "It's okay, darling. You go right ahead and cry."

"Uncle Jesse is a cop!" wailed the little girl. "He could get shot by a bad guy, or his car might go off the road when he's chasing somebody—"

Glory kissed Liza's temple. "He could also live to be a very old man, honey, like his grandfather."

After a while, Liza began to settle down. "I g-guess you'd better measure me for my costume," she said, sniffling. "I have to go and practice for the pageant tonight, and Aunt Ilene will be here to pick me up after she closes the store."

With a nod, Glory set her daughter on her feet and went to get her sewing basket. She measured Liza according to the printed directions.

It was Jesse who came by to pick the child up a few minutes later, not Ilene. He sent Liza to wait in the car and lingered outside Glory's door, his hands in his coat pockets, his expression guarded and remote.

"You told her," Glory said, standing there in the doorway. She knew he wouldn't come in even if she invited him.

Jesse sighed. "Yeah. I told her part of it." He paused for a moment before dropping the bomb that blew Glory's tentative dreams to bits. "Liza's been through more at nine than most people endure in a lifetime," he said. "I want you to stay away from her until everybody gets their emotional balance back."

For a moment, Glory held on to the hope that she hadn't heard him right. "Stay away?" she echoed in a small voice.

"I don't want her to get attached to you, Glory, only to be hurt later when you decide small towns and kids aren't 'you' and move on."

There was, unfortunately, no doubting what he'd meant that time. "I won't let you do this, Jesse—I love that child as much as you do."

His response was a quietly furious, "You can talk about love, but it takes a hell of a lot more than that to raise a kid. You've got to be able to stick out the tough times, and I don't think you know how to do that."

He turned then, and started to walk away. Glory started to call him back, then stopped herself. Jesse had obviously made up his mind and, for now, there would be no reasoning with him.

She closed the door quietly behind him, spread the white synthetic taffeta for Liza's costume out on the kitchen table and tried to focus her tear-filled eyes on the printed instructions. She worked straight through dinner and by ten o'clock she had the outfit finished, right down to the tinsel halo and gauze wings trimmed with silver garland.

The next morning Glory dressed and went to work as usual, dropping off Liza's costume at Ilene's bookstore without saying more than a muttered, "Good morning." Reaching the bank, she got out Pearl River's thin phone book and looked under "attorneys" for the name of a lawyer.

There were only two in town, and the first one, Glory recalled, had been one of Jesse's closest friends since kindergarten. She called the second, a man named Brock Haywood, and made an appointment.

He agreed to see her during her lunch hour.

ON SATURDAY MORNING, Glory bought a tree from the straggly group displayed in front of the supermarket. One of the bag boys tied it to the roof of her car, and she headed straight home.

Whatever Christmas spirit she'd mustered was gone—she was only putting up the tree for appearance's sake. Delphine and Harold would be worried if she didn't do something to observe the holiday.

She was putting lights on the tree, having set it in its stand in front of the bay windows in her living room, when Jill pulled up. Glory was relieved to see her friend, but she also felt a desire to hide.

Of course she couldn't since Jill had seen her.

"I thought you were going tree-hunting with Jesse and Liza," Glory's friend commented as she divested herself of her coat, hat and gloves. "I wouldn't have stopped, if I hadn't caught a glimpse of you through the window as I was driving by."

Glory repeated a silent litany of reasons why she must not burst into tears and then said, in an awkward attempt to change the subject, "Weren't you supposed to be skiing this weekend with that new boyfriend of yours?"

Jill rolled her eyes. "He turned out to be another creep." She plopped herself down in one of Glory's chairs. "I swear, if I ever do find a man I like they'll probably feature him on 'Unsolved Mysteries' as an ax murderer."

Glory laughed, despite the pain of her own situation. "How about some hot cider, or a *latte*?"

"A *latte*? You sophisticated creature! I'll have one of those."

The process of brewing two of the concoctions

gave Glory time to pull herself together. It was inevitable, after all, that Jill would ask again why she wasn't spending the day with Jesse and Liza as planned.

She sprang the question as soon as Glory returned with the two steaming cups and sat down on the sofa. "What happened between you and Jesse?"

Glory sighed. She'd never told Jill the whole truth, but it spilled out of her now, all of it. She related how the judge had forced her to leave town, how she'd come back and discovered that the daughter she'd given up had been adopted by Gresham and Sandy, how Jesse had ordered her to stay away from Liza for the time being.

"And you're letting him get away with it?" Jill demanded, her face a study in disbelief.

"No," Glory answered, shaking her head. "I've filed a suit for visitation rights." She glanced at her watch and sighed again. "Jesse should be getting the papers soon."

Jill put down her cup and covered her ears with both hands, as if expecting an explosion. After a moment, she grinned shakily and dropped them to her lap. "This ought to give tonight's Christmas pageant a high degree of dramatic tension. You are coming, aren't you?"

Glory nodded. "Nothing could keep me away."

"Good for you," Jill answered resolutely. That was easy for her to say, Glory thought. She wasn't playing with emotional dynamite.

"JESSE BAINBRIDGE?"

Jesse stopped in the hallway of Pearl River's tiny courthouse, frowning at the old man who stood before him. "You know who I am, Harry," he said. "I used to deliver your newspapers."

Harry flushed. "I'm sorry, Jesse," he said. And then he held out a folded document.

Jesse muttered a curse and accepted the papers without asking for a further explanation. He knew a summons when he saw one, and nobody needed to tell him who was behind it.

DELPHINE AND HAROLD arrived at Glory's apartment at six o'clock sharp, bringing a potted red poinsettia. While Delphine set the plant on the coffee table, Harold sniffed the air and smiled appreciatively.

"Something sure smells good," he boomed in his big voice. "I'll bet you're as good a cook as your mother." He put an arm around Delphine's slender shoulders and squeezed.

Glory made an effort at a smile. "It's my specialty, Spanish rice," she replied.

Harold said he was looking forward to supper and sat down in one of the living-room chairs to watch the news on TV. Delphine joined Glory in the kitchen.

"You look like hell warmed over," she told her daughter bluntly. "What's happened?"

Glory made a major enterprise of taking the casserole dish from the oven and getting the salad out of the fridge. "Thanks for the poinsettia, Mama," she said, hoping to deflect the conversation. "It's lovely."

"Glory."

She sighed and faced her mother squarely, setting the Spanish rice on a trivet on the counter. "Jesse declared war a few days ago, and I fired back."

"What do you mean, Jesse declared war?"

"He told Liza that he's her father. Then he told *me* to stay away from her until further notice. So I saw a lawyer and filed for visitation rights."

Delphine's normally pink cheeks went white for a moment. "Uh-oh. What was Jesse's response to that?"

"I don't know yet," Glory said. "He probably didn't get the papers until this afternoon."

Delphine gave a deep sigh, then put her arms around Glory and hugged her tightly. "Well, what's done is done. Harold and I will stick by you, of course."

Glory returned her mother's embrace before stepping back. "I'm sorry this had to happen now, Mama, right before your wedding and everything."

Delphine and Harold were to be married on New Year's Eve, in a candlelight service at the First Lutheran Church. "You have enough to worry about without fretting over that," the older woman said. "We'll all just have to take this one step at a time."

"You're on my side?" Glory asked, surprised, as, still wearing oven mitts, she picked up the casserole dish to carry it to the table in the dining area. Delphine followed with the salad.

"Good heavens, sweetheart, did you expect me to take Jesse's part? I'm *your* mother."

"I know you like Jesse."

Delphine kissed Glory's cheek. "Maybe so, but I *love* you."

After that, she and Delphine and Harold had a quiet dinner amid the twinkling sparkles cast by the tree. As soon as they'd cleared away the dishes, it was time to leave for the Christmas pageant.

"When you get home tonight, after seeing Liza again," Glory said to her mother, when she was settled in the back seat of Harold's car, "I want you to take a good look at that old picture of your grandmother Bridget."

Delphine nodded, but her smile was tempered with sadness, and she was quiet as they all drove to the church.

The requisite snow was falling as they left the car and followed the crowd up the steps and into the building. In the sanctuary, fragrant garlands of evergreen decorated the altar railings, and someone had constructed a remarkably authentic stable on the dais, complete with straw. There were candles waiting on the pews, and each person took one before sitting down.

Glory quickly scanned the crowd for Jesse and was relieved not to see him. Maybe, she thought in a spate of wild optimism, he was somewhere battling crime and wouldn't be able to attend the pageant, at all.

He came in about one second after she'd formulated the idea and took a place in the pew directly in front of hers, turning to give her a challenging stare.

Harold, who suspected nothing, thrust out his hand and said, "Hello, Jesse. How's the lawman business these days?"

Jesse's face thawed visibly as he shook Harold's hand. "Unfortunately, it's thriving." He looked at Delphine and gave her a roguish wink. "By the way, Harold, congratulations on marrying the prettiest girl in town."

His friendliness to Harold and Delphine, which clearly shut her out, was almost as difficult for Glory to cope with as the cold anger he bore toward her. It was a tremendous relief to her when the organist started the prelude and everyone sat down.

Candles were lit, and the lights turned down, and the
pastor delivered a short sermon on the significance of
the season. Glory tried to concentrate on the real meaning of Christmas, but all she could do was stare at the
back of Jesse's head and ache because even after all
these years they couldn't be civil to each other.

Presently the pastor finished speaking, and the pageant began. Mary and Joseph came up the center aisle
to a cardboard door set up at one side of the dais, and
Joseph knocked, causing it to waver dangerously.

The innkeeper opened it and, with audible prompt-
ing from Jill, who was sitting in the front pew, informed the weary couple that there was no room at
the inn. They could, however, sleep in the stable if
they wanted to.

Mary and Joseph trekked wearily over to the makeshift barn. They knelt in the straw, as if to pray, and
there was a moment of dramatic import before Jill
rushed up and put a baby doll in the manger.

Meanwhile, shepherds came up the aisle in burlap
robes, with bath towels on their heads and sandals on
their feet, and angels fluttered in through the doorway to the pastor's study. Glory's heart surged into
her throat as she watched Liza take her place with the
others, resplendent in her costume.

There were songs and Bible verses, but Glory had
eyes and ears only for her daughter. Like Mary, she
pondered the miracle of birth in her heart.

All too quickly, the evening ended. As the players
filed down the aisle to collect their reward of cookies
and hot cider in the church fellowship hall, Liza's eyes
linked with Glory's, and Glory felt a stab at the sorrow
she saw in her child's gaze.

Obviously Jesse had announced his decision to keep Glory and Liza apart. An anger entirely unsuited to her surroundings welled up inside Glory, and she rushed out of the sanctuary, through the narthex, and outside into the biting cold. There she stood gripping the stair railing, her eyes burning with furious tears.

She sensed Jesse's presence a moment before he came to stand on the step beside her.

"Glory—"

She crammed her hands into her coat pockets so she wouldn't start pounding at his chest in an hysterical rage. "Did you think I wouldn't fight back, Jesse?" she whispered. "Did you think I'd let you take Liza away from me, like your grandfather did?"

"Glory, listen to me."

"No, I won't listen to you!" Glory blurted out, moving the rest of the way down the steps. "I've heard it all, Jesse. You say you're afraid I'll make Liza love me and then desert her, but the real truth is you want to punish me for hurting *you*! You're not thinking about her, you're thinking about yourself!"

Although most people had gone downstairs to share in the celebration and the refreshments, there were a few souls trailing out to go home. Both Glory and Jesse lapsed into a stiff silence until they were alone again.

Then he took her arm and hustled her a little way down the street. "Maybe I am thinking about myself— after all, I'm the one who's had the most experience with your methods—but you're not operating out of pure altruism yourself, lady. You want to soothe your conscience, and you're not going to use Liza to do it!"

"She'll guess, Jesse," Glory said evenly, having made a great effort at keeping her temper. "It doesn't take a rocket scientist to count backwards ten years and look at the pictures in a high-school yearbook!"

"I'll handle that when it happens. Right now, I want you to leave her alone."

Before Glory could reply, she saw an angel with pigtails standing on the church steps and gazing wistfully in their direction. Glory ached with everything in her to gather the child into her arms and tell her that she loved her, that giving her up was the single greatest regret of her life. "Let's call a cease-fire for now, Jesse," she said with a sigh. "An angel has just stepped into range."

Jesse turned and saw Liza there and instantly he was in motion. "You were fantastic!" he told his daughter, scooping her into his arms and starting up the church steps. "Let's go get some of that cider before it's all gone."

Over Jesse's shoulder, Liza stared forlornly back at Glory and wiggled her fingers in farewell.

Struggling to regain her equilibrium, Glory waited on the steps until Delphine and Harold came out a few minutes later. Maybe Jesse was right, she thought miserably, as her mother and future stepfather drove her home. Maybe she was just thinking of herself, and it would be better if she moved on and started a new life somewhere else.

After saying good-night to Delphine and Harold, Glory went into her apartment and flipped on the Christmas-tree lights, leaving the rest of the living room dark. Then she sank down onto the couch, still wearing her coat and gloves, and murmured, "Oh, Dylan, what should I do—stay or go?"

She supposed talking to her dead brother—a foible

that seemed excusable when she was standing beside his grave—meant she'd finally gone around the bend in the river and would never be able to paddle back, but she didn't care.

The radiators clanged, but Glory knew that wasn't a message from the other side. It just meant the landlord was too cheap to put in a modern heating system. With a sigh she took off her coat and gloves, kicked away her boots and flipped on the television set.

Glory watched one program and then another and then another, and if her life had depended on it she couldn't have said what any of the shows was about. Awakening to find herself hunched up on the couch, cold and achy, she rose, switched off the TV and the tree lights and went to bed.

Tomorrow was another day, and the war between her and Jesse would undoubtedly continue. She'd need her strength.

In the morning, Glory went through her usual routine of showering, eating breakfast, putting on her makeup, blow drying her hair and getting dressed. She felt like a wooden mannequin, caused by some unseen magician to move and function but not quite brought to life.

Since the bank didn't open until ten, and Glory reported to work at nine, she used her key to let herself in. The two tellers smiled and said "Good morning" in chorus, and Glory, still the mannequin, responded as if she'd been programmed.

She'd no more than put away her purse and gotten out her appointment book for the day when Shelby, one of the secretaries, came in with coffee. She was a pretty dark-eyed girl with long chocolate-brown hair.

"Someone evidently came by to see you either last night or this morning," Shelby said with a smile, producing an envelope and setting it on Glory's desk, along with the coffee. "I found this in the night depository."

A feeling of dread clenched Glory's heart and stomach as she picked up the envelope. Her name was written across the front in teetering cursive letters. "Thank you," she said distractedly, wanting to be alone.

Shelby left, and Glory opened the envelope and took out the folded page of notebook paper inside.

Dear Glory, the same childish hand had written, and Glory groped blindly for the telephone receiver as she read on.

LIZA STOOD UNCERTAINLY beside the railroad track, holding her Uncle Jesse's high-school yearbook under one arm and her piggy bank under the other. When the train stopped—as yet, there was no sign of it—Liza meant to climb into one of the freight cars just like she'd seen a girl do in the movies once.

Her feet were cold, even though she had two pairs of socks inside her boots. She'd worn jeans and a flannel shirt and thermal underwear so she wouldn't get sick and die, like Beth in *Little Women*.

She sniffled. She probably shouldn't have climbed up on the concrete edge that protected the flower bed at the bank and dropped that stupid note into the night-deposit box, because Glory would most likely call Uncle Jesse as soon as she read it.

Glory. Awkwardly, Liza set the piggy bank and the yearbook down in the snow and hugged herself. If Glory didn't want to be her mommy, it was all right. Liza didn't want to be Glory's daughter, either.

Much.

In the distance the train whistle hooted, and Liza drew in her breath. She was afraid the tears would freeze in her eyelashes if she cried, and she *really* wanted to cry.

She supposed she'd known Glory was somebody special from the first time she'd met her. Last night, lying in bed, all wide awake from the excitement of the Christmas pageant, the whole thing had come to Liza in a shattering flash. The words she'd heard Glory say on the sidewalk in front of the church had come back to her, their meaning crystal-clear.

She'll guess, Jesse. It doesn't take a rocket scientist to count backwards ten years and look at the pictures in a high-school yearbook!

Uncle Jesse was her father, he'd admitted it himself. And he and Glory had been in love ten years before, and Liza was nine years old. It took nine months for a baby to grow inside a woman's stomach, according to a special she and Aunt Ilene had watched on PBS. Besides that, Aunt Ilene had told her just the other day that Uncle Jesse was always mad at Glory because he'd loved her very much once upon a time and she'd gone away.

Liza wiped her nose with a mittened hand. If she could have had any woman in the world for a mommy, besides the one she'd lost in the plane crash, of course, she would have picked Glory Parsons. That made the thought that Glory hadn't wanted her, that she'd gone off and left her all alone in some hospital right after she was *born*, for pity's sake, impossible for Liza to accept.

She'd decided to go away somewhere and raise herself. Even the fact that it was almost Christmas and she probably would have gotten a Nintendo from Uncle Jesse couldn't make her stay.

The train chugged around a corner, coming out of the snowy trees, making a great clatter as it approached. Liza had seen it stop in just this place about ten million times, so she stooped and picked up the yearbook and the piggy bank and prepared to jump on board.

The whistle shrieked a greeting, and Liza waited patiently, hoping that raising herself wouldn't cost more than 15.87.

"JESSE!" GLORY GASPED the moment the sheriff of Pearl River County came on the line. "Liza's run away! She left a note in the night depository—oh, God, Jesse, *do something*!"

His voice was surprisingly calm. "Glory, take a deep breath and get a grip on yourself. Did she say where she was going?"

"No," Glory burst out, half sick with panic.

"Read me the note," Jesse said evenly.

Glory began, the lined notebook paper crackling in her hand because she was trembling so hard.

Dear Glory,

If you don't want me, that's okay, because I don't want you, either. You left me at the hospital. The reason I can't stay is, I don't want you and Uncle Jesse to fight about me anymore. And I don't want to see you in the bank and know you didn't like me enough to keep me. I know Uncle Jesse and Aunt Ilene will miss me a whole lot, and I would have got a bunch of presents at Christmas.

I guess they can take back whatever stuff they bought and get a refund.

Love, Liza

"Listen to me," Jesse said, his voice stern. "We're going to find her. I'll send a deputy to the bus station and we'll cover all the highways leading out of town. *Liza will be all right*, Glory."

"Like Dylan was all right?" Glory cried. "Like Sandy and Gresham—"

"Stop it, Glory. I don't have time for this."

"Come and get me, Jesse. I want to go with you."

Jesse gave in, but reluctantly. "I'll be there in five minutes. If you're not waiting on the sidewalk, I won't even slow down, let alone stop and twiddle my thumbs until you come out of the bank. Is that clear?"

Glory was already out of her chair and groping for her purse. "It's clear, Jesse. I promise it's clear."

He hung up with a crash, and Glory ran to tell Mr. Baker there was an emergency in the family, but she didn't explain the details. He very kindly excused her to go and take care of it, calling after her that he hoped everything would work out all right.

Jesse's patrol car appeared an instant after she stepped out of the bank and, as good as his word, he just barely stopped at all. The tires were spinning again before Glory had managed to close her door or fasten the seat belt.

"I hope you're satisfied," Jesse rasped, just before he reached for the microphone to radio the men he'd dispatched to different parts of town.

Glory bit into her lower lip and said nothing. If anything had happened to Liza, she was never going to forgive herself.

CHAPTER NINE

"THIS IS ALL my fault," Glory fretted as she and Jesse began the search for their runaway daughter. "If I hadn't come back here—"

Jesse's jawline hardened for a moment, but then he reached out and touched Glory's knee. "Take it easy," he told her. "Liza's nine years old—she couldn't have gotten far."

Glory didn't find it at all comforting to realize that Jesse was taking the road that led to the small park down by the river. The water would be frigid at this time of year, even frozen over in places, and Glory's whole being seemed to clench in terror as she prayed Liza hadn't gone there.

"W-why the river?" she managed to ask, when Jesse brought the patrol car to a stop in the small, freshly plowed parking area that overlooked an array of snow-mounded picnic tables and barbecue pits.

"We've had some happy times here," Jesse said in a hoarse, distant voice. "Watch out that you don't break your neck in those damn high heels."

Only then did Glory realize that she wasn't suitably dressed for a search in her gray Ultrasuede suit, ruffly blouse and charcoal eel-skin heels. She was out of the car as fast as Jesse was, but keeping pace with him immediately proved impossible.

He started down the pristine slope toward the picnic area, his strides long, his plain boots perfectly suited to the task. Cupping his hands to his mouth, he yelled, "Liza!"

Glory picked her way along behind him, moving as fast as she could, her eyes scanning the river, with its shards of sun-glittered ice. *Please God*, she prayed, *don't let her be in that water.*

Jesse gave the landscape around them what Glory perceived to be a cursory examination, then announced, his breath white in the crisp air, "She isn't here."

"How do you know?" Glory demanded. Even though she'd just prayed that Liza hadn't come near the river, she wanted to leave no stone unturned.

With a sweeping gesture of one arm, Jesse took in the whole park. "No tracks in the snow. Nobody's been down here in the last few days except us." His brown eyes ran over Glory's inadequate clothing with a sort of tolerant contempt. Then, without a word of warning, he strode over to her, lifted her up into his arms, and started carrying her toward the parking lot. "You're heavier than you look," he commented.

Glory tried to ignore what being held so close to Jesse did to her, even under such uncertain circumstances. If she'd known Liza was safe and warm somewhere, Glory would have wanted him to make love to her. "Thanks," she retorted.

Reaching the parking lot, Jesse set Glory back on her feet with an exaggerated sigh of relief. Moments later, he was in the front seat of his car, the microphone to his radio in one hand.

Glory heard the blunt, static-ridden answers to his

questions as she snapped her seat belt in place, but she couldn't make sense of what was being said.

"They didn't find her at the bus station," he said, staring out at the river as he put the microphone back in place, "and there's no sign of her along any of the roads leading out of town."

Panic rose around Glory like invisible floodwaters, threatening to drown her, but Jesse offered her hope as he started the car and shifted into reverse.

"That probably means she's still somewhere in Pearl River," he said.

Shivering with cold and fear, Glory hugged herself. "Maybe she went to your house, Jesse. There are a lot of outbuildings there, if I remember correctly, and she probably has happy memories of the place."

"It's worth checking out," Jesse agreed. And then he headed back to the main highway.

It took a full forty-five minutes to search every nook and cranny in the Bainbridge mansion, and there was no sign of Liza anywhere between the wine cellar and the attic. The stables, carriage house, storage sheds and the guest house were all empty, too.

In the mansion's huge kitchen, Jesse made instant coffee for Glory, lacing it generously with brandy, and then grabbed at the wall phone and punched out a number. Glory knew without being told that he was calling his office, hoping against hope that there would be some word.

She thought she'd faint with relief when, after barking a greeting, Jesse grinned. "Liza's been found," he said to Glory. "She went to the diner after she missed her train, and she's okay."

Glory swayed against the counter and took a restorative sip of her coffee. *Thank you, God,* she thought, closing her eyes. *Thank you, thank you, thank you!*

After a few more words, none of which Glory was able to grasp, Jesse hung up the receiver with a triumphant crash.

Glory started to set her coffee aside, but Jesse stopped her with a crisp, "Drink it down. You're white as hell." Then he took her arm and led her to the bench beside the big trestle table.

Knowing Jesse wouldn't take her to her daughter until she'd done what he said, Glory sat down on the bench and drank her spiked coffee as fast as she could swallow it. Then they returned to Jesse's squad car and started toward town.

Instead of heading toward the diner, Jesse took the first right turn after they crossed the city limits and brought the squad car to a stop in front of Dr. Cupples's humble office. It was a small blue house with white shutters, and the doctor's shingle hung from the scrollwork above the porch.

Glory hadn't been near the place since that day a decade before, when she'd learned she was pregnant with Jesse's baby. Despite the unhappy memories, she was right behind Jesse as he strode up the walk.

"I thought you said Liza is all right!" she cried breathlessly, when he reached the porch and wrenched open the front door.

"Johnson brought her here, just to make sure," Jesse answered shortly. And then he was looming over the receptionist's desk, demanding, "Where's my daughter?"

"Right in there," the middle-aged woman replied, pointing toward a doorway, not in the least intimidated by the sheriff's manner.

As quickly as Glory moved, Jesse was through the doorway first.

Liza sat on the end of an examining table, wrapped in an oversized, old-fashioned felt bathrobe with Indian designs on it, sipping hot cocoa. Her eyes went wide when she saw Jesse.

He shook his finger at her. "You're just lucky I'm too glad to see you to tan your hide!" he told the child furiously.

Liza looked from Jesse's face to Glory's, then sighed like a ninety-year-old woman. "I'm sorry," she said, her little shoulders stooped.

Glory spoke far more gently than Jesse had. "Why did you do it?" she asked. Even though she was sure she knew, she still hoped she'd been wrong. "Why did you run away?"

Liza's gaze was level. "Because you didn't want me. I would probably be halfway to California by now, if that darned train had just stopped."

Just then Dr. Cupples appeared in another doorway. He was an old man now, with white hair and kindly blue eyes. "Hello, Jesse," he said. Then hesitantly he added a greeting for Glory. "Ms. Parsons. I wonder if I could speak with the two of you in my office."

Jesse nodded shortly, and his brown eyes were hot as they swung back to his daughter. "I still haven't decided against spanking you," he warned, "so don't you dare move!"

Glory, for her part, was swamped with memories as she preceded Jesse into the doctor's small office. Here, the physician had given her happy news that was to have tragic, far-reaching results. She felt weak as she sank into one of the chairs facing Dr. Cupples's desk.

Jesse took the other, lifting one booted foot to rest on the opposite knee.

The doctor carefully closed the office door, then went behind his desk to sink into his swivel chair with a weary sigh. He pressed a button on his telephone and said, "Doris, will you please hold my calls for a few minutes?"

Jesse shifted uncomfortably in his chair, then leaned forward, his brows drawn together in a frown. "What's this all about?"

The old man sat back, making a steeple of his fingers beneath his double chin. "I have a confession to make, and it's not an easy thing to do, Jesse Bainbridge, so I'll thank you to keep your pants on until I get it said!"

Still glowering, Jesse subsided a little, settling back in his chair. Glory, meanwhile was perched on the edge of hers, sensing that Dr. Cupples was about to make an important announcement.

"After you came to see me that day ten years ago, Glory," he said with resignation, "I betrayed your trust—and my own vows as a physician—to call my friend Seth Bainbridge and tell him you were expecting a baby, and that Jesse was the father."

Glory wasn't surprised; she'd deduced that long ago. But Jesse straightened in his chair, poised like a rocket about to shoot off the launchpad.

"What?" he rasped.

"I thought I was doing a friend a favor. Now, of course, I wish I'd just stayed out of the whole thing. That little girl out there might have been a whole lot happier if I had." Dr. Cupples sighed and leaned forward, bracing his forearms against his cluttered desk.

"The judge thought it was important for you to go to college and marry well, Jesse, so he paid Ms. Parsons to leave town."

Jesse shot a lethal look in Glory's direction. "Don't blame yourself too much, Doc," he rasped. "The plan wouldn't have worked if Glory hadn't been so damn willing to be bought off!"

Glory would have liked to think Jesse didn't mean what he was saying, that he was just reacting to the unavoidable stress of losing a child and finding her again, but she knew he meant every word. And she was too crippled with hurt and regret to defend herself.

"Glory was eighteen," Doc Cupples pointed out kindly. "A fatherless girl, with nobody to take her side." His blue eyes shifted to Glory's face. "You have no idea how sorry I am for my interference, my dear, or how much I wish I'd done something to help you."

Jesse thrust himself out of his chair and stormed out of the office, and Glory followed him, after one apologetic look at the doctor.

In the examination room, Jesse scooped Liza up in his arms, borrowed bathrobe, and all, and held her tightly against his chest. His gaze punctured Glory's spirit like a lance. "You and your lawyer wanted a fight," he breathed. "Well, lady, you've got one!"

Before Glory could work through the wall of pain that surrounded her and respond, Jesse strode out, carrying Liza with him.

Dr. Cupples laid one hand on Glory's shoulder. "Jesse's a good man," he said quietly, "even if he is hot-tempered. He'll come to his senses if you just give him a day or two."

Glory felt broken and bruised inside. She nodded distractedly and went out.

Walking to her mother's diner, she heard Liza's words over and over in her mind...*you didn't want me....*

When Delphine saw her daughter, she was visibly horrified. Stepping back to admit Glory to the little apartment over the diner, she said, "Glory, sweetheart, what's happened? I thought you'd be happy, finding Liza safe—"

Glory sank into a chair and kicked off her eel-skin shoes. They were completely ruined, but she didn't give a damn. "You were right," she said brokenly. "You were right."

Delphine bent to unbutton Glory's coat, as she might have done when her daughter was a child, and pushed it back off her shoulders. Then she took the crocheted afghan from the sofa and draped it tenderly around Glory's legs. "There, now," she whispered soothingly. "What was I so right about?"

"I shouldn't have come here," Glory fretted in utter despair. "All I did was mix Liza up. She ran away because she thought I didn't want her. And, Mama, she could have been hurt or even killed. Someone awful might have picked her up—"

"Hush!" Delphine interrupted with affectionate harshness. "The child is safe and sound, Glory—that's all that matters." She moved toward the kitchen to brew the inevitable cup of tea, always part of her solution to any heartbreak. "You were right about one thing," she said cheerfully. "That little girl is the spitting image of Bridget McVerdy!"

Glory began to cry softly. Liza might have been

saved all this trauma if Glory had just kept her promise to the judge and stayed away from Pearl River. But no, she'd had to come here and blow the lid off everything. Now Liza would not only grieve for Sandy and Gresham, she would suffer with the knowledge that her birth parents had failed her.

When Delphine returned with tea, a little plate of colorful Christmas cookies and a packet of tissue, Glory was slightly calmer. She dried her eyes, no doubt smearing her makeup all over her face, and then blew her nose. When that process was completed, she accepted one cookie and the strong, fragrant tea.

"There is one obvious solution to all this, you know," Delphine said gently, sitting down on the sofa facing Glory and folding her hands.

"What?" Glory sniffled, taking a disconsolate bite out of an angel's wing.

"You and Jesse could get married. Then the two of you could go about making a life for yourselves and your daughter."

Glory shook her head. "I'll admit it, Mama—I'm just crazy enough that I'm as much in love with Jesse as I ever was. I g-guess I'm one of those women who loves pain. But there's no hope for us. Jesse's furious with me—he can't see past the fact that I took money from the judge when I left Pearl River. I hurt him far more deeply than I ever dreamed I could, and he's never going to forgive me."

"Why don't you decide that after you've gone to him and told him the truth, Glory—that you love him desperately?"

Glory imagined the scenario and shrank from the

accusations she knew she would see burning in Jesse's eyes. "I can't."

"It would seem you're not all that crazy about pain, after all," Delphine observed with a wry twist to her mouth. She reached for a reindeer cookie and bit off its antlers.

Glory sighed. "You know, Mama, I wish I were more like you. You've had lots of heartache in your life, but it never broke you. You were brave. You just kept putting one foot in front of the other and, lo and behold, here you are with a business of your own and a man who adores you."

"Do you think I never ran away from a problem?" Delphine asked, raising her eyebrows. "If you do, you don't have a very good memory. When we came here to Pearl River, you and Dylan and I, we were on the run from a very bad situation."

"But you started over. You made the best of things. What would you do if you were me?"

"Knowing what I know now? I'd stand toe to toe with Jesse Bainbridge and tell him I loved him. Then I'd work at my job and I'd find a way to build some kind of relationship with Liza."

Glory set her teacup aside. She wasn't as courageous as her mother; she couldn't endure Jesse's hatred, or the knowledge that she'd done her own child more harm than good. No, the best thing to do would be to go away.

Eventually Liza's wounds would heal over and so, hopefully, would her own.

She set the afghan aside and rose shakily to her feet. "I'd better go home," she said. "I have things to do."

"I'll drive you there," Delphine told her, standing and going to the closet for her own coat.

"That won't be necessary, Mama," Glory protested woodenly. "My car's at the bank."

"You're in no shape to walk even that far," Delphine insisted. "And you've ruined your shoes. I doubt they'll even stay on your feet."

Sure enough, the high heels were destined for the rubbish bin. Glory accepted a pair of her mother's slippers, since any of her shoes would have been too small, and obediently followed her downstairs to Delphine's little silver car.

Delphine didn't take Glory to the bank parking lot, she took her directly to her apartment. There, she undressed her like a child, put her into a warm flannel nightgown, turned up the heat, and tucked her into bed. Then Delphine brought her a cup of hot lemon juice mixed with water and honey and two aspirin tablets.

Glory dutifully took the aspirin and sipped the lemon concoction. "I'm not sick," she protested.

"You will be, if someone doesn't take care of you," Delphine responded firmly. And then she left the room, and Glory heard her talking on the telephone, telling Harold she was spending the night at her daughter's apartment.

When Glory had finished her drink, she settled down into the covers and closed her eyes. She'd just rest for a few minutes, then she'd get up and telephone her attorney, and Mr. Baker at the bank.

When she awakened, she was instantly aware that hours had passed. Delphine was humming along with Christmas carols on the radio, and something smelled heavenly.

Glory got out of bed and, after a short visit to the bathroom, ventured into the kitchen. The tree was lit, belying the fact that suffering existed anywhere in the world.

Pulling back a chair at the table, Glory sat down. "Hi," she said.

Delphine kissed her forehead, and once again Glory thought how much she'd missed having someone to fuss over her when things were going wrong. "Hi, sweetie. I cooked your favorite for supper—spaghetti and meatballs."

Glory sighed. "That was a good trick, since I didn't have anything in the cupboards or the fridge—I was planning on going shopping tonight after work."

Back at the stove, Delphine was stirring the savory sauce she and she alone could make. Her slender shoulders moved in a pretty shrug. "Harold stopped by the supermarket for me."

"You should have invited him to stay for supper," Glory said, feeling guilty. Here she was, a grown woman, getting in the way of her mother's romance.

"I did," Delphine answered. "He said we needed this time together without him hanging around, getting in the way. Those were his words, by the way, not mine."

Glory propped her chin in one hand. "He's a great guy," she said. "I think if I didn't love you so much, I'd be jealous."

Delphine smiled. "You might find that Jesse is a 'great guy,' if you'd just wade through all that hostility until you reached the real man."

"That calls for a braver soul than mine," Glory answered softly. "And what makes you think Jesse is so wonderful, anyway? Some mothers would resent him, you know, for making their teenage daughter pregnant."

After dishing up two plates of spaghetti and meatballs and bringing them to the table, Delphine went back for salad, wine and garlic bread. Not until everything was ready and she'd taken her seat at the table did she respond. "Jesse had more privileges than you and Dylan did," she said in a thoughtful voice as she and Glory began to eat. "But he's had just as much unhappiness, if not more. First his parents died, then he lost the girl he loved, then Gresham and Sandy perished in that plane crash. I'll wager that on some level Jesse's afraid to let you know how much he still cares for you, thinking you'll either die or disappear again if he does."

Glory bit her lower lip for a moment to keep from crying. She'd done enough of that. "What makes you think Jesse still loves me?"

Delphine chuckled softly. "I *should* have realized it that first morning you were home. He watched you every single minute, except when you were looking at him, of course. And his rage tells me a lot, too. Fury isn't the opposite of love, Glory—indifference is. And Jesse Bainbridge is *anything* but apathetic, where you're concerned."

Swallowing, Glory remembered the night she and Jesse had gone to dinner and ended up making love in his grandfather's car. His passion had been partly anger, but he'd taken the utmost care to please her. Still, when it was over, things hadn't been any different between them. "Face it, Mama. You were right in the first place—I should have stayed away from Jesse and Liza, even after I discovered the truth. Once your wedding was over, I could have gone on to San Francisco, and nobody would have been any the wiser where Liza's parenthood was concerned. I really blew it."

"I'm not so sure of that, darling. A little girl needs a mother, and there's no doubt that that child's been lonely, even though Jesse and Ilene have done their best by her."

Glory's throat thickened. "Big girls need their mothers, too, sometimes," she said, grateful that Delphine had come through when she needed her. Glory had wanted to be there for Liza, but she'd botched everything, and the damage seemed irreparable.

Delphine made a bed on Glory's sofa that night, and Glory slept better, knowing she wasn't alone. In the morning, though, her resolve was as firm as ever. She would make the necessary arrangements and leave Pearl River before she did anything else to hurt her child.

Since it would take time to orchestrate everything, Glory didn't give notice when she reported to work at the bank that morning. She just threw herself into her job and avoided every attempt anyone made at conversation. Everyone from Mr. Baker down to the lowliest file clerk, of course, was wondering exactly what had happened the day before, although most of them had probably gotten the general details by means of the grapevine.

After work she drove to the mall in Fawn Creek, where she bought Christmas presents for Liza, Jill, Ilene, and her mother and Harold. The bright decorations and happy music that had pleased her so much before, when she'd shopped with Liza, were a mockery now. She could hardly wait for the holiday to be over.

Later, at home, she wrapped each present with great

care and placed them under the tree as she went. When the doorbell rang, her heart fluttered, but she knew better than to expect Jesse. He'd made his feelings perfectly clear the day Liza ran away.

When Glory pulled back the door, however, there he was.

"Delphine told me you're planning to leave," he said, and he might have been wearing his mirrored sunglasses, his eyes were so devoid of any emotion.

Glory nodded, knowing she should say something but unable to think of anything. And even if she'd managed that, it would have been hard to force words past the twisted knot in her throat.

"Could I come in?" She heard in Jesse's voice what she hadn't seen in his eyes; the effort he was making at self-control.

Still unable to speak, Glory stepped back, and he crossed the threshold warily, moving without his usual confidence and purpose to stand beside the Christmas tree.

Glory had just put a package underneath with Liza's name written on it in big gold letters, and she waited for him to say *his* daughter didn't need any presents from her. If he did, she knew she'd go at him like a wildcat, kicking and screaming and scratching.

But he only said, "Nice tree."

Reluctantly, Glory closed the door. "Thanks," she managed to croak.

He turned to face her. "Liza's doing okay," he said hoarsely.

Glory folded her arms, shielding her heart. "Good," she replied.

Jesse sighed. "I suppose it's for the best. Your leaving Pearl River, I mean."

Glory prayed she wouldn't cry. She had so little pride left as it was. "I suppose," she said.

He took a step toward her, and there was something tender in his eyes, behind the cautious expression she realized now had always been there, even when they were kids. "Glory," he murmured, and the name was a sentence in itself. It was a plea, a reprimand, a shout of fury, a kiss.

His hands rested on the sides of her waist, and Glory gave a despairing whimper, knowing that even now, with her world lying in pieces around her, her need for Jesse was as great as it had ever been.

He pulled her into his kiss and she went willingly, wrapping her arms around his neck. He cupped his powerful hands under her bottom and pressed her to him, while his tongue conquered hers.

"Jesse," she gasped, when he finally broke the kiss, but he didn't hear her. He lifted her T-shirt off over her head, and she let him—she let him because she knew this time was going to be the last, that it would have to sustain her for the rest of her life.

He pushed her bra down, without bothering to unsnap it, so that it rested around her waist in a gossamer pink circle, then lifted her high, so that her plump breasts were level with his face. Glory wrapped her legs around his lean hips and thrust her head back with a cry of relief and welcome when she felt his warm mouth close over a nipple.

Jesse was greedy at her breasts—it was as though he couldn't get enough of them. He went from one to the other, suckling, nibbling, nipping lightly with his teeth. But after a time, he carried Glory into her room and laid her on her unmade bed with her hips on the edge of the mattress.

She tossed her head from side to side and clutched at the sheets and blankets as he lowered her jeans and panties and then tossed them away, along with her shoes and stockings. Then he parted her legs and slid his hands under her bottom to raise her to his mouth.

When he captured her, she arched her back and clawed frantically at the bedclothes. The last bit of her pride was gone, shriveled to cinders in the heat of his passion. "Jesse—oh, yes—please—*Jesse*—"

He brought her swiftly to a scorching release, stroking her quivering bottom as she flailed under his tongue, stripping off his own clothes while she lay trembling in the aftermath of her satisfaction.

Jesse entered her in one powerful thrust, and she raised her hips to take him to her very depths. He buried his face in her neck as they moved together, now nibbling at the skin there, now raising his lips to her earlobe.

Glory threw herself against him with all the strength she had, desperate for the sweet union that would not be complete until she and Jesse collided in that final, explosive contact, their cries mingling in the velvety darkness of the night.

Jesse burst out with a ragged oath when passion finally overtook him, making him drive deep into Glory's body and remain there, trembling violently as she forced him to give up his seed. Beneath him, she sobbed his name, clasped her hands behind his head and dragged him into a kiss.

"We'll always have that to remember," he said a

long time later, sitting up and reaching for his clothes, "if nothing else."

Glory pulled the covers up to her chin and stared at the darkened ceiling. It took all her remaining strength to say the words.

"Goodbye, Jesse."

CHAPTER TEN

ILENE BAINBRIDGE'S USUALLY serene eyes flashed with annoyance and frustration. "*Grow up*, Jesse!" she snapped, making no effort to keep her voice down because the bookstore was empty of customers and Liza was still at school. "Here's a bulletin for you, Sheriff: you're not the first guy who's ever been hurt. And if you don't change some of your attitudes, you're going to end up a bitter, vindictive old man, just like Seth!"

Jesse stared at his cousin in amazement. He'd never seen her so angry. "Next you're going to tell me I should expect three ghosts to drop by tonight and point out the error of my ways," he said, trying to lighten the mood.

Ilene went back to unpacking a new shipment of books then, and her movements were still angry and abrupt. "Just go away, Jesse. I don't want to talk to you right now, because I'm going to end up saying a lot of things I'll regret."

He remained where he was, standing beside the counter with his arms folded. "What do you think I should do?" he asked quietly. Jesse wasn't one to let others dictate his opinions, but he had a lot of respect for Ilene. Ever since Gresham and Sandy's death, when custody of Liza had fallen to him, Ilene had been there to provide the female companionship the child needed.

She sighed heavily. "That's not for me to say, Jesse.

But if I were you, I'd examine my feelings very closely before I let Glory leave my life again. And I'd try to understand what it is to be eighteen and intimidated by a powerful man like Seth, and I'd be a little forgiving. After all, 'tis the season."

Jesse's beeper went off just then and, frowning, he reached for the telephone behind the counter. Quickly he punched out his office number. "Bainbridge," he said, when his secretary answered.

A car accident had been reported, five minutes north of town, the woman told him, and the State Patrol was shorthanded because of all the holiday travelers and the uncommonly heavy snow. They wondered if Jesse's department would take care of this one.

"Tell them I'm on my way," he said. "Are there ambulances on the scene?"

"They're en route," the secretary answered, and Jesse thanked her and hung up.

"Merry Christmas," he said to Ilene in a distracted tone of voice, as he wrenched open the door of the bookshop and headed out into the cold. Once he was inside the patrol car, he switched on the lights and siren and made a wide U-turn.

All during the drive, he braced himself for what he might find when he reached the scene of the accident. "Just don't let there be any kids," he muttered, in case some guardian angel was listening.

LIZA CAME SLOWLY toward Glory, who stood by the little Christmas tree they'd decorated together a few nights before, there in one corner of Ilene's cozy little bookshop. Glory was holding the presents she'd bought for her daughter in arms that trembled slightly.

"Hello, Glory," Liza said cautiously, as though speaking to a bird that might take flight at any instant. Ilene put the "closed" sign in place, locked the door, and retreated behind the counter to empty the cash register.

Glory held out the presents, and Liza accepted them shyly, with a murmured, "Thank you. I've got something for you, too, but it's upstairs."

Don't let me cry, Glory prayed desperately. *Please, just get me through this, and give Liza a happy life, and I won't ever ask You for anything else.* She waited, not trusting herself to speak, and the child hesitated, too, as though afraid that Glory would leave if she turned her back for a moment.

"You'll wait?" she asked. The slight quaver in the little girl's voice was almost Glory's undoing.

"I'll be right here," she said softly.

With that promise, Liza set the packages Glory had given her on the seat of the rocking chair and scampered upstairs.

Glory swallowed and turned her gaze toward Ilene, who was watching her. "I guess Liza's going to stay right here with you, even though she knows Jesse's her father," she said.

Ilene shook her head. "Jesse's hiring a nanny and a housekeeper," she said. "He wants Liza to live with him."

"Won't you miss her?" Glory asked, putting her hands in the pockets of her coat in an effort to keep them still.

Ilene smiled. "Of course I will. But I'll see her often."

Before Glory could say any more, Liza returned,

proudly carrying a small box wrapped in red-and-white striped paper and tied with curling ribbons of both colors.

"Would you please open it right now?" the child asked.

Glory's heart caught at the carefully contained eagerness she heard in her daughter's voice. Unable to speak, for the moment at least, she began undoing the ribbon and paper. Inside a plain white box, nestled on a bed of cotton, lay a beautiful silver locket.

Sinking her teeth into her lower lip, Glory opened the locket and found a miniature photograph of Liza inside. Several awkward moments passed before she dropped to her knees and took the little girl into her arms. "Oh, Liza, thank you. It's the finest present I've ever had, and I'll wear it always. Whenever I touch it, I'll remember you."

Liza stepped back in Glory's embrace. "Remember me?" she echoed. "Are you going away?"

Glory felt the tears she'd sworn not to shed stinging her eyes. "Yes, baby."

"Why?" The word was plaintive, despairing, and it practically tore out Glory's heart.

Glory took the time to put the locket around her neck and clasp it, needing those moments to get a new grip on her composure. Then she laid her hands on Liza's small shoulders. "Sweetheart, the things I'm going to say might be hard to understand, but I hope you'll try very hard, because it's so important.

"I love you, and I've thought of you every single day of the nine years since I turned you over to the adoption people. And there will never be a day in the future when I don't hold you in my heart and pray that you're happy and well.

"But I know now that it was a mistake for me to stay here in Pearl River, once I realized who you were. Sweetheart, all I've done is cause you trouble and pain, and I'd rather die than go on doing that. So I've got to go away."

"No!" Liza cried, twisting out of Glory's grasp only to fling frantic little arms around her neck. "No! You're my mommy, and you can't go away and leave me— *please* don't—"

Glory held the child close. Walking out that door in a few minutes was going to be the hardest thing she'd ever done, more difficult even than leaving Liza the first time. But she and Jesse couldn't go on pulling their daughter back and forth between them. "Darling, I promise I'll write, and when you're older, if it's all right with your dad, you can come and visit me." She pulled back far enough to take Liza's quivering chin in her hand and look straight into her tear-filled eyes. "And I want a promise from you, too, Liza Bainbridge. I want your word that you won't ever, ever run away again."

"Glory, *please*—"

She swallowed and held her chin high. "Liza."

"I promise."

Glory kissed her daughter's forehead. "Good. I love you," she finished. And then she got slowly to her feet and went toward the door.

"Glory!" Liza wailed brokenly.

"God forgive me," Glory whispered, as she wrestled with the lock and then opened the door to go. The thought of Jesse came to her on the cold wind. "God forgive us both."

Without looking back, she hurried out into the dark, chilly night, half blinded by tears and grief.

Back home, she packed her suitcases, threw away all the food in the refrigerator, and took all the lights and ornaments off the Christmas tree.

Then, after taking a long, hot bath, she dressed and got into her car. Glory drove by Jill's place, but didn't stop, since she'd left an awkward farewell message on her friend's answering machine. And then she went past the diner.

Through the colorfully festooned windows, she saw Delphine and Harold presiding over a punch bowl full of eggnog, and the place was packed with friends. They were expecting Glory, but she couldn't bring herself to stop and go in. She'd telephone later, from somewhere down the road, and hope Delphine and Harold would understand why she was skipping out before their wedding.

There was just one more place she needed to go before leaving Pearl River forever. With a glance toward the little potted Christmas tree she'd bought at the supermarket earlier, Glory headed for the cemetery.

"DRUNK DRIVER," ONE of the ambulance attendants confided to Jesse when he arrived. The man paused after wrapping the patient in warm blankets and strapping him to the stretcher.

Jesse swore and scanned the scene, seeing a large car that looked relatively unmarked and a little one that appeared hopelessly battered. "How many people were hurt?"

"Just this guy," the attendant answered. "He's had a few too many, and his head's banged up pretty good, but my guess is he'll be out of the hospital in time to have turkey dinner with his family tomorrow."

"If he was driving with more than the legal limit of alcohol in his blood," Jesse said quietly, "he's going to spend Christmas in the county jail. Have you got a reading?"

The attendant gave Jesse a number that made him swear again and handed him the man's driver's license. After checking the identification, he bent over and looked down into the party boy's face. "Hey, buddy," he began jovially, "I want to wish you a Merry Christmas on behalf of the Pearl River County sheriff's department. I'm here to offer you our hospitality, since as soon as they're done with you over at the emergency room, we'll be coming by to pick you up. You have the right to remain silent, Mr. Callahan. Anything you say can and will be used against you in a court of law…"

"You don't understand, Sheriff," Mr. Callahan whined, when Jesse had finished reading him his rights. "I only had a couple of eggnogs. Damn it, it's Christmas!"

"Ho, ho, ho," Jesse replied. And then he turned his attention to the shaken family huddled in the small, dented car on the side of the road.

He walked over, smiled and bent to look through the window as the driver rolled down the glass and said, "Hello, officer."

Jesse saw two kids with freckles and pigtails sitting in the back seat, clutching their dolls and looking scared, and silently thanked the benevolent fates for sparing them. "Merry Christmas," he said. "Is everybody sure they're okay?"

The driver, a man about Jesse's age, sighed. "We're fine," he said. "Just a little shaken up, that's all."

"How about the car? Does it run?"

The Christmas traveler shook his head. "The ambulance people radioed for a wrecker," he said. "But there probably won't be room in the cab for all four of us, and it's getting pretty cold in here."

Jesse nodded and thrust his hands into the pockets of his jacket. "I'll drive you into town," he said. "But before we go, I need you to tell me exactly what happened here. Is somebody expecting you in Pearl River?"

The woman leaned forward and smiled wanly, and Jesse watched her for signs of shock. "My grandmother, Alice Northrup. She's probably been watching the road ever since noon."

Jesse didn't remember the woman in the car, but he knew right where to find her grandmother. Miss Alice was a little old blue-haired lady who was always hearing prowlers in the her backyard. He grinned and opened the door so the little girls in back could get out. "I'll radio the office and have them get in touch with her," he said.

The children looked up at him with serious faces. "Are we arrested?" one of them asked.

The young parents laughed affectionately, but Jesse squatted down to look straight into the child's eyes. "No, ma'am," he said. "If I were to do a thing like that, Santa Claus would be real put out. And he's one man I don't like to cross."

"We've got presents in the trunk," said the other little girl.

Jesse settled the woman and the two kids and the presents in the patrol car, with the heater going full blast, then radioed the office. Deputy Johnson promised to let Mrs. Northrup know that her loved ones were safe and would be arriving soon.

While the three females sang Christmas carols, Jesse and the husband went over the accident scene. Soon, Jesse's report was complete, and he drove the family to Grandma's house.

He felt a little envious, watching the old woman run out to greet them. That was what Christmas was all about, he thought to himself, and wondered why he couldn't get things right in his own life.

Stopping by the office, he left the report to be typed by Deputy Johnson, who'd drawn duty that night, took a package from the top drawer of his desk, and went back to his car.

The lights of a huge tree were visible through the big front window of the nursing home when Jesse arrived, and he heard the voices of carolers from one of the churches as he came up the walk. The residents, male and female alike, were gathered around the main room, singing, their faces splashed with color.

Jesse smiled and greeted a few of the patients as he worked his way through the room toward the hallway. He'd known without looking that his grandfather wouldn't be among the merrymakers; Seth had never cared much about Christmas.

Reaching the door of the judge's room, Jesse paused and knocked.

"Come in," grumbled a familiar voice.

Jesse went in grinning. "Well," he said, going to stand beside his grandfather's bed, "if it isn't Scrooge himself. Merry Christmas, Gramps."

"Humph!" said Gramps, but he reached out for the

present Jesse had brought. "Probably slippers. Or another box of chocolates."

"Wrong," Jesse replied easily, dropping into a chair. He wanted to be home with Liza and Ilene—how he wished Glory would be there, too—but he loved this old coot, for all his cantankerous ways.

The judge ripped open the paper to reveal a kit for building a ship in a bottle. Despite his effort to appear singularly unimpressed, he opened the instructions with fumbling, awkward fingers and peered at them. "Get me my glasses!" he snapped.

Jesse chuckled and took the familiar leather case out of the drawer beside Seth's bed, handing him the bifocals. "I figure it'll take you till next Christmas to put the thing together," he teased. "Then you can just wrap it up and give it back to me."

Seth laughed, in spite of himself. "The hell I will," he said. "Don't you have anything better to do on Christmas Eve besides pick on an old man?"

Sadness touched Jesse's spirit as he thought of Glory again. "I can hang around for a while," he told his grandfather quietly.

"That woman still in town?"

Jesse felt his hackles rise, but he reminded himself that it was Christmas, that Liza and Ilene were waiting for him at the mansion, and that Alice Northrup's family had made it home, safe and sound, to hang up their stockings. Maybe that was all he could ask of the holiday. "You mean Glory?" he asked.

Seth nodded.

"She's leaving soon," Jesse said, and the words left him feeling raw and hollow inside.

"I paid her off, you know."

"Yes, Gramps," Jesse sighed. "I know."

"Told her I'd send that brother of hers straight to jail if she didn't leave you alone," the judge reflected proudly.

Jesse sat bolt upright in his chair, feeling as though somebody had just goosed him with a cattle prod. *"What?"* he rasped. "You involved Dylan in this?"

The judge chuckled, obviously reveling in his own cleverness. "He was a troublemaker. It would have been easy to have him sent up."

Standing now, Jesse gripped the lapels of the old man's bathrobe. He didn't want to scare him, just get his undivided attention. *"You told Glory if she didn't leave, you were going to frame Dylan?"*

Seth nodded, his beetle eyebrows rising a notch. He looked somewhat less amused. "I wanted to protect you, Jesse. And she wasn't going to take the money. I had to do something—"

"Fool," Jesse rasped, turning away, and he wasn't talking to the judge. He was talking to himself. "You damn fool!"

"Now, Jesse, I—"

It was too late for the old man; he'd probably go to his grave believing he'd done the right thing. But Jesse still had time to undo some of his mistakes, and he didn't want to waste a minute.

"Merry Christmas," he said, excited as a kid, giving Seth a quick, affectionate slap on the back. "I'll come out tomorrow and make sure you eat all your turkey and stuffing. But right now, I've got to go!"

"Hey, wait a—"

Jesse was gone before the sentence was completed, striding down the hall, joining a chorus of "God Rest

Ye Merry Gentlemen" as he hurried through the main room and out into that cold, snowy Christmas Eve.

He went to Glory's apartment first, breaking the speed limit all the way, but when he pulled up out front, her windows were dark. She was probably with Delphine, over at the diner.

Making a wide turn, Jesse bumped the tires over the sidewalk on the other side of the street and sped toward Delphine's.

There were people jammed inside the diner—mostly folks who didn't have anywhere to go—and carols were being sung at ear-splitting volume. Jesse waded through the crowd until he found Delphine, gripped her gently by one elbow, and hustled her into the kitchen.

"Where's Glory?" he demanded.

Delphine glanced at her watch and frowned. "I don't know. She should have been here by now. I'd better call."

Jesse's throat felt tight for a moment, then he managed to grind out, "I was just at her place. It was dark as a mole's fruit cellar."

Glory's mother gave him an accusing look. "She's been depressed lately," she said pointedly. Then she marched over to the wall phone and punched out her daughter's number. A long time passed before she hung up, her teeth sunk into her lower lip, her brows drawn together.

Before Jesse could say anything else, Jill appeared in the doorway. "I come bearing sad tidings," she said dismally. "It's bad news, bears."

"What?" Jesse snapped.

Jill glared at him. "Don't you get smart with me,

Jesse Bainbridge. As far as I'm concerned, this whole thing is your fault!"

"Jill, please," Delphine pleaded, her voice small, and Jill put an arm around her.

"When I came home from doing some last-minute shopping just a few minutes ago, there was a message from Glory on my answering machine. She said she hoped everybody would understand, but she had to leave Pearl River while she still had some of her soul left." Jill paused to narrow her eyes at Jesse, holding Delphine tightly against her side. "She left for San Francisco tonight."

Delphine looked as if she was going to cry, and Jesse hadn't seen her do that since that night ten years before, when he'd come to her half drunk and begged her to tell him where Glory was. "Without saying good-bye to Harold and me?" she whispered disbelievingly.

"I'm sure she means to call you later tonight," Jill said comfortingly.

"I guess Glory isn't very good at saying goodbye to anybody," Jesse muttered, and then he left the diner by the back way, unable to face any more holiday cheer.

As he slipped behind the wheel of the patrol car, soft, fat flakes of snow began to fall.

"You're not getting away with it this time, Glory," he whispered, reaching for his radio mike. He contacted the office, and got the long-suffering Deputy Johnson. "Call my place, will you, and ask Ilene if Glory's been by."

"Roger," replied the deputy.

A few minutes later, as Jesse was cruising the main street of town, the answer came. Glory had stopped by the bookstore briefly, just about closing time. She'd said goodbye to Liza and left.

Swearing, Jesse pulled over to the side of the road and went into a phone booth. One quarter and three long rings later, Ilene answered his telephone at home.

"Bainbridge residence. This is Ilene."

"How is Liza?" Jesse blurted, rubbing his eyes with the thumb and forefinger of one hand.

Ilene sighed. "She's doing okay for somebody who's lost two mothers and one father."

"What the hell did Glory say to her?"

"She said she loved her," Ilene answered somewhat acidly. "Terrible woman."

"Damn it, Ilene, I don't need this right now. I just found out that Gramps forced her into leaving town ten years ago by threatening to throw her brother in jail. I've got to find her."

"Are you thinking what I hope you're thinking?"

"If—*when* I find Glory, I'm going to admit I'm an idiot and beg her forgiveness. And then I'll propose, and if she says yes, we'll go drag Judge Jordal away from home and hearth to issue us a special license and perform the marriage ceremony."

"That would be one jim-dandy Christmas miracle if you could pull it off," Ilene said eagerly. "Good luck, Jesse."

"Thanks," Jesse said, and even though he was grinning like a fool, his voice came out sounding hoarse.

THE CEMETERY WAS WELL-LIGHTED, and Glory wasn't surprised to see other people visiting lost loved ones on Christmas Eve. It was the most difficult time of year for the bereaved.

She dusted the snow off Dylan's headstone and then put the little potted tree in front of it. "Merry Christmas," she said, putting one hand to her throat and sniffling once. She squatted down beside the grave and rested one hand against the cold marble stone.

"I know, I know," she said. "I've got to quit hanging around here this way. But you must remember how I was always tagging after you." Glory took a tissue from her coat pocket, dried her eyes and dabbed at her nose. She sighed, and a smile crept across her face. "Remember that Christmas when we hid flashlights under our mattresses and practically synchronized our watches so we could peek at the presents after Mama put them out? You got a baseball glove, and I got one of those dolls that talked when you pulled the string."

Suddenly Glory began to cry. Hard. She put her hands over her eyes and sobbed.

"There now, miss," said a kindly voice, and strong fingers closed around Glory's shoulders and lifted her to her feet. "I like to think them that went before are having Christmas tonight, too, somewhere."

Stunned, Glory lowered her hands to stare into a gentle, weathered old face. "Who are you?"

"Name's Clyde Ballard," the elderly gentleman said, touching the brim of his snow-dusted fedora. "My wife Sylvia is buried out here, and I like to come by of a Christmas Eve and leave her a poinsettia plant. She always loved those pretty red blossoms, and she could make 'em bloom year after year, too. Used to fill our living room with the things."

Glory dried her eyes with the back of one mitten, since she'd already exhausted her tissue supply, and squinted at the man. He didn't look familiar. "You must miss her very much," she said, a little ashamed of her outburst a few minutes before.

"Oh, I certainly do," agreed Mr. Ballard, bending to read the words and dates on Dylan's stone. "And you miss this young fellow, too. It's a pity he died so early."

Glory nodded. She was beginning to feel better. "He was killed in an explosion a couple of months after he joined the air force."

"That's real sad," said Mr. Ballard sincerely. "But I know he wouldn't want you here in the graveyard, crying your pretty eyes out, on Christmas Eve!"

Glory chuckled. "You're right about that."

"Of course I am," the old man responded. "I'm on my way over to Delphine's Diner for some pecan pie and eggnog. You ought to come along—there's always room for one more when *she* throws a party."

Nodding, Glory smiled. "I know," she answered.

Mr. Ballard started to say something else, but just as he opened his mouth, Glory saw a patrol car pull up down by the gates, lights flashing. Her heart surged into her throat.

"Jesse," she whispered.

Mr. Ballard gave a pleased cackle. "You wanted for some crime, young lady?" he teased.

"I'm an incorrigible jaywalker," Glory confided, and Mr. Ballard laughed.

"I'd better run along before the pie's all gone. You sure you don't want to come along?"

Impulsively Glory kissed his cheek. "Maybe I'll be by later," she said. Her heartbeat was loud and fast now, pounding in her ears. "Merry Christmas, Mr. Ballard."

"Merry Christmas to you, little lady," he responded. He passed Jesse on his way down the hill and touched the brim of his hat in that same courtly manner as before.

Jesse didn't even seem to see Mr. Ballard; he was looking up at Glory. Reaching her, he took her shoulders in his hands.

"I thought you left for the money," he said gruffly. "But tonight Gramps told me he threatened to have Dylan framed for some crime if you stayed."

"Or if I said so much as a word to you," Glory clarified, swallowing. "What are you doing here, Jesse?"

He grasped her hand and led her to a nearby bench. After dusting off some of the snow so she could sit, Jesse pressed her onto the bench and dropped to one knee in front of her. Snow and mud were probably seeping through his pant leg, but he didn't seem to care. "Glory, I was wrong. I was stubborn and prideful, and you were right when you said I was only thinking of myself. Will you forgive me? Please?"

Glory blinked, uncertain that any of this was really happening. Maybe it was all an illusion. "Well—okay."

Jesse gave a jubilant burst of laughter, rising to his feet and hauling Glory with him. He put his arms around her and kissed her thoroughly. "I love you," he said when it was over.

She stared up at him. This was real, all right. No fantasy kiss had ever felt like that. "Well, I love you, too, but—"

He laid a finger to her lips. "But nothing. Will you marry me, Glory? Now—tonight?"

She kissed the tip of his finger and then reluctantly shook her head. "No, Jesse. We have too many things to work out. But I'll marry you in the summer if you still want me."

Jesse held her close, and it felt impossibly good. His lips moved against her temple. "But you won't leave again—you'll stay right here in Pearl River?"

Glory cupped her hands on either side of his face, feeling a new beard scratch against her palms. "I'll stay, Jesse. I promise," she said, and then she stood on tiptoe to kiss him.

CHAPTER ELEVEN

THE LIGHTS OF the Bainbridge mansion glowed golden through the snowy night, and as the patrol car reached the top of the driveway, the door burst open and a small silhouette appeared in the opening.

"Today Ilene told me to grow up," Jesse confessed hoarsely, as he brought the car to a stop in front of the garage, "and I think I finally have. No matter what happens between us over the next six months, Glory, Liza is your child as much as mine, and I won't ever try to keep you away from her again."

Glory squeezed his hand and pushed open the car door. "Liza!" she called in a happy sob.

The little girl scrambled toward her, her voice shrill with surprise and delight. "Glory, *you came back*!"

Glory enfolded her daughter in her arms and held her close, right there in Jesse's snowy yard. "I'll stay if you want me to," she managed to whisper. "Oh, baby, I'm so sorry for the trouble I've caused—I never meant to hurt you..."

Liza pulled back in Glory's embrace and looked up at her, and for a moment it was as though their roles were reversed, and Glory was the child. "I understand, Mom. Aunt Ilene explained about all the things that happened to make you and Uncle Jesse—Dad—unhappy."

The word "Mom" had brought a sheen of tears to Glory's eyes. "Here you are, outside without a coat," she scolded good-naturedly. "Let's get inside before you catch pneumonia."

The interior of the mansion was decorated with cheerful good taste. The scent of a live tree filled the air, and instrumental Christmas music provided a cozy background.

Ilene came forward to kiss Glory soundly on the forehead, Jesse on the cheek. "It's about time," she said, and then, claiming she had to baste tomorrow's turkey, she disappeared into the kitchen.

Jesse put one hand on Glory's back and one on Liza's and ushered his family into the huge living room, where an enormous tree towered in one corner and a fire snapped on the hearth. He took Glory's coat and laid it aside before removing his own and squatting down to look into Liza's eyes.

She was seated in one of the leather wing chairs, her face shining brightly enough to rival the star of Bethlehem. "You're going to marry Mom," she said with the confidence of a seasoned game show contestant.

Jesse glanced back at Glory over one shoulder and grinned before facing his daughter again. "Yeah, I'm going to marry her. But how did you know? Things have been pretty bad lately."

"I wished it, that's why. And I asked my other mommy and daddy to talk to God about it special. After all, they're angels, and they're right there in heaven with Him."

Glory's throat was tight again. She perched on the arm of Liza's chair and laid a hand on her shoulder.

The beautiful man and child before her blurred for a moment.

Jesse reached out and tugged affectionately at one of Liza's braids. "I'm sorry I was so bullheaded, sweetheart," he said, his voice low and a little husky. "Will you forgive me?"

She threw her small arms around his neck. "Sure I will, Dad!" she crowed. "I'm not some immature kid, you know!"

Jesse laughed and held her tightly, but the look in his eyes was strictly for Glory, and so was the saucy wink. "I think you'd better call Delphine," he said after a few moments. "Jill reported you officially missing from the fold, and it didn't exactly make your mother's Christmas."

Glory nodded and scanned the room for a telephone. There was one sitting on a desk over by one of the towering windows. She dialed the number at the diner and fiddled with the silver locket Liza had given her earlier, while she waited.

Delphine answered almost immediately, and she sounded breathless. "Hello?"

"Mama, it's me, Glory."

"Mr. Ballard said he saw you at the cemetery!" Delphine cried. "Sweetheart, are you all right?"

Glory lifted her eyes and saw Jesse sitting in the wing chair, with Liza balanced happily on his knee. "Oh, I'm more than all right, Mama. Jesse and I have agreed to try to work things out, and I'm staying here in Pearl River. With any luck, I'll be a bride this summer."

It was plain that Delphine was crying, and that her tears were happy ones. "Oh, darling, that's wonderful."

"And Jesse has promised not to try to keep me away from Liza even if we don't end up as a family."

"You will," Delphine said with certainty. "I swear, this Christmas is just like in the movies. I wouldn't be at all surprised if there was an angel involved somewhere."

Glory watched her daughter's glowing, animated face. "There's an angel involved, all right. Merry Christmas, Mama. I'll see you sometime tomorrow."

Delphine made a sound she called "kiss-kiss," bid her daughter a magical night, and hung up.

Liza was about to hang up her stocking, when Glory returned from making a call. It was an enormous thing, almost as tall as its owner. Jesse lifted his daughter by the waist so she could reach one of the special hooks set into the underside of the mantel.

The knowledge of those hooks eased a tightness in Glory's heart. Knowing Seth Bainbridge had once been a little boy, eagerly hanging a stocking above this same fireplace, washed away the last of the bitterness she'd held toward the old man. Even better was the relative certainty that other Bainbridge children would celebrate their Christmases here, too. Her children and Jesse's.

"I've got to get back to work," Jesse said with a sigh when he'd set Liza on her feet again.

Liza nodded, evidently used to his erratic schedule. Then her eyes shifted to Glory. "You'll stay, won't you? You'll be here in the morning, when I wake up?"

Under any other circumstances, Glory would have gently refused. She didn't have any compunctions at all about sleeping with Jesse—as far as she was concerned, he was already her mate—but she hadn't planned on sharing his bed with Liza in the same house until after the wedding. Still, Liza had been through a great deal in her young life, and she deserved to have her mother nearby on this special night.

"I'll stay," Glory said with a shy glance at Jesse.

His dark eyes smoldered with teasing passion as he gazed at her, making a blush rise from her breasts to her face. After kissing Liza good-night and sending her off to find a favorite storybook, Jesse took Glory's hand and pulled her close to him. "I'm going to make very thorough love to you tonight," he vowed quietly.

Glory trembled against him, feeling the promises his body was making to hers. "Jesse—"

"I know," he interrupted, his lips almost upon hers. "It's only for tonight, and you're not moving in until after the wedding. Which is not to say I won't have you at *your place* whenever I get the chance." He kissed her, his tongue seeking entrance to her mouth with gentle insistence and then breaking down the barriers to conquer her utterly and give her a foretaste of what awaited her.

When he finally released her, Glory was clinging to the front of his shirt with both hands just so she wouldn't slide to the floor. "D-do you still sleep in the same room?"

Jesse grinned. "No, ma'am. That room is Liza's now. I'm in the big master suite at the other end of the hall."

Glory blushed and swallowed. Where this man was concerned, she had no pride, at all. But then, she'd always known that. "I'll be there waiting when you get home, Jesse," she promised.

He took a teasing nibble at her lower lip before responding, "Don't expect one ride over the moon and the proverbial long winter's nap," he warned, his voice throaty and low. "We've got a lot of time to make up, and I intend to show you what you've missed."

She let her forehead rest against his shoulder for a moment, then looked up at him with a soft smile. "You enjoy the idea that I'll be thinking about all the things we're going to do, and wanting them, don't you?"

"Yes," he answered without hesitation, and then he kissed her again, swatted her once on the bottom and went out.

Moments later, Liza returned, her storybook gripped in both hands. "Will you read this to me, please?" she asked hopefully. "It's *A Visit from St. Nicholas*."

Sitting down in Jesse's chair and pulling the child onto her lap, Glory uttered a silent prayer of thanks and began to read. Ilene crept in, with hot buttered rums for both herself and Glory, and listened to the old favorite with a smile on her face.

When she'd completed the poem, Glory just sat, reveling in the fact that she was holding the daughter she'd once thought she'd never see again. It was pure bliss knowing they wouldn't have to be separated anymore. And then there was the sweet certainty that later, when the presents had been set out and Christmas Day was about to dawn, Jesse would take her to his bed and make love to her.

Presently, Liza laid her head against Glory's shoulder and yawned hugely.

"I think somebody needs to say good-night," Ilene observed gently.

Liza looked up at Glory's face. "But you won't go away, will you, Mom?"

Glory touched the tip of Liza's nose with an index

finger. "I won't go away," she promised. "Not only that, but I'll tuck you in and hear your prayers, too."

A few minutes later, mother and daughter climbed the stairs, with their intricately carved banister. Jesse's old room had been so thoroughly changed that Glory wouldn't have recognized it. Pink-and-gold striped paper covered the walls, and there was a four-poster, billowing with lace and ruffles, where Jesse's water-bed had been. Teddy bears and dolls lined the window seat, instead of model airplanes and copies of *Popular Mechanics*.

After brushing her teeth and putting on a flannel nightgown in the small adjoining bathroom, Liza knelt down beside the bed, and Glory took a place beside her.

"Thank you, God, for letting me have a mom and dad again. And thank you that it's Christmas. You've been real good to me, so if Santa Claus—" Liza paused here to looking meaningfully at Glory, letting her know she was speaking in the figurative sense "—if Santa Claus doesn't bring me a Nintendo game or a Prom Date Barbie, I'll be perfectly happy. Good night, God, and Merry Christmas."

Glory rested her forehead against her folded hands for a few moments to hide the tears in her eyes. Although they sprang from joy, not sorrow, she was afraid Liza would misunderstand them and be worried. "Thank you, God," she echoed in a broken voice.

After that, Liza climbed into bed, and Glory tucked the covers in around her and gave her a sound good-night kiss.

"I'm so glad you came back," the child whispered.

"Me, too," Glory answered, her voice shaking. "I love you, sweetheart."

"I love—you," Liza replied, stopping once to yawn.

Downstairs, Glory found that Ilene had reheated her buttered rum, and she raised it gratefully to her lips. "This has been quite some day," she told her friend.

Ilene smiled. "Yes, it has." She paused to sip from her cup and gaze at the glowing embers in the fire. "Jesse was planning to roust Judge Jordal from his bed and force him to marry the two of you this very night."

Glory laughed as an image of Jesse strong-arming an old man in a flowing nightshirt and matching cap filled her mind. "We've agreed to wait six months before we get married. Not that I have any doubts. I want to show Jesse that I'm in for the duration this time."

Ilene reached out to pat her hand. "You're a wise woman, Glory Parsons. By the time June rolls around, our stubborn Jesse should be in a very flexible frame of mind."

The two women sat and talked for about an hour, and then Ilene excused herself. "Liza will be up early, tearing into the presents," she said. "Therefore, I'm off to get whatever sleep I can."

Glory nodded and, when Ilene had been gone for a few minutes, she went to the fireplace and threw in another chunk of wood.

A little after midnight, Jesse returned, smiling when he saw Glory sitting there, enjoying the quiet, the fire and the lights on the tree.

He approached and pulled her out of the chair just long enough to sit in it himself. Then he placed her carefully on his lap. "I stopped a fat guy for speeding tonight on my way home," he told her, looking solemn as he traced her jawline with a chilly finger. "He was driving a sleigh, if you can believe it, pulled by eight tiny reindeer."

Glory laughed, thinking if she loved this man any more, she'd burst like an overfilled balloon. "I *don't* believe it, Sheriff. I think you must have been hallucinating."

He shifted and pulled a small velvet box out of the pocket of his coat. "If I was hallucinating," he reasoned, "how come he gave me this?"

Glory stared at the object. "Is that...?"

Jesse attempted to look very exasperated. "Of course it isn't the same ring I bought for Adara. Don't you think I have any class, at all? I persuaded Harvey Milligan to open the jewelry store." He set the box in her palm.

Her fingers trembled slightly as she lifted the lid. Immediately a cluster of diamonds caught the lights of the Christmas tree and the flicker of the fire and held them fast. "Oh, Jesse, it's beautiful."

He took the ring out of its little slot and slid it onto her finger. Only then did he ask, "Will you marry me, Glory?"

She kissed him, treating him to previews of coming attractions. "Yes," she finally answered. "Next June, just like we planned."

Jesse sighed philosophically. "Next June," he agreed. Then he gave Glory a swat and set her on her feet. "Let's get busy, wife-of-Christmas-future. We've got a stocking to fill, and toys to set out. Then I'm going to take you upstairs and do right by you."

He peeled off his jacket and tossed it aside, then removed his gun and holster and locked them carefully away.

Glory had never had so much fun as she did filling Liza's stocking with an orange and a candy cane and a variety of other goodies. She helped Jesse set out the video-game center Liza had wanted, along with the Barbie doll she'd asked for, a set of delicate little china dishes and a huge stuffed horse.

Jesse and Glory stood holding hands for a while, admiring their handiwork, then Jesse checked the screen on the fireplace and turned out the Christmas-tree lights. Glory was caught by surprise when he swept her into his arms, Rhett Butler-style, and carried her up the stairs and along the hallway.

The master suite was enormous, with its own wood-burning fireplace and room enough for a couch and two chairs, not to mention the bed. There was a table, too, beside bay windows, and Glory dreamed of sitting there, watching the moonlight play on the snow.

"Do you always work nights?" Glory asked.

Jesse set her down and immediately started unbuttoning his uniform shirt. "My hours are crazy," he sighed. "Sometimes it's nights, sometimes it's days, sometimes it's twenty-four or forty-eight hours straight." He bent his head and nipped at one of Glory's nipples, causing it to push against the fabric of her bra. "I guess you're just going to have to figure I'm going to be making love to you at some very weird times. I can promise you one thing, Glory—it'll happen often. Want to share my shower?"

Glory nodded, and her eyes drifted closed as Jesse began unbuttoning her shirt. He stripped her slowly, pausing to kiss and nibble on everything he bared, and Glory was trembling by the time he took her hand and led her into the bathroom.

After making sure both spigots in the double shower were spraying warm water, Jesse stepped into the stall and pulled Glory after him.

She knew if she didn't take the lead right away, Jesse would, so she reached for the soap and a large sponge and began to wash him gently. He gave a low groan and braced himself against the wall of the shower with both hands when she reached his manhood and knelt to rinse him under the spray.

He cried out like some magnificent, wounded beast when she began treating him to some very deliberate attentions. "So long," he moaned after several moments of hard breathing. "Oh, God, Glory, it's been so long..."

"Ssh," she soothed, and then she made a circle with her tongue and Jesse's buttocks tensed under her hands.

He pleaded raggedly, and she gave him what he asked for, along with a series of little bites and kisses calculated to drive him crazy. Finally, in a fever, he hauled Glory to her feet and devoured her mouth in a kiss that left no doubt who was in charge.

She was dazed when he'd finished, and nothing could have made her protest when he turned her and set her hands on the steel safety bar affixed to the inside of the shower. He set her legs apart, and she drew in a deep breath because she knew actual intercourse with Jesse was going to be better than anything her fantasies could offer up.

His hands caressed her naked breasts for a few moments, then went to her hips, holding her firmly, setting her in position. "Do you want me, Glory?" he asked, his lips moving against her neck, the warm water streaming over both of them.

"Oh, yes," she answered. "Yes, Jesse." And she felt him at the center of her femininity, seeking entrance.

He gave her an inch of himself, just enough to tease. She was expanding to take him in, and the sensation was urgent and sweet. He continued to taste her neck. "I could make you wait," he reflected sleepily. "I could make you wait for a long time."

"No, Jesse—I want you—I need you *now*—" Because she was not without power herself, Glory gave a little twist of her hips and wrung a long groan from Jesse's throat.

He muttered words of surrender, and love, and then he drove deep into her, and she welcomed him with a gasp of joy.

At first their movements were slow and measured, but as the friction of that most intimate contact increased moment by moment, passion drove them before it, like a giant, swelling tide threatening to swallow them up.

When they were breathless from the chase, Jesse suddenly stiffened and uttered a warrior's low cry, his hands tightening over Glory's breasts. Glory felt his warmth spilling deep inside her and welcomed him, and in the next instant she went soaring over the precipice herself. Hoisted high on his shaft, his fingers working her nipples, Glory quivered repeatedly and then collapsed against the shower wall, exhausted.

But just as he'd promised, Jesse was far from through with her. He vowed to spend fifty years making up for the ten they'd sacrificed to pride and youth, and Glory looked forward to every minute.

After they'd gently washed and dried each other, Jesse took his bride-to-be to his bed and laid her there, watching the firelight play over her skin with solemn, hungry eyes. "You're so beautiful," he rasped, "and I need you so much."

Glory put her hands behind his head and pressed him to her breast, where he drank hungrily, while his fingers trailed over her thighs. Presently, Jesse caught Glory's hands together and held them high above her head, and she whimpered at being made more vulnerable to him.

It was only the beginning of vulnerabilities, and of pleasure. Over the course of that night, Glory surrendered again and again as Jesse put her through her paces, changing their positions and his demands regularly. Sometimes it was Jesse who submitted, but more often it was Glory.

And during those brief moments when her thoughts were at all coherent, she wondered how she had survived ten years without Jesse tuning her body and then causing it to play symphonies.

They slept for an hour, but then Jesse awakened Glory in a most delicious way and had her thoroughly, all over again. She was allowed to shower in peace only when Liza was up and around.

Her suitcase was lying on the bed when she came out wrapped in a towel.

"I stopped by your car and picked this up on the way home last night," Jesse said, watching her with those brazen brown eyes of his. "Can you imagine the speculation that must be going on? I can hear it now: 'I tell you, Mavis, she parked her car at the graveyard and disappeared without a trace.'"

Glory laughed and took out clean underwear, a pair of jeans and a roomy aqua-blue cable-knit sweater.

"Give the gossips their due, Jesse," she said, beginning to dress. "They're saying I've been in your bed all night, and they're right."

He stopped her as she would have hooked her bra and gave each nipple a warm suckling before snapping the front catch himself and pulling the straps up onto her shoulders. "I love you, Glory."

Her cheeks heated as she looked up at him because, after all of it, she found herself wanting him to lay her back on the bed and take her again. She didn't know how she was going to wait six months to share this room with him on a regular basis, but she was determined to do it, because she wanted their marriage to be long and unshakably solid. "Oh, Jesse, I'm so wanton."

Jesse laughed. "Patience, Glory. There's always tonight at your place."

She smiled and put her arms around his neck to kiss him, teasing his lips with her tongue. "Since it's my bed, Sheriff," she said, "I'm going to be calling all the shots."

Reluctantly Jesse backed away, but not before Glory lightly touched the front of his jeans and found him reaching for her.

They went downstairs separately, Glory first, and Jesse about five minutes later.

It snowed on New Year's Eve, but that didn't stop Harold and Delphine's guests from attending the wedding. The church was still decorated with poinsettia plants from Christmas, and candlelight flickered romantically.

Glory stood at the front of the church, wearing her royal-blue bridesmaid's dress. Happy tears dropped into her bouquet of roses and carnations, and soon the vows had been exchanged and the bride and groom were hurrying down the aisle to strains of joyful music. As Glory turned to follow, she made eye contact with the man who would be her groom when summer came, and six months seemed to be a very long time.

On the other hand, when you compared it to forever, half a year was nothing. Glory and Jesse had arranged for special counseling with the pastor, for themselves and for Liza, and they were already working hard at learning to be a family.

She'd messed up badly once, and Glory didn't intend to make the same mistake again. She knew now that love doesn't just happen, it has to be nurtured and cared for.

Jesse was waiting at the foot of the aisle, his arm out for Glory, and she went into its curve willingly. "I'll drive you over to the reception," he whispered into her ear, managing to trace it once with the tip of his tongue, "but I can't promise to take the most direct route."

Glory was grateful that everyone was looking at Delphine, who made a lovely bride in her pale rose dress and big picture hat, because she herself was blushing. "Jesse Bainbridge," she scolded. But she let him put her into his grandfather's fancy car, and she didn't say a single word when he turned off down a sideroad and headed for the rest area overlooking the river.

Her protests were cut off with a kiss that made her go damp all over, and when Jesse made the seat go back, she just went with it, already too weak to sit up without support.

"Jesse, they'll miss us—my mother's wedding—"

"We'll be back in plenty of time for the pictures and

the cake," Jesse said, raising her billowy skirt to find
her with his hand and caress her.

Instinctively, Glory raised her knees up, then let
them fall wide apart. Her hands gripped the tufted
seats as Jesse ducked under her skirt and petticoats to
tease her through the thin, tautly drawn panty hose.
When he peeled them down, there were no protests
from Glory, because he'd already created a need that
made it hard for her to lie still.

He parted her, and she heard his muffled chuckle
under all those ruffles. She would have sworn he said,
"Glory, Glory, Hallelujah!"

* * * * *

Mr. and Mrs. Harold Seemer
request the honor of your presence
at the marriage of their daughter,
Glory Ann Parsons,
to Mr. Jesse Alexander Bainbridge
on Saturday
June twenty-second
at 2:00 p.m.
First Lutheran Church
Pearl River, Oregon

"I like you, Shane. You seem like good people. You know the house, you take care of the yard, and I could really use the extra income right now while I'm settling in and looking for work. So, if you want to stay on, I'll have the attorney send over the lease."

"I want to stay."

"Good. Then it's settled."

"Same rent?"

"Same rent."

He stood up, crossed the short distance to her and held out his hand. "I appreciate this, Rebecca."

"Of course, the old lease only accommodated for one pet. We'll have to change that to account for Top."

"I'll pay an additional pet deposit, if you'd like."

"No." She shook her head. "I'm just grateful that you saved her. Any news when she can come home?"

"Tomorrow."

"That soon?"

He nodded.

"That's wonderful, Shane. Caleb is going to be over the moon when he hears. I'm going to warn you now, he's going to beg you to see her."

"He can come see her."

"Well, if either of my boys starts to wear out their welcome with you, don't be shy—just tell them the truth and they'll respect it."

He gave her another nod.

"Well, I'd better get back to work. Those boxes aren't going to unpack themselves."

The last time, she had something to add to the conversation—this time, it was Shane who stopped her from leaving.

"I forgot the thank you. For the lunch."

It wasn't his words that made her pulse quicken; it was the way he looked at her, like he really saw her. When Shane looked at her, it felt as if he was able to read all of the secrets of her soul. It was unnerving and, if she was being honest with herself, exciting.

"It was my pleasure, Shane."

Get 4 FREE REWARDS!

We'll send you 2 FREE Books plus 2 FREE Mystery Gifts.

FREE Value Over **$20**

Both the **Romance** and **Suspense** collections feature compelling novels written by many of today's best-selling authors.

YES! Please send me 2 FREE novels from the Essential Romance or Essential Suspense Collection and my 2 FREE gifts (gifts are worth about $10 retail). After receiving them, if I don't wish to receive any more books, I can return the shipping statement marked "cancel." If I don't cancel, I will receive 4 brand-new novels every month and be billed just $6.74 each in the U.S. or $7.24 each in Canada. That's a savings of at least 16% off the cover price. It's quite a bargain! Shipping and handling is just 50¢ per book in the U.S. and 75¢ per book in Canada*. I understand that accepting the 2 free books and gifts places me under no obligation to buy anything. I can always return a shipment and cancel at any time. The free books and gifts are mine to keep no matter what I decide.

Choose one: ☐ **Essential Romance**   ☐ **Essential Suspense**
            (194/394 MDN GMY7)   (191/391 MDN GMY7)

Name (please print)

Address   Apt. #

City   State/Province   Zip/Postal Code

Mail to the Reader Service:
IN U.S.A.: P.O. Box 1341, Buffalo, NY 14240-8531
IN CANADA: P.O. Box 603, Fort Erie, Ontario L2A 5X3

Want to try two free books from another series! Call 1-800-873-8635 or visit www.ReaderService.com.